A
Garland Series

VICTORIAN

FICTION

NOVELS OF FAITH
AND DOUBT

A collection of 121 novels
in 92 volumes, selected by
Professor Robert Lee Wolff,
Harvard University,
with a separate introductory volume
written by him
especially for this series.

BEYOND THE CHURCH

Frederick William Robinson

Three volumes in one

Garland Publishing, Inc., New York & London

1977

———

Bibliographical note:

Volumes I and II of this facsimile
have been made from a copy
in the Library of Congress (PZ3.R56Be)
and Volume III from a copy
in the British Museum (12624.aaa 2).

———

Library of Congress Cataloging in Publication Data

Robinson, Frederick William, 1830-1901.
   Beyond the church.

   (Victorian fiction : Novels of faith and doubt ;
52)
   Reprint of the 1866 ed. published by Hurst and
Blackett, London.
   I. Title. II. Series.
PZ3.R56Be9 [PR5233.R16]   823'.8   75-1501
ISBN 0-8240-1576-2

BEYOND THE CHURCH.

" The shadow cloaked from head to foot,
Who keeps the keys of all the Creeds."
IN MEMORIAM.

IN THREE VOLUMES.

VOL. I

LONDON:
HURST AND BLACKETT, PUBLISHERS,
SUCCESSORS TO HENRY COLBURN,
13, GREAT MARLBOROUGH STREET.
1866.
The right of Translation is reserved.

PROLOGUE.

WHEN Doctor Watts makes a youthful
pietist request that

> "In books, and work, and healthful play,
>   May 'his' young hours be past,"

it is more than probable that the
worthy, though prosy, hymnodist was
scarcely thinking of the advantages of an
university education. And yet it would
be hard to find a system in which the
three elements are so well combined. Let
'books' equal a course of private study,
'grinding' and coaching, grant that work is
not badly represented by the routine of
lectures private and public—and very hard

'work' it is too sometimes when the lecturer understands neither his subject nor the powers of comprehension of his audience—by chapel-keeping, and hall-going, by collections and all the various public examinations, and I do not think we shall quarrel about the merits of cricket, boating, hunting and athletic sports, which make up the last item of 'healthful play.' It is true, some people may wish that the two former were more cultivated, and 'healthful play' did not quite so largely predominate—nay, may even compare their relative proportions to Falstaff's bread and sack; but then Doctor Watts has laid down no exact canon of proportion in the hymn aforesaid, and that is sufficient for our purpose.

Of all seasons of relaxation at Oxford, that which is called the summer term is certainly the brightest; nor could a stranger, desirous of learning in what

manner the hopeful young students or
'collegians' as in all probability he calls
them, unbend their tightly strained bows,
select a better time for enquiry than
between the hours of one and three. Just
then the college gates are pouring out their
groups on pleasure bent. The drags are
conveying their living loads to the various
cricket fields. Little knots of lightly clad
and much be-flannelled heroes are wending their way to the river side. Daintily
dressed youths of languid mien saunter
slowly down to the gate, where the low
basket-carriage which poor John Leech
used to caricature so inimitably awaits them,
or the well-groomed hack is led to and
fro. And to those whose idleness or inclination leads them to seek pleasure within the precincts of the venerable city, there
are the tennis courts and the billiard or
the auction rooms, where bargains worth
nothing can be obtained, for that indefi-

nite premium, ' next to nothing.' Add to
all this the delights of the genuine constitutional, shared in alike by dons and men,
the main end of which appears to be the
getting over a certain space in a certain
time with the least possible result, and the
stranger will acknowledge that the *réper-
toire* of healthful play is sufficiently extensive, and that those whom the Professor
of poetry calls ' our young barbarians,'
not only know how to play but do it very
thoroughly.

One bright June afternoon in the summer term of 186—, when the commemoration was already drawing nigh and becoming the principal subject of conversation and thought, the usual groups of
idlers were be seen at the gate of St.
Margaret's College. We use the name,
St. Margaret's advisedly, because, firstly,
there is no college in Oxford blessed by

that name; and, secondly, as we have no special house of learning in 'our mind's eye,' and do not intend to bepraise or abuse the Collegiate staff of any such, the title appears to us in all ways unobjectionable. So the University reader may save his brains the labour of trying to discover for what college St. Margaret's is a *nom de plume*, and whether it gives on High Street, Broad Sreet, or St. Aldates, sufficient for us that it was a picturesque Perpendicular erection, with low gables and frowning gateway built of a peculiar crumbling stone, which resembles mouldy pound cake in texture and a wet sponge in colour.

To this gate, almost at the same moment, come three men from various parts of the college, two of whom greet each other with certain feints and passes of their canes after a fashion much affected in the University. Let us look at them. One of the fencers is the very model of a young John Bull.

In figure somewhat stumpy, but tremendously muscular; with a face scarcely good-
looking, but full of good-temper, perseverance, or suppose we say obstinacy as
that is what we mean, and a certain careless trust in circumstances with determination to take them easily. You can
see his bent is rather for athletic than
mental exercise; but he is no fool notwithstanding. His name is Charles Burke,
and he is the only son of a rich banker,
and will be taken into the firm of Burke,
Thellusson and Burke as soon as he can
write B.A. after his name. Verily his lot
has fallen in a fair ground, and so,
like a true born Briton, he grumbles thereat and execrates the fate which has made
him a banker rather than a sailor. But
his troubles do not seem to affect his
health or spirits. To him Edgar Purcell
forms a sufficient contrast. Small and
delicately moulded, he scarcely escapes the

charge of effeminacy; nature has omitted all angles in his composition, so that if he fall, he will roll, I should think, a long way. He looks made of lilies and roses, with rose water for blood. He is not naturally a fool however; but there is a want of muscle, rigidity and back bone which shows weakness somewhere. He is one of those young fellows who are said to have an elegant mind, fond of the society of ladies and the clergy, a tasteful arranger of bouquets, an amateur with an alto voice, a dabbler in water-colours, and a furiously hot Puseyite, emotional but not logical. Of my group, I have kept the most remarkable till last; and Cyril Ponsonby though not handsome was remarkable. Rather above the middle height, but spare in figure, with dark brown hair already a little thin and grizzled about the forehead, and yet possessing a pair of keen light grey eyes, which for some reason are generally kept half shut, with bold aquiline nose and small firm set mouth, with thin nervous lips which have a tendency to work satirically when not closed—his is a face you would hardly pass without a second glance. He has a weary listless look about him, and lounges down to the gate as though his destination were not only a matter of doubt, but complete indifference. And him Charlie Burke addresses in his out-spoken hearty tones.

"I say now, you are just the man I wanted. Can you tell me where your cousin is ?"

"My dear Burke, how should I know ? Am I my cousin's keeper ?"

"No, but he is Brydges' keeper apparently, and I want to see him."

"I thought it was I whom you wanted just now ; never mind, you won't have to wait long, for here comes their basket-carriage."

"I never knew two men so thick as Fordyce and Brydges, they are just like a pair of those little birds who sit side by side and say ' tweet' to each other. Parroquets, amadovats, what d'ye call em? They are together driving, riding, walking—everything in fact."

"Well," remarked Ponsonby, who had subsided upon a stone seat the gateway afforded, as if standing were an unnecessary exertion. "Well, what of it ?"

"Nothing of course, as far I am concerned," replied Burke, "I like men to be thick together, and your cousin is no end of a good fellow."

"Yes, John acts up to his lights, but—"

"But you were going to say he is a ' leetle' too fast for you. Well, I don't know, you see I am not particular myself, not that I know of at least; but I must say I think Fordyce and Brydges make the running rather quicker than I care for. Brydges is just as bad."

"Of course, because my good cousin is his tutor in all. Brydges is exactly like an empty glass, you may fill him with what you please."

"Mr. Marbecke said to me the other day," interrupted Purcell, with blushing energy, "that he was afraid both Fordyce and Brydges were going on badly."

"My dear Purcell," replied Ponsonby, having carefully pulled each whisker as if to ascertain whether they agreed in length, "if you can only quote Marbecke, let me advise you as a friend to 'shut up,' to use Burke's pet expression."

"But you know he's a very good man, Ponsonby."

"I know nothing of the kind, my good fellow. And even so, that does not prevent his being a fool. I think now that all the 'good men' I ever met were fools more or less, generally more."

"But why do you dislike him so ?"

"I'm too good a Christian to dislike any one, my dear child, especially a Marbecke. Why, he amuses me, he's a kind of ecclesiastical Don Quixote or a mediæval masquer, who performs his antics for our delectation—we ought to be grateful to such men. But take their opinion—I think not. And here he comes, I declare."

As he spoke, a tall, grave, cleric approached, clad in the long black straight cut coat, and the white linen hoop which is or was the distinguishing garb of the orthodox High Churchman. He was gentlemanly in appearance and not unkindly in face, although small eyes and a large firm chin gave him a look of ungovernable obstinacy and self-satisfaction which formed the ground work of his character. As he approached, the three young men slightly raised their hats, for he was a high college dignitary, being not only tutor and fellow, but bursar and dean as well. I should have said that two raised their hats slightly, and the third which, as you may guess, was Edgar Purcell, saluted with deep respect. At the same time he drew near, and it was evident that he had been waiting for Marbecke.

"I fear I am behind time, Purcell, ah, yes, I see—fifteen minutes late. I am sorry, but have been detained on rather an important business with the Head. However, we shall get our walk now, so let us start." And pupil and preceptor went off arm in arm.

"There goes an illuminated MS. in vellum, and a folio in parchment and boards," remarked Ponsonby, who had risen to watch them.

"What do you say to a small squib and a Roman candle?" echoed a voice behind, and as a heavy hand was laid on his shoulder, Cyril turned and saw his cousin John Fordyce, and his inseparable friend Brydges. I have already in this chapter drawn three portraits in my rough way, and so I shall certainly spare the reader any more just yet—especially as Fordyce can wait for the present very well.

Arthur Brydges was little more than a good-looking lad, on whose face utter indecision was only too plainly written. He looked dissipated, languid, and weary, and two dark rings round his eyes told of late hours and amusements scarcely conducive to health. He leant on Fordyce's arm as though unable to stand alone, and echoed Fordyce's words as though incapable of independent thought.

"Do you know, John," said his cousin, "that you almost said a smart thing?"

" Never mind, Cyril, it was an accident not likely to happen again. Hallo, Burke I didn't see you, what are you two loafing here for ?"

"I am waiting for something to happen," replied Cyril calmly.

" And I came to the gate to meet you two," said Burke. " Where on earth have you been hiding ? I want you both, and Ponsonby too to come to wine to-night."

" You're a brick, old fellow," was Fordyce's reply, as he walked with his friend to the little basket-carriage. " All right for both of us. Seven, I suppose ?"

"! Seven, and you'll come too Ponsonby ?"

" Stop a minute, is it going to be a squash ? because if so excuse me, but I am not as young as I was, and there are such things as nerves."

" Never fear, man, there will only be about half a dozen"

" Any out college men ?"

" Only one, and that's a man I know you like, Maxwell of St. Catherine's"

Now Maxwell of St. Catherine's was what is called a swell. He was the scholar of his year, and a double first to boot. He was now up for Divinity Lectures and was much sought after by the younger men. A curious smile stole over Cyril's mouth, and he answered.

" All right, one more question and I've done. The claret—will it be the ' Burke' ?"

" It will be the ' Burke' as you call it; got a fresh supply from home."

" My dear fellow, consider the matter settled, I wish you a delightful ride."

Just then a handsome grey was led up to the gate, and in another moment Charlie Burke was mounted and prancing down the street with that sidelong movement in which horses will sometimes indulge. Cyril watched the little cloud of dust for a minute or so, and then apparently forgetful of whatever had brought him down to the college gates, retraced his steps murmuring softly to himself, " I think I'll go to my rooms and wait for something to happen," which was his favourite phrase for being idle. And accordingly he went to his luxuriously furnished rooms, where flinging himself into an easy chair with his legs on another he managed to pass the afternoon with a novel and many cigars. After Hall, those invited duly assembled in Burke's rooms with two exceptions, Fordyce and Brydges.

It is not my intention to undertake the description of that wondrous party, called an university ' wine.' All the world knows that it is simply the meeting of friends after dinner for the purposes of desert.

Whereas the fellows and dons of colleges assemble in Common-room for the discussion of that repast; undergraduates, who are a sociable race, meet in their own rooms, where the banquet is more or less prolonged, according to the wealth of the host or the inclination of his guests. The thing has been described over and over again, with varying success, from the piquant chronicles of our friend "Tom Brown" to the beer and tobacco-stained pages of "Mr. Verdant Green's Adventures." Of one thing the reader may be sure, that at 'wines,' as a rule, the guests neither quote Latin and Greek, and talk Essays, nor on the other hand do they drink to excess. There may be a few pedants and a few drunkards, but they are the exception. Besides Burke, Ponsonby and Purcell, whom we have seen before, there were three other St. Margaret's men of not sufficient individuality to need description, and the great gun of the evening, Maxwell of St.

Catherine's, a pleasant intellectual-looking man senior to most there, who endured with much good humour the "chaff" which was levelled at his newly acquired honours.

"I say, old fellow," remarked the host "it is no end good of you to come, I was half afraid to ask you, you know, I was indeed."

"Did you think I had become too great a don, Burke, then? No, no, I am only a sucking don as yet, I have not yet developed into the full-grown porker."

"I hope," said Ponsonby, "that you are too human ever to sink so far. And yet I don't know, I have known several really nice men who have been utterly spoilt. Evil communications corrupt good manners."

"Then you might be made a don with impunity," replied Burke, "for you've no manners to speak of."

"I am a child of nature," was the answer, "and I am awaiting a further development."

"It is almost time it came, I think," said Maxwell laughing. "But, of course you'll scream at the idea, but I really think that most of the dons mean very well to us—there let me include myself as a youngster—to us undergraduates."

"Mean? Quite possible. Only they are like the seven holy sleepers of Ephesus, I have no doubt you know their names, Purcell, for it's in your line, who on awaking knew neither the world nor the age they were living in. The Commonroom after all is a kind of Sleepy Hollow."

"Come, come, that's a little too much, you cynic. In the first place you are confusing your similes, Rip Van Winkle was not one of the brothers of Ephesus, at least, I never heard so; and, secondly, you argue from a very few particulars

ᴄ 2

to a sweeping general conclusion. The greater part of the fellows are not only energetic, but very anxious for the good of their pupils."

"I am sure, Marbecke is," burst in Purcell, who had been waiting an opportunity long.

"Yes, and by the good of his pupils, he means their utter slavish subjection to himself; he means bringing them to confession, like whipped children, forbidding their having an independent opinion, and keeping them eternally playing parts in that Mediæval masquerade of which he is leader and director."

"I say," remarked Burke, "poor old Marbecke! I can't say I am particularly fond of him, he's not my sort, you see; but you are rather savage against him, Ponsonby, on my honour. There fill your glass, man, and don't get hot."

"What Marbecke may have said or done

to hurt you, of course, I don't know," said Maxwell, with rather a marked manner, "but you certainly are not only savage, but unjust also. I dislike those extravagant High Church notions he upholds as much as any one; but I believe him to be a perfectly sincere, single-hearted man, the object of whose life is to do good."

"My dear Maxwell, I never argue, certainly not when it is as hot as it is now; *most* certainly not with a double first and fellow of St. Catherine's. So, if you please, we will change the subject; nay, if you like, I will drink the worthy Marbecke's health. At the same time I may observe, *en passant*, that some people's good lives do far more harm than other people's bad lives."

Perhaps the host feared that the Parthian shot might rouse the battle again, for he broke off a conversation about the Henley race, to exclaim: "That's right, both. And now that is settled, what on earth has became of Fordyce and Brydges, you know it's too bad to say they'll come, and then stay away."

"My cousin never was in time for anything," replied Ponsonby. "It's his way, I believe he upset all my aunt's calculations, and came into the world very much after he was due."

There was a laugh, and then Burke continued in a grieved tone, "I'll tell you what, the ice is spoiling and I've a great mind to send the scout's boy over to their rooms to see whether they've come back."

After considerable shouting, that young gentleman was duly found and despatched, only to return with the news that "Mr. Fordyce was not in his rooms, nor Mr. Brydges neither."

"I'll tell you where they are very likely,

as they were not at Hall. Send to the Mitre, and see whether they are at dinner there. At least, if it is worth the trouble," added Ponsonby lazily.

" By Jove, the very thing. Here, Jack, you go as hard as you can to the Mitre, and ask who is dining there. Look sharp, and cut back again."

In a few minutes after, a cab was heard to drive furiously up to the gates, and Purcell, who was near the window, reported that he saw a man run across the grass plat, and go into the Master's lodgings.

" A frantic candidate for matriculation, perhaps," suggested Ponsonby, laughing.

" More likely the bearer of some bad news," said Maxwell, rather gravely, and his manner seemed to cast a chill over them all.

At the same moment, Jack returned with his broad face unusually pale, and dismay in his eyes. "They were neither of them there, Sir; and, oh, Sir, they do say that something has happened."

The party rose simultaneously, and put down their glasses.

"Something, you fool, what do you mean by your somethings?" indignantly demanded Burke, "speak up, man, and say what."

"Do you mean an accident, my man," asked Ponsonby, very quietly, though his pale olive face had become paler than usual.

"Yes, Sir; yes, Mr. Ponsonby, that's it; and please, Sir, they're bringing it down the High."

'It'—that little word told the tale. No longer a living man but a corpse. One of these two young men who had gone out so full of health and strength but six hours ago was dead!

"Who is it?" enquired Ponsonby, in

his restrained voice. "Did you hear?"

"No, Sir, I don't know which it is rightly, but the trap is smashed and the pony killed."

It sounded bad enough certainly. But Ponsonby's keen eye detected the boy knew more.

"You have heard some name mentioned; tell me, I insist."

"Mr. Fordyce, Sir, they did say, but 'tisn't known for true."

Cyril turned slightly aside, and quickly filling and emptying a glass of wine, said rather unsteadily : "I'll go to the gate, I think, very likely its only a rumour," and he ran down. But as he reached the gate through the quad, already filling, he saw that the large folding leaves were closed and only the wicket open ; and he heard a regular measured tread outside, and a surging throng beyond. In a minute more 'It' was brought in, stretched on a shutter, and covered with a sheet on which was one little spot of blood. And after 'It,' came John Fordyce with his head bare, and his coat torn and dust covered, but alive and uninjured.

"Jack was mistaken then, it was Arthur Brydges who was killed."

Cyril went up and put his hand in John's, but John neither spoke nor looked, his gaze was fixed upon the ghastly burden in front. Nor when the Master approached with some words of comfort, did he look up or reply. He followed the corpse until it was deposited in what had been Brydges' rooms, opposite his own, and then without a word or sigh turned away to his open oak, which, in a moment after, those outside heard slammed, bolted and locked.

Before long the whole college knew that on their return Brydges, who was not quite sober at the time, had insisted

on driving. Something frightened the
pony and caused it to run away ; before
Fordyce could seize the reins in his
firm grasp, one wheel had gone over a
fallen tree and flung them both out—John
unhurt, Brydges killed on the spot, and
the pony injured so as to necessitate its
instant death.

That night, between eleven o'clock and
twelve o'clock, the Rev. Thomas Marbecke
descended the staircase whereon his rooms
were situated, and came into the moonlit
quad. Having crossed the grass-plat, he
ascended staircase No. 3, where were
Fordyce's rooms, and knocked at the
oak. That done, he turned his face to the
opposite rooms, where 'It' lay, and I
think read something from a little red
edged book he carried with him. As no
answer came, he accompanied the louder
knock he next gave with the intimation
that it was the Rev. Thomas Marbecke,

dean and bursar, who demanded admittance. And that potent name was successful, for in a minute after the door was flung open, and he entered the dim dark room. John Fordyce cast himself again into the chair from which he had risen, and leant his tearless face upon his arms. Marbecke took up a situation on the hearthrug.

Now this man, as we have said, was neither bad nor cruel, but when he spoke, his words fell on John's ears like drops of vitriol.

"I am not come, Mr. Fordyce, in my capacity as your tutor or dean of this college. Nor am I come to make any enquiries, or pronounce any censure. Tomorrow, of course, you will go before the Master, and the Master will act by his own discretion as may seem best to him. But I am come in a far higher office; I am come as a priest of the holy Catholic

Church, of which you are a member, however little you may esteem it. And I am come to point the warning which this awful catastrophe brings with it, to exhort you to turn from your resolute course of evil living, and to seek the only true way of peace according to the method which alone is authorised by the Holy Mother Church. I, a priest of that church, come to you, I hope a penitent sinner, to invite you to that wholesome confession by which alone can you obtain remission of your many sins. And when you hear my voice pronounce words of absolution, you will esteem it as the voice of Christ from whom I have received my commission."

As he ceased, he laid his right hand upon the head of Fordyce as though to give the preparatory Benediction which, in the Roman ritual he imitated to the best of his power, precedes the form of confession. But he was mistaken, for John drew himself slightly up and replied in low but respectful terms.

"Mr. Marbecke, doubtless you mean kindly ; but if, as you say, you are not here as a college officer nor as a friend, excuse me if I say I am too ill and sad to listen to you in any other capacity. Please leave me alone."

And then he laid down his head without another word. Marbecke's small black eyes glittered with disappointment and anger, and regretting that John was not in a more fitting state of mind, he turned away. But though John was all alone, there was with him, I imagine, a better presence, and a more powerful voice than that of the baffled Anglican Priest.

CHAPTER I.

"FROM all shams, good Lord, deliver us." At which exclamation, I see and hear in my mind's eye a chorus of bull-frog voiced old ladies and gentlemen, who straightway accuse me of blasphemy, ribaldry and all the collected sins of Korah, Dathan and Abiram. I am condemned—untried—and executed. Be it so. Then my ghost uprears itself, and in hoarse tones repeats, "From all shams, good Lord, deliver us."

Aye, in very sober and sad earnest, dear brothers and sisters, have we not all need to pray for deliverance from shams? to fight, and work, and struggle for escape

from the clutches of those unlovely birds
of evil and foulness, which grip us tight
and flap their narcotic wings in our eyes
till light and darkness appear the same ?
Indeed we have, and none the less because
we won't acknowledge them to be evil
and unclean birds, preferring to call them
innocent doves and such like harmless
fowl. We intreat deliverance from a devil
and all his works—ten times more should
we ask deliverance from 'shams' which
are the very breath of his nostrils, coming
with brimstone perfume from the bottom-
less pit and choking us ere yet we are
aware of it.

Let us have war then with shams,
unrealities and delusions, be they political,
religious, or domestic. Let us pull down
the gauze curtain on which these Chinese
shadows are reflected, and look the Truth
in the face. Better be blinded at once by
a sudden in-pouring of pent-up angry

daylight, than grope for ever in the Cyclops, dark cavern, bone-strown and blood-bedaubed, swearing that the illumination thereof is the completest, genteelest thing we ever yet beheld. And for this reason chiefly, that when we have once accustomed ourselves to a daily diet of shams and unreal viands, our taste and appetite does gradually loathe all wholesome food, and we sit down contentedly for ever by the side of those unhappy flesh-pots, the end of which is death. And so, I end as I began, " From all shams, Good Lord, deliver us." " And what in the world," asks the enraged reader, " what in the world has that to do with your hero, or your story ? Leave shams to Mr. Carlyle, and, remember, " ne sutor ultra crepidam." Very good, worthy reader, we will resume.

John Fordyce was the only son of the Rev. Henry Everett Comberland Fordyce,

Rector of Easimore-cum-Slugabed in the
Fens, with its comfortable Rectory, spa-
cious conservatory, pinery, melon-pits,
and fruitful garden, the envy of the
county. It was evident that the labourer
who lived there must be very well worthy
of his hire, and so indeed he mostly
thought himself. The parish consisted
of a closely packed population of five
hundred, whilst the great and little tithes
amounted to eleven hundred pounds per
annum, so that for the care (or neglect)
of each single soul, the Rector received
two pounds four shillings annually.

Now let us see how Mr. Fordyce became entitled to the prefix of Reverend.
He was the second son of Squire Fordyce, of Chesham Hall, and in his early
days was more remarkable for riding well
up to hounds, never missing his bird,
and the numbers of tumblers of whiskey
punch he was able to carry, than for

much study, or any devotional tendencies.

Algernon, the eldest born, who, of course, would succeed to the entailed estate, had come out a "First" at Oxford. Henry, on the other hand, "scratched" more than once, and escaped plucking by the skin of his teeth; but what he wanted in honours he made up in debts, such a cloud of which followed the prodigal down to the Chesham roof tree, that the poor Squire, groaning under the difficulties of an entailed estate and three unmarried daughters to provide for, threatened to cut off supplies, and hinted at emigration; but at the critical moment, the creaking of wheels and pullies is heard, and a goddess descends from the machine.

Goddess this ! old, lean and ill-favoured. Parnassus knows her not, nor Olympus,

nor the waters of Helicon. By mortals
yclept, Aunt Grizzel; she wears a nim-
bus of banker's cheques, and at her
shrine much incense is consumed, and
many a votive taper lit. With an old
lady's usual preference of highly flavoured
black sheep, to tasteless innocent lamb,
her affections passed over the immaculate Algernon, over Jemima, Sarah and
Ethelinda, the virgin daughters of Chesham, to fix and centre upon the reprobate Henry Everett Comberland; and this
was her scheme for his help.

" With a golden pitchfork, my nephew,
will I hoist thee from the mud heap, and
land thee straight in—the church. Too
idle for a lawyer, too empty for diplomacy, too foolish even for a guardsman,
the church is your vocation; into it
you shall go."

And so the good lady advanced, waving
her cheque book in one hand, and the

Advowson of Easimore-cum-Slugabed in the other. To choose between a harpy chorus of creditors shrieking for blood, and the dulcet title of Reverend—who could hesitate? Not the high flavoured black sheep at all events; with so loud an outward call, that from within could not be long in following, and so Aunt Grizzel—a modern Minerva—bore off in triumph her young Telemachus to be crammed for his examination for Holy Orders. What with wet towels, pale ale and soda-water, he managed to pass tolerably, and so at the end of a year's apprenticeship as a curate, stepped into his living. Thus was he pitchforked into the Church, and falling on his back in a heap of rose leaves and vine clusters, became that lump of inutility and plague spot to the eyes of angels, a fat, lazy parson, a pig who could not even say " Humph" for his food.

This a strong specimen, we grant, and the state of things which allowed, almost encouraged, such evils is rapidly passing away. For all that, such men have flourished as clergy and are to be met even now. In all that has gone before and all that follows, let the reader remember that the Rev. Henry Fordyce is a picture drawn from nature, from actual facts existent, for all we know, at the present time, neither extenuated nor exaggerated.

To such a one what will say the stern Three—rigidly-unalterable assigners of the fates of men? Perhaps on this wise. "You there, by Nature, man, by vile pot-love and lucre-hunger, so-called priest, man, half-hog, half-sloth, what can you say for yourself? How came *you* by a shepherd's crook—having it, how have you used it? Was a flock, yours, only to receive the fleece money? Was it for you

to sit by your vile flesh-pots with much
onions and cucumbers, while rams, and
ewes, and lambs went straight into the
jaws of such wolves and grizzly beasts as
waited on your idleness? What of the
wolf, do *you* know? Bearest thou the mark
of his fangs and claws, or he of thy staff?
What of thy flock? didst care to close
and fold it, at eve when the storm
winds arose? Look at thy fair linen and
trumpery, what are those spots we see?
The blood-stains of the wounds of each
sheep the wolf has torn, each lamb let
stray, and wander, and lost. Go, sorry,
impudent wretch with thy pot-hunger and
onion-greed, go vile intruder into a fold
not thine by the eternal laws, go into
such depth of Malebolge as natural gravity
shall sink thee to."

Only, remember, dear ladies and gentlemen, that neither the author nor the
genteel world makes the above-mentioned

remarks. They proceed simply from a trio of the Three stern judges of the infernal kingdom, with a little growling obligato for Cerberus. We must excuse such radical murmurs coming from so low a place.

In the meantime, how should the world speak of him save as a worthy and decorous member of society ? For he has not trodden on the corns of said society, and so men swear he is an excellent fellow-traveller. And truly—but on what road ? He pays his debts, restores his church, gives good dinners, and splendid wines, is staunchly Conservative and sends beer-gruel to sick women. What more would you have ? He quietly eats his his way to Heaven as men keep their terms for the Bar—though perhaps he may find the reckoning harder to pay than a barrister and in other coin, I ween; possibly tear-drops, possibly very heart-drops, and sighs, and groans.

O, Ministers in holy things and waiters on the Altar, see that ye obscure not its flame by those seething cauldrons where-with Belial, the belly god, is served. O men, whose carcases need all your care and thought, what time have you for the bodies and souls of John Hodges and all his family of cow-herds and earth delvers ? And yet, I trow, if for the bread they ask of you, you give them stones—yea, be they never so much polished and chipped by custom, said stones will one day return upon your heads in an altogether unexpected and other manner than you look for. For, at least, if Nature does not prevent her children acting the parts of swine, mules, and sloths, she requites them with their fate and more.

After two years' bachelorhood, mail-phaeton driving, hunting, shooting, danc-ing, and the like, after two years' utterance of boyish themes to Sunday

congregations, after marrying, baptising,
burying, and neglecting various and all
of his parishoners, the Rev. Henry
Fordyce availed himself of the license of
Anglican orders and took to himself a
wife. As he did nothing in his parish,
it was evident that he needed not a
curate to help him thereat, but a wife
would in every way enhance his position
and enable him to fulfil his duties to
society the better.

The lady whom he chose for this purpose,
was admirably suited to him. Miss Arabella
Lovaine, daughter of a neighbouring
squire, pretty, silly, and with a nice
little sum of her own. As she danced
herself into his affections, so did he take
by storm the heart of the worthy squire,
who, generally disliking what he elegantly
called, "black cattle," never failed to
pronounce Fordyce " a right down good
sort of chap, with no methodistical non-

sense about him, and not a bit of a parson
or a fool."

The stomachs of the Easimore flock
were bettered by the match, for the Rector
was in the main both good-humoured and
liberal enough to them, only needing some
one to suggest such ways of benevolence
as required no exertion.   So beer-gruel in
plenty, yea, and old port, too, was given
to those who needed; black draught and
cholera mixture were kept ready for
emergency, and Christmas was celebrated
by all the village stomachs with much
plum-pudding and meats various.

Mrs. Fordyce was very popular: for
when people have been accustomed to
nothing, a little goes a great way.   Not
only did she say " Good cheeild" to every
curtseying or lock-pulling rustic she met,
but would ask Joan after Darby's rheumatism, and whether " our Tummus" was a
good boy.   Three old women and two old

men did she occasionally visit, and to them
read aloud Blair's sermons ; but then
as they were mostly deaf, no harm was
done.   And once a-quarter did the mail-
phaeton convey her to the leading farmers'
houses, there to admire their old-fashioned
china, praise their clove carnations, and
taste their ginger-wine, which she "infinitely preferred to sherry."   A notable
Phyllis, this careful Pastora of the
ovine fleeces.   I wonder if she ever
thought there was more of them than
fleece and stomach.

Nor was this all.   Passing over such
items as hunt breakfasts, tea-drinking,
and school-prizes, works of supererogation
at which angels must clap hands and shed
tears of joy, we come to the crowning
point of all.

Need I say that the Rector was a Tory
of the purest kind, and utterly determined
to conserve and preserve all our "old

ancient Institutions"—especially Rectorial tithes ? When therefore the Tract movement commenced, it was at first regarded by him with suspicion. By degrees, however, as High Church began to ally itself with Conservatism, and Low Church with Whiggery, the Rector thought it time to take in and trim his sails. He had his library furnished by a great London bookseller with the chief 'Anglican' divines. He did not read them, it is true, and if he had, would not have understood them; but then their morocco and gold backs gave a pleasing warmth to the study, and altogether looked well. He then restored three gable crosses, and as he found this offended the Dissenters, and annoyed the rural Dean (a Whig;) in great glee, he proceeded first to restore the venerable broken nose of St. Frideswide, and at length to repair the whole fabric of the church, with due regard to ancient example. That eminent little High Church architect, Gluepin, was selected for this work, and managed to introduce as much Romish scenery and accessories as the occasion allowed; although, as he confessed afterwards, he was afraid Mr. Fordyce had not "a really Catholic mind."

In other things, the parish went on much as usual, the stream of Blair and water being turned on for half an hour once a-week, whereat all the thirsty might drink as they listed.

A large proportion, comprising, perhaps, the more earnest part of the parish, preferred the stronger drams of Jabez Dutton, of the new connection, and went some four miles, wet or dry, to hear him. But these were Dissenters, of whom the Rector used to say, "he'd as lieve meet a toad."

In course of time a son, our hero, John Fordyce, was born, and greeted with much joy. As his father destined him to succeed to the living, it was only natural that he should train him after that fashion which had succeeded so well with himself; and, accordingly, undertaking the rudiments of Latin and Greek to his own part, morals "and all that" were left to be instilled into the neophyte by Tom, the groom, and Jerry, the stable-boy. All which progressed charmingly and with effects altogether noteworthy. From ten till twelve the mental development went on by means of Delectus and the Analecta; then for the rest of the day the boy was given up to such able tutors as the devil could spare. And very excellent ones he *did* provide, choosing them with that admirable tact which, to do him justice, he usually displays.

The ingenious reader need not think from these remarks that poor Tom and Jerry were desperately wicked specimens of their class, or that all association with that class is a thing to be avoided by gentlemen's sons. Doubtless, there are excellent Toms and most virtuous Jerries to be found, only we would venture to hint that such are rare, and that, in the meantime, unlimited association with stable-helpers is slightly apt to tinge the mind and twist such morals as belong to young gentlemen of twelve and thirteen.

John Fordyce was a gentlemanly boy, that is to say, he neither swore in ladies' society, gorged himself at meals, nor broke the Queen's English, always opened the door for a lady and sometimes wiped his feet on the hall-mat. Well-dressed, nice-mannered, healthy, and athletic—was not this enough? However, there was yet something more, to wit, a heart, not utterly spoilt by a father's neglect and a mother's folly; a taste not necessarily vicious, only vitiated, which had blundered

into quagmires, because not trained to
see the advantage of a well-paved road.
And so, this said, John was sent to
Eton.

"Spare us his Eton school life, if you
please, Mr. Author!" With the greatest
pleasure in life, good reader, and for
one very excellent reason, if not more,
viz., that never having been to Eton myself, my description of and opinions about
it would necessarily be somewhat foggy.
Of course, you know I could write after
a fashion, either in the muscular or rose-
water styles. I might delineate his
youthful form gathering laurels, now at
the classic contest, now as captain of the
boats. I might dwell sweetly on the
quiet converse at the hour of eve, the
earnest argument on some deep point in
which he and some favoured companion
should argue like St. Thomas Aquinas and
Duns Scotus. Or I might draw that

wondrous supper up in the dormitories,
and enumerate the ducks, the pies, the
tarts, the punch, the wine, and—the
consequences. But as I don't think this
would be particularly interesting to my
readers, I beg to refer them to the many
charming accounts of Eton life existing,
and request them to fill in the *lacunæ* as
they please.

Neither worse nor better than any other
lad was John Fordyce, and his actions
were those only that might be expected
from such training as he had received.
"Oh, but the thought of his mother kept
him straight." Indeed, my romantic friend ?
why should the remembrance of a well-
dressed, good-tempered, middle-aged lady,
particular about the set of her point lace
cap and the due proportion of clotted
cream to plum pudding, influence him in
any special manner ? Certainly she was
most careful about the airing of his linen,

and liked to see him well brushed and
well dressed, kept him liberally tipped
while at school, and sometimes wrote to
say how his dogs and pony were. But
that was all. No seeking for boyish
confidence, no gentle warnings or kind
advice.

I would humbly suggest that in the
fiery trial and hand to hand devil-fight,
quite other ideas than of good-tempered
and sugar-lipped mothers must come to
rescue their children.

Let them picture a kneeling form heart-
riven in earnest prayer and intercession,
eyes half brimming over with tears, half
smiling unspoken encouragement; let them
imagine a soft pleading hand placed in
tender confidence upon the arm, and better
than all this let them know that this is
the truth, that such a mother does exist,
does pray, does weep for them miles
away; and if after this they turn to mud-

baths, away with all such to the brook
Kishon, or other suitable slaughter ground.

But then how inconvenient all this
would be to the mothers. " Well, then,
the athletic sports of course would render
his mind healthy." Not so fast, good Sir,
athletic sports alone can never make men
or boys more than strong men and boys,
of course that is very much better than
weak men and boys ; but what I mean is,
they wont make them Christians without
some collateral training, and that is exactly
what our hero had never received. Grace
was said before meat, on Sundays he
went to church once, and that was the
extent of his Christianity.

Prayers are soon forgotten after nursery
days, and even if not, where acts are not
prayerful, words do not go for much.
When he went to school, his mother told
him to be careful of his clothes and to
put on flannel in October. His father

told him to stick to his books and not get into debt. Behold, the whole duty of man! And, so when John Fordyce left Eton, which he did at the age of nineteen, he left it a clever, tolerably well-read, athletic gentlemanly heathen, possessor of a somewhat extensive acreage sown chiefly with tares and wild oats, of which the harvest was yet to come.

CHAPTER II.

IT has been mentioned that the three daughters of Squire Fordyce were named respectively, Jemima, Sarah, and Ethelinda. With the two former, as with their brother Algernon, this history has nothing further to do. On their father's death, they betook themselves and their money to Cheltenham, Bath, or other such paradise of unmarried ladies of that age which is usually called 'certain,' and doubtless lived happy, and died respected and regretted. But with Ethelinda it was otherwise, and her fortunes demand a certain amount of attention from us. Soon after her brother Henry's elevation to the Easimore Rectory, she had the good luck to be introduced to no less a personage than Horatio Powys Gerald Ponsonby, Esq., late Secretary to the Rag, Bag, and Bone department, and a member of that most respectable family, the Ponsonbys. It is true that, as a family, they were somewhat pompous, possibly even a little dull, but then *so* respectable! No one could say a word against them; except, of course, those little good-natured remarks whereby we show our love for one another. But I mean, they, the Ponsonby family, had never been cited before the world's tribunal for certain crimes and misdemeanours, they had never had to hold up their hand and plead; on the contrary, they were entitled to pass judgment upon and fulminate edicts against other their offending neighbours. And really in these troublesome, high-pressure times, this is saying much; for of late the Publicans have been busy with some most respectable Pharisees, and try to insist that they are like other men after all, very much disturbing the even tenor of their prayer, as they stand in the inner place. But bold would be the man who could accuse the Ponsonbys of aught. They did all by rule.

They were neither extreme nor emotional. Everything answered their expectations, no disappointments, no mistakes, no blunders ever occurred; they never had to confess themselves wrong, and indeed if they had been wrong, wouldn't have done so. No *mauvais sujet*, no black sheep, no questionable character under a cloud, ever made his way into the Ponsonby fold. Fleeces of the thickest, whitest, softest, cleanest, adorned each Ponsonby back, nor did any desire to wander from their eligible pasturage. And thus they walked merrily

along the broad path of honour, arm in
arm with the world and the flesh, while
the third member of the firm swept the
road clean before them and opened the
gates. Now of this family, Horatio &c.
&c. Ponsonby was a good specimen. He
was one of those men whom Nature
evidently intended for a courtier. Even
as a child, it was noticed that he crawled
on all fours later than most of like age,
while his early playthings were a tattered
old copy of Burke's Peerage, and a gilt
crown from the frame of a portrait of
George III.

Later in life, though still in boyhood, he
developed a marvellous love for natural
science, shown chiefly by a curious collection of British toadstools and other
fungi, gathered together at some cost
and labour.

At College, he distinguished himself
by coming out as 'honorary fourth' at

the same time as the Earl of Walford,
whose acquaintance he had cultivated
with assiduty. Nor was this all, for
shortly after he became private secretary
to Lord Dustye Perriwygge, whose
son, the Honourable Bob Tayle, he had
extricated from some escapade into which
his joyous spirits had led him.

Here his talents had full range and
scope. It was soon known that the
masterly series of articles upon the Treaty
with Van Diemen's Land, which en-
tranced the readers of the " Scourge,"
proceeded from his pen, nor was virtue,
in this case, her own and sole reward.
When the Secretaryship of the Rag, Bag,
and Bone department fell vacant, by
the translation of Mr. Aston Poker
to a higher sphere, the Perriwygge
influence was strong enough to secure
that important place for Mr. Ponsonby
who filled it worthily for many years,

ultimately to retire upon his pension of
£800 per annum. And then he fell in
with Miss Ethelinda Fordyce, and seeing
in her all those charms he desired, laid
such successful siege to the blushing
damsel of thirty-five, that finally she
was persuaded to become Mrs. Horatio
Ponsonby. But before we pass to the
description of this good lady, let us
remark the personal appearance of her
husband.

He was tall, with an habitual bend in
the back and twist of his head, which
seemed to imply an incessant assent,
a kind of "exactly so," which alone
showed his fitness for Court atmosphere.
His glistening bald head, with its fringe
of hair, his curved Roman nose, and his
keen grey eyes, made the resemblance
to a vulture very striking, especially as
he had a habit of nervously rubbing
together his bony white hands with their

long almond shaped nails, as though
about to pounce, and sharpening his
talons beforehand. *Du reste,* he was
politic, grave, shrewd, and desirous his
family should do well in the world.

And Mrs. Ponsonby? Well, she was
not good-looking; but then you could
not call her "ugly." She had far too
good taste to be anything so distinct
and pronounced. She was plain—yes,
that is the word, plain; just such
features as you would pass by without
a second glance, and forget as soon as
seen. She had the look of having been
sent bodily to a careless washer-woman,
who had taken all colour and stiffness
out of her. Her face was nondescript;
pale, grey-green eyes with white lashes,
a nose which, once intended to be an
aquiline, had signally failed, and now
presented an obtuse angle, slightly flat-
tened on one side, as though it really

had not the courage to advance upon
you straight; a small mouth, buttonny
and vague, such a mouth as never could
say "I will," or "I won't;" and feeble
curls of straw colour supporting what
upholsterers call a "swag," like the
drooping fold of a curtain—and you
have Ethelinda Ponsonby.

The colours she chose in dress being
somewhat faded and vague, harmonised
admirably with her complexion. Pale
dove colour, soft greys and greenish
drabs were the hues of her choice,
which had the result of making her
resemble a moulting canary. She had
a weakness for bracelets and brooches
of a feeble and imbecile kind, as Tunbridge ware or imitation mosaic, and
her caps quivered with so many flowers
and butterflies as to resemble a botanical
garden.

Her character I need not describe, as

she had none. Possibly in her youth
she may have possessed some ideas, if
so, time had woven them into such a
tangle as no power could unravel; but
as she always did as she was told and
had no independent action, this did not
matter.

The Ponsonby family consisted of three
children. Cyril, with whom we are already acquainted, and two daughters.
Charlotte and Annie were two good-looking, lady-like girls; but more than this
they had each chosen their *spécialité* or
line of their own, the family respectability of course being paramount. Char-
was a " blue," an *esprit fort*, a nineteenth
century Hypatia, with a slight dash of
Madame de Staël. Her talk was of systems and theories, and " isms " and
" cosms ;" while on the question of the
origin of species she had held a long
correspondence with a certain great man,

which reflected equal honour on her head and heart. And Annie, dear Annie, was the innocent foil, slightly silly, slightly fast; but oh! so natural and genuine that it did your heart good to see and hear her.

Until the age of twelve or thirteen, Master Cyril had been brought up at home under the special supervision and care of his father, and in the continual companionship of his mother and sisters; from which ensued mainly two results, that he was thoroughly well grounded in French and English, and that already at that early period had begun to imbibe his father's ideas and philosophy with regard to mankind.

Retaining somewhat of the old diplomatic leaven about him, Mr. Ponsonby looked upon every man as an habitual liar until his truthfulness was made clear. "All men are by nature and inclination rascals," he was fond of saying, " but some are fools also and they are found out. We are all virtuous when it suits our purpose, and the fear of discovery is the only restraining motive from crime. Should I quarrel with my neighbour because he is a rogue? Certainly not, good taste forbids it : but I am on my guard. It is diamond cut diamond, and the sharpest wins." Now, of course, I do not mean to say that the good diplomat habitually used these words in addressing his son. Far from it, he was one of those really clever men who inform and mould without advising. No man ever goes to ask a friend's advice with the serious determination of following it out. Even supposing he should do so, that innate spirit of contradiction which dwells deep in the human breast would at once rise up in arms. No, no, we make up our minds first and then we visit our friend, if possible to gain confir-

mation, at least to pay what is supposed
to be a compliment. And this Mr. Ponsonby knew well, and accordingly never
advised Cyril to one course or another.
He laid them before him and drew his
attention to the consequences. "And an
excellent plan too, Sir, one calculated to
exercise and improve the lad's judgment
and power of decision." Possibly, only when
a father becomes so strictly impartial, it
is very apt to lead sons to suppose that
as long as they bear the consequences
themselves, their actions matter little,
indeed that there is no such thing as a
guiding principle of life.

Gradually, Cyril became so accustomed
to hear everything regarded as a matter
of opinion or sentiment, that he fell into
the same way of thinking himself. At
twelve years of age he was to go to
school.

The Ponsonby finances would not allow

Eton, Harrow, or Rugby, and Mr. Ponsonby was somewhat puzzled to know where to send his boy. In a happy moment, however, he thought of St. Athanasius, Yoxholme, which not only had a good reputation for its scholarship and gentlemanly tone, but also was admirably suited to his rather moderate means. And so to Yoxholme Cyril Ponsonby was sent. It was a modern High Church school of limited dimensions, and for such an establishment did its work well. Now-a-days if an M.A. fails in other lines, he has only to get possession of a house, more or less convenient, inveigle some Bishop or dignitary into becoming Visitor, call his house a College and himself a Warden, issue a prospectus in the 'Watchman,' professing to give a sound classical education on church principles, and the thing is done. But, however, you must understand that St. Athanasius, Yoxholme, was none of these scholastic fungi. The college *was* a college, as far as a handsome and commodious mediæval building could make it. It had its great dining hall, its chapel, its studies, and its dormitories. There was abundance of carving in stone and wood, square feet of stained glass, yards of painted texts, and all the rest of the paraphernalia which constitute the stock in trade of such places.

But the gentleman who was called the warden, *was* a gentleman, yes, and a scholar too, and the masters and assistant-masters were of the same pattern. If a boy showed aptitude for work, they certainly were sufficiently ready to help him, and some very good scholars they sent out. And there was a very fair allowance of muscularity also, and though there was much in the system that was painfully ridiculous and affectedly mediæval, yet on the whole the Athanasian lads on leaving carried away a fair amount of culture, mental and physical.

"Then why, Mr. Author, this sub-sarcasm and acidity, what was it that you in your plenary wisdom disapprove in the Yoxholme plan?" Simply this, oh, ingenuous reader. Instead of being content to leave much to the natural principles of uprightness and honour which are to be found in every boy, if you know how to look for them, and to aim simply at making them honest, God-fearing and manly, the clerical staff were always striving to make all their pupils little duodecimo editions of the saints, little ecclesiastical partizans of the hottest kind. Now one "saintly Billy" with a passion for his "catechee" is all very well, but one is apt to get rather weary, not to say doubtful, when saintly Billies are met in dozens.

A boy with strong predilections for

altar lights and flowers, and a decided
opinion upon the Real Presence, is rather
a portentous creature. And such very
many of these gentle youths proved. They
returned to the parental roof-tree with a
combination of dogma and ritualism in
their heads, which made papas open wide
their eyes and sisters listen with admiration and rapture. This was bad, but
there was worse yet. To have your son
a dogmatical and bigoted partizan of any
special form of doctrine is bad, but to
have him profoundly sceptical as to religion
itself is perhaps worse. But such many of
these lads became, through the injudicious proselytising and clerical *espionage*
to which they were subjected. And among
these was Cyril, already predisposed that
way by his father's example. He saw
that those of his companions who talked
loudest of their religious principles, and
were best up in High Church 'slang,'

were in reality no better than their neighbours; and boylike, he drew the very unnecessary conclusion that Religion itself was in fault and a mere sham. His was a lazy, languid, indifferent nature, hard to rouse into action, although quick enough to move when the advantage of so doing was made manifest. He was one of the passively selfish, not one of those who would build his house upon the ruins of his neighbour's home; but one to allow his neighbour's house to fall to ruins, rather than exert himself so much as to raise a finger to prevent it. He had not the slightest objection to the happiness of the rest of the world, as long as it did not interfere with his own.

Such was his character when he left Yoxholme at seventeen. His career had not been specially satisfactory to his father. Not that he had managed to get into any particular hobble, or *escapade*, while there, but rather that his *insouciance* appeared likely to prevent his attaining that distinction to which his abilities entitled him. It seemed almost impossible to interest him in anything, and he came back with the reputation of being a young man who might do anything, if only he could be persuaded to apply his mind to it. He was very gentlemanly, and possessed a natural air of weariness and boredom which many a Mayfair dandy would have given much to acquire. His father surveyed him with pleasure, and looked forward to his career with hopes of success.

CHAPTER III.

ONE day, as the time for Cyril's departure for Oxford drew nigh, he was lounging round the garden after breakfast, accompanied by his eldest sister Charlotte. She was his favourite and chief companion at home, and perhaps understood him better than any one else.

" Charlie, my child, do you know that in a very short time you will have to do without me ?"

" Indeed I do, Cyril, and heartily I wish I were going too."

" You ? Why what on earth would you do with yourself at Oxford ?"

"Anything would be better than this dead weight of idleness I am condemned to bear. I am always wishing I were a man, and had some sphere of action worthy of me."

"That's a mistake, Charlotte, I should say."

"Why, what have I to do here that is useful? I read and study, as you know, and laugh at the reputation of a blue; but that is not enough. I cannot always be at my books. And what else? Would you have me descend to tract distributing, sermon reading, and sick visiting like the Vicar's daughter?"

"Heaven forbid!" murmured her brother devoutly.

"Well then, what is there for me to do? I feel to be wasting my energies, Cyril, and merely vegetating instead of living."

"Do you know, I half suspect nature

has made one of her usual blunders in
the composition of us two. You have a
double allowance of energy, your own
and mine."

"Ah, Cyril, I wish you had more. You
of all men ought to have ambition. Look
how our father succeeded in life."

"The worthy late secretary of the Rag,
Bag and Bone department is a very
estimable person. Yes, you may laugh,
Charlotte; but I assure you I positively
respect him. Regarding myself as his
son, I know I am a failure. That, you
know, I cannot help, because no man
can be his own father—at least I suppose
not. But, my dear child, for all that I
mean to succeed in my own way. My
way isn't his way, that's all. I take
things quietly, and never put myself out—
he is all fuss. Ah, there he is, you
see."

Just then Mr. Ponsonby put his head

out of a little glass door opening on the garden and called out,

"Cyril, I wish you would come in to me, I want to speak to you."

"Would five minutes hence do as well?" was the calm reply.

"Well, yes, I suppose it would: but why not now?"

"Simply because I am smoking a perfect Trabuco which it would be sinful to waste, and I know you abhor smoke in your study. Five minutes more, I regret to say, will finish it." The glass door was closed hastily.

"Cyril," said his sister, laughing, "you really should not, you have made him angry."

"Not a bit, my dear, he has too much good taste. Besides, he only wants to lecture me *à la* Chesterfield; of course it is all right and proper and so on, but why people continue to give advice which they know will not be followed I can't conceive. I suppose it's a way he caught at the Rags and Bones."

"I know he wishes us all to be happy, Cyril."

"Of course he does. The geatest happiness of the greatest number. There now, isn't that sound political economy, Charlotte?"

"Much you care for political economy, or any other sort of economy I expect, either."

"Well, I confess economy is scarcely in my line," replied the young gentleman, modestly. "And now, look, my cigar is out, so I must go and be talked to."

As he entered, his father was seated on one side of the empty fireplace, softly shaving his chin with one hand, according to a habit in which he often indulged. Cyril, with a politely restrained yawn, cast himself into an easy chair, and having selected a paper knife as a convenient plaything, composed himself to listen.

Mr. Ponsonby was one of those men who like to begin a set speech with a quotation.

" Rochefoucauld says, my dear Cyril, that the greatest minds are those which avail themselves of the least opportunities."

As a matter of fact, Cyril knew very well that Rochefoucauld says nothing of the kind ; however, he gravely replied,

" Ha, not a bad idea of his."

" Like all the other apothegms of that great philosopher, it is remarkable for sound good sense. Do you see its application, my dear Cyril ?"

" I can't quite say that I do, Sir. Do you mean that you expect me to show the greatness of my mind by making the best use of a small allowance ?"

" Hum, that is one way of putting it

certainly. Perhaps we shall have to come to that subject presently. The particular matter to which I desire to direct your attention, is to your going to College. I have had a letter from your uncle, Cyril."

"What, Bluebeard, Sir?" I am sorry to say that by this *soubriquet* was the Rev. Henry Fordyce known to his nephew.

"Your uncle Fordyce, Sir," with severity, "and he is pleased to say some very handsome things of you in it."

"Very good of him, I am sure. I wish he'd act as handsomely as he writes."

"That depends on yourself, my son. He writes to say that your cousin John is going to St. Margaret's, and that if it falls in with my plans he should be glad if you both went to the same place."

"Does my worthy uncle expect me to

become Mentor and bear leader to that Centaur, my cousin John?"

"Your uncle and your father, too, expect you not to be a confounded fool, Sir. If you don't take care, Cyril, you'll lose every friend by your sneering ways; It's not good taste, I tell you. I wish and expect, yes, and desire that you and your cousin should be good friends at Oxford, as is only proper."

"Of course, Sir, that's enough for me. If you wish, I will rush into his arms and swear an eternal friendship with cousin John before the Vice-Chancellor."

"Look here, my good boy. To a certain extent I may speak to you as a man of the world. You are, I think, as free from prejudice and sentiment as I could wish any son to be. Indeed, if you had only a little more energy I could not complain; but let that pass. Well, you know me sufficiently to be

sure I should not want you to do anything unless something were to be gained
by it. Your uncle Fordyce is a man
of few words, and means more than he
says. When he says he wishes you both
to go to the same college, he knows
my income is nothing like his, and depend upon it he means to afford such
assistance as is necessary."

"To that I say Amen, Sir, with all my
heart."

"You have no quarrel with your cousin,
I hope, Cyril."

"I've no quarrel with any one on
the face of the earth, nor can I conceive any possible point worth quarrel-
ing about. Set your heart at rest, Sir.
I like John well enough. For a good-
hearted man he is no fool, and I have
no doubt we shall get on famously."

"I'll tell you what, Cyril, you must
make only a few friends at Oxford; but

let them be of the best; those who
will be of use to you. The men who
get on in the world are not those who
can tell you the altitude of Chimborazo,
but those who climb it, making use of
every shrub and projecting point they
find. You'll have to fight your own
battle, Cyril, and perhaps it will be
hard; for the allowance I can make
you is small, very small." Cyril winced
slightly. "My income is not large,
and I have many calls upon me. Your
education at Yoxholme was expensive,
far more so than I had reckoned for;
and then, too, my insurances and other
matters I need not detail to you con-
sume much. Now you must particularly bear in mind that I will have no
debts—mark me—no debts. They are
low and ungentlemanly, and besides they
are a continual clog round a young man's
neck. I think I see my way clear to

your uncle's helping you. He is rich,
and has only one son. If I were you,
I should cultivate his acquaintance. It
is never time thrown away. As for
your cousin, you know, good taste and
your own interests must make you very
good friends. Not too intimate, remember, for that kind of thing is quite old-
fashioned now-a-days. I think you have
your wits about you, Cyril, and you
will have to use them at Oxford. And
now that is all I have to say at present."

When he regained the garden, Cyril
selected a warm comfortable lounging
place, free from spiders and such small
deer, and then casting himself upon his
back and lighting a second Trabuco—they
were Hudson's and cost a shilling a piece
—moralized under the shade of a lime tree.
" It is a great pity," thought he, " that
our feelings are not consulted prior to our

creation. We could then hint at the kind of *rôle* we should prefer. Ah, but of course there is no 'we' then. It is scarcely fair after all to hang a man who commits a murder, the fault is with his parents. If ever I get into the 'House' I will suggest that view of things, if I remain an old bachelor that is to say. Now why did nature give me the tastes of a rich man, when circumstances doom me to the life of a poor man? It is a mistake, and not of my making. I suppose a moralist would tell me to adapt myself to circumstances; I don't see that at all. Why should I violate my nature, the nature of which I am conscious. A cow does not pass its life in trying to bark, of course not. No more will I. After all what does it matter? does anything matter? By Jove, my cigar is out! Charlotte bring me a light."

CHAPTER IV.

IN due time the cousins were matricu-
lated and members of St Margaret's,
and I may add very good friends. Cyril
went at once to call on his cousin, and
soon made his way to John's open
heart.

"Look here, cousin John, the govenors
want us to be great chums, and all that
sort of thing as cousins ought. I don't
believe much in friendships to order as a
rule, but I am sure I don't see why we
should not be very good friends indeed.
Let me see, when last we met we
were boys. I think we quarrelled, didn't
we—and you blacked my eye for me? I've

no doubt I quite deserved it, though perhaps I didn't think so at the time."

"At all events, Cyril, we're not likely to come to fisticuffs now," laughed his cousin.

"I hope not, certainly for my own sake, you look horribly strong and muscular. Are you in any set? I mean riding, boating, cricketting and that sort of thing?"

"Well I'm in with all at present; you know I was always one for athletic sports. Not much in your line, are they?" looking at his cousin's spare figure.

"Why, you know, of course I *can* both ride, take an oar or manage a bat; but I don't believe in doing for amusement what I find only bores me. And if you get in a clicque they tyrannize over you so. So I just do enough to escape botheration, and find I am let alone and liked none the less. Have you any cigars, John, my case is at my rooms. Thanks, this looks decent, I'll try it. Shall you read?"

"Well, Cyril, you know I can't call myself a reading man. I have a fair amount of brains, I suppose, but I wasn't with a reading set at Eton and that's the truth. I don't see the fun or the use of it for me. A plain degree will do just as well for me as honours. I shall have the living just the same, you know."

"In that case reading would be a work of supererogation, and contrary to the doctrine of the English Church," replied his cousin with a laugh. "I wish it were my case."

But the scheme of this little tale will not allow us to linger long over our hero's early college days, which must be given in a condensed form. Oxford wrought little or no alteration in his character. It was merely changing the *venue* of his pleasures. There is no occult power in

Oxford buildings, or institutions, to
change a heathen into a Christian; for I
will undertake that a man shall go through
them all, and yet come out unchanged.
His momentary impulses he shall have,
his rhapsodies, and inspirations. He shall
quote the orthodox poets at the sight of St
Mary's, or the Radcliffe, or Magdalen
Tower, he shall thrill at sight of a certain
stone cross, mud-stained in Broad Street,
and shall draw in his breath deep in the
Bodleian Library. But all these momentary transports and gushes of " effusion,"
as the French call it, don't make a man a
Christian.

I have known worthy heads of families
among the lower middle class, grow devoutly rapturous after supper on Sunday
night—perhaps stewed kidneys and mashed
potatoes, Scotch ale, and a glass of
whiskey punch. Jemima and Kate sang
" before Jevovah's awful throne," or,

"Come ye sinners haste along," till the good man was not only ready to defy the Pope and all his myrmidons, but full of a kind of religious, "won't go home till morning" feel, talked largely of subscribing to the Society for the conversion of Gorillas, and training the youthful Pongos. But then, Monday morning? what remained but a headache and a vague sense of folly. Nor do these rapturous Oxford sentiments last as soon as the excitement is over, because a man must have some principle of faith to work upon. The barbarians of Melita were wrong in both their inferences from what they saw, but then they did believe in something after all.

But with John, although his mind and imagination were occasionally tickled by what he saw and heard, the feeling did not penetrate and abide. The thorns choked it.

Of course his first tutor, Mr. Crammer,

duly hoped, on his matriculation, that his pupil would be regular at lecture and chapel, and sometimes stay the communion, so that of course John regarded them all as different kinds of routine drill. Young men, unless they have had some previous training, are not apt to make nice distinctions. Then his careless good humour, and high spirits made him take men too much as he found them, without much doubt or inquiry. What was he that he should judge or criticise others? And so what with loose companions, and the impulse of a rather headlong disposition he scarcely satisfied the college authorities, and was pronounced as sinning against all Ten Commandments at once by being "irregular."

Alas! was it not because he had not been taught the Great Eternal law underlying, though oft concealed by so-called regulations? was it not because he was unaware of any master, whom, Chistopher like, he might serve and yet retain his strength ? For serve a man must; and which is healthiest, noblest, truest, the Delilah service of Samson in the Vale of Sorek, or that of the Christ-bearing ferryman ? I leave you, O reader mine, to judge.

Still there was just this difference between him and his cousin. John sowed his wild oats broadcast, as if inviting all his friends to come and see how admirably his farming operations were getting on. He turned up his trousers and his sleeves and went to work with a will, basket in one hand, handsful to the right, handsful to the left.

But languid Cyril really left the world in doubt as to whether he had invested any capital in the said wild oats. In truth, he dropped a little handful here and there in bye corners where there was no one to see him, and so when the world came upon them, they thought they belonged to others.

I am sorry that my hero is not an immaculate one, a Sir Galahad, but I fear such are only to be found in the pages of "Mort d'Arthur," and the Pre-Raphaelite studios.

And so, poor John sank deeper and deeper in his mud-bath, and the worst of it all was that to ordinary eyes he appeared quite right. There are few outward marks and signs of the devil's sacraments, and often the outer man seems to canter along gaily enough, while the inner is being dragged over head and ears in unsavoury slime. Not a pleasant topic, is it, dear friends? Suppose we burn some pastiles and sprinkle lavender water. Brimstone is not nice, undoubtedly. Yet, though we certainly can stifle and conceal it with that fluid called "wilful ignorance,"

I question whether it were not better for us occasionally to pause and sniff at this strange smell coming " betwixt the wind and our nobility ;" for where such a smell is, is corruption, and where corruption is, is death.

For John to be irregular was bad, but to be the cause of irregularity in others was worse. And yet his manners were so genial and taking, that many a silly youngster fell under his spell and adopted him for his model. But the chief among these was that Arthur Brydges, whose melancholy end the reader saw in the first chapter. With a weak body and a weaker brain, he was cursed with abundance of money and no self-control.

At Eton he had been in the worst set. At a private tutor's he had scarcely been pulled out of numerous escapades, and when he came to Oxford, had nearly destroyed the remains of his digestion by his immoderate use of brandy. Weak and foolish, he could never stand alone but was ever in want of some companion. And strange to say, John took to him and actually bore him a very real affection, so as to cultivate his acquaintance and become in time his inseparable friend. A friendship which bore no good to either, a friendship to be ended as we saw by the violent death of one, and as we *shall* see by the moral upheaving and life-long remorse of the other.

CHAPTER V.

ONE morning about the middle of the second term that the cousins had spent at Oxford, when they had both ceased to be freshmen, Cyril Ponsonby was seated alone in his rooms after breakfast, that is to say about eleven o'clock.

As the said chambers will convey a good idea of what a cultivated taste, in combination with either a long purse, or what is for the nonce as useful, long credit, will effect, perhaps the reader will be so kind as to undertake a tour round them. The suite comprised three apartments and consisted of two sitting-rooms, one large, the other smaller in size, and a small

bedroom. The former looked upon the
Quad, the latter upon some mysterious
stable-yard and out-buildings, which were
supposed to belong to the head of the
College. The large sitting-room was
employed by Cyril for the reception of
ordinary friends, and the general purposes of society as understood at Oxford,
the inmost *penetralia* were reserved for
special visitors, and for his own particular
enjoyment. And so a marked difference
was observable in the style of their decor-
ation and upholstery.

As trials of strength, gymnastic exercises
and such like exhibitions of what Ruskin
styles the " Northern energy," are to be
expected from, and indeed appear to form
part of, the ordinary life of undergraduates, and as these little amusements
occasionally have a detrimental influence
upon furniture and crockery, Cyril had
borne this carefully in mind when furnish-

ing. He had been content to retain the greatest portion of the commonplace, stout old fashioned articles which had satisfied his predecessor, and for which he had paid his "thirds." Although, therefore, he abhorred the noisy outbreaks and crapulous revelry which delight the ordinary undergraduates, he was able to look on with tolerable composure and still be master " of *himself* though China fell," whenever his guests proceeded to the *argumentum ad hominem*, as exemplified by throwing a trencher-cap at an opponent, whom syllogisms were powerless to vanquish.

There was nothing more valuable to break than a few plaster casts and statuettes, which looked down upon the Saturnalia before them with impassive solidity. The book cases were well filled with classical works; Cyril had in an idle moment bid for, and carried off a set of

Delphines at Richards' sale rooms, the
presence of which imparted a studious
character to the apartment. The regular
freshman's pictures, Ansdell's and Land-
seer's, decorate the walls, and a rack of
pipes, whips, canes &c., complete the
fittings of the room. Stop here and you
would see nothing more than any economical gowsman might possess, and would
leave it, if with no high opinion of Cyril's
taste, yet at least with admiration of his
prudence. Open sesame, and we are in
the *sanctum sanctorum.* Walls of sea-green
with cream colour and gold pattern, and
gold mouldings; curtains, green chintz
with rosebuds and lilies of the valley;
carpet, crimson, with geometric device in
white and gold; a charming couch, on
which to recline is to dream; luxurious
easy chairs; tables of all sorts and sizes;
queer cabinets; charming china and glass
ornaments; all the little luxuries for

the writing table which betray the amateur and dilettante; choice engravings,
water colours and photographs—in a word
all the belongings which augur good taste
in the possessor, accompanied by a long
purse, or an easy conscience.

The former of these we know Cyril had
not, the latter he certainly owned. "If
you want a thing, get it," he used to say
"it's much nicer than longing for it, and
I am sure is far more wholesome.   I
always find that if I want a thing, after a
time it comes."   And as he happened to
wish for a good many things, after a while
a somewhat startling number of things
' came.'   You see Oxford tradesmen sometimes make mistakes like other men, and
naturally fancied that the son of an ex-
secretary of the Rag Bag department must
necessarily be a wealthy man.

"All these things arrange themselves
somehow," remarked Cyril, "and the less

a man worries his head about money matters the better."

Certainly he does not appear to be worrying himself at the present moment. As we have before said, he had finished that rather heavy meal which undergraduate digestions do not scorn under the name of breakfast, and having pushed the table away, had wheeled his easy chair round to the open window, where he was able to enjoy at one and the same time the scent of the beautiful flowers with which the window-seat was crowded, the busy doings in the Quad below, his pipe and—a pleasure he seemed in no hurry about—his morning's correspondence.

Two or three letters lay on a table near him, but though his hand wandered often enough to the ornamented tobacco jar by their side, the letters remained undisturbed for a long while. At length, with a gentle sigh, he took up one on which he had recognised his father's bold hand-writing and initials.

"I cannot conceive," he mused to himself, for need we say how very rare that wonderful animal the Soliloquist is, "I cannot conceive what is the use of fathers, they must be a consequence of the fall of man. But for that unlucky Ribstone pippin, I have no doubt that mankind would have been all *autochthenes*, or come up promiscuous like Cadmus' warriors. As men, they are all very well. I don't object to my father as a man. Fussy and fidgety of course, thinks himself awful knowing, and fancies he has a taste for wine. But all that's pardonable. It is only when I regard him as a father that I am compelled to confess him a failure, not worse than other paternities, perhaps, but a failure all the same. Above all though, why write to me? Or if he must write, and I suppose he 'had the

honour to be' so long at the Rag and
Bone office that he has never got rid of
the *cacoethes* yet, why expect me to
answer? However, I suppose he must
be humoured, so here goes."

He broke the seal, and commenced
reading the following epistle, which we
are privileged to read over his shoulder.

"My dear Cyril,

"Your not having replied to my letter of
the 12th ult. has given rise to much speculation as to the cause of your silence,
which, I may add, has been productive
of much annoyance. Method and punctuality in all epistolary concerns are most
necessary to be acquired by one who
intends, as I trust you still do, serving
Her Majesty in her Civil Service. Although
it is, I believe, far from my nature to lay
claim to any merit, however humble, which
I do not possess, and, as you are aware,

I always reprobate the foolish vanity of those who are in the habit of extolling those deeds of which they have been the authors—"

" Mercy on me," murmured Cyril, "why it's worse than a Latin sermon, or the maze at Hampton Court."

" Yet I think I may lawfully boast that the regularity and despatch with which the affairs of that Department, over which I once presided were conducted, has been the subject of praise—I may say warm praise—in very high places. I merely mention this that I may incite you to emulate your father in a quality which at present appears to exist in deficiency in your mental organization. I shall now pass to business, merely premising that I write under the hypothetical assumption that no serious matter or accident has prevented an answer to my last letter, but that your silence has proceeded from

an indisposition to exertion, which I
should regret to have to call by its proper
name of idleness."

"Now, doesn't this just bear out my
ideas about fathers in general, and my
own in particular? I think I'll try some
bottled ale after that, before I go farther."
The ale, duly opened by his scout, he
proceeded.

"I have had an interview with my
brother-in-law, your uncle, the Rev. Henry
Fordyce, and I think that you will have
reason to be pleased at the ensuing results.
My interview was by appointment on his
part, and related to your position at the
University. He is evidently desirous that
you should be on terms of intimacy and
companionship with your cousin John,
and expressed himself to that effect with,
I may say, considerable energy. Aware
of the great difference existing between
your means and his son's, and confessing

—tacitly—that this intimacy may possibly entail upon you expenses which my limited means would be quite unable to meet, he has come forward with a very generous proposition. He offers to allow you—and I need scarcely say that I have readily accepted in your name as well as my own—the sum of £150 per annum, to supplement that allowance which I already make you; and this he will continue for the three years you remain at College."

"Now, really," remarked Cyril, as if to an imaginary third person, "I decidedly think I should prefer my father and uncle to change places. Blue-beard never writes letters, and, as long as he continues his supplies, will meet with my approbation. Well, what next?"

"Pray do not imagine, my dear Cyril, in the first flush of your improved and augmented income, that the advice I gave you respecting the management of your

expenditure is any the less requisite.   The
man who is unable to manage upon £200
per annum, will never be able—"

"Oh, bother! my dear sir, that's just
like Joseph Surface, in the 'School for
Scandal.'   H'm, h'm;   hallo ! what's
this ?'"

"I regret to say that since your departure, bills in your name, to the amount
of £56, have come in to me, of which I
enclose you a list.   I have before this
remonstrated with you upon your careless
and reckless extravagance, and feel much
satisfied that in the present case the
remedy is in my own hands.   I have,
therefore, deducted this sum from that
which I to-day have paid into your account
at Messrs. Parsons, through my bankers,
and would impress upon you the need of
great caution in your employment of the
residue."

The letter then went on to some family

matters, given with elaborate detail; and ended with a *coda*, as it is called in musical parlance, a *resumé* of all that had gone before. Cyril had just laid it down on the table, his eyebrows arched to the utmost, when with no small amount of noise and bustle, or, in Shakespearian language, "Alarums, excursions !" his cousin John bounded into he room.

"Hallo ! Cyril, my boy; what are you mooning here for, you lazy dog ?"

"Now, don't be boisterous, there's a good fellow; it's your weakness, you know, to fancy all men are as nerveless as yourself. You have just come in time, and can oblige me, if you will. It isn't filial for a man to abuse his father, at least so people say, but he may abuse his uncle if he likes. Will you be so kind as to call my father a beast, or a jolly old shark, or anything else expressive and abusive ? Don't laugh, I mean it, upon my honour;

I must let off my feelings somehow. I have just received and done him the honour to read a regular Grandisonian letter, and then at the end I find the sting. Some idiot has been fool enough to send him a bill of mine, and he is mean enough to stop some money which is passing through his hands.

"And so you are 'hoist with your own petard.' Poor Cyril! it is rather hard, I grant you. However, for all that, I won't abuse my respected uncle, especially as I believe him to be a most worthy old gentleman."

"Well, if you won't do that, sit down and smoke. There's some Bass and there are the cigars. I say—I have something to tell you which concerns us both. Do you know that our respective and respected fathers have been laying their heads together with one consent."

"And are confederate against us, I suppose?"

"Well, no, not quite; but the joke is, that your father, my uncle Blue-beard (you don't mind my calling him Blue-beard, do you?) has so high an opinion of my prudence, sagacity, modesty and ingenuosity, that he thinks you cannot but profit by my society, and therefore desires us to be no end friendly."

John roared with laughter.

"Wants you to be my Mentor, I suppose, and keep me out of harm's way. Upon my word and honour that's about the best thing I have heard yet. "*Sed. quis custodi et custodes ipsos?*' Eh, Cyril! I think now if my dear old dad could have seen you the other night, he would have rather thought me qualified to look after you and guide your tottering steps."

"My misfortune, John, and not my fault; you should never reproach a man who is under the pressure of adverse circumstances."

"If you call tumbling under the table 'the pressure of adverse circumstances,' I've done. However, to do you justice, I must confess such occasions are rare; and when you are so, you don't talk fustian, you speak like a philosopher full of indignant virtue."

"Yes, in *vino veritas*, my true nature asserts itself. However, in spite of your chaff, I shall accept this honourable post and look after your morality closer than ever."

"Hadn't you better keep like the Pharisee, 'afar off,' lest your own should be contaminated? Never mind, Cyril, I think we shall jog on very well together, whichever of us is Mentor. And privately, I think that Cæsar and Pompey are very much alike, only I am like a noisy stream, and you are a piece of deep water. Don't frown, man, it's only my joke. Give me another cigar, this won't draw.

And now I'm fairly settled, let me hear what this report is about your having been hauled up for a speech at the Union."

"It's absurd nonsense," replied Cyril, with some signs of vexation, "and only proves what I have always maintained, that Oxford is a priest-ridden nest of superstition."

"That's elegant and terse too, because it refuses to hear the voice of its Ponsonby, I suppose. Well, tell me all about it."

"I don't often go to the Union, as you know; I think it is a kind of patent society for affording special opportunities to men to make fools of themselves. However, the other night I went. The debate was upon the Irish Church, and men were talking awful nonsense; Redclyffe and Latham, and some of the Puseyites were for abolishing it, because they declared it to be schismatical. Where a branch of the Catholic Church was already established, the people were and ought to be nothing else but 'Roman Catholics. Then the Baliol and Utilitarian party were for abolishing it also, because they said it was a national robbery perpetrated upon the Irish, and a defiance of their feelings and prejudices. Some wanted the revenues secularised and devoted to the improvement of the land. Then the Synagogue and Low Church men set up a howling, and pronounced the Protestant Establishment in Ireland to be a Missionary Church, whose mission was to convert the poor deluded idolators. It was the only spiritual light in the land. And then at last I couldn't help it, and up I got. And I told them, that if it were a light—which I doubted— it was under such a very thick bushel as to be of no use, and certainly its first

missionary efforts might very well be
diverted towards the Evangelicals, to teach
them a little charity and christianize them.
And then I let fly at the Puseyites, and
told them that if our church was to give
way to another, they were right in wishing that their own imitation of Romanism
should yield the *pas* to the real article—
that if we must drink, it was better to
drink either water or wine, than a maw-
kish mixture of both. And then I went
in at all parties together, and said that at
the present time when no two religious
parties or even clergy could agree, I thought
that it only showed how much better all
parties would live without any religious
profession whatever. Practically, religion
did not influence people, then why retain
ridiculous outward forms and cumbersome
confessions of faith which we denied by
our actions. There could be no doubt
but that Christianity had failed."

"I say, Cyril, you're coming it rather strong."

"Just listen and don't interrupt—Had failed to bring in anything like peace or goodwill. The amiable spirit of Paganism was utterly opposed to any form of persecution for religious matters, and was tolerant of all religions as religions; christians were only persecuted for political reasons. But intolerance and persecution had followed, and gone hand in hand with Christianity, and until we had learnt its maxims a little better, I thought it better to give up anything like Church establishments and all the tribe of priests and ministers, who thrust themselves between nature and a man's heart. Think and talk as we might, one thing was plain, that what we called Christianity had brought Ireland into a far worse state of superstition, bigotry, hatred and jealousy, than any form of Paganism could have done. Well, you never heard such a howling and groaning in your life, as greeted me then. They shouted 'Infidel —Pantheist,' and showered down compliments on my head. At all which I laughed, as you may imagine, and all the more when I caught sight of Marbecke's awe-struck face from one of the galleries, looking as if the world were coming to an end, and his coat-tails already on fire. Well I rose and left them, flinging mud at me and my Pantheism as they were pleased to call it, and next morning came a summons from Marbecke. I went prepared for a tilt, and I think I may say I upset him pretty well.

" He began by saying, that he was aware the Union debates were to an extent privileged, and that the course he was pursuing was, perhaps, somewhat out of order. Still what he had heard last night seemed to augur the existence of such grave evil, that he felt compelled to speak to me, and insisted that I would answer him as to a priest, and not merely the college officer.

"To this, I said that I should much prefer speaking to him as one gentleman to another, and that I was quite obliged to him for his interest in me.

"He looked very queer for a moment, and then began upon my speech, in which he said I had advocated directly infidel and anti-Christian views; was he to conclude from that that my faith was shaken, if not worse?

"'Certainly not,' I replied; 'I was sure he had read and seen enough of religious discussions, not to feel that speeches and even published opinions were no index to real belief, nor indeed to practice either.'

"'Had I then spoken what I did not really believe—sad as this was, of course it would be preferable to the other hypothesis !'

"So I said that as long as I did not openly quit the Established Church—you know that word 'established' always riles Puseyites—and conformed to all her ceremonies, I thought that was sufficient *primâ facie* evidence that I was a Churchman ; and as such, it really did not matter what views I chose to ventilate, or what speeches to make. I was quite ready to speak on the other side if he liked.

"'Then was he to understand that I habitually spoke what I did not really believe.'

"Certainly not, only I made a considerable difference between matters of fact, and mere matters of opinion and sentiment."

"'And did I consider religion simply as a matter of opinion, about which any one view would be as good as another?'

"Well, there I had him, for I said that even if I did, I could quote good authority on my side, as our good Head, Dr. Field himself remarked in his work on 'The Evidences,' that Christianity must be judged by its moral teaching, which was to be preferred before merely barren facts as an evidence of its truth! This shut him up completely; for he said, flushing up red as he always does when angry, that he regretted I did not meet him in the spirit he wished. To which I retorted that the meeting was not of my seeking, and that he had himself settled the terms upon which we should address each other. If I had committed any offence against the College or University, I was quite ready to answer for it; but that I had an objection to be catechised gratuitously.

"And then it all ended in his saying that he saw I was in no fit state for religious

matters, that I was full of spiritual pride
and puffed up by my own conceit; in fact,
a regular ' dearly beloved' kind of homily,
at the end of which he either blessed me
or delivered me over to Satan, I forget
which. And now you have the true, full,
and particular account of the whole transaction."

" Well, Cyril, do you know, I think you
behaved rather badly. I know old Marbecke is a bigoted, disagreeable kind of
would-be pope; but he means kindly, and
speaks for the best."

" So, I suppose did St. Paul, when he
delivered over Hymenœus to the tender
mercies of Satan, that he might ' learn not
to blaspheme.' That proves, by-the-by,
that the devil is a Quaker."

" No, no; don't be a fool. I think he
wishes us to consider him as more than a
mere tutor—you know what I mean as
well as I do."

"There, Jack, shut up and pass me over the beer, or shout for lunch or something, but don't talk utter rubbish. If Marbecke wants to be my 'guide, philosopher, and friend,' as your father wishes me to be to you, he is frightfully mistaken, that is all I can say. As a tutor I consider him a muff, but then he is a necessary evil; as a priest I can only call him a fool, further than that I go not. And now for lunch, if that beast of a boy will only come. Hullo! was that a knock? Come in!"

And accordingly Mr. Henry Burton entered.

CHAPTER VI.

AND who was Mr. Henry Burton ?
To answer which question satisfac-
torily, it is necessary to go back, if not as far
as the Siege of Troy, yet a very long way,
and to enter upon a discussion respecting
the state of society in Oxford. Perhaps
there is no drawback to the University
system of education, as pursued at Oxford,
more serious than the entire want of
female society which is entailed upon the
undergraduates. It is no exaggeration to
say that a young man may go through his
three years, or three years and a half,
without having had one opportunity of
speaking to a lady during all that time;

nay, more, that those who are fortunate
enough to possess reputable female acquaintances and friends, must be regarded
as rare exceptions to the general rule.
But why is this ? Certainly not by design,
or in observance of university statutes ;
mainly, it would appear, by mere custom,
and that of the foolishest. The state of
the case is this. There are in University
and city three grades or circles of society.
The first is that charmed and sacred ring-
fence, which contains the amiable, accomplished and affable families of those
mighty pundits, the Heads of Houses.
These form the *crême de la crême*, and are
looked upon as the undeniable aristocrats
of the place, blue blood, arched instep,
and all other properties of aristocracy
being theirs by right divine.

To these are united by alliance, offensive
(in many senses) and defensive, the
county families, who make common cause

with the Heads, and agree mutually to
keep at their proper distance the presuming and upstart town. Never having
pierced the inmost penetralia of this
charmed circle, we can only describe their
mystic gatherings by report. We have,
however, had the inestimable privilege of
knowing those who have been made free
of convivial gatherings and dinners of the
Oxford *huut-ton*, and not only have they
survived the honour, but with one accord
pronounced them unutterably dreary. They
resemble, we are assured, a polite cock-
pit, where female dons and Heads of
Houses pit daughter against daughter, for
the delectation of the unmarried Fellows
of Colleges, and the few noblemen and gentlemen commoners who have been collected
for the occasion. As a rule, it will be
found that the families of College dignitaries—I refer to the female portion—
have more hauteur, ignorance, and less

grace and affability of manners than any other young ladies of their rank and station. Mixing only in a small, exclusive, and very peculiar clicque, with its own laws and customs, they gradually attain to an ostrich-like indifference to the outer world, and believe themselves unseen because they know nothing of it. With very few chances of meeting young men of their own age, they are thrown mainly upon the society of middle-aged and elderly clergymen, most of them engaged in the work of tuition; and pick up, with a remarkable and most unpleasant quickness, all the dogmatism and prejudices characteristic of that body. At an university party you see a formidable group of ladies, young and old, demoiselles and chaperones, round whom flutter or stumble the white-throated gentry, the Fellows and parochial clergy, who are their privileged cavaliers. At the door clusters an unhappy group of undergraduates in *academic* costume—that is to say, with a yard and a half of black stuff, decorated with more or less of queer shaped appendages, dangling behind their backs. They tread on each other's feet, and perform various figures of awkwardness, for the space of two or three hours; seldom getting beyond the fatal door, seldom sitting down, never being introduced to anyone, and ever wishing themselves at the Antipodes.

It is a species of dress parade ; and as such it is attended. If one or two present are known to possess musical powers, they will be invited to charm the company by an exhibition of their skill; at the end of which, crimson and hot, they return under a fire of matronly eye-glasses, to their former position, and "as you were" becomes the word. Of course, you must understand that a little more geniality is attainable by any young ' tuft,' or noble-

man; but, to do them justice, their visits
are like those of angels, "few and far
between." It is quite useless to speculate
upon the different results which might
ensue from a rational mingling of the
undergraduates with the fair ladies, forming the female aristocracy of Oxford.

Perhaps it is asking too much to expect
that the privacy of the domestic circle
should be disturbed; but, in the name of
common sense, if hospitality be extended
by Heads of Houses to the *alumni* under
their charge, let it be a reality, and not a
Barmecide's feast—let it be something to
please, refresh, and instruct, not a period of polite boredom, anticipated with
shuddering, and looked back upon with
disgust.

It is not too much to say that a very
great influence for good might be obtained
over the young and impressible, accustomed to the pleasures and amenities of

the home circle, if some human attempt
were made to supply its place during
their separation from it. It would take
a most important place in a scheme of real
education, and would be at the same time
a motive and incentive to good and pure
lives, and a restraint from that *ennui*
attendant upon a bachelor life, which is
always dangerous and frequently the cause
of ill. However, the eternal fitness of
things, and the ineffable wisdom resident
in the brains of Heads of Houses have
willed it otherwise, and what is to be
said ? " *Stet pro ratione voluntas.*"

Before we descend to the external circle
of society, formed by the city or town's-
people, as they are called, pause we for a
moment to examine one which, like the
coffin of Mahomet, hangs poised in mid'
air. It is that which, though formed of
town residents, mostly professional men,
may lay certain claims to University

respect, inasmuch as the avocations of its members brings them into contact with the sacred upper ten thousand themselves. Lawyers, medical men, and professors of the arts of music and drawing, if possessed of families, may, and generally do, include a fair sprinkling of undergraduate friends among their guests; nor would such social gatherings be unpleasant, if only the sound good sense which directs the business relations between host and guest were extended into their social connection. But, alas, like the bat in the fable, this little group, unable to mingle freely with that immediately and conventionally above it, and fearing to sink entirely into that beneath, only succeeds in attaining the stiffness and frigidity of the first, without the geniality and real hospitality of the latter.

The success of the party is almost universally marred by the presence of a

little knot of dons, or College Fellows,
who, from the Alp-like whiteness and
sublimity of their starched neckerchiefs,
survey both host and fellow-guests with
"mingled pity and contempt." Aware
that they have left their cozy corner in the
Common-room and bottle of sound port,
for the ill-grouped gathering of—let us say
—a medical man, whom, in their heart of
hearts, they do not regard as their equal;
they expect due homage to be paid them
by the guests in recognition of this fact.
Failing this, they talk in little groups;
obtaining it, they patronise in a manner
to be seen in perfection in Oxford alone.

So it happens in the end, that what
might really be a very pleasant. meeting for
young and old alike, becomes a funereal
ceremony resembling faintly that *custom*
of the sacred upper circle which I attempted to depict, but without the mellow,
religious twang about it which elevates

the former almost to the level of a devotional exercise.

The outer circle—circle ignored by the sacred Brahmin caste, and even unloved by the hybrid middle rank of society—consists of the town's-people unadulterated; which, of course, comprises all classes, from the wealthy tradesman up to the civic magistrate himself. Here is, if not refinement, at least good sense and geniality. Here the University Brahmin seldom, if ever, strays. The parochial clergyman may be met at these *réunions*, and sometimes, in consequence of the bonds of freemasonry, a sprinkling of undergraduates, members of the 'Alfred' or 'Apollo' lodges; but the noble College Fellow is but rarely found, and if met, proves to be of the convivial, rather than the exclusive or starched type.

Now, considering that a large proportion of the undergraduates are intended for the

ministry, and that the sphere of their
future work must be very much among
the middle classes, what better opportunity for their making mutual acquaintance could be devised than social meetings
of town and university habitants?

It is a fact, however, that they are rare,
and looked upon with dislike and suspicion
by the College magnates. And thus it
happens so frequently, that the clergyman
of a parish knows about as much of
the life and manners and spirit of the
middle classes, to whom he is appointed
to minister, as he does of the idiosyncrasies
and habitat of the Dodo or Apteryx.

CHAPTER VII.

BUT all this while the question, " Who is Mr. Henry Burton?" remains unanswered. Some years before the course of this veracious narrative commenced, there resided in the city of Oxford, a merchant of the name of Charles Burton. I call him a merchant by courtesy, on the same principle that my grocer calls himself a provision merchant, and his little shop a mart. At the same time we may, if you please, anglicize the French term and describe him as one who "made affairs." What his merchandise, business or affairs were, it would puzzle most people to discover.

He always left home about ten o'clock in the morning, and walked with an important air to his "office," a little squeezed-up building in a back street, with the lower half of its windows dabbed over with putty, and "Burton, Agent," inscribed in large letters thereon. Now agent means a person who does something or other; but Mr. Charles Burton apparently did nothing whatever except smoke, read the papers, drink brandy and water, and periodically go through the Bankruptcy Court, which he did with great regularity, always emerging rosy, portly, and hopeful. He was a tall, bulky man, with a deep red face, a deeper red nose, small, twinkling grey eyes, and white hair and whiskers. He dressed carelessly, walked slouchingly, and took snuff constantly. As he grew in years and gradually declined in his worldly affairs, the slouching, sham-bling gait became more apparent, and I am sorry to say the aroma of French brandy was permanent.

This worthy had married in early life a very pretty, good-tempered and foolish girl, who, at the time to which we refer, had become a pleasant-looking, homely, and intensely foolish matron, about as much fitted to educate, train, or control a family as she was to drive a flock of emus or llamas. She dressed up to her face, that is, with a very tolerable amount of vulgarity, was an excellent cook, and a notable housewife. She had her cares and her troubles, poor thing, and turned a brave face to them accordingly. Many an anxious day and weary night had she passed for Charles' sake, and often when deviling the kidneys for breakfast, which her lord and master loved, did the warm tears mingle with the catsup in the gridiron. So we will forgive her and speak well of her, though she did let her daughters "go on so," though she did prefer to call asparagus "grass," and eat it grasped in her fingers.   Those daughters —yes, certainly before we answer the question thrice asked,   "Who was Mr. Henry Burton?"   They were three in number, Barbara, Marian and Lizzie, of whom the two latter were as lovely as you could wish, and the former plain—well, rather more than that; suppose we say as the Americans, "real ugly."   She possessed a broad, flat, good-tempered looking face, with a complexion of light leather colour, frizzly hair like a gosling's down, grey green eyes with a dash of yellow, a nose like the ace of clubs or a button mushroom, a wide gash which did duty for a mouth, displayed when open a wild array of teeth like Stonehenge in size, but fortunately good in colour.   That and her

good-humoured expression were the only
redeeming points in an uniquely hideous
visage.   But she was emphatically a good
creature.   Like Mr. Gargery senior, she
was "that good in her hart."   You forgave her her forty-horse-power flirting,
her slang, her brusquerie, when you
knew her great warm heart, so uncultivated, so uncared for, so neglected.   Of
course her dress and appearance were
fast and *prononcée* in the extreme, and
to this her manners corresponded.   She
very wisely adopted the course of a frank
acknowledgment of ugliness, which is
much the best way.   The ugly faces
which you remember with dislike are
always those which attempt to deny the
stamp of nature, and affect a beauty
which they never can possess.   At the
same time, there are faces and people
which accept and confess their ugliness with
so frank and simple a manner, that after a

time you really forget they are ill-favoured.

Marian and Lizzie, however, possessed beauty enough to atone for their elder sister's failings. The former was a pensive beauty with half-shut, sleepy blue eyes of a violet tinge, and long dark lashes sweeping her delicate rosy cheeks, a small straight nose, scarlet lips and dainty little teeth complete her face. Lizzie resembled her sister, only being of a sparkling and vivacious type. Her nose was a quaint little *nez retroussée*, her eyes bright blue and sparkling, her mouth expressive alike of scorn, coaxing and fascination generally. She was a dangerous little witch, and she knew her powers and used them accordingly. Both sisters were thorough mistresses of the art and mystery of the toilette, which was the more useful, as like all the rest of the family they lived upon credit. The brightest of silks, the airiest of muslins, the most piquante of woollens, the quaintest of petticoats, the daintiest of Balmorals were always to be seen on the Misses Burton, and if Barbara did not attempt their style of elegance and fashion, at least, she possessed a dashing style of her own which made her no bad contrast.

Henry Burton, their only brother, the eldest of the family, was a medical man, or rather a general practitioner. In his youth, he had been a very decidedly black sheep of the woolliest and very deepest die. He had all kinds of terrible escapades at school; he had walked the hospitals, like Satan, seeking whom he might devour, and apparently with such vigour as to come home almost barefoot to his irate parent; he had set up for himself and speedily become bankrupt; he had removed to the neighbourhood of Leicester Square, where it is said he

was a billiard marker; he had sown
wild oats—pecks, bushels, sacks, with
all his hands; he had all kinds of bad
things said of him, and all kinds of dismal prophecies prophecied. When lo !
just as all his "friends" thought that
the last act had arrived and he must
flee the country, he suddenly turns up
clothed and in his right mind, sleek
and prosperous-looking; yes, and more
than all, with ready money and no debts.

It was a world's wonder whence he
obtained his means; whether he had
betted and won, or maimed and murdered
—the idea of his having earned it occurred
to no one. But it was even more of a
world's wonder, when he gave out quietly
that he intended settling down and prac-
tising in Oxford, which in course of time
he did. And now came a somewhat
curious transaction.

In the old days, his father had expressed

in language strong, if not select, his resolve to have nothing to do with son so
abandoned. Now the tables were turned,
and the Burton *fils'* scale was in the
ascendant. The old gentleman began to
discover that there was a limit to the gul-
libility even of his own favourite creditors;
that they began to look shy at his bills,
decline his I. O. U's., and express a not
unnatural preference for ready money.
Cigars and French brandy are perhaps
not very unreasonable requirements, still
their vendors are in the habit of expecting
something more than mere promises in
exchange.

Things looked ill with old Burton; he
went to the office, it is true, and of course
was still an agent, but his Cognac had to
be exchanged for Old Tom, his Havannahs
and Cabanas for a Broseley clay or London straw.

At this juncture came forward his son,

and proposed terms, which ultimated in a species of concordat, as follows. The freehold house in which they lived was made over to him, in return for which he undertook to make an arrangement of the paternal debts and allow his father a certain annuity, not to be exceeded.

He thus became virtual head of the house, and issued his edicts with authority. He then proceeded to banish his father from the house, save only at meal times, and to promote his mother from being universal drudge to the position of cook and housekeeper. Thus, two important points were secured, good cooking and the absence of vulgarity. To his sisters it was not so easy to dictate. He made them understand, however, that for the future they must look to him alone, that their chances of marrying depended entirely upon his exertions, and that, therefore, he should expect the most thorough and willing compliance. His practise, he said, lay chiefly among the under graduates, and his intention was to make his house a pleasant evening resort for them. Having thus brought the birds to the net, it was for them to do the rest. To each was alloted her part.

Barbara must give up all hopes of flirting on her own behalf, and must be willing to support her sisters, receive flank attacks and cover retreats when necessary. In other words, she must be always in good health, spirits, and temper; ready to take a spare hand at whist or écarté, join in at croquet if needed, allow herself to be teased, accompany bashful gownsmen in '*A che la morte,*' pour out tea and coffee, listen to confidences if offered, and lead up to them if not, do her sisters' hair, mend their gloves, and, in fact, be generally useful.

To Marian was given the sentimental

rôle, the album photograph, pensive ballad, water-colour sketching, moonlight wandering line, for which she was very much adapted. She had beautiful arms, and so bagatelle and Thalberg's pieces were put down to her; while Lizzie, whose brachial muscles were not so well developed, but yet had pretty tapering hands, was better suited for chess, saucy ballads, and the lighter style of flirting. To the aforesaid Lizzie, also, were handed over the young and timid, the smokers, whose cigars "she didn't mind the least in the world, in fact, she sometimes smoked a cigarette," and that extensive line which we may call the College chapel and garden business.

To the uninitiated, we may explain that certain colleges have choral service in their chapels, that admission to these chapels can only be obtained by an order from a Fellow of the college, and that in the asking for, and employment of these orders, followed, perhaps, by a promenade in the beautiful College gardens, lies no small part of the Oxford system of flirtation.

Certain general rules attended these more particular orders, such as that all quarrelling should take place in the bed-rooms, and not be extended to the drawing-room, that mutual help should be given by the three sisters, and that spiteful and severe remarks should be directed only towards externals, the family privilege of mutual criticism being suspended for the general good.

With regard to Burton himself, I need only say as follows. He was a clever and skilful practitioner, and managed to make himself agreeable to his patients, although his manners were neither specially easy nor gentlemanly. He was a first rate hand at billiards, whist, and écarté, he inherited his father's taste for spirits with, however, far more than his father's powers of carrying them, and was an excellent judge of (his friends') cigars. His various experiences of London and elsewhere, the nature of his profession and his own tastes, combined with a good memory, had made him a walking "*Chronique scandaleuse*," and, to some minds, a very agreeable companion. Add to all these charms the advantages of three sisters, two pretty and one useful, and you will see that the firm of Burton and Co. had a very nice little game to play.

But cautiously and warily was it played. No scandal ever was connected with the Misses Burton. They were flirts, it is true, but then they were—women; they were tremendous flirts, it is true also, but then how many others came under that category? Lastly, they were successful flirts, for after a year or two's campaign, Marian enslaved a gentleman commoner of some third rate college, and became Mrs. Adrian Hesketh, and proprietress of a husband worth £2,000 per annum. And now there was only Lizzie, counting Barbara for nothing; and for her great hopes were entertained, as we shall see. Nor were these the only gains. A man does not play at whist and écarté night after night without result, and Henry Burton had learnt both these games, and gone through his apprenticeship in a far more likely school than the raw undergraduates who were his guests. I do not hint for a moment that he cheated, indeed there was no need of it—only he won.

You certainly might spend an evening worse than at the Burtons'. There were always good coffee and tea, abundance of music, chess, écarté, whist, and flirting; then came sandwiches, in which the meat really *was* meat, and not greasy fat, and. the bread both fresh and well buttered; add to this abundance of bitter beer, and, after the ladies had retired, spirits, cigars, pipes, and still more cards, and you will see that for young undergraduates, weary of eternal bachelordom, the attractions were many.

CHAPTER VIII.

MR. Henry Burton entered. Place a
weasel on its hind legs, and you have
a tolerably clear idea of Mr. Henry Burton's
appearance. He was short, fair, indeed of
a washed-out appearance, with eyes unpleasantly red and down looking. He
stooped somewhat, and had an odd way of
approaching crab-wise, that is sideways.
Not prepossessing, but perhaps repulsive,
rather than actually ugly. Never mistrust
instinctive likes and dislikes, for there
is more in physiognomy than some are
willing to allow. Nature's royal stamp
is inimitable, ineffaceable, unmistakeable.
Her golden pieces may be worn, and bat-

tered, and knocked about in the wear and
tear of life, but *Dei gratia* is on them, and
woe to the man who cannot read it, or
descry the ring of the metal. Good or
bad looks have nothing to do with it.
Give Nero the mask of Apollo, and he who
is called Apolyon, Alabbon, or simply Shaitan, will still peep through the eyes, twist
the mouth, or contort the brow, to prove
his right of habitation. And give Fénélon
or John Howard never so much of the
ugliness of Scarron, and for all that, his
face shall shine with a light which is
celestial. When, on looking at a man,
you feel the same thrill and shudder of
aversion run through you as when you
tread on a snake, be on your guard.
Mischief will come to you from him, and
his face is to him in the place of a rattle
to warn the beholder of the shadow of
death.

"Hullo! Burton," exclaimed Cyril,

"you are just come in time, we were going to have lunch. Come and sit down like a good fellow, and tell us some news."

"Thanks. Good morning, Fordyce. How are you? Well? that's right. Lunch? Well, one might do worse. You college men live so well. I suppose you know that lunch is perhaps the most unwholesome meal you can eat."

"Exactly so, et cætera et cætera. You doctors are of all men the most inconsistent. Who ever knew a doctor who did not abuse supper? who ever saw a doctor refuse one, hot or cold?"

"True; but you ought to be all the more obliged to us; the truth is, we are martyrs to science, and for the good of our patients we experimentalise on our own constitutions, to be able to tell our invalids what to eat, drink, and avoid."

"*Fiat experimentum.* Well, doctor, you can try an experiment upon a *pâté de foie*

gras which has just come from Cooper's.
Edward," as the scout boy entered,
" lunch for three. What soup will you
have, Burton ? I can recommend the ox-
tail. Very well; three ox-tails, stiltons,
butters, and celery; bring up a bottle of
brown sherry. Is there any news going ?
Where have you come from ?"

" St. Catherine's; news ? well, none;
yes, by-the-bye, Maxwell has been elected
Fellow."

" By Jove," shouted John, " and I am
very glad to hear of it. He's about the
only reading fellow I ever met who wasn't
a bit of a humbug. He's no end of a
swell at cricket, and on the river. But he
does not pretend never to open a book,
and then sap all night on green tea and
wet towels."

" I shouldn't think any one could accuse
you of that, John," observed his cousin,
" your nights are not spent so profitably."

" Never you mind, old fellow, I dare say my name will come out as well as those of men who fret their lives out with worry and work. We can't all be such sobersides as you. Eh, Doctor?"

" 'Pon my honour I never knew Ponsonby was particularly sobersided. If he be, he ought to keep you in better order. Where do you get your wine, Ponsonby, this is simply first rate."

" I meant it to be; it happens to be College port."

" College port?"

" College port."

" Come, nonsense, draw it mild, old fellow, how on earth could you manage to get it?"

" The easiest thing in the world. Marbecke was lecturing me the other day, so I thought I would get a rise out of him. When I had heard him to the end, I remarked that my lungs were pronounced weak, and I was ordered everything strengthening, specially good Port. I lamented the extortion and adulteration of Oxford wine merchants; and wound up by asking him whether he thought under the circumstances he could get me some of the St. Margaret's Port, which I heard was very good. To do the old boy justice, he was intensely polite; said he would get me a dozen in his name, for which I could settle when I liked, and here it is."

"Upon my life, Ponsonby," remarked Burton, "you have the old gentleman's own assurance. Why, I'll engage to say that Marbecke has never done such a thing before in his life. It was regularly spoiling the Egyptians."

"Or seething the kid in his mother's milk," said John. "For all that, I wonder at your acceptance of a favour from a man you dislike so much. I should have thought your pride would have come in the way?"

"Pride! My good John, I have none; certainly not when I can gain by humility. Pride and conscience are two luxuries reserved for the rich by a bountiful Providence."

"Hear, hear," said Burton; "our noble host has spoken the words of wisdom. I looks towards him," and he drank off his glass and replenished. "Marbecke is one of those men intended by nature to be cheated. Mankind is made up of dupes and dupers."

"No," said Cyril; "of dupers who are and those who are not found out. We all cheat each other with more or less adroitness, and the weaker goes to the wall. Have some more wine, John, to wash that truth down. 'Truth lives at the bottom of a well.'"

"But my throat is not that particular

well, my dear Cyril. No, I must be off in a minute. I am going to drive with Brydges this afternoon."

" Ah ! that reminds me, Fordyce," said Burton, as he rose to get his hat. " Brydges is coming round to my place after Hall, and I think Purcell, too; you'll come, I suppose, and you, Ponsonby, if you have nothing better to do."

" I shall be delighted to have one of my usual tournaments with Miss Burton, I am sure," replied Cyril, " it is a long time since we quarrelled. John will come with me."

"Yes," replied Fordyce himself. " I had another engagement, it is true, with Brydges; but I suppose he has forgotten it. By-the-bye, you owe me my revenge, Burton."

" All right, you shall have it. *Au revoir.*"

" My dear and very simple cousin," began Cyril, as soon as the door was closed, " how much a term do you think your acquaintance with that inestimable doctor costs you? I don't mean for medical attendance alone."

" Oh! hang it, Cyril, you have always some suspicion or suggestion to make. What's the matter now ?"

" I simply asked a question, cousin."

" Ah! but I know well enough what you mean. Why, man, he plays as fair as the sun in heaven."

" And always wins."

" Well, you know, he can't help that if he's the better player."

" Ah! it's a way he has, I suppose. And it's a way you have to lose. But that's not all; he may be as just as Rhadamanthus for all I care, only he has two strings to his bow, one called écarté, and the other Lizzie. Now I guess he has touched the bull's eye pretty often from the one, what luck has he with the other ?"

" I'll tell you what, Cousin Cyril, you are too clever by half, and like all too clever people you are always turning mole hills into mountains. I am about as likely to marry Lizzie Burton as you are to marry Bab. Why, man, you must be able to see through a millstone, if you can see any affair of that sort. She happens to be the only respectable woman I know in Oxford to speak to, and I like her well enough to laugh and talk and chaff with— but marry! Pooh, Cyril, you make me laugh. Now if you had said Brydges, there might have been something in that."

" Poor, unhappy, deluded idiot; to be brother-in-law to that little varmint, who cannot look you straight in the face. Well, there's no accounting for tastes. At least I am glad to hear you are safe. There's no telling where to have you impetuous fellows. And if anything

happened, Blue-beard would be sure to
say it was my fault. Miss Lizzie is a
dangerous little witch, there's no doubt,
although her fascinations are lost upon me.

> " ' I know a maiden fair to see,
> Take care, take care.'

Now if it were Marian, it might be
different."

"My dear sneering Cyril, she's a married woman; perhaps you are not aware
of that little fact."

"But in that little fact would lie the
charm—the attraction to me. Unmarried flirts are to be found any day in the
week. But your married woman who has
graduated in coquetry is quite a different
matter. *Il y a fagots et fagots.*"

"If you are going to talk French
morality, I'm off, Cyril. After all, I
begin to think I am a good deal better

than you. Give a dog a bad name, you know. Now, goodbye for the present, for I am late and must be off."

Truth compels us to confess that the good taste which ruled the toilettes of the Misses Burton did not extend to the arrangement of their drawing-room. Perhaps because the successful adornment of an apartment requires powers of a different kind from that of a dress, a bonnet, or a bow. External neatness, I do not mean mere mechanical ordering, is seldom found without a corresponding inward sense of fitness and good government. Your thoroughly untidy man lives, thinks, speaks, and acts in an untidy and slip-shod manner. His thoughts push one another out of their place, tread on each other's heels, and never advance steadily and of purpose. Half his life is spent in trying to catch the other half. However, *revénons à nos moutons !*

The Burton drawing-room was large, straggling, and untidy. It seemed as though it had never made up its mind to be a drawing-room altogether, but still had vague longings after bed-room, dining-room and boudoir belongings. A pair of shoes is not generally considered a desirable ornament for the chimney-piece, nor is a wine-cooler often seen in a drawing-room; yet both of these articles have mine eyes beheld in the Burton *salon*. Then, too, bonnets, gloves, shawls, might be seen in all manner of strange and uncomfortable places; and if an unwary or nervous visitor went so far as to open the lid of any of the ottomans and settees with which the room abounded, there would be no end to the surprises which might be discovered. Articles of necessity, and (very) plain work thrust aside hastily on the approach of some unexpected visitor, dog's

eared novels and slatternly work-boxes.
Some one declared that he once found a
rouge pot, but I doubt this, because nature
had supplied her rose madder so liberally,
as to leave nothing to art. Of course,
there were all the modern apparatus of
photographic albums, stereoscopes and
views, a scrap-book to which many gene-
rations of undergraduates had contributed,
and other such female implements of war.
A few scrambling flowers—a handful of
flowers rather, than a bouquet—occupied
the centre of the table, and together with
a dirty pair of gloves completed its adornment.

Edgar Purcell, who was the first to
arrive, found the fair Lizzie robed in
white muslin (N.B. a little soiled, but
still good enough for the occasion) and
sky blue ribbons. Her fair forehead was
bound with a velvet band of the same
colour, and her hair hung in a rippling

mass on her shoulders; and as she bent over her book, she appeared to the ardent young Puseyite like a very beautiful Christian martyr—say a St. Catherine. Although the book in her hand, 'The Curate of St. Ethelburga's,' suited this character well enough, we may be permitted to inform the reader, that under the cushion of the sofa on which she sat, might have been seen the second volume of "The Three Musketeers."

"Oh, we are so glad to see you, Mr. Purcell, Barbara will be here in a minute. It is such a *long* time since you have been here. I began to think you had forgotten all about us." The blue eyes looked reproachful.

"Oh no, Miss Burton," replied the youngster in a delightful state of blushing, "certainly not that. I have been reading very hard indeed. You know I am in for smalls soon."

"Ah, yes, I suppose so," replied Lizzie, who knew nothing of the kind, "but then I am sure *you* have no cause to be afraid." The blue eyes looked hopeful. "You are not like some of Harry's friends, so horribly fast and idle. Do you know I think it is quite shocking to think how some collegians waste their time. And preparing for the church too! I am sure I couldn't do so." The blue eyes looked in despair at the wickedness of the ungodly.

"Mr. Marbecke—you know whom I mean, he is my tutor, and very kind to me, in fact I do not know what I should do without him—says that a regular course of study is absolutely essential for one who is to become a priest. He has marked out all my day for me."

"Oh, how very nice. That is just what I should so like, to live by a rule, and have fixed times for everything. It is like those dear Sisters of Mercy. Ah, Mr. Purcell, do you know I sometimes think I should like to be one. So peaceful and happy, to walk about the hospitals and to nurse the sick, and say the Hours and all that."

"That's just what I think," exclaimed the enthusiastic youth, "I am sure those sisterhoods do an immense amount of good; I wish all ladies would belong."

"But you see one's friends dislike the idea so much. Now if I were to—"

"Oh, Miss Burton, how charming that would be. I am sure the Mother Superior would be so delighted to gain *such* a daughter."

The infatuated one looked unutterable things, but that was not enough.

"Ah, dear Mr. Purcell, if only we could act as our hearts bid us!" and she clasped her hands in pious raptures at the thought, "if only you knew what obstacles—how much we poor women have to undergo. But I am only wearying you, and I have no right to do that."

"Wearying! Oh! Miss Burton, if you knew the pleasure it is, I could listen for ever; oh! if I could but help you!"

And then Brydges and the two cousins entered.

"Hush! I will tell you another time."

And she swam across the room to her visitors, being at that moment re-inforced by the redoubtable Bab.

"I am sure I don't know where Harry is," began that lady, "and I don't very much care, either; he has been as cross as two sticks all day long about something. I hope you men will put him in a good humour."

"Is it possible that friend Burton is ever cross with you, Miss Bab?" asked Cyril, with affected incredulity.

"Now look here, Mr. Ponsonby, how often am I to tell you I won't be called by that name. In the first place, it is very ugly, and secondly I am Miss Burton,"

"Never mind, that is your misfortune, not your fault; that will be mended some of these days."

"That is adding insult to injury. I dare say the remedy would be worse than the disease—it would with you."

"Cruel Miss Barbara, barbarous creature, to dash all my hopes to the ground. Just fancy how well it would sound, 'I, Cyril, take thee, Barbara,' and all the rest of it."

"If you are not civil, I will not give you a drop of coffee. You grow worse and worse every time. Mr. Fordyce, why don't you keep your cousin in order?"

"Why, he is supposed to be keeping me in order, I believe. He is big enough to take care of himself. Hullo! Burton."

Just then the worthy host entered, and dispensed his nods around.

" Give me some coffee, Bab ; no milk, if it's all the same to you. Well, Brydges, where have you been all the afternoon ?"

" Fordyce and I have been over to Bullingdon in my new basket trap. About the neatest little turn-out you ever saw, Symonds says there is not another like it in Oxford; crimson leather and silver for the harness. I'll tell you what, Miss Lizzie, you must see it. Will you come for a drive some afternoon ?"

"Oh, Mr. Brydges ! I'm surprised at you. How can you think of such a thing ?"

" Well, but what have I done that's wrong ? Ponsonby says I never open my mouth, but I put my foot in it."

" Why, how could you expect me to go alone with you without a chaperone ?"

" Oh, hang chaperones !" exclaimed the ingenuous youth, "that's all fudge, you know, you and I should be immensely jolly together, now shouldn't we?" he sank his voice, thereby intimating that he thought the proper time for a tête-à-tête had arrived.

The young lady, however, observant of Edgar Purcell's eye, thought otherwise. So she threw out some question in a loud voice to her brother, and, under cover of the answer, half whispered to her attendant swain. "Perhaps I might with you."

As they rose from the table, good-natured Bab began to question Purcell on his chances for smalls, which gave Brydges another chance with the fair Lizzie.

"I say, Lizzie—I may call you so, may I not?"

"Certainly not, Mr. Brydges; it is very wrong of you. Gentlemen don't call their lady acquaintances by their christian names, at least, they ought not."

"Oh, but we are more than acquaintances, you know; I wish you would call me by my name."

"So I do, I call you Mr. Brydges, do I not?"

"Bosh! I mean my christian name, you know, Arthur; do you think it a pretty name?"

"I don't know. Let me try 'Arthur,' 'Arthur,' yes, I think I like the name."

"Oh, if you would only like the bearer. Oh, Miss Burton!"

And he seated himself on a little stool at her feet.

"Get up directly, and don't be absurd, Mr. Brydges. I never saw anything so ridiculous as you are."

"I won't get up until you call me Arthur; there now, just once. No, it is no good frowning."

"How tiresome you are. I will not. Well, if you are so absurd, then,—Arthur. Now go and talk to Bab."

And the fair strategist rose and walked across the room to join the rest of the party.

"Come, come, good people all," exclaimed Barbara, "what are you all going to do to-night?"

"A pretty question for a hostess to ask," said her brother. "There, go along, Bab, and give us some music. If you are not ornamental, I suppose you can be useful."

"That's how I am treated, Mr. Fordyce," she said, with a little laugh, as John followed her to the piano. "Do you speak to your sisters like that?"

"I wish I had any to speak to, Miss Burton; but I am all alone in my glory at home, and rather dull I find it at times."

"So you say, but I can scarcely believe you. You men can do so much we poor women cannot. You have all

your active out-door amusements, hunting, shooting, fishing, and all that; and
then you have politics, and reviews, and
magazines. Oh, if I were a man, I would
do so much."

"You forget how much you would have
to leave undone which you do now. We
should lose by the exchange."

"Come, come, Mr. Fordyce, no compliments from you, please. I like you
too much—you know I always speak
my mind—I like you too much to wish
for any such compliments as your cousin
pays. No, I always feel an useless piece
of goods."

"Labelled 'Fragile, this side upwards,'
I suppose," said Cyril, who had come
behind.

"What, you again? Whatever brought
you here, you torment?"

"The mention of my own name. I
know how fond you are of praising me,

and wished to hear what pretty compliments you were paying me."

"Well, now you are here, make yourself of use and sing something. I would rather hear you sing than talk."

"And I would rather hear you talk than sing," retorted he.

Bab had the voice of a peacock, and so there was a general laugh.

Cyril sat down and sang the serenade from "Faust," with considerable energy and taste.

"That just suits him," said Bab to John, "it's sneering like himself."

By this time, Purcell, who had been irresolutely turning over some photographs, managed to steal round to Lizzie.

"What a beautiful view that is of Tintern Abbey, Miss Burton. How I hope some day it will be restored to its old use again."

"Ah, yes! That would be sublime. So romantic, so peaceful and quiet."

"Yes, I really think the English Church is coming round to the old true Catholic state. That unfortunate Reformation!"

"Very true," murmured the young lady, thinking it time to cast her best made fly; "but there were some gains, you know. The clergymen can marry now, which they couldn't before." And she rolled her half-closed eyes at him.

"Yes," responded he, after a long pause, "yes; but I almost doubt whether that is a gain. I think celibacy is more Catholic, you know, more primitive."

He spoke as if he had some little hesitation.

"But how dreary for a solitary clergyman, with no one to cheer him or sympathise with all his troubles and joys. Oh! I could almost die as a clergyman's wife, such a glorious work, so different from the weary life I lead in this world,"

She quivered her eyes and clasped her hands, and looked more like St. Catherine than ever.

" St. Elizabeth of Hungary was a married woman," thought Purcell, " and yet she was a glorious saint."

Poor child! he had not read his Carlyle, you see.

" Here, Liz," called out her brother, " we want you to sing. Brydges won't sit down to cards until you have sung him something."

" Very well, what is it to be? Only one, mind."

" Oh, sing that jolly German thing, ' Do, do,' something or other, I forget what."

" Oh, I know which you mean."

And accordingly she sat down to the piano, and sang " Du du liebst in mein

hertz," with all the expression of which
that dangerous little ballad is capable.
Then came " Juanita," and then " Come
into the garden Maud," which, by the
bye, she had no business to sing, as it
is a male song and for a male voice.
However, her admirer made no objection.
And then last of all came the seductive
" Di parlate d'amor," by which time
Arthur Brydges was about as much prepared to play whist as he was to ascend
Mount Chimborazo. Oh ! those ballads,
what mischief they do ! Why don't
young ladies follow St. James' advice,
and when they are merry sing psalms ?

Fancy singing the Old Hundredth,
or the Hundred and Fiftieth new version
to an ardent lover ! However, in some
hands, or rather mouths, I believe these
even might become perilous weapons.
Surely a Sister of Mercy might sing
them to a sucking curate ; but then

how about the celibate priesthood? The
effect upon Edgar Purcell was to make
him conjure up wonderful dreams of a
dimly lit oratory, an organ, and a black
robed figure pouring forth dulcet Gregorians. Somehow these got mixed up
in his mind with visions of a country
Rectory; curtains drawn, lamp lit, and
a little muslin-clad fairy warbling
Longfellow's "Psalm of Life!" Oh!
Marbecke, Marbecke, where wert thou
then?

After that they sat down to business.
John and Burton, that is, to écarté,
Cyril and Bab, Brydges and Lizzie to
whist. Purcell was asked, but he belonged to a brotherhood which did not
allow its members to touch the "Devil's
books," so he sat by and pored over
photographs. I don't think he quite
liked to see St. Catherine playing at
whist; but then was not Naaman par-

doned for bowing down in the house of
Rimmon?

The result of that evening may be
summed up thus. To Brydges, the loss
of one heart and sundry coins of the
realm; to Purcell the great disturbance
of his celibate ideas; to John the loss
of twenty pounds—so that Cyril was
the only one unscathed.

CHAPTER IX.

TO the others, however, lords of themselves and their destinies, loss of heart or money was but as a very small thing; but not so to our little Puseyite friend. To him there was a dread creature, called a spiritual director, begot of superstition on fear, and by mortal undergraduates named the Rev. Thomas Marbecke. Many a man's conscience held he in his thumb and finger to rule and guide as he listed. He was a mystery man, a sayer of dark sayings, a dabbler in deep waters stirring up much mud, perhaps to some minds somewhat of pearls also; but to Purcell he stood in a double light, not simply guide and philosopher but friend also, a walker of walks, a giver of teas where there were exhibited jam and semi-Romish doctrine, and a lender of little holy books, such as the life of St. Ulularius, who lined his mattrass with darning needles and sang hyms without ceasing, or a monograph of St. Parcelblinda, who always screamed when a man approached, and never kissed her father after her third year.

Such food, oh, Marbecke, didst thou give thy disciples as they sat at thy feet, and picked up the crumbs thou didst let fall. Honour to thee, good but pigheaded, as to all others who try to do what they consider their duty. But would it not have been better to look on the world and its duties with the eyes God had given thee, rather than with the smoke-coloured glasses of pre-

judice and self-conceit? He undertook
to guide the youth under his charge,
but unhappily he treated them as though
they were a herd of wild pigs, ever longing to scatter and hurtle headlong into
the deep, forgetting that nature and
reason are sufficient guides to those
whom Homer calls "articulately speaking, mortals."

With this Mentor, Purcell was wont
to take a constitutional, let us say, once
a week, during which doctrine and discipline was driven into him, interspersed
with little holy jokes, such as Elisha
might have made to the sons of the
prophets. Now such a walk was due
for the day after that evening spent at
the Burtons', and when Purcell thought
thereon he trembled. Had it been a
flirtation—horrible word! a flirtation?
Had he unawares slipped into that whirl-
pool of iniquity? He had certainly called

her "dear Miss Burton" an unnecessary
number of times; he had tried to whisper
Lizzie once, only it stuck half-way; then,
again he had pressed her hand very hard
on leaving; and again, as a separate count,
when asked to play at whist, instead of
replying that his conscience and the rules
of the Guild of the Blessed Gengulphus
forbad him, he had been cowardly enough
to say that he did not care much for
cards. Bad, very bad; but was there
nothing per contra?

After all, that sweet, ah! too sweet
conversation had only related to the bles-
sedness of the monastic and religious life;
had he not painted it in seductive colours?
had he not tried to remove obstacles?
Certainly he had, that must not be forgotten.

Nevertheless, the little man, after some
of those complicated gymnastico-religious
exercises involving the employment of

prie-Dieu, candles, crucifix and rosary, which supply the place of prayer to many modern High Churchmen, retired to his couch with a troubled mind.

However, the day dawned bright, and the face of the august Marbecke shone with amiability, as about three o'clock in the afternoon he and his pupil started on their way. Up the High Street wended they, and up the hill of Headingdon where a gentle wind arose and caught the Marbeckian coat-tails as they flapped, until he resembled a rara avis indeed, or an ineffective aerial machine painted sable. On still, on to Cuddesdon episcopal and beloved of the curate species. They went like the oxen of Bethshemesh, turning neither to the right nor left, and as they went they lowed. Let us listen.

"I cannot agree with you, Purcell," Marbecke is saying in reply to some remark. "I cannot agree in thinking this new gymnasium of any service. Indeed, I fear it will only add one more to the already many distractions from a course of disciplinary study. For boys, with a certain moderation, gymnastic exercises are useful and healthful. But 'when I became a man I put away childish things.' The training of the mental powers for the service of the Church, is the great object of your presence in Oxford. There is no objection, certainly, to such relaxation in walking as we are now taking. The Apostles appear to have been great walkers. But even then, it is always desirable to have some object in view, such as some interesting church to visit, so as to improve your archæological knowledge."

"But you don't think gymnastic exercises wrong, do you?"

"Certainly not for the laity, who may indulge in such amusements; but for a priest, and even a candidate for the priest-

hood, I think them undesirable. There is
a tendency in them to encourage the development of the merely muscular as
opposed to the spiritual energies, the
hylic as contrasted with the *psychic* principle; I look with grave distrust upon
this. The Catholic must never forget that
his is a spiritual warfare, and that any
carnal weapon, such as mere muscularity,
is only an impediment. Look at St. Paul,
he was mean in stature and—there is a
tradition—had weak eyes. You will find
an interesting note on that subject in
the Triplex Expositio upon Galatians. I
advise you to read it. Then again I
think that the outward aspect of the
priest should contrast with his priestly
and spiritual powers. In these he is
terrible, in those contemptible. His
weapons are the power of the keys
and the ministration of the sacraments.
Compared with this, mere muscu-

larity is valueless, nay more, is harmful."

"But would not some acquaintance with athletic sports tend to popularise a clergy—a priest, I mean, in his parish?"

"That is exactly what we should not aim at, and I am surprised to hear you fall into a vulgar error. A good priest can never be popular. He hastens to wrestle with the carnal powers, and the world accordingly will hate him. Of course, a few holy and devout souls will be found occasionally who will recognise his powers and love—hem—his office; but popular he can never be. My dear Purcell, I hope you don't dream of popularity?"

"Oh, no, not in that sense; but I should like to do my duty and be loved too."

"Love is a thing you will learn to dispense with. Remember how many blessed saints have purposely made their appearance loathsome and uncleanly, for fear they might be liked by their follow-men. The true ascetic is above the respect or love of his fellow-creatures. He prefers to be despised and abhorred. Of course there is a medium. There is a prejudice in these days in favour of cleanliness, which I do not think it would be well to oppose. But remember, we have no business with making Catholic Truth palatable and acceptable to the world. Truth will prevail but by her own powers. In fact, my dear Purcell, you must not seek to gild your pills."

Then followed a ghastly little laugh, and the conversation flowed into other channels. The charming nature of A's sermon, the beauty of St. B's church, the splendid retort which C had given to D in the House of Lords on the matter of religious processions. At length generals led round to particulars, and Marbecke remarked,

"By-the-bye, I did not see you at St. George's last night. Reading hard, I suppose."

Now St. George's was the famous and most Puseyite church in Oxford, whither Purcell and his friends were wont to resort. He knew his time had come, but replied bravely, "Well, no. The fact is I was at the Burtons."

Upon which the sun went behind a cloud instantly, and Marbecke uttered an "oh" of portentous significance, followed a little later by another "oh" of increased severity. Now Marbecke's "oh" was capable of as much meaning as Lord Burleigh's nod. Being interpreted, it meant at present, "at one time I had hopes of the ultimate salvation of this young man; but now from the confession he has just made, I fear these hopes were ill-grounded and that after all he is utterly abandoned like the rest of this vile world."

Then he said, "I was not aware you knew them."

This regarded grammatically is the statement of a fact, but Purcell knew well it was intended as a question, and with spluttering began to answer, "I can't say that I know them intimately, at least, you know, Burton is my medical man—that is to say the young ladies—" and then stopped short, crimson.

"That is enough, Purcell, quite enough —I do not wish to know what you are unwilling to tell. We will change the subject, if you please. I thought I had your confidence that is all."

"No but, indeed, Sir, there is nothing to tell, nothing at least that I wish to keep from you. I have only been there a few times of an evening."

"A few times! My dear Purcell, are you sure that you are wise in forming indiscriminate acquaintances—ahem—lady acquaintances, you in particular who are training for the priesthood, and just now when time is of so much importance."

"But surely there is no harm is there, Sir?"

"If you ask me to judge, you place me in a difficult position. It depends upon circumstances, I only said that I thought it *unwise*. If you reflect, you will perceive that already it has caused you to neglect a duty, your attendance at Vespers at St. George's. Let us hope that is all."

"I am very sorry for that, very. But surely you do not know any harm of the Miss Burtons, Sir?"

"Harm? no," in a tone which spake volumes of suppressed information of murders and thefts. "I am not aware, however, that they are very desirable companions for you. Was Mrs. Burton present during the evening?"

"No, Miss Burton said she had a headache."

"Oh! you know if I speak at all on this, hem, unpleasant matter, it is desirable that I should speak my mind thoroughly. Let me earnestly advise you, Purcell, as your spiritual director and your friend, not to seek to prolong such intimacies. I say nothing about the Burton family. They may be estimable in their way, and act up to such light as they have received; but they can scarcely be called Church people."

"I know Burton is not very particular in his opinions; but I assure you, Sir, Miss Lizzie, I mean his youngest sister, has really most correct views; she was telling me only last night how unsatisfactory she. found the worldly life. and how great her desire was to become a Sister of Mercy."

"Indeed," said the ecclesiastic, somewhat puzzled, "indeed, her change of mind must have been rather sudden, I think. Observe, I do not for a moment doubt her sincerity, at least, I wish to express no opinion upon the matter, only I must say that she has made a somewhat strange choice of a confidante, in selecting a young undergraduate as her adviser."

Purcell blushed scarlet.

"May I enquire, unless your conversation was of a private nature, may I enquire whether she has decided upon taking any steps towards the accomplishment of her wishes, and if so, whether you are to afford any assistance?"

"Oh no, Sir, you quite misapprehend me. Miss Burton only spoke generally of the charms and excellencies of the religious life, and regretted the obstacles in her way."

"Oh, oh! Well, Purcell, you will understand that I speak entirely for your good, when I say that such conversations

between one in your position and a young
lady are dangerous—dangerous. They
have an unsettling tendency upon the
mind, and a perilous approximation to
that most reprehensible habit of vain conversation—called in the world, 'flirting,' I
believe—against which, as of course you
remember, the Guild of the Blessed Gengulphus has a special rule. Let me urge
upon you to avoid interviews of such an—
hem—exciting nature, and to be content
for the future with such society as is
suited to a candidate for the priesthood.
We will say no more about the matter
now. I have no doubt that your conscience will suggest to you another time
and place when it may better be discussed."

And Edgar Purcell, glad to escape so
for the present, hastened to admire a
distant church, of which they came in
sight just then. Amiable and well-mean-

ing little coward that he was! To what
purpose a mind, a heart, a conscience, if
they were all to be locked up in Marbecke's
breeches' pocket and aired only when he
pleased? Perhaps the ordinary reader,
whose happy fate has not thrown him
among the hybrid breed of semi-Romish
priests which the Tractarian movement
has hatched, may consider the above
ridiculously exaggerated and over-coloured.
Far from it, good reader, far from it. The
palette is only set on too light a scale, and
where I have been content to employ gray
and brown, I might have placed black
with all truth to nature. The entire
subjection of the will is a leading doctrine
with those of the Marbecke kind; the
crushing out natural passions and desires,
a much-urged necessity. The merely
human bonds of love which unite parents,
children, and husband and wife, are to be
flung aside and superseded by those higher

relationships which the Church has sanc-
tioned, and of the necessity of which they,
the priests, are, of course, sole and infallible judges. And yet, wonderful to
relate, these men are good sons and
brothers, and occasionally, nature tri-
umphing over artificial laws, good hus-
bands.

But is not the Romish Church of this
opinion also? Yes, indeed; but then, at
least, she has the merit of being outspoken
on this point. Her doctrine of the confessional and of religious vocations is no
obscure mystery, nor does she profess to
be a Reformed Church. But to hear
members of the Established Church (a
title they hate little less than that of
Protestant) talk the hideous rubbish which
Marbecke poured into his pupil's ears, is
somewhat remarkable, and certainly shows
on how very broad a basis the Church of
England must be constructed.

As their walk drew to a close, Marbecke suggested to his companion that, as they were late for Hall, they had better go on to service at the Church of St. George of Cappadocia. At the time to which we refer, the church dedicated to that saint was the favourite house of the Puseyite clicque, as it possessed advantages peculiarly adapting it for the gorgeous spectacle and elaborate musical display in which that party delights, and which render it so popular among young ladies. The parish was small and well to do, so that the incumbent was able to devote his time, thoughts, and superfluous income to the cultivation of ritual and musical science, and the main-tenance of a staff of irreverent lay figures and boys who constituted his choir. Of course, if a little clicque of clergy, and third-rate musical amateurs, with their enthusiastic and æsthetic tail of young ladies and gentlemen choose to play at

Romanism, perhaps their peculiar type of mind could not be much etiolated by their musical exercises; but, nevertheless, the bulk of English congregations are not ready to accept this as religion.

As it was, the parishioners mostly stopped away with the remark, that if they wanted to hear an opera, they could hear "Le Prophète," or "L'Etoile du Nord," with a better band and *mise en scène* than at St. George's, while if they wished to say their prayers, they must go to a real church, and not to an Ecclesiastical Concert Room. Nevertheless the incumbent, who cared not for parishioners' scruples, likes or dislikes, held bravely on his own way, and on the whole contrived to turn the Church of England Service, into a not bad imitation of that of a third rate Romish Chapel, as far as theatrical appearance, noise, and confusion are concerned; indeed all but the realty, which the nature of things rendered impossible.

The rich furniture, varied hangings, brilliant lighting, and skilful posing of the bands of choristers in combination with an organ as big (and noisy) as the tower of Babel, produced great effects upon the congregation which attended. But then, said congregation was composed of materials most easily affected by such things. Romantic young undergraduates, great at ritual, dunces at Greek; enthusiastic young ladies, thirsting for excitement and spiritual dram drinking; elderly spinsters professing celibate principles, and a strong taste for that form of flirtation known as confession—these were the items of the congregation of St. George of Cappadocia, and thus, to satisfy the unwholesome craving for excitement in silly minds and the love of display in idle amateurs and semi-Romish priests, was one of God's

Temples desecrated by effeminate trash and absurd display.

Thither, however, went Marbecke and his pupil, and received, we doubt not, much satisfaction and edification from the sight of flowers, candles and dirty boys in white surplices, which they occasionally used as pocket-handkerchiefs. They also heard a neat imitation of thunder upon the huge organ, and a curate with a cold in his head who sang the service very much through his nose, and then gave way to another, who preached a dreary little sermon, in which he made a feeling allusion to the fact of its being the vigil of the festival of St. Shallabala, and congratulated his beloved brethren on the great comfort it must afford them. Then the choir who had been engaged in running pins in and making faces at each other, woke up and sang a hymn very fast to a tune as much on one note as is possible. Some one held up two fingers and a thumb to render impressive the act of Benediction, and everyone trooped away, except a Sister of Mercy, who had a difficult case to refer to the Senior Curate—him of the sermon—and who stayed behind.

When Purcell shook hands with his Mentor and departed to his rooms, he felt the afternoon had been well spent, and he had done his duty. So he had; but still, Lizzie was very charming, almost as charming as St. Shallabala.

CHAPTER X.

IT is scarcely necessary to observe that ultimately St. Shallabala triumphed over that dangerous St. Lizzie. The hottest fire, if not plied with fuel, must after a time go out and resolve itself into a little heap of ashes cold and lifeless. Acting upon Marbecke's injunctions, Purcell devoted himself more than ever to the Greek Plays and Horace, which were to form his *pièce de résistance* for the examiners in that school which is profanely called "Small." He breakfasted on Euclid, lunched on Latin Prose, and supped himself into indigestion upon the fore-named classical authors. No more visits to the

Burtons, no more dalliance with fair enti-
cing Saints, no more doubts to the absolute perfection of the celibate state.   After
all, was not the Gregorian warbling of St.
Cecilia infinitely preferable to all the dainty
songs of Lizzie the fair, but perilous.   Yes,
she should sing to him in that visionary
Rectory to come, and no daughter of Eve
becrinolined and false.   So the good little
man swept away resolutely all the cobwebs
from out of his brain, and settled down to
work in a vigorous, sensible manner.

In this at least did the counsels of Marbecke work for good, for to a certainty nothing but vigorous work could have saved
him from ignominious failure, yclept plucking. And Burton soon perceived that he had
made a mistake in respect to this guileless
Israelite. We need not say that the fact of
his being heir to some thousands a year had
weighed rather more with him than any
personal excellencies he might possess. But

when his visits suddenly ceased and his
bows, to the female portion of the Burton
family, became rather more restrained in
character, Mr Henry Burton saw reason to
congratulate himself on having two strings
to his bow. And this other string? By
name Arthur Brydges, young, rich, impres-
sionable, horribly dissipated, and with about
one fifth part of a constitution remaining
to him. He would be richer than Purcell,
and certainly there were no awkward
scruples to be overcome in his case. Poor
lad, he was one of those beings in the
composition of which nature seemed to
have omitted some absolutely vital ingre-
dient, a mammal lacking a vertebral column,
a tree without a root.

It seemed to be a necessity of his life to
defy all natural laws. He was morally
colour blind, and where others saw pink
he saw black, when others shuddered at
black, he swore it was white. Poor lad!

you meet such at school, at college, in the army, where not ? These are they whose wild and outrageous actions, defying all decency, occasionally turn up to shock us in the police courts, and elsewhere, and cause us to ask whether they are responsible for their deeds. He was good-tempered, generous and obliging, but he was eminently what Scripture calls a " fool."

It would be worth our while to study the significance of that word and character, inasmuch as we use it far otherwise from Scripture, mainly, indeed, for mental deficiency, whereas the sacred writers seem to denote moral. So, the fool who says in his heart " there is no God," is not simply a man of weak intellect, unable to reason from effect to cause, but one who has resolutely closed his eyes, lest he should have forced upon him a fact unpleasant to him, because condemnatory of

his course of life.   But fools, Scriptural or
not, provided they have money, contrive
to get on very fairly in the world, nor is
the general judgment on them very harsh.
There may be no royal road to learning,
indeed, but there is a road paved with
gold, along which fools can travel, both
swiftly and safely, towards their hearts'
desire.   Their desire may not be ours,
nor their high road ours; but after all,
each man can but be happy in his own
way, and "*chacun à son goût.*" Aristotle's
definition of happiness, is not universally
accepted as yet in practice, however incontrovertible it may be as a theory.
Arthur Brydges, at all events, had made up
his mind as to what was necessary for his
well-being, and had decided that unless he
married Lizzie Burton, Heaven and earth
might go to general ruin.   And this he
announced—being, like all young hounds,
prone to give tongue on the least provo-

cation—to all his friends, and notably to John Fordyce.

And now came about a curious masqueing, as it were, or change of character. Both of them were what the world calls fast, let us say somewhat immoral, if you don't mind the expression. But then Brydges was a fool, and John was not; specially was he not fool enough to consent to such a marriage as this. So, while the fool in his love passion talked morality, the wise man to gain his end had rather to laugh at morality.

"I'll tell you what it is, Jack," grumbled Brydges, one night, as they sat over their brandy and water and cigars, "it's no use talking, if I don't marry that girl I shall go mad."

"Don't be a fool, Arthur Brydges, you'll do nothing of the kind; you'll not go mad, Arthur Brydges, because you haven't brains enough. And you'll not marry Lizzie, because I fancy you have just brains enough to keep you from such a matrimonial suicide."

"Why on earth do you speak like that to a fellow?"

"Simply because that is the only way of speaking to a fellow like you. Look here, Arthur, you and I have been great chums, haven't we? Well, do I ever sponge on you? no. Or do I owe you any money? no. Or do I expect to get anything out of you?—you know I don't. Well then you really may take my advice as that of a disinterested man; you see, it is nothing to me personally whether you marry Lizzie Burton, or your scout's daughter; only I should be horribly cut up to see my friend, a gentleman by birth and education, a fellow who will have a position in the world, throw himself away upon a regular little flirt—don't swear, man—the daughter of a notorious old drunken rascal, and sister to another rascal, as big, but not as drunken."

"Don't sit there sneering, man, like your jackanapes of a cousin, Ponsonby—I hate Ponsonby, he's always sneering at me—she can't help her family, can she? I never knew a chap as illiberal as you are."

"In one sense of the word she *can* help her family pretty considerably by marrying you. I'm not in the least illiberal, Brydges. If she were better than her family, or different from her family, I should not say a word against her; but they are all cut from the same piece of wood, there's not a pin to choose between them. Come, you can't deny she is a regular flirt, can you?"

"She has never flirted with me, I know, and what she says I believe. She told me she was very unhappy at home, nobody cared for her, and all that; I dare say that rascal Burton is awfully unkind to her."

" Oh, Arthur, Arthur, what a simpleton you are ! Why, he is the manager of the puppet-show, and pulls the strings ; don't you see they mutually depend on each other in the games of cards and matrimony ? 'Pon my honour, though, his game is innocence itself compared to her's ; you know your losses at écarté, but you never find out all your losses in matrimony. I just know this, that Hesketh, who married Marian Burton, is about the most pitiable object you can see. She was all in the mild and pensive style before marriage, and now she has turned out a Tartar. The poor fellow cannot say his life is his own, and she is always carrying on a flirtation with some of his brother officers. But even putting all that aside, remember that a married undergraduate is about the greatest absurdity to be seen."

" Thank you for nothing then.   When
I am married I shall cut the concern, and
take my name off;   why you surely didn't
think I meant to go to a Hall, and vegetate
there ?"

" I don't know, you seem mad enough
for anything, as far as I can see.   And so
you would actually leave Oxford, you who
are only just one-and-twenty, and retire
into the country to settle down on married life ?   By Jove, Arthur, I begin to
think you are well nigh crazed, in very
earnest."

" Well, laugh as you like, but it strikes
me I was never so sensible in all my life.
I know you fellows think me no end of a
fool, and perhaps I *am* a little soft.   I
know I'm not good at Virgil and Homer,
and all those old swells.   But then I
always knew I should have plenty of tin,
so what on earth use would there be in
my breaking my back in working at

them? Well, now look here. Here have
I been these three years just going the
pace, spending my money on a lot of
fellows and girls who don't care a pin for
me, and playing old gooseberry with my
health, and you never say a word to stop
me; but now that I want to turn round
and pick up, and lead a decent life and all
that sort of thing, just because I mean—
for by Jove I do—to marry a girl whom
even you can't say isn't respectable, you
turn round, cut up rough and slang me,
and call me a fool. It's deuced unfriendly,
John, that's what it is."

The poor weak little man was maudlin,
he had been drinking raw brandy, tears
stood in his silly blue eyes, and his thin
hand, as he stretched it out towards the
bottle, trembled and shook like a leaf. But
there was truth in what he said, however
grotesque his utterance. And John felt it,
for a quick bright flash flamed up in his

cheek, and his brow contracted nervously.
However, the unpleasant thought which
had arisen in his mind was put on one side
for further consideration; and he spoke
not unkindly to his friend, just removing
the bottle out of his reach.

"I think we've had enough of this jaw,
old fellow, and I am sure you have had
enough and more than enough of that
stuff. I can't have you laid up again with
D. T. I know both you and I have been
great fools, perhaps it's time we turned
round again; but whether your way of
righting yourself is the best, remains to
be seen. At all events we wont quarrel
over it; and now if you will be good
enough to walk off into your bedroom I
will blow your light out, as a lighted
candle, though very well in its way, is
scarcely the thing to put on your bed when
you go to sleep."

With some little difficulty all these

manœuvres were accomplished, after
Brydges had several times addressed his
friend as 'dearest Lizzie,' and then with
some inconsistency offered to fight him.
When in bed, he suddenly became very
grave, and expressed a determination to
begin reading Homer for smalls. This
being frustrated by John, he dropped
asleep—promiscuous—muttering to himself, "It's all a mistake—it's all a mistake."

John had blown out the candles and
turned off the lamp, but the moon was
pouring in great beams of green light
through the half-closed curtain, so he
strode up to the window-seat and flung
himself down there, resting his head on
his hands and looking out upon the moonlit quad. Brydges' words rang in his ears.
"It's all a mistake," what was the
mistake? who had made it? was it his
life that was the mistaken thing? was it

possible that after all he was a fool and
leading a fool's life? He stopped and
asked himself for a moment those terrible
questions, "what am I? and why am I here?
and what do I here?" and he found the
answers all unready. He had yet to find
out what life is, by learning what death is.

It seemed a great tangled mystery to
him. He was young, he was strong, keen
of wit and healthy of mind, and with all the
gifts fortune could give him. What should
life be to him but a time of enjoyment, of
pleasure, of happiness. Was it? Was he
happy?

Be sure, good reader, as soon as you
begin to ask yourself this question, something is wrong. You are happy when you
do not question and analyze your happiness.
Put it in the crucible, and puff! it is gone
in vapour, or comes out dull and alloyed.
Was he happy? well, he supposed so.
He certainly attained the kind of happiness

he strove after ; but then, after all, was this
the only, or the best possible ? He was
like all strong youths and most young
men, a splendid, healthy, magnificent
heathen, a materialist, a worshipper (though
unconscious) of that great beneficent
tender goddess Hertha, whom to love we
need no teaching ; we are all by nature and
instinct Pagans, after-years bring us,
perhaps, to Christianity, but by birth we
are and must be Pagans, and some of us
continue so all our lives.

John Fordyce as he gazed dreamily out
upon the moonlit quad, felt that perhaps
the life of dissipation which he had been
leading was not as satisfactory as it might
have been, but nothing more. He did not
feel that his life had really been a defiance
of nature's precepts, that he was out of
harmony with her eternal beauty, he did
not feel that his energies had been misdirected, and that misdirected energy is

after all sin. Nor did he feel then, that on his shoulders rested the burden of those whom he had caused to stray, whom he had led wrong, or neglected to help on their way.

"It was a mistake," certainly. But then life was such a great mystery, that how could a man keep straight? As for Brydges, poor fellow, he would do what he could for him. If he wanted to turn round he would not prevent him. Ah, too late! horrible words, too late! The next day they went out on that fatal drive, and Brydges was killed.

CHAPTER XI.

I DO not know whether it would be possible, I am not sure whether it would even be desirable to attempt to describe John's feelings, as he sat alone the night of the accident. Marbecke's entry and departure formed no interruption to his thoughts, more than a buzzing fly might that he had brushed away with his hand. We said that when he was left alone, a Mightier Presence was with him than any the priest could summon up. John was face to face with his conscience, and making its acquaintance for the first time. At length he was forced to pause and think, and ask

himself questions. Nothing less would
have brought this about. As a daring
horseman, accustomed to gallop along at
his own pace, and making light of all
such obstacles as hedges and ditches
never so high and broad, is at length
compelled to rein up and swerve aside
from the awful black chasm of some unused shaft, so John, on whom pages
of advice and volumes of remonstrance
would have had no effect, was suddenly
checked and stopped short by the violent
death of his friend. Strong natures need
strong remedies. And this appealed to
just that part of him which was most
respondent.

If any living man had come and told
John he was a sinner and exhorted him
to repent, he would have replied by telling
him to mind his own business; but a
corpse speaks far more eloquently than
any living man, and it has the last word

ever—you cannot reply. Although he had
loved his mother with the warmth of an
affectionate nature, he had stood by her
coffin with less emotion than he now did
by that of Arthur Brydges. There was
a special bond beteeen them; the lad,
weak and foolish as he was, had looked
up to, and imitated, and loved John; and
John remembered now that no word of
restraint, warning, or advice had ever
come from his lips. How should it?
What was he to advise? And now it
was too late. The face of the dead in
its icy calm revealed no secrets, told no
tale, it had carried them with it, and
it was too late.

There is nothing so terrible to contemplate as the irrevocable Past. Future
evils, however near, are softened and al-
leviated by hope. Present troubles bring
their own cure by enforcing action; but
for the Past there is neither hope nor

remedy. The Past with its burden of miserable sin, of fruitless sorrow and suffering, of neglected opportunities and wasted hours, with its ceaseless dirge of "too late," the saddest sound which language frames, is like an impenetrable. granite rock which no efforts can pierce, or tears melt.

"It might have been," "I once could," "If I had," "Oh, that I had not," whose life memory is free from these ghastly echoes of the past? And if all were too late—as it seemed to him—for Brydges, how was it with himself? Cloud after cloud rolled back from the past, until in the mirror of conscience he saw his own past life. Now she had much to say to him, nor were her remarks of a pleasant kind. A palate thoroughly accustomed to a diet of Dead Sea apples loses the taste of the ashes therein. Restore the tone by a good tonic, and the cindery, nauseous bitter becomes evident as compared with wholesome food. For long there was anarchy within him. The old *régime*—namely, that of brimstone pagods—had abdicated, or rather been chased from its thrones as soon as its incapability was recognised. As yet no permanent government was declared. Much dust, uprooting and down-tearing, partial cannonading, and very sufficient uproar characterised this change, for the great vessel rolled about masterless with no hand to guide her into port.

In the fog and dissatisfaction which possessed him, one thing alone was clear— not consolatory, perhaps, but at least a negative fact. Hitherto, his twenty-three years had simply resulted in the presentation of so many testimonials of respect to the powers of evil. Perhaps on the whole, that was not sufficient; might not testimonials of respect be needed elsewhere also?

For twenty-three years he had neglected the only culture which could repay him—self-culture—and had devoted his time to wild oat sowing and deadly night-shade planting. Now for a better style of farming. But still what system was he to pursue? Of course, "become religious" you will say; but his difficulty was to discover what was meant by this, and how he could be so without also being a fool or a hypocrite.

Being religious at home meant, of course, duly going to church, and, if possible, keeping awake during sermon. At Oxford, it meant being either of the Low Church clicque, going to hear Mr. Chisholm, not turning round at the Creed, talking a conventional language and attending the meetings of the Undergraduates' Synagogue, as a certain religious society was called; or belonging to the High Church clicque, at-

tending the choral service at St. George
of Cappadocia, turning round and bowing at all possible intervals, wearing a
cross on your chain, reading little red
edged books, talking a conventional
language, and being a member of a
Guild. And between the two factions
John Fordyce was quite unable to decide,
regarding them as rather complicated methods of going to Heaven.

But he met with a friend. Maxwell,
the fellow of St. Catherine's, of whom
you have heard as a double-first and rising
man, was this friend. He was one of
those clear-headed, bright-eyed men, the
very sight of whom seems to do you
good when in a mental tangle. While
he discoursed to you sound good sense,
you found afterwards to your surprise,
that it was religion also; but then with
him religion was practical. If he advised you to do a thing, you knew both

that it could and ought to be done. He
dealt not in hair-splitting mysteries and
dogmatical theology. When you asked
him for bread, he did not hand you a
neat specimen of quartz or granite. He
didn't expect you to diet on ashes and
swear you enjoyed it; but he gave you
the truth, and was rigid in condemning
what he knew to be wrong. No prag-
matical babbler, or quoting scripture on
all occasions like a yard measure, and
as narrowly. When he did quote, however, the spiritual weapon he used, came
out bright and sharp, and cutting through
muscle and flesh. He never gave an
opinion unasked; when requested, he gave
an unbiassed, unreserved opinion. And
so while John was eating his heart and
finding it particularly nasty, while he was
regretting that his nature was such as
to allow him to go neither to the good
or the bad, save with his head turned back

over his shoulder, Maxwell came to him,
and by his calm good sense shewed him
really what he wanted.

That a man cannot live without some
rule and motive for action, that the mere
indulgence of every animal desire of pleasure cannot in the end satisfy—that a man
must serve and obey some power, surely
best then, that power who was both God
and Father—that this service was simply
obeying the instincts of the higher nature
and the voice of conscience, and regulating
and restraining the lower nature. That
Religion did not simply mean the bare
acceptance of certain facts, or the bare
assertion of certain doctrines, and denunci-
ation of all those who did not hold the
same, but love and trust in God, and love
and trust in all men as the children of God;
finally, that the life of the great Example
" who went about doing good," was ex,
actly that practical life, which in our

measure we are bound to imitate. In a word, Maxwell possessed the inestimable gift of a good digestion, combined with common sense. If we only knew how much depends upon that good digestion, we should surely attend to it more. Half the ignorance, vice, misery, hatred, and violence in this world, will be found to proceed and spring from indigestion, physical and moral. For the two are intimately connected.

Given a certain amount of physical indigestion, and the moral sense shall become weakened, and depraved. Exactly as physical indigestion renders the organs incapable of performing their functions and duly disposing of the food which the appetite craves, so a man, who suffers from moral indigestion, is utterly unable to deal with the mental and spiritual food circumstances throw in his way. He is unable to draw from it the nutritious juices

it may contain, to reject what is useless
to retain the bone and muscle-producing
portion. Poison and healthy food gradually become alike in taste, until the mind
actually craves the detrimental and loathes
the life-giving.

I said that Maxwell possessed a good
digestion, and common sense. It was
the *mens sana in corpore sano*. He was
able to take a singularly clear unbiassed
view of any matter brought before him,
to examine its bearings and to discrimi-
nate accurately between the more or less
advisable. He had already made his mark
in the University, and appeared one of those
men of the time who manage to infuse
their character into their surroundings.
He had hitherto cut out his own way, and
the College of which he was fellow was
beginning to look forward to his becoming
a tutor. And, indeed, it was no small thing
for the poor widow's son, sent to the Uni-

versity at God knows what cost and priva-
tion to the brave souls at home, to become
a fellow of one of the richest Colleges in
Oxford.   Henceforth his future was made,
he should sit with the best and wisest in
the land, he should rise again higher and
higher, and who knew what mitres the
future should hold in store?   So did good
widow Maxwell sing her touching little
Nunc dimittis, believing, like all good
mothers since Eve, that the world held no
better son than her hero.   Nor were the
rest of his family slow to recognise his
good fortune, each in his own special
way.   Rich Uncle Goldsby, who had
snubbed the little widow and advised her
to apprentice her son to some useful trade,
now wrote to congratulate Maxwell on his
well-merited success, and to request that
he would procure for him six dozen of the
College Port.   And the poor uncle—it is
immoral of uncles to be poor—who had

hitherto confined his attentions to paying his nephew flying visits at Oxford, and tasking the resources of his modest cellarets, took advantage of the joyful occasion to borrow ten pounds of his "dear boy," remarking, that his word was as good as his bond; a statement which I regret to say proved strictly true, as his dear boy afterwards found to his cost. And how did Maxwell himself regard his success? Often did he smile in after life to recal the eager hopes, the frothy plans and wild expectations in which he indulged.

Happy all-golden time of youth, when a man can look back if not without, yet at least with but small remorse, and forward with such infinite hope and confidence! The horizon there is always tinged with sunrise colour; the day has not grown grey and old. In but few years we sit cold and cheerless by an empty fireside, and trace in the dim white ashes which

lie before us, only shattered hopes, broken
vows, resolutions unrealized, friendships
sundered.   Maxwell was commencing a
new era.   He had been poor—very poor.
Now he had an income which to his ideas
seemed riches.   He had been obscure in a
crowd, now he might take his true position
among his equals.   He had known what
trouble and hard work meant, now if he
chose he might rest on his oars and watch
poor struggling mortals toil against wind
and tide, free from care like the gods of
Epicurus.   But, at least, not that was his
resolution.   Rest—aye—but not rust, not
fruitless unhelpful idleness.   Now that he
had climbed the mountain, surely he might
help some weary traveller up the same.

And so he resolved to the best of his
powers to identify himself with the body
of undergraduates to which he had so lately
belonged, to endeavour to employ whatever influence he possessed for their good,

and for the breaking down the barrier
which too often separates the tutor and
pupil at the University. Men of his
spirit are, thank God, not so rare now as
they were some years back, when youth
was left alone to flounder helplessly into
Heaven only knows what of darkness
and misery and sin, to be stripped and
wounded on his ways to Jericho, while
Priest and Levite alike daintily gathered
up their robes and walked by decorously
with averted head and upcast eye. And
for this change, we must be grateful mainly
to that party which has obtained the name
of Broad Church, and to such writers in
especial as Kingsley and Hughes. While
High Church was deep in its coquetries
with Rome, and confined its care of its
younger members to a kind of patronage,
based on the confessional, calculated to
destroy all independance and manliness;
while Low Church had its pet under-

graduates, who could talk sweetly of irresistible grace, original sin, and the inward call, and were usually the greatest dunces in the University; the Broad Church party has manfully stepped forward, teaching tutor and tutored alike. To the former, that he is no mere machine, warranted to feed another machine with a certain amount of Latin and Greek per diem—but a living, acting, thinking man, whose experience of life must be brought to bear upon those young hearts with which he had to deal. And to the latter, that the University system is one of *education*, not mere cramming, education and development of all powers, both of mind and body, and that it is the due union of both these which makes the true man. And in this spirit did Maxwell enter upon his work, and chancing on John Fordyce, and attracted by his many good qualities, proceeded to render such aid as

lay in his power to extricate him from the
Slough of Despond into which he had
fallen. Thus separated from dogmatic
theology, quibbles, squabbles and glosses,
Religion was set before John Fordyce in
so plain a form, that he wondered now he
had never seen it before. Repentance for
the past, and faith in the future was to be
his motto, and on this he started the new
life.

However varying in degree, there can
only be two kinds of mutation, from good
to bad, or from bad to good. They may
be sudden, or deliberate, in action; they
may be noisy and vehement, or quiet and
imperceptible, but one of these two is ever
going on in each one of us. When Aaron
cast the Israelitish gold into the fire, and,
to use his expression of naïve hypocrisy,
"There came out this calf;" that was an
example of a change for the worse, good
gold had been transmuted into a vile thing

vile in itself, vile as art, vilest in its use; but when a man is moved to cast the calf, or beast-like part of his nature into the furnace of fiery self-examination and judgment, the stream of pure metal which flows forth clear when the furnace door is opened is glittering, pure and priceless, fit for the king's diadem, for it has been tried and refined.

And this was the change which had taken place in my hero, Low Church may regard it as a conversion, if they please, High Church may regret he didn't go to confession; for himself, he could say, "One thing I know, that whereas before I was blind, now I see."

CHAPTER XII.

THE Commemoration was over, and
the undergraduates hurrying down.
Three weeks had elapsed since the accident, but that time had sufficed to materi-
ally alter John's plans. He and Brydges
were to have gone together on some
foreign tour, and though Cyril professed
himself ready to take the vacant place, the
death of his friend had made John averse
to travelling. He wanted to be quiet,
least of all was he in the humour for
Cyril's cynicism and sneers, although the
two cousins were very good friends. So he
contented himself with a half promise
of coming down to the Lindens.

"Where," remarked Cyril, " you will be bored to death by the ghost of genteel poverty," and then betook himself to Easimore Rectory. There he found the Rector, as usual, doing nothing, and doing it very thoroughly indeed. His time was usually spent somewhat thus. After breakfast, the great labour of reading the " Standard " of the day commenced. This arrived about ten o'clock, and occupied the worthy gentleman two hours in perusal; but then he read it in a truly Conservative manner, commencing with the leading articles, that he might know in what light to regard the news of the day. Then came the Home Department, police reports, awful murders, and the political news, and the like; next, his eye passed (with considerably diminished interest) on to such trifles, in the way of revolutions, assassinations, and the like, which might be going on abroad, as detailed by "our own correspondent;" last of all came the light brigade of gigantic gooseberries, extraordinary births, and centenarian deaths, which are so useful in filling odd corners and still odder brains. The advertisements generally occupied a good half-hour, during which, perhaps, he was engaged in trying to answer the enquiries as to whether he did or did not bruise his oats, double up his perambulator, or use Thorley's highly spiced condiment for cattle. And in this way the "shining hours" were passed, much to his delectation, interrupted only by a visit from the housekeeper, to receive his orders for dinner, or any household matters.

It was rarely he received or had to answer any letters. Their reception was always attended with much grumbling, the necessity of answering them acknowledged tardily and with much stertorous puffing and groaning. If we were to say

that on these occasions frequent reference
was made to a certain work of that great man
who is called our English lexicographer, we
should not be wrong. You see, ordinarily,
no one inspects a sermon but its author,
so that spelling is not so necessary.
Besides, do we not read advertisements
in highly respectable clerical papers stating
that MS. Sermons may be obtained at
prices varying from one shilling upwards ?
The good Rector was not a lunch eater.
He denounced the custom, and was only
in the habit of partaking of a glass of
sherry and an Oliver biscuit which, as he
said, did not interfere with his dinner and
left him light and active. The afternoon
was taken up lounging and pottering about
his grounds, seldom extended to a walk.
There would be the gardens to be visited,
the fruit inspected, the stables reviewed,
possibly a servant to be scolded for idleness—for a " fellow feeling" does not

always make us "wondrous kind." And
then came the golden hour of the day—
dinner-time—that hour for the preparation
for or retrospect of which all the others
existed. To delay or interrupt this was
an offence of the highest character. If
parishioners wished to die, they must select
some other hour out of the twenty-four,
but *that* was sacred.

Although no drinker in the bad sense of
the word, the Rector had his own ideas
respecting his wine and, to do him justice,
an excellent taste for it. After dinner, he
would sit for an hour or more sipping his
half-dozen glasses of Port, and mechanically
breaking up the Oliver biscuits in which he
delighted, staring intently before him the
while, a bovine creature, stall-fed, chewing
the cud. He was habitually a silent man,
and cared but little for society or conversation. When John was there, they kept
up a straggling conversation much inter-

rupted by stretches of silence on days when venison or pheasant graced the board.

He liked well enough to listen to his son's sayings and doings, any news of his neighbours was acceptable, or a little political patter as long as it tended to the glorification of the Tories. He would utter occasional grunts and snorts of assent or dissent; he never argued or reasoned, but then he would contradict you flatly and that did as well. Occasionally he would warm up, and with a sly twinkle of the eye relate some anecdote of his young days, some escapade belonging to that time when he was not the elect of Aunt Grizzell, but then he would suddenly pull up and assuming a face of ludicrous gravity remark that times were very properly changed now, byegones were byegones.

After all he was a good-hearted, positive, unreasoning and obstinate old gentleman, not a bad type in himself, but not that which we generally select for a clergyman. He would go to bed, say his prayers and doubtless sleep very soundly after a day spent as we have described, without the slightest misgiving as to any part of his duty neglected or left undone. Towards his parishioners he was liberal enough in all money matters; if they were ill, he did not go to them himself it is true, but then he paid for the doctor, which certainly was of greater service. We have been thus particular in describing the daily life of the Rector of Easimore, that the reader may see how entirely John was left to his own devices for amusement and occupation. He paid his father rather more attention perhaps than he had done before, read him his daily "Standard," and wrote for him the few letters to which were required any replies. Some hours of his time also were taken up with his books, as by Max-

well's reiterated advice he had decided
to try for honours. The time he had
wasted at Oxford had naturally thrown
him back somewhat.

However, it was merely a case for some
hard reading, and he fell to with a will,
and devoted his mornings to the necessary
studies with marvellous perseverance and
steadiness, his father wondering, but
silent. His afternoon rides soon became
his chief amusement, and after a little
while were generally in one and the same
direction.

How was this?

My fair readers—if I have the good
luck to possess any—have already guessed.
John was in love.

Dear fair readers, I cannot express the
delight with which I have piloted my hero
safe into this port, which I longed to
make before. If I possibly could have
managed it, he should have fallen in love

earlier—in the first chapter, let us say, and then how much of dry theological and controversial matter would you have been spared. How smooth would the course of our narration have been, how many sunken rocks should we have avoided!

Alas! that it could not be so, that we had no power to direct it otherwise. However, according to the old Greek proverb, "if you can't sail you must row;" and so we hasten to bring on the scene, albeit somewhat tardily, the fair young lady who will be—but, by-the-bye, that is telling too much, so we will say the fair young lady with whom our hero chose to fall in love.

About four miles from Easimore lived a Mr. and Mrs. Masterman, who had one only daughter, Edith. When Mr. Fordyce thought himself too fat to continue hunting any longer, he made over John, then quite a lad, to the care and guidance of his friend Masterman, who took a great liking to the promising youngster, and was proud of showing off his powers.

And thus John became acquainted with Edith, then a little damsel some two years his junior, though I cannot say that he felt more than the good-natured contempt with which big boys regard little ladies.

As Time wore on, and Miss Edith went to school at Cheltenham, they met less often, and for nearly a year before this particular long vacation, she had been abroad with some friends. So that when John's rides over to Masterman Park were resumed, she had grown into a tall self-possessed young lady, and he was a man— I won't say bashful, for this is not an Eton fault, but one, at least, scarcely accustomed to young ladies' society. Women always have men at a disadvantage, they are always older, and more self-possessed, and of quicker instinct.

It was the old story of the witch's son
and the snowy Florimel. There was not
much in her, it is true; but to him an
universe, and so he straightway fell down
and burnt incense and sang orisons to the
deity of his imaginations. She was good-
looking, I will grant. Grey eyes, bright
chesnut hair, rich complexion, and trim
figure. Fairly instructed, too, though
not accomplished; French passable,
Italian enough to read " I Promessi
Sposi," drawing enough to criticise, music
enough to accompany. She entered a
room with grace, dressed and danced
well, and talked just that amount of
inanity which is bearable. She was good-
tempered, had a class at Sunday School,
and carried a neat little Church Service
bound in ivory and gold. She liked
Cathedral service, especially the organ
and chanting, and thought architecture,
" lovely," " so calm and peaceful, you

know." She observed all the proprieties, and yet was no prude, knew just how much was proper to give to Cæsar, and gave it to him. Thus she went to the meets, but did not hunt; to church twice on Sunday, yet didn't dislike friends dropping in to lunch; and when her mamma was an invalid and she became housekeeper, never forgot to order egg sauce with the salt fish on Ash Wednesday and Good Friday.

On the whole, she was just the girl to make a faithful, unimaginative and reasonably obedient wife; and many would prefer her on the principle on which some men prefer driving a blind horse as unapt to gib or shy. She had not the faculty of surprise or admiration. She could be shocked, certainly, at some great breach of the proprieties; but the course of her ideas soon returned into its usual channel, and flowed on as destitute of casual eddies and whirlpools and impediments as it was free from flowers or leaves.

But all this to John seemed perfection just now in the depths of his humility. The abyss of his Malebolge made her brightness shine the more, just as stars are clearly seen from a coal-pit, which to those on higher ground are invisible. And so after some weeks of this silent worshipping, he resolved to try his fate, well perceiving that the parents were willing enough.

But like an honest man, he resolved to tell his lady-love how much in the past he had to regret and lament, and by way of practise, he thought he might as well make a similar revelation to his father, who had of late been very kind to him. It would be unpleasant, it is true, but it would be salutary at least.

Father and son are seated in the study —so called on the *lucus a non lucendo* principle. All the respectabilities of English clerical life are there,—Turkey carpet, well filled book-cases, writing table and its appurtenances, also some articles not so generally included in English respectability—such as " Bell's Life," gun-case and powder flasks, fishing rods, whips and ferret muzzles.

Other business than sermon writing is transacted here, I ween. The well polished mahogany table bears port and sherry, and a jug of claret, biscuits and fruit are there, and silver mounted horse-shoe bearing rectorial snuff. The possessor of all these pleasant things, and spiritual pastor and master of Easimore, is a tall, portly, somewhat stern-looking man, of about fifty-four, firmly and well-made, with rather a sportsman-like cut, something like Nimrod of old, only dressed in loose alpaca trousers and a shooting-jacket. He sits sipping his wine, and pulling at his grapes almost in silence; not that he is cross, only, having but few ideas, he likes to let these germinate and fructify in quiet undisturbed.

"Help yourself, John, as you drink claret; it isn't bad stuff in its way, none of your cheap and nasty tariff articles. Rascally shame it is to keep on malt tax, and let in red hog-wash at twelve shillings a dozen—that comes of your new fangled statesmen; however, it doesn't concern me, I stick to my glass of port; is it still good at St. Margaret's?"

"We haven't the luck to get it, Sir, you forget I am not a member of Common-room exactly yet. It seems to agree with the dons very well."

"Humph! Dare say it does. Ah, nearly all the old set I used to know are dead, or have taken livings. Man there of the name of Rogers?"

"A man, Sir? Well, there's a tremendous don of that name, Senior Fellow, and a lot of other things, the Rev. William Rogers, I think ; is that your man ?"

" To be sure, to be sure.   Senior Fellow, is he? When last I saw him he had just taken a First in classics, and was as drunk as a lord, he offered to fight the Dean when he came out."

The Rector gave a grim chuckle; he liked to recall College dignitaries as " drunk as lords," and could, had he listed, have spread dismay in many Common-rooms by a few of his remembrances of old days.

" I can't say he ever does so now, Sir ; he's the straightest of the straight."

" Quite right, too, when he has to do with a lot of careless young dogs like you young men.   There's a time for everything. When are you in for your next examination ?   I don't understand these new statutes and new-fangled arrangements."

"Not for some time to come, Sir, I shall be able to make up for lost time, I hope."

"Lost time! what d'ye mean? Haven't you been reading, then? what is the good of going to Oxford if you don't read?"

John, who had been building up a pyramid of maccaroons which a misguided housekeeper thought a fitting accompaniment to port wine, suddenly swept them away, and began.

"No, Sir, I don't exactly mean that. I certainly haven't read, though, enough. I am pretty sure of a fair class, my friends say; but since that accident—you know what I refer to—I have been thinking much, and see how much there is to regret in the past. You know I have been what men call fast, and certainly have not done my duty as I ought to you, or," with a slight blush, "to God."

"Why bless my life and soul if I can

understand what you are driving at, with your fine words about duty and life, and all that. Now, look here, if you've been making a confounded fool of yourself, and getting into any scrapes or debt, say it out at once; it won't be the first time, you know that, but don't beat about the bush."

"On my honour, Sir, you are quite mistaken, I don't owe twenty pounds all over Oxford. You have allowed me too liberally for that.

"Then what on earth do you mean?"

"What I mean is, that having lived carelessly and badly before, I am heartily ashamed of it now, and mean to try and do better for the future. I don't want you to think better of me than I deserve."

"I can't say I have ever thought particularly about you. I know young men will be young men, and, of course, I have heard of your goings on. However, let bygones be bygones—if you want money, I'll draw you a cheque; but don't be Methodistical; whatever you are I couldn't stand that. I always did hate Dissenters, and, please God, I always will. And now I shall go to sleep, I think."

"Stop a minute, please, Sir, I just want to tell you one thing more."

"Why, bless the boy, what's come to him; you are like a double-barrelled gun, first one and then the other. What on earth is it now?"

John smiled, and dashed into his fresh subject.

"You know Miss Masterman, father?"

"Since a baby in arms. Well?"

"Do you know, Sir, I was rather thinking of proposing—that is to say, you see, of asking her to be my wife, if you have no objection?"

The Rector gave a little gruff laugh, and replied,

"Objection! Why, my boy, I have always meant her to be your wife since you were a lad, you couldn't do a thing that would please me more. Now you speak like a man of sense, and I'll back you up in it. And now you had better leave me for my nap."

The next day Black Bess was saddled and conveyed her master over to Masterman Park. On his way he encountered the Squire, and jumping from his horse walked by his side as far as their ways went. He explained the nature of his errand that day, and met with nothing but encouragement.

"My man," said the kind-hearted Squire, "I have known you since you have been a little lad, so high; and I can safely say that there is not another young fellow in the county, no, nor in England, whom I had rather have for my son. And so will mamma say, I

know, when she hears of it. As for
what you tell me, why I like you all
the more for your manliness in telling
me. Although, you know, I pretty well
knew it all before. However, you were
quite right, my lad, quite right to say
so. Bless your heart, I know what
young men are, and when a fellow says
he's sorry, why what more do you
want? But you know, as for Edith, of
course, I can't answer for certain. You
two must settle that, for I never will
interfere with her free choice as long
as it is a gentleman. A little bird tells
me you will have no difficulty—at least,
I think not. Look here now, go on
at once and settle the matter. I left
her in the old beech walk. Of course
you'll stay to lunch. I shall have a
turn at the birds in the afternoon, and
you'll come too."

So the Squire stamped off full of

business, or what he thought was such, and John hastened on to the house. Was it necessary to make his confession to Edith? That was the question being debated within, to which inclination said "No," and conscience "Yes." Oh, vile wild oats which bore the meal of this bitter cake, this humble pie, and oh, vile folly which planted them. Never again, never again! And so he crashed through underwood and shrubbery to that part called "The ladies' garden," where the beech walk was. Plainly did he see a flash of bright blue silk glinted with golden sunlight among the great brown boled beeches, and as it approached, and Vixen the Skye terrier began to bark, his heart gave a great thud and then stopped still. As he entered the avenue, Edith turned round, and greeted him with frank welcome.

" Mr. Fordyce; why we all thought you

had forgotten us. But I am so sorry papa is out, he went out only half an hour ago."

"I know it, for I met him on the way, and walked some distance with him."

"Oh, if so, then he has told you all about the poachers, who turn out after all to be Easimore people. It is so tiresome, isn't it, that they won't leave the game alone; I am sure papa is very good to all his tenants, and gives away, oh, ever so much meat at Christmas. Did he seem angry about them?"

"Why, to tell the truth, we did not speak of them at all; indeed, this is the first I have heard of the affair."

"Why, what could you have been talking of, Mr. Fordyce; for I know papa thinks of nothing else, and if you had not come to-day, meant to ride over to you?"

"Shall I tell you what we spoke of?"

"Well, yes, if you like."

" It was about you, Miss Masterman, and I was telling him the hope which has been growing in me for long, and which has brought me here to-day. May I tell you, Edith ?" She was silent, but continued to walk by his side. Then he went on, " I told your papa, and I now tell you, how much I love you, how I want you to be my wife; your papa said 'yes,' and now Edith, it all rests with you." He bent down and took her hand, which trembled a little. As it was not withdrawn, he was encouraged to go on." " But I must not deceive you, Edith, or let you think me better than I am, I scarcely know how to tell you how bad I have been—it is so painful to me, I hardly know how to begin. You have heard men called fast and wild, have you not ? It means more, it means really wicked, and such I have been. Perhaps it is only since I have been so much with you, thought of you so much, and loved you so much, that I have seen how bad my life has really been, and how degraded I am. But now, when my future hangs on your lips, let me tell you that I regret and hate the past, and am heartily sorry for it. I cannot undo it, but I will mend the future if you will help me."

When he ceased, there was silence for a minute or so. Edith had not removed her hand, but kept her head bent down, her colour slightly raised. At length she looked up, and said,

"And do you really love me?" Of course, he spluttered out incoherent protestations. "That is enough for me, John, where I love I trust fully."

As to what followed, I leave the reader to guess. This happened about twelve in the morning, and the two o'clock lunch bell rang in vain for a long while, so I suppose their conversation was interesting.

CHAPTER XIII.

BOTH the Squire and Mrs. Masterman
had welcomed John gladly as a son-
in-law, and taken him to their hearts. She
was one of those who are called by their
fellow-women a "dear good creature,"
which generally means an amiable fool.
Very simple-minded and good-humoured,
she loved mankind too much universally, to care very much for anyone in
particular.

She liked to see the Hall filled with
pleasant guests; but she liked one quite as
well as another, and regretted them, when
departed, equally little. She considered
herself too great an invalid to take a very

active part in their entertainment, regarding her friends from her sofa like an amiable Indian idol, placid, inert, smiling. To make up for this, however, she maintained a vast correspondence with a host of "dear friends," was a delightful confidante, invariably forgetting all she was told, and a most indefatigable philanthropist; she always had some scheme of universal benevolence on hand, of which she spoke in superlatives of admiration, lasting, on an average, quite a week. With the best intentions, she possessed no powers of thought and reflection, and continually embarked in undertakings of the most contradictory kinds. However, she filled her place in the background of society well, was a good wife and mother, an agreeable hostess, and made a very fair neutral tint acquaintance.

"Here's the letter-bag!" exclaimed the Squire one morning, looking up from the devilled kidneys he was devouring. " Now let us see what there is for us. I'll tell you what, Cecy," to his wife, " if you have such a frightful amount of correspondence you must have a bag to yourself. Eight letters, I declare. Well I am glad you, and not I, have to answer them. Edith, one for you, and in a gentleman's hand-writing too ; if I were you, John, I should not allow it. One for you young man, sent on from · Easimore. And now, my dear, if you will give me another cup of tea, I'll try and read my paper."

This was the daily formula, and after being hidden for half an hour behind the huge columns of the Standard, he would emerge with the same remark, " There was nothing in it."

" Mamma," exclaimed Edith, looking up from her letter, " the Pongo Bazaar at Arlington is fixed for Thursday next, and here is a letter from Mr. Royston, inviting us to lunch at his lodgings in the Close, before going. What shall I say?"

"My dear child, you will accept of course. My going is unhappily out of the question in my present state of weakness, but you and John can drive over together and join the Mason's party. Squire, I'm afraid it's no use to ask you to go?"

"My dear Cecy, I hope you won't, for as you know I refuse you nothing; but the Pongos or Ponchos, or whatever you call them, are certainly out of my line. What will you be after next—why it was the South African Baby-Linen Society, you were 'cadging' for last."

"My dear John, pray dont listen to him. The Squire always laughs at my charitable schemes. I particularly want you to know all about the poor dear Pongos, because it may be useful to an intending clergyman, you know. Now you must not confound them with the

Pongees, they are quite a different race. The Pongees are black, the Pongos a nice copper colour, or what you may call a whitey brown. Then again, the Pongees are horrid cannibals, but my Pongos, poor creatures, never eat anyone."

"Hulloh, Cecy," interposed the Squire, looking up for a minute, "how about Mr. M'Stringer?"

"Oh, that," replied his wife, blushing slightly, "that was proved to be a mistake. They ate him it is true, but I don't think they meant him any harm."

"As a mark of affection, perhaps," suggested John, "I have heard women say to their children that they could eat them."

"Ah, well, I see you are laughing. However, I assure you you must go to the Bazaar and escort Edith."

"Oh, that I shall be ready for, Pongos or no Pongos."

" If you had only heard the dear Dean speak so feelingly about them at Arlington —the Bazaar is all his idea. And then, too, his scheme of importing some of the best to England as parish-clerks, and then after a few years' residence send them back as missionaries—so simple and practical. You know they would soon pick up our Protestant religion, and then go back and teach all their friends."

" I'm afraid, Ma'am, that the negroes when in contact with whites, learn our vices quicker than our religion."

" Ah, I fear you are as bad as the Squire. However, you will go I know. Edith, my love, write to Mr. Royston, and say how delighted you will be to come to lunch, state it is impossible for me to attend the Bazaar, and say that Mr. Fordyce comes with you."

" Who is Mr. Royston ?" asked John.

" I'll tell you what he is, my boy," re-

plied tho Squire, " he's about the jolliest
specimen of a parson going. Bill Royston
is one of the Minor Canons of Arlington,
and a jollier man does not live. Good-
tempered, easy going, kind-hearted chap,
a capital Tory and Churchman, one of
your out and outer style—true blue. He
has a beautiful voice and chaunts like a
bird, knows a good horse when he sees
him, and a good bottle of Port when he
drinks it, and lands a salmon in better
style than any man I ever met. I'll tell
you what, John, you cut up like him when
you're japanned, and you will be all I could
wish. As for these Pongos, the rogue
cares no more for them than I do, it is
only an excuse for a merry party and a
good feed."

" Mr Royston is papa's great favourite,"
remarked Edith with a smile, as John and
she left the room, " and he certainly is a
nice, good-tempered little man and makes

everyone laugh. I am so glad you are
going John, and hope it will be a fine day
for the bazaar."

The Bazaar at Arlington was the project
of some half-a-dozen great ladies of the
Close, that is wives of Canons and Prebendaries who had the inestimable privilege
of residing within the sacred inclosure of
the Cathedral. When I say that it was
their project, I believe I ought to say that
the idea first emanated from the Decanal
mind, and was then eagerly caught up by
the bevy of fair ladies who formed the
" Guardia nobile" of the very Rev. Archi-
bald Gurnington D.D. Dean of Arlington,
Rector of Poggledike and Starkey-cum-
Taberdar. He was a very great, and his
friends used to add a very good man.
Howbeit his greatness which was carnal,
perhaps, made more impression on the
observer than his goodness, which was
purely spiritual. He was tall, portly and

of a healthy brick-dust colour, with a gleaming blue eye and somewhat curling grey hair, and an eagle nose of formidable dimensions. He had a very white hand and very white teeth, and he managed to display both belongings very freely. If the degree of love for his neighbour could have been estimated by that of his hatred for his enemies, his neighbours might with reason have felt very happy. But then you see as he was the friend and champion of Religion and truth, all his enemies must be the enemies of Religion and truth, and those according to the Very Rev. the Dean were a hideous majority. So practically this "neighbourhood" was limited to a very small number indeed, just those who contrived to say "Shibboleth" with the exact accent in which he delighted. But then to this particular clicque he was omnipotent, the very incarnation of wisdom, infallibility and power. If he frowned, they trembled; if he smiled, they beamed with delight; if he made a little holy joke, they shouted; if he condescended to contradict anyone, the person so honoured at once made a banquet of his own words.

There are some Protestants who seem to have exchanged one Pope for many, and who take pleasure in making doormats of themselves for their own particular pastor to wipe his feet upon, just as their forefathers believed and trembled under the yoke of the triple-crowned successor of the fisherman of Galilee. The distinction appears to us subtle and nice, but then our eyes have not been spiritually enlightened and as yet can only see matter of fact. And so the Very Rev. the Dean ruled supreme in Arlington, and dictated laws from the sanctum of his decanal retreat, which his marshals and generals, the ladies of the Close, carried out and dictated in their turn to their several followings. More than half of the Canons were of this particular persuasion, including their wives and families. Those who were recalcitrants, simply confined themselves to the execution of their Canonical duties, and interfered but little with those high aims and universal undertakings which delighted the Decanal party.

The Bishop was, as of course bishops ought to be, charmingly neutral. He was indeed an overlooker, for he managed, like Nelson, to turn his blind eye towards all that it would have been inconvenient to notice. Perfectly impartial, he balanced his mild little compliments to one party, by amiable little nothings to its opposite. When any proposition was made to him he had ever one answer ready, that he was scarcely prepared to go as far as that, although he could not deny that there was very much in the arguments used.

Still, on the whole, he thought that with moderation something might be effected; only "*festina lente.*" We need scarcely remark after this that the amiable prelate was the offspring of a temporary coalition between the Whigs and Tories, who on a memorable occasion had agreed to sacrifice party prejudices (and principles) for the good of their country. A logician would have best described him by the sign O, or a particular negation. A satirist might have been reminded of an ass between two bundles of hay. However, all the world knows that a Bishop is less than no one in his own Cathedral, possessing only pomp without power, while the Dean is really the mayor of the palace and actual potentate. So although the consent of the Bishop was asked, *pro formâ*, for the Bazaar scheme, it would have gone on just the same had he refused it. But he did no such thing, and so shortly all Arlington became involved in that delicious whirl of religious dissipation which a Bazaar creates.

Of course a ladies' committee was appointed, consisting of four wives of Canons and Prebendaries and three county ladies headed by Mrs. Gurnington nominally, and really by the Lord and master. Then a sub-committee of town ladies was found absolutely necessary, and it was proposed that same sub-committee should be presided over by the Mayoress. Here, however, a hitch occurred. For it appeared that the worthy lady did not see the matter in the same light, and being assured that the word "sub" intimated inferiority, declined the presidency of any such committee, which should be inferior to that of the Close. She would be no Triton among minnows, and, unmindful of the good old fable, resolved to have a swim with the brazen vessels, or remain

on land. It was nimble-witted Mr. Royston, the handy man of the decanal party,
whose good temper and indefatigable
energy was held to cover a multitude of
sins, who extricated the Dean's ladies
from their difficulty. An affair like this,
without the support of the Mayoress
would never do; there were potent
reasons why there should be no quarrel
with the town; but then, on the other
hand, all Cathedral precedent was against
the admission of a mortal into the Olympian
council.

"Remove," said the jolly little man,
"remove the word, 'sub' and the thing
is done; you will have two committees;
the cathedral committee most properly
presided over by the good lady of our
universally respected Dean, and the town
committee, over which, of course, the
mayoress will be the fitting president."

"But will not that be an *imperium in*

imperio, Mr. Royston," enquired the Dean, who was present when the matter was discussed, " we must have no unseemly collision, no clashing of opposing interests. How will you prevent that ?"

" Oh, leave that to me, Mr. Dean, and I will undertake that all shall go smoothly. We might divide the command, and yet manage that all the real arrangement, all that demands a cultivated taste and elegant mind shall be alloted to one who alone, I am sure, can be equal to the occasion." And he bowed to Mrs. Gurnington. " You see, there really are many matters with which the town ladies will be more conversant—ordering the tents, hiring the band, getting loans of statuettes, all that kind of thing which is so effective; besides, there is the croquêt and the Aunt Sallies,"

" The *what*, Mr. Royston ?" demanded the astonished Dean.

"The Aunt Sallies, Mr. Dean. It is a new invention, but one that takes immensely at bazaars."

"And of what, pray, do these Aunts—Sallies, as I believe you called them—consist. The pastime, if it be one, is new to me?"

"Well, Mr. Dean, it is very simple. There is a carved head of wood, in many cases, of black material, which you know would be very appropriate under the circumstances, in the mouth of this is inserted a tube—ah, a pipe, in fact—which the byestanders attempt to break by casting sticks at it."

"Oh, indeed," replied the Dean to this lucid explanation, "oh, indeed! There appear to be several objectionable features about this—pastime. In the first place, the name, why Aunt? and, again, why Sally? I particularly object to the employment of a diminutive without due

reason. Sarah, I should prefer, although
the use of a christian name and a Biblical
name savours of levity. Let me see,
ladies, as this is a Bazaar for the poor
Pongos, why not call it the Pastime, or
Diversion of the Pongo Chief? I think
that would be far more appropriate than
the other appellation. Then again there
is that pipe, you know—all the world
knows my firm opposition to the vile and
unchristian habit of smoking; how then,
with consistency, can I permit the introduction of that instrument of sin, a pipe,
and, as I hear, a clay pipe, into my very
grounds and garden? Oh, no, never! Is
the—pipe absolutely indispensable, Mr.
Royston?"

"I fear so, Mr. Dean; at least it must
be something capable of being broken."

"But, Mr. Dean," suggested one of the
county ladies, Lady Augusta Middleton,
"by throwing at these pipes should we

not display most strikingly our abhorrence of the habit of smoking ?"

"Very true, Lady Augusta, very true, and that puts me in mind of a way in which we may protest, as it were, at one and the same time against two superstitions. By casting a stick at a black figure, we show our abhorrence of heathenism, even as the Jews did of disobedience, by casting stones at the tomb of Absolom. Now substitute a little clay cross for a—pipe, and not only should we thus display our abhorrence of Popery, of which it is the symbol, but also show how intimate is the connection between them. In this way, you see, Mr. Royston, the pastime you mention may be made unobjectionable, instructive, Protestant, and remunerative. Be good enough to remember my suggestions. Ladies, I wish you all a very good morning; success attend your deliberations !"

T 2

And in this manner was not only the sub-committee difficulty, but the Aunt Sally perplexity tided over. The Mayoress fell into the trap laid for her, and consented to head an independent committee, which undertook the management of finance and the more substantial arrangements; to the Close ladies was left the department of "taste and the musical glasses," the dressing of stalls, selection of stall-holders, and the generally ornamental line. Both Town and Close parties alike were to contribute, gain contributors, and torment all their available friends into gifts and loans. And so, finally, the great bazaar scheme shaped itself thus. It was to be held in the Dean's gardens, which were extensive and well kept, and had, moreover, an opening into the town. Three, out of six stalls were to be held by the ladies of the Cathedral, two by titled ladies of the county, and the remaining

one by the Mayoress.   This was found to
be an absolutely necessary concession to
civic dignity.   There was to be a refresh-
ment-stall with fancy prices, a flower-stall,
where the prettiest girls were gathered
together, a post-office and wild beast
show, and the Pastime of the Pongo
Chief, *alias* Aunt Sally.   This was put
under the care of Mr. Royston, to whom
was entrusted the task of explaining the
alterations which had taken place in the
appearance of the venerable lady.   The
band of the —th was to be in attendance,
and to play alternately with that of the
Arlington Band of Hope, a company of
young gentlemen of tender years, who
had bound themselves to raise their
testimony against the demoralising habits
of beer and tobacco.   Last, but not least,
that great missionary and traveller, the
Rev. Theophilus Centipede, was expected
to deliver an address on behalf of the

Pongo mission. It is true, he had never been to the Pongo Isles, but as he seemed to have been everywhere else, that would do quite as well. Some little anxiety was felt about his appearance, as his travelling engagements were so many and so close, that he was apt to turn up only at the last moment, and then prove insufficiently supplied with information upon the subject of his speech and appeal; indeed, he had been known to wander altogether from the matter in hand, and finish by appealing on behalf of quite a different mission from that upon which he had begun descanting. Still he was a wonderful great gun, if only he could be got properly sighted and charged and rammed down; and to Mr. Royston was his care finally committed.

CHAPTER XIV.

EDITH had her wish, in common with all the other young ladies of Arlington, for the day dawned bright and warm, and all seemed as if the bazaar were to be a great success, as far as the weather was concerned. Since their walk and conversation, John and Edith had fallen into the regular lovers' routine, and were generally occupied in mutual adoration to the exclusion of all other objects. John made a very ardent and attentive lover. As we have said, he had seen so little of ladies' society previously, that Edith's somewhat commonplace charms and character appeared to him as divine. To hover round her, fetch and carry for her, and anticipate her wishes was his happiness.

Their conversation seldom proceeded much farther than mutual endearment, or discussion of indifferent matters. He had not yet tried to guage the depth of her mind, and find what chords there rung responsive to his touch. She was affectionate, simple and ladylike, and, for the present, this was enough. These are good foundations to build upon, but it is not every architect who can erect the fair tower of his planning upon them. And often the sufficiency or insufficiency of foundation is only discovered too late, when the tower lies a mass of sherds and scattered ruins. However, as we said, John was happy, and Edith was happy, and they had neither studied the doctrine of elective affinities.

The lunch at Mr. Royston's was to precede the Bazaar; and accordingly John and Edith started in the pony carriage together. On the way, with a true woman's missionary instinct, she tried to rouse an interest in him in the Bazaar itself. He, however, honestly professed his indifference to the matter.

"I am delighted to go with you, Edith, but then it's the being in your company, certainly not this precious Bazaar. I honestly confess that I haven't thought much about this kind of thing; but it seems to me that if you want money to convert the poor Pongos, it would be so much easier to give it at once, without all this bother and commotion."

"Ah, but then you know, dear, that people like to get as much as they can for their money, and if it were not for the Bazaar, many would give nothing at all."

"That is just it, my pet. Don't you see people give for their own amusement, or because their friends bother them; not

for any interest they take in your dear delightful Pongos.   Never mind, Edith, I
mean to buy heaps of things, and I declare
when you know what has happened, you
shall go to a Bazaar a week if you like;
as long as you don't want to hold a stall."

"And why may I not hold a stall, eh,
Sir?" asked Edith, laughing; "do you
know Lady Augusta wished me to assist
at her counter?"

"Lady Augusta is an old goose for her
pains.   You are a great deal too pretty to
be stared at by a heap of jackanapes.   If
you had held a stall, I should have stood
by and scowled at all the men who came
up until I frightened them away."

"I don't see why my being what you
call pretty has to do with it.   I can see
you are a jealous monster, and I am
ashamed of you.   No, don't look like that,
it is not the least use, and the pony is
going across the road, and—oh! good

gracious me, John! how can you be so ridiculous, squeezing my new white bonnet?"

I don't know what driving has to do with squeezing young ladies' bonnets, but I *do* know that the pony Hassan disapproved so entirely of the proceedings behind his back, that he tossed his head, snorted, and finally stood quite still until the attention of the lovers was recalled to him, and sublunary matters generally. And in this way they proceeded, and presently Edith made another little attempt at forming John's mind.

"John, when are you going to begin your reading again? you used to say that you must read so hard, and now you are doing nothing."

"My dear child, whose fault is that? did I not read most pertinaciously until I fell in with you?"

"If you are going to tell such horrible

fibs, I will get out of the carriage and
walk home. How can you say I have
anything to do with your idleness? you
know I want you to be very very clever,
and take a great degree, and be made a
clergyman at once."

"Don't you think I am clever enough?"
interrupted John.

"No, I don't, Sir, I think you are dreadfully conceited and horribly idle ; and I
shall not be contented unless you go and
do more than that friend of your's, that
Mr. Maxwell you are always talking of.
And then you must settle down, and
become a good clergyman, and keep
bees."

"Is that absolutely necessary, my
dear ?"

"Well, no, I suppose not, but you
know all good clergymen in books do
keep them, and walk about after breakfast
and look at them."

"I think pigs would do almost as well," suggested John, "but then remember that all good clergywomen in books wear thick boots and linsey petticoats and old sun-bonnets, and carry a basket full of soup and gruel, (I wonder how they do it without spilling) and packets of tea and snuff. Are you prepared for all this?"

"Oh, John, how absurd! Of course I mean to go about, and visit, and teach, and all that; but I shan't wear any thick boots or sun-bonnets, and I know all about soup, you take it in a cold jelly, so it can't spill; but as for snuff, I shall never give any, for I think it a horrible custom for women, and only fit for you good-for-nothing men."

And in this style the conversation proceeded, until the pony drew up with a dash before Mr. Royston's lodgings in the Close.

Mr. Royston was, as we have said, one of the Minor Canons of the Cathedral of Arlington. As such simply he would have been a mere nobody, alternately patronised and bullied by the higher powers, a little higher than a singing man or verger; but he was far more than this, he was certainly the most popular man in Arlington, welcome at all tables, alike clerical and lay, tolerated by the Dean and caressed by the Mayor. He took patronising, snubbing, and sugar-plums with equal equanimity and imperturbable good-nature; he was like one of those absurdly amiable Newfoundland puppies, who is always begging you to do something to it, feed it, play with it, caress it, kick it, anything rather than leave it neglected. He was always ready to fetch and carry for any of his friends, who employed him accordingly; nothing could be done without Royston, and his good-tempered

cherubic face was always turning up when
least expected—weddings, funerals, picnics,
balls, synods, arhidiaconal visitations, at
all of these could he answer ' adsum,' and
wherever he was, he managed to be the
leading spirit.   Of course he had not one
atom of dignity, that could not be expected;
his aim in life was to make other people
happy and himself well liked, nor did he
care what fools' tricks he played to attain
those ends.   His popularity was perhaps
greatest in the town, where his special
talents for a hand at cribbage or whist, a
hot supper, punch and comic songs, and
his very convenient deafness when any
word of too warm a character slipped out
unawares, were more appreciated than in
the select society of the Close.   However,
in these chaste mansions was he also a
guest, as his sweet tenor voice was found
useful in duets and glees, and his inex-
haustible small talk bridged over many a

dead pause in conversation. His lunch
on the occasion of the Pongo Bazaar was
intended as an acknowledgment of hospitality received from his civic friends, and
was select and *recherché*.

Of the guests, the Masons alone were
known to Edith, who was considered to
be of their party and under Mrs. Mason's
chaperonage.

This good lady was the wife of the
lawyer most in repute with the county
and clerical party, a man of no little
standing and importance. She was a
lady-like, amiable woman, and came accompanied by two quiet well-bred daughters, whose only failing was a weakness
for diminutives and superlatives. There
was also present a Mrs. Gulrick, the wife
of Dr. Gulrick, the fashionable physician
of Arlington, together with her sister and
a Miss Fillister, aged about forty-five, a
" gusher " and great fern collector and

naturalist. This worthy lady might almost count for two, she was able to talk for at least half-a dozen, and her entry into a room generally produced the impression of a sack of coals having been suddenly upset near at hand.

These and Edith composed the corps of ladies to entertain whom Mr. Royston, John, and another Minor Canon—so mild and retiring that he scarcely deserved so military a title—Willison by name, were the available bachelors.

The quaint old-fashioned rooms in the Close, which formed Mr. Royston's lodgings, were decorated with much taste, and a lavish display of bouquets and *couvrettes* of snowy whiteness. The bachelor bed-room formed the ladies' retiring-room and boudoir, being remarkable chiefly for the liberal supply of scent and hair-pins on the toilette table, and for the enormous number of Mr. Royston's boots which stood on a shelf above, "enough," as Mrs. Gulrick observed, "for a centipede."

The lunch was charming, everything being cold save the vegetables; *pâté de foie gras*, pigeon pie, cold ducks, tongue, lobster-salad, creams, iced pudding and jellies, Sauterne, Sherry, and sparkling Moselle. Oh, Mr. Royston, Mr. Royston ! how stood thy banker's account after this little banquet, how about that little tailor's account so long due? But we must not look our gift horse in the mouth, so let us take the goods the gods provide, and eat what is set before us, "asking no question for conscience sake." At all events, his guests agreed to do so, and did full justice to the delicate catering of their kind-hearted little host.

"What taste you have, Mr. Royston," exclaimed Miss Fillister, as some beautiful fruit was placed on the table set in a little nest of leaves and flowers, " I really never saw such admirable grouping ; why, here you have that lovely fern, the Asplenium Septentrionale, or forked spleenwort; I declare it is far more beautiful than the peaches and nectarines—oh ! and I declare. there is the Hymenophyllum Tunbridgense ; the darling ! where do you get them, you wonderful man ? I should like to go fern gathering with you."

" My dear Miss Fillister, you make me blush with your praise. I shall be most delighted to go fern hunting with you any day you please, however, our excursion need not be further than the nearest nursery gardens, whence those came. Do you admire ferns, Miss Masterman ?"

" I think them very pretty indeed, but after all not more so than many common wild flowers which are almost unnoticed."

" Oh, excuse me, Miss Edith," burst in Miss Fillister, " there's the greatest differ-

ence; so much more interesting you know,
no true root and no flower; oh, I assure you
there is no comparison—none at all. You
know the family of Filices is my hobby;
I am never tired of looking at them, sweet
little creatures."

"Where do they live?" asked matter of
fact Mrs. Mason. "I have visited about
Arlington for many years now, and never
met any family of that name."

"Oh, Mrs. Mason, how can you say so?
Never seen any of the Filices about Arlington? If you will come with me to-morrow, I will show you a charming group of
them thriving and growing down a well,
at the back of the Close."

"What, ma'am, a family living down a
well! I never heard of such destitution;
does the Dean know of it? If not, I am
sure I must tell him. But who are these
Fillisses? are they respectable, industrious
people? How came they in such poverty?"

"Oh, now I perceive," exclaimed Miss Fillister, with long drawn note, "*I* was speaking of the Filix or Fern family, and *you* were speaking of some human creatures. Oh, I understand nothing of that kind of thing. I adore Nature, she is so grand and calm and peaceful. Are not you very fond of Nature, Mr. Fordyce?" She turned suddenly on John with a snap like a dog.

"Oh yes," responded our hero, who was most decidedly bored with the whole discussion, "she is all very well in her way, but on the whole I regard her rather as a failure. Artificial flowers last longer than real, there is more certainty in a hot water apparatus for a house, than there is in the sun's shining; and as for the moon, I have seen far better at Covent Garden, or the Princess'. Lime light has made the moon quite *passée* now. The sun certainly does some good sunsets now and then, but then they are rather poor copies of Turner. Nature is in her infancy, Miss Fillister, there is room for improvement. And as for ferns, everyone knows they are only flowers which have not sense enough to blossom."

"There, stop his mouth someone; I declare it is perfect blasphemy to hear him. You bold, bad man, I wonder someone does not keep you in better order."

"Now, ladies, will you allow me one moment?" said Mr. Royston, who had been waiting for Miss Fillister's North-East blast to drop. "You see, to my grief, I cannot always be with you to look after you and protect you, and as I shall have to attend to the Aunt S——, I mean the pastime of the Pongo Chief this afternoon, I have selected a most devoted ladies' champion— don't blush, Willison, you know you are— to be my deputy. Fordyce, too, is up to any amount, so you see you will be well looked after. Mrs. Mason, I dare say you will keep Willison in order. If I were to tell you all I know—ah, then !—"

"Now really, Royston," expostulated the crimson-eared Minor Canon, "what will all the ladies think?"

"Yes, that is just it; what will they think when they know it? However, you be on your good behaviour this afternoon. And now, ladies, as I see you are beginning to look anxiously at that clock, and as the poet says, 'Tempus fugit,' let me give you one toast before we part, 'Success to the Pongo Bazaar, and may the Pongos do as much for us as we are about to do for them.'"

The toast was drunk, and then as a corollary Mrs. Gulrick, who had been conspicuous by her deep and solemn silence, remarked, with an awful gravity, "The Doctor, (to her there was but one doctor) the Doctor has a theory that unless the system of miscegenation is fairly tried, the coloured race—in which he includes the black, red, copper and whitey-brown varieties, are destined infallibly to supersede and supplant the whites."

"Then, I think, perhaps, we had better put on our bonnets," observed Mrs. Mason, scarcely relevantly, but with a sincere desire to ward off an impending discussion.

And so the ladies all retired to put on their bonnets, and the Misses Mason also plucked up courage to try Mr. Royston's trencher cap on their pretty little heads.

"Upon my word, Mr. Royston," said John, as they were waiting, "you clerical bachelors manage to have very snug quarters, and lead very snug lives. If this is a specimen, I shall not mind this kind of life myself."

"Ah, my boy," sighed the good-tempered little man, as he furtively unfastened certain buckles behind his waistcoat, " *Deus aliquis hæc nobis otia fecit.* It isn't all like this though, I wish it were. We have to moil and toil like the rest of mortals. However, *æquam memento,* you know the rest. The great secret is to take things easily, and not fret and grizzle. I am glad to see you giving pledges of joining our glorious body."

" What do you mean ?"

" Tut, man, never blush. I mean your engagement to that charming Miss Masterman, who, I dare say, is at this moment tying on the sweetest little bonnet in the world. A man is never a good clergyman until he is married or engaged."

" Does not that press hard upon you then ?" asked John, much amused.

" Me, sir ? No. I belong to the regular, not the secular priests, you know ; I am a monk in fact, and as such, am bound to mortify the body."

"Well, as long as that mortification includes pigeon-pie and Moselle, I don't think you have much to complain of. Here come the ladies."

And as he spoke, the door opened, and the ladies duly appareled, entered.

In the meantime, all the preparations for the bazaar were completed, and the Dean, having gathered his female staff around him, invoked the Divine blessing upon the pin-cushions and pen-wipers, before the great gates were thrown open to admit all comers.

Bazaars are very much alike after all, the only great difference exists in their being in the open air or in a room. The former is less unbearable than the latter, as there is some little escape from the artificial glare and noise and hubbub all around. At all alike is there the same collection of rubbish, dignified by the name of fancy work and sold at exorbitant

prices, the same half-faded flowers,
dispensed at five shillings a-piece by forward young ladies, who affect with
indifferent success, the *piquante* pertness
and brusque slang of race gipsies. There
are the same articles of *vertu*, "kindly
lent for the occasion," the washy smudges
called water-colour, the apocryphal auto-
graphs, the tag-rag and sweepings of
penny toy-shops, the same combination
of the rubbish of the Lowther Arcade and
the atmosphere of Exeter Hall. This was
neither better nor worse than any other.
Young ladies, half dishevelled, ran after
you and solicited—no, bullied is a better
word—bullied you to put into their lottery.
Lady Augusta's stall of pretty girls proved
almost as attractive as the window of a
sewing machine shop and far more remunerative. Young men chaffed, and
young ladies flirted zealously in the cause
of charity and religion, but, strange to say,

the "poor Pongos," though much talked of,
seemed to be regarded rather as an excellent joke, and if not witty themselves
the cause of wit in others, than as matter
of serious consideration and thought.
The Dean perambulated the gardens like
an evangelical policeman, and occasionally
indulged in sallies of what might be styled
' awful mirth,' to the unspeakable delight
of his followers.

To the great pleasure of the ungodly, that wicked little Miss Mostyn had
contrived to sell him, as an Algerian purse,
a highly embroidered cigar-case, and so
he afforded to the beholders the marvellous
spectacle of the great denouncer of
the vile habit of smoking, walking
about with the very emblem of it
in his hand. When afterwards he
discovered it, he never forgave Clara
Mostyn.

The duration of a bazaar may be divided

into three periods. During the first, people walk about shyly and languidly, and the stall-keepers, unused to their position and privileges, are afraid it will be " a horrid failure." By the time that the second period arrives, things look more cheerful, all parties have been gradually worked up to the necessary pitch of excitement, and all goes briskly, post-office, lottery, Aunt Sallies—all are besieged. Then comes the reaction of the third period, young ladies have had their crisp muslins torn and trampled out of shape, lovelocks have fallen down limp, bandoline and cosmetique have lost their power; they know they are limp, dirty, bedraggled, and oh, how weary! They long for a cup of tea and bed. This is the last stage, during which a cheap admission price reigns, and economical townspeople come, but neither purchase nor admire, then go away disgusted, and remarking that they don't think so much of that beautiful Miss Mostyn after all. It was at this period, when Royston had shouted himself hoarse at the Pastime of the Pongo Chief, and Mr. Centipede had arrived very late, and without the slightest notion of what subject he had to speak upon, calling the Pongos, Mangoes, and finally going off at a tangent upon the woes of the Irish Protestants, that John suggested the desirability of return to Edith. She was perfectly ready; for, to tell the truth, she had been both disappointed and disgusted.

"You were right, dear John," she said, on their way home, "there is a great deal I dislike about it; and oh! how glad I am I did not help at a stall."

"My darling! I knew your good sense would lead you to that conclusion. No one respects people who try to do good more than I do, but I cannot see that what we have seen is the best way of doing it. As for the Pongos, I sometimes think they have as much reason for sending us missionaries to teach us what Christianity really means, as we have for sending out to convert them. No, my dear Edith, I would rather see you with the basket and soup, and flannel and gruel, than behind the counter talking slang and refusing change at the Pongo Bazaar."

CHAPTER XV.

THERE is no life which more combines the elements of the picturesque and the comfortable, than that of the country squire of fair estate and good rental. There is nothing very heroic about it perhaps, but at least it forms a pretty pastoral. There is the old Hall, with its quaint rich Elizabethan or sturdy Georgian architecture, half hidden among the venerable oaks and elms which gird it round; its trim verdant slope of lawn, which forms the setting for many a jewel-like bed of flaming colour. Behind are the stables and kennels, with the great turret clock above, whose deep sound is

is echoed by the clear bell-like tones of
the pent up hounds; add to all this the
half feudal interest which attaches to an
old family name, the *prestige* of unbroken
succession from father to son for many,
many years, the atmosphere as it were of
chivalrous noble deeds, of personal courage and strength, of the old Saxon love of
feats and daring adventures, and you have
in some degree the kind of halo which
surrounds country squirearchy. Nor, to
complete the picture, must the Parsonage
be forgot. Clinging somewhat close to
the Hall, as if mindful of the times when
the parish priest was half-chaplain, half-
lackey, half-buffoon to the feudal lord,
stands the snug respectable country parsonage; itself, perhaps, a copy in little of
the style and bearing of the lordly mansion, only with the clerical added grace of
humility and modesty. The trim deep-
porched house half hidden by westeria

and clematis and ivy, the small-paned windows peering curiously out of the bower, the glimpses they reveal of the good man's study, with its learned litter of papers and books and dust; or the she-parson's little sanctum and its tables overflowing with flannels and lindseys and calico; and then again the delicious old-fashioned garden with its medley of flowers and vegetables, and its southern wall laden with peaches and nectarines, the solace of many a sick bed—in all these we have the religious element of our pastoral.

But the village itself; what of that? There it lies picturesquely seated down in the hollow; the stream brawling through its midst, Hall and Parsonage in its front, as emblematic of Religion and Power protecting innocence. Each cottage is a separate study for the artist, its rugged time-stained walls, its roof a mass of picturesque mouldiness, with its wreath of fungus and stonecrop and moss and lichen, the well-worn steps, the massive oaken door, the humble interior, the groups of children; surely, in all this, we have the finishing touch, the rich background of our Pastoral. Here we have the trio whose mutual existence implies so much; the union of Power and Religion and Humility, the commonwealth of all the virtues. And the reality?

The finest Turner, Wilson, Cuyp or Constable will be found on examination to consist of a certain combination of oils, resins and pigments, more or less poisonous and nasty, laid on a canvas background. The sweetest idyll of Theocritus or Tennyson is but so much parchment or paper, stained with blood of cuttle fish or ink. What does the rest? The creative and imaginative faculty. Be it so. Let us be content with our

" bainting and boetry ;" but in the name of
all sweet illusions, let us have nothing to
do with the race of analysts, with those
unpleasantly persevering enquirers, who
" want to know" whether the forbid-
den apple was a pippin or codlin, and
whether Abraham patronised the system of breeding in and in. For do but
look nearer, and how often will that picturesque cottage, abode of innocence and
content, resolve itself into a mere human
pig-stye, whose inmates live a life worse
than bestial, because against the very
instincts and principles of nature; where
the day of long, unthinking, ox-like toil, is
succeeded by the night of sodden over-
crowded rest, foul, verminous, pestiferous.
How often is this, the home of the English
labourer, a social hell, where morality,
decency, innocence, cannot exist—a bru-
talizing, unchristian den, where all natural
laws, by very necessity, are set at defiance,

and parents and children, brothers and
sisters, alike wallow in one common stye of
filth and crime. Nor is this an over-drawn
or exaggerated view. Were the facts that
substantiate these statements to be printed
in these pages, this would become a sealed
book to be read with tearful eyes and
burning brow.

The facts relating to between five and
six thousand of these "happy English
cottage homes," as put forth by authority,
may be read by those whom these matters
concern. Of one thing let us all be sure,
that to preach Christianity to those whom
our wicked selfishness compels to live in
utter Paganism and bestial heathendom,
is in very hypocrisy to utter lies which, if
they do not blister our lips, will bring, one
day to come, their own proper brimstone
showers upon our heads. Let us permit
our fellow countrymen to live—well, if not
like men, yet at least as well as our

hounds and hunters, before we expect
them to care much for that Evangel which
speaks of goodwill towards men, and
which our acts render negative. And this
neither chasubles and incense and banners
and confession will effect, oh, dear brother
Ritualist; nor tea-drinkings, hymn-sing-
ing, Rome-hatred and the doctrine of
Faith without works, oh, dear brother
Simeonite; but simply the little understood doctrine of common-sense, and hard
earnest work.

We simply ask for stone and wood, and
bricks and mortar and space, and you
answer us with tracts strong with
doctrine, gruel weak with water, many
words, many wishes, many warnings,
and an infinite amount of forms and
ceremonies. We want to work, and you
ask us to sing hymn No. 367, we want to
build and you beg us to stop and admire the
cut of your stole or cotta; we want to

consult about the best way of draining, lighting, ventilating, cleansing, Christianising, and you beg us to unite in an Association for Promoting the Use of the Salisbury Ritual, or extending the devotion to St. George of Cappadocia, or sending out crucifixes to some interesting and most Catholic-minded Abyssinians, who dwell in the Marshes of the Dismal Swamp. Ah, dear friends! the energy with which you pursue these bubbles, and squabble and tear each other to pieces every week in the columns of the " Watchman " or " Chronicle," would serve to rebuild every cottage in the kingdom, and raise the English labourer from being a mere patient beast to a Christian manhood.

I do not mean to say that the village in which Masterman Hall was situated, was by any means one of the worst specimens of the class to which I have referred. Squire Masterman was far from a bad, or

even selfish, man, nor was he one of those
landlords who at the same time improve
the picturesqueness of their estates and
the condition of their purses by pulling
down cottage after cottage, and driving
the inhabitants either to crowd together
closer in those remaining, to the ruin
alike of health and morality, or to take
refuge in the nearest town.   But though
not thus actively selfish, he was one of
those who effect nearly as much mischief
by looking on quietly and letting things
take their own course.   If the bailiff said
that a cottage wanted repairs, they were
executed in due time—in hard seasons he
would sometimes lower the rent, and he
had always a nod and good-tempered word
for his tenants and labourers when he met
them ; and Mrs. Masterman was liberal
enough in the matter of beer-gruel and
delicate puddings, and milk and port wine.
How was he to know that seven, eight, or

ten human beings had one room to sleep
and dress in? how was he to know all the
foul details of life among the cottages?
Things had been so in his father's time,
rents were paid, cotters looked healthy
enough, and multiplied fast enough—too
fast, perhaps, if a certain mark attached
to certain baptisms in the church registry
book meant anything—he heard no murmurs or discontent, and walked out of
church down an avenue of uncovered
heads. Was not this Arcadia? what
more could be desired, wished, or expected, save by demagogues and radicals?
Possibly the rector, Doctor Sleepwell, had
a suspicion that certain evils were curable
by a little thought, reflection, and resolute
application of the shoulder to the wheel,
accompanied by loosened purse-strings.
But who was to play Nathan to that good-
tempered, easy-going David? Nathans are
rare at all times, specially in country par-

sonages, and few know how difficult it is to say " Thou art the man " to David, after David and Nathan have been hob-nobbing together as friends.

Is not this a state of things to fill the observer with something like despair? To see so much vague desire of good, such infinite falling short, to see the reign, not of terror, not of tyranny, not of cruelty and blood, but of amiable incapability and idle self-satisfaction. Was the Moloch to whom Israelite mothers made their children to pass through fire a cruel and blood-thirsty god, or rather was he not the deified Power of Indifference, which slays its tens of thousands? And yet after all, shall strict reckoning be made with these prisoners of hope, with these victims of selfishness and idleness? happily their judge will not be Man, who has forced them into crime, but the God who alone knows the history of natures perverted and corrupted by faults and errors not their own. There is one aspect of nature, surely the most hopeful, which moralists are too apt to overlook. Nature is too often compared with human nature to the disadvantage of the latter. The entire recognition and fulfilment of divinely imposed law by the great inanimate world around us is brought into sharp and unfair contrast with the discords, rebellions, and contradictions of the human soul within us. And yet we entirely forget how much easier it is to comprehend and fathom the laws and movements of the outer world, than those which are supposed to regulate the world within us. In the one case, we examine, test and analyze at our ease; in the other case, we are necessarily prejudiced by our own personal interests, our soul involuntarily shrinks, and our hand trembles, under the infliction of the lancet and scalpel. If, in the outer world of nature we recognise, with trembling though it be, the fact of wind and storm fulfilling His word, if we are careful to acknowledge the fact of good consequent upon evil, even when we most acutely suffer under that very evil, should not all this encourage us to reason in a similar way as to those laws regulating the human soul?

The primal law of the universe must indeed be one of calm and peace and fruitfulness; if, therefore, we sometimes find this superseded by another law, calling into existence the powers of storm and drought, may not the condition of the human soul be analogous? Thus, while carefully guarding against any theory of necessary evil on the one hand, even in the face of statistics of the regularity of crime, we shall be saved from those painful doubts and difficulties respecting human nature and its place in the uni-

verse on the other. That sin is entirely
the consequence of the Fall must be purely
impossible, since had not man possessed
a previous fallibility, the Fall itself had
been impossible. Is this not—with all
due deference be it asked—one of the
questions where dogmatic theology
" darkeneth counsel with words ?" may
it not rather be removed from the sphere
of dogmatic theology altogether, and be
safely committed to those natural instincts
and feelings which were planted in man
when God breathed into his nostrils the
breath of life, and man became a living
soul ?

Not yet, however, did thoughts such as
these arise in John Fordyce's heart. He
was in. no mood for discovering or com-
menting upon any difficulties in the
system of the world; his engagement
seemed to have put the seal upon all his
new resolutions of good, and he looked

forward to the time when they should be
called into active service hopefully, because
ignorantly. He did not regard his future
life as a country parson with any great
enthusiasm or romantic hopes; but then,
looking at it as he did, how could he?
The neighbouring clergy seemed very
happy, very comfortable, very good-
tempered, possessing just that quiet
confidence in themselves and the world
which follows naturally upon good appetite, good feeding, good digestion.
They had their High and Low Church
bias of course, their little likes and dislikes, and prejudices; but after all said
and done, the result appeared very similar
in all cases—Pompey was very much like
Cæsar. They were very good men doubtless, doubtless also cared very much for
their flocks, but that did not in the least
interfere with their amusements and
private enjoyments; why should it? They

were able to hunt (some did), fish, shoot, ride, go to archery and croquêt parties, dine out continually, go abroad or touring in the autumn, and, in fact, enjoy and deport themselves just like all the rest of the world. Why then should a young man contemplate future ordination with any special dread or misgiving? John and Edith had talked the matter over, and drawn little fancy pictures of what was to be their future life.

"You know, dear," the lady would say, "I don't think you ought to hunt when you are a clergyman. I know your dear papa used to do so, and Mr. A. and Mr. B. still do now; but I think that times are altered since they were young, and the bishops don't seem to think it right. You know you never saw a bishop out with the hounds, did you now?"

"Well, perhaps, I can't say that I ever did, though I don't know how much that goes to prove. However, to set your little heart at rest, I may tell you that I shall not hunt when I am a parson. I do not see there is any more harm in my riding over hedges and ditches after the hounds, than there is in my riding on the turnpike road ; but the world in its infinite wisdom sees fit to condemn the practice, and as, after all, it is very immaterial, I do not care to run my head against popular opinion. Any other suggestion, young lady ? have you any ideas respecting the cut of my coat, or the hemming of my pocket-handkerchiefs ? I am quite ready to listen and drink in your words of wisdom."

"Don't be a dear old goose, John ; I only want to keep you from offending what Dr. Sleepwell calls, 'the weak brethren.'"

"Do you know, my dear child, that those 'weak brethren,' as they are styled, appear to me very often to be simply very selfish and uncharitable brethren ; don't look so shocked. Of course, we ought to respect their prejudices in matters really of religion and importance; but many people go farther than this, and pry into a clergyman's private life and habits and customs in a most unwarrantable manner—in fact, they look upon a clergy-man as a man in a social pillory, at whom they may throw all the rotten eggs and vegetables they list."

"Oh, John, don't say anything so horrible ! I am sure no one will ever venture to do anything like that to you. Now come in and practise your scales."

For she had taken it into her head that John had a fine natural uncultivated tenor voice, which would be very useful in leading the psalms and chants, and so she had taken him in hand and made him go through various Sol-fa exercises daily, much to his amusement and the general discontent.

Before the end of the Long Vacation, and John's departure for Oxford, by the united powers of persuasion of the whole household, the Rector of Easimore was persuaded to come over to Masterman Park to dine. He was very gracious in his somewhat grim way, and endeavoured to show the unqualified pleasure he felt in the match. He brought Edith over a beautiful bracelet of carbuncles which had belonged to his wife, and actually put it on her arm himself, kissing her and telling her to be a good little girl. He and the Squire stayed behind after John had left the dinner-table, and then he began to unfold his views.

" I'll tell you what, Masterman," said he over their Port, "you've known me a long time now, and I can tell you nothing ever gave me more pleasure than this

match of our children. I like Edith as
much as if she were my own daughter,
and I don't care who knows it. I think
them just the pair to step well together.
As for John, though he is my son, I can
warrant him. He has been a good son to
me, and I think will make your daughter
a good husband. As for his having been
fast—well, you know, Masterman, between
ourselves, I think we know what we
were when we were young, and I can't see
we are any the worse for it—young blood,
you know, young blood."

"You are just about right there, Rector,
and that's the truth; when I have to ride
or drive a young horse with plenty of blood
and spirit in him, I like to take it out
of him the first few miles. Galop him into
a bath of sweat—bless you, he's soon glad
enough to quiet down and take things
easily. And that's the way with young
men; so long as he is true to my girl,

now, I don't care a hang for the past."

" Now, look here, Squire," continued the Rector, " I'll just tell you what I mean to do for John, that there may be no misunderstanding about the matter.   I have always meant him to have the living, and he has always known it. If he had crossed me, he would have had nothing at all except a little property of his mother's settled on him, which I cannot touch.   However, he has known this, as I said, and means to take up the living.   Well, I do not mean to keep him waiting for my death—that would not suit either of us.   Between ourselves, Masterman, I am not the man I was some years ago.   I have seen Doctor X——, and he says I ought to have perfect rest and quiet ; and so as soon as John is ready to be ordained, I mean to retire and go to live in Bath, or Clifton, or some other place where I have old friends, and settle down quietly. Now, the living's worth £1,100—till he's a priest he must have a *locum tenens*, which will cost say £100. I shall reserve £400 a-year to myself—so you see the long and short of it is, that when they choose to marry, the young people will have £600 the first year, and afterwards £700 a-year to go on until my death, when they will drop into the whole £1,100 besides all the private property I have to leave. What do you say to that, Squire?"

"Say? Why, I think you mean to act uncommonly liberal, Fordyce; upon my word, I never expected as much as that. I always thought you would have had John for your Curate, or something in that line. Well, I will do my best to meet you, though my income is not as good as the world gives me credit for. You know, the Hall goes away by the entail to my nephew Geoffrey, as I have no son of my own—still for all that Edith will not be badly off. I shall make over to her £15,000 on her wedding-day, to be settled as we shall arrange with those rogues, the lawyers, and I dare say there will be a trifle at my death. That's square isn't it, Fordyce."

" I am perfectly satisfied with it; and, as for John, he would marry Edith if she had but one frock to her back. So now we understand each other. No more wine, thank you."

END OF THE FIRST VOLUME.

LONDON: PRINTED BY A SCHULZE, POLAND STREET.

BEYOND THE CHURCH.

" The shadow cloaked from head to foot,
Who keeps the keys of all the Creeds."

IN MEMORIAM.

IN THREE VOLUMES.

VOL. II.

LONDON:

HURST AND BLACKETT, PUBLISHERS,

SUCCESSORS TO HENRY COLBURN,

13, GREAT MARLBOROUGH STREET.

1866.

The right of Translation is reserved.

CHAPTER I.

THAT happy long vacation came to an end, as all things must, happy or otherwise. It had begun in clouds and sadness with John; but the clouds had lifted, the rain had cleared off, and an all-golden prospect seemed opening out to him. He had not forgotten poor Brydges and his tragical end, but he was able to regard that event now in its true light without exaggeration. His engagement to Edith had changed the whole current of his life, and given an object and aim to that which had been vague, unsettled, meaningless. He was able to look back upon the past without that black remorse which leads to

despair.   Edith seemed the silver clue
to the dark labyrinth.   And so he went
back full of high hopes and resolutions.
In spite of the interruptions of croquet
and riding parties, to say nothing of the
almost constant presence of Edith, he had
managed to get through a very fair
amount of reading, and to hope for tolerable success in the schools.   Need we
say how he was spurred on by his lady-
love ?

"You know, John, dear, I would not
for worlds have you overwork yourself, or
read yourself into brain-fever, as I have
heard of some doing, but I *should* so like
to see you come out first in the list.
Isn't that what you call double first?"

"No, my dear child.   Let me tell you,
if you want to see me a double first,
you must dismiss your hopes.   In the
first place, I am only going in for honours
in one school, and in the second place, I

shall think myself very lucky if I get a second class."

"Oh, nonsense, John. I am sure the Vice-Chancellor, or whoever it is, wouldn't be so unfair. I shall call him a horrid old monster if he does not make you something very good, indeed."

"Very well, then, you had better write to the examiners, whoever they may be, and hold that threat over them. Could not you offer to bribe them to favour your humble servant? I think, if you were to come into the schools, and do as the Duchess of Devonshire did to the butcher, that might have some effect."

"And what did her Grace do?" asked Edith, innocently.

"Like this," replied John, very ungrammatically as he added a practical illustration.

"Then she was a nasty, horrid creature!" said Edith, "and you ought to have been ashamed of yourself also to think of such a thing. But, John, dear, I want to know one thing. Has your examination, your class, as you call it, anything to do with your ordination ? Has the Bishop any connection with it ?"

"You dear little goose, your ideas are all abroad on that subject. Once for all, then, my getting a first, second, or no class at all, concerns my ordination not one jot. The Bishop will think neither better nor worse of me; I shall not become a clergyman the least sooner, nor shall I be any better off for the exhibition of wisdom or folly I may make. It is the proud pre-eminence of the English Church to choose her ministers quite irrespective of their mental acquirements. As long as they can pass an examination which almost any charity school-boy in the first class might undertake successfully after a little cramming, they are ready for ordination,

and without previous training of any kind
are allowed to teach and preach those
flocks committed to them. I have wondered much of late, since I have had to
think of these things, how it is that in
other learned professions young men have
so long a probation, such rigid tests, such
deep study—and why a mere school-boy
smattering of sacred subjects should be
held sufficient for the Church."

"Well, but, John," objected Edith, with
a woman's regular conservative instinct,
"you know it has always been so. The
Bishops must know what is right best.
I have heard Dr. Sleepwell say that a
clergyman becomes valuable only by age
and experience."

"Oh, doubtless, my love, doubtless,
very much as wine improves by keeping;
but what of the unhappy congregation
while our model curate is gaining his
experience? is it any consolation to you

when the dentist's apprentice has just drawn the wrong tooth, to be told that he will be a skilful dentist ten or twenty years to come? We want men who can *do* their work, not those who are only just learning to do so; of course I know that time will do wonders, but without asking for wonders, I think there ought to be a certain standard of simple requirements, and that those who fall short of this should be inadmissable.   Now, a man really ought to be able to put together common sense and common grammar in a sermon, for instance; but just think of that effusion of the worthy Doctor's we heard last Sunday."

"Well, yes," replied Edith laughing, "that was rather dreadful, certainly, but, you know, I have heard it so often that I am accustomed to it. He keeps them in a regular heap, and goes through them by order, so that I know what to expect; he

told me that he had not written any since
he was a young man."

"Which must have been sometime in
the days of Noah, I should think; his coat
tails have a decided flavour of the ark
about them, and remind me of a pea-
green Shem in the playthings of my
childhood. I should very much like to
dip the dear old Doctor in a pot of
emerald green and see how he would
look."

"Now, John, you really are too bad,
and I won't listen to you any longer; the
Doctor is a very good old man, and I
only hope you will be as good when you
are a clergyman."

"So do I, dearest," said John gravely,
his over sensitive conscience causing him
to find reproach where none was meant,
"I feel the solemnity and importance of
what I shall undertake as much as any
one can, and if I can only do some good

and mend some of the evil past—" At which Edith placed her little soft hand on his arm confidingly, as though to remind him that all that was condoned. " If only I could feel I might do good, I should be perfectly content, so that if ever I seem to speak slightingly or laughingly of Church matters, it is not in disrespect, but in jealousy to see ' fools rush in where angels fear to tread.' I may sometimes have doubts and misgivings, but I have none about my own sincerity. I have a double pledge now to do my work honestly, my duty to the living," and he looked lovingly at his fair companion, "and my duty to the dead."

He raised his hat slightly as he thought of poor Brydges, and Edith understood his feelings too well to break in upon his silence. After a while she said,

" I sometimes think the future is almost too bright and that I am almost too happy.

I always said to myself that I would marry none but a clergyman, and now—oh, my dearest, how happy I am !"

At which point I think this conversation had better be left, as it ceased to have any interest for the reader, consisting mainly of purring interjections and words of endearment, used with that reckless profusion and disregard of Lindley Murray for which lovers are famous. Is it better to be a fool in a fool's Paradise, or to be a wise man in the Inferno of dissipated illusions ? Answer, oh, my reader! and answer truly, if thou hast ever known the sweet madness, and then, when cured, hated the physician, his medicaments and nostrums. At least John was happy.

And then like knight of old to the wars, he departed on his crusade, with his lady's benison, to do or die. As he had truly said, he felt that he had a double pledge for well-doing in the present and future alike,

and he had accepted his responsibility in
no coward spirit. And so he went back,
braced up for the work before him and
ready to do with diligence what his hand
found to do. There was a round of visits
to pay and receive; one of the first to his
friend Maxwell, now the Rev. A. Maxwell,
for he had been ordained in the September
ordination, in compliance with the requirements of his fellowship. His principal
sitting room—for he had two—was a
large old-fashioned apartment, with low
ceiling, panelled walls and a deep bay
window. Book cases ran round two sides,
chiefly remarkable for the absence of books
and the presence of various extraneous
matters which had no possible business
there. Books it is true there were in
abundance, to be found in any place
rather than their lawful home. On and
under tables, chairs, couches, piled in
window seats, and littered on the Persian

rug in front of the fire. A few prints in old-fashioned black and gold frames, a cast of Michael Angelo's head of Christ, and some oddities in the way of bronzes, old keys, tesseræ of Roman pavement, lamps, and such like, picked up in continental wanderings and cast about in wild disorder, constituted the adornments of the room.

In front of the fire lay a disreputable looking rough terrier, which had followed Maxwell home in a state of abject misery, and from the guest of a night had gradually become his adopted child and lawful pet. It was a fond and foolish beast, always overflowing with gratitude, which it exhibited in an inconvenient fashion by casting itself down at its friend's feet as before a Juggernauth car, whence generally ensued stumbling, confusion and not blessings, the animal all the while executing a tatoo of thankfulness with his stumpy tail. Maxwell was seated writing near the window, a huge cup of his favourite beverage, cocoa, at his side. To this mess he was inordinately attached, drinking it at all possible and impossible hours, and sometimes letting it stream down his moustaches and great beard in little cascades, much to the amusement of his friends, who used to call these the "falls of the Swallow river."

When John entered, he pushed aside his papers and jumped up to greet him, putting his hands on his shoulders and swaying him backwards and forwards with a friendly vehemence.

"John Fordyce, John Fordyce, a sight of you is good for sair een. Come and sit down and have a talk. Have some cocoa? No! Oh, I forgot, you are not yet thoroughly enlightened and don't know what is good for you. Sit you down—no not there, please, for I left an inkstand on that chair, if I remember; nor there, for there is a lot of MS. which must not be disturbed—there's an empty seat for you." It was made empty, we may remark, by the simply process of upsetting its contents upon the ground. " Now tell me all about it."

John knew this meant his engagement, of which he had conveyed the intelligence briefly in a letter. He complied with his friend's request, with perhaps not more of the blushing, tautology and repetition than are usual under such circumstances. Of he course was the happiest man alive, he didn't deserve such bliss, Edith was the most lovely, the most charming, the most accomplished, &c., &c. We all know it, we have all gone through this form of epidemic, or attended friends in the like case. Let your love-sick friend talk, dear reader, let him talk. It amuses him, it relieves him; and after all it does not very much annoy you, for you need not listen with your inward ears, or believe in your heart of hearts. When the clock had run down, Maxwell, who had listened with a pleasant smile and occasional pulls at the cocoa cup, took up his parable and made reply.

"Dear old boy, I am so glad, you cannot think. It is just what you wanted, just what I wanted, and just what ought to have come about; I always tell you that *le bon Dieu* always arranges things best, when we don't interfere and make ourselves too busy. You acted wisely and rightly in doing what you did, and Miss Masterman acted generously, as women on the whole generally do. And when are you to be married?"

"Well, you know, I shall be in for greats, and take my degree this time next year, so I could be ordained the Lent after, that is in about fourteen months, and then, of course, I should be married at once."

"Bless the lad! That's taking Time by the forelock, indeed—degree, ordination, marriage, all in a lump, and at express speed! Well, I suppose there is no lawful cause and impediment why those three events should not succeed each other with the rapidity you mention. Then you will read for schools and for the bishop's examination at the same time? You can do it easily enough, I think, and perhaps will find relief in turning from one to the other. Do you know what books your future Bishop requires?"

"Yes, Bible and Greek Testament, Butler, Pearson, Blunt and Robertson, first three centuries, Hooker and Latin writing—of course a fair knowledge of the Prayer-book."

"None of those will trouble you much; in fact, the examination is little more than a farce, as I found; it implies too often a merely technical, and not practical knowledge of things. But, however, do not let me discourage you, and let me for a moment speak as one newly ordained. The main thing is a firm hearty resolve to do your duty like a man and an Englishman; of course, a knowledge of the history of the Church of which you are to be a minister is useful and desirable, but don't search into Church History simply as one raking in a muck-heap for all the heresies and squabbles and miserable little disputes which have disgraced God's Church, so that you may be able to throw an ill-name at an opponent. It is of far more consequence to understand well how to deal with a great town-parish in these days, than it is to know what St. Cyril did, or, more probably, did *not*, hundreds of years ago. I don't undervalue Church History for a minute, but I want to see it regarded as something more than an antiquarian amusement. Well, John, well, I have said enough, I see you are looking as puzzled as a moon-calf already. What are your thoughts, man?"

"I'll tell you what, Maxwell, I don't think it would be a bad thing if I were to go to Arleigh Theological College for a term before my ordination, to coach up a little practical knowledge, eh? what do you say to that?"

"Say? Oh, most simple youth! why that very question of your's proves the peculiar state you must be in. Practical knowledge! Arleigh! How can you hope to reconcile the two? Arleigh is simply a place where fast men are white-washed and made respectable members of society and the Church, where classical dunces are transformed into so-called theologians, and where, with costly *matériel*, infinite well-meaning, and much

waste of time, a man is rendered as unfit
to cope with the difficulties and requirements of the nineteenth century as may
well be. You may learn there a certain
narrow theology, but you will learn
nothing else — nothing of humanity,
nothing which may render religion
charming, or even palatable, to men of
any intellect, experience, or culture.
There you will find excellent dinners, a
sufficiently comfortable and ornamental
system of fasting, charming gothic archi-
tecture, diluted Romanism, sweet little
cells, and *dilletante* parochial visiting,
all cut and dry for you. But the system
does not turn out good hard practical
men, able to speak to men as fellow-men
and not as would-be monks. The spirit
of the age is against these semi-monastic
institutions, and the spirit of the age is
right ; you can't reform a man by illuminated texts, and singing Gregorians

through your nose, so don't you try, John Fordyce. I'll tell you what we will do, please God. I should like to spend next Long with you, reading together. I shall have work on hand, writing I mean, and you can be grinding up and having the last polish put on for the schools, and, moreover, we can bestow some time on theology also. What say you to that? Aye? Then so let it be. And now I have said my say, and you have talked your talk, and I want to be busy. I have a book on hand which promises me much amusement and some profit. If you like to stay and be quiet, there is a pipe, and there is the tobacco jar—rest and be thankful; if not, depart in peace, and to-night, if you come, I shall be able to talk about your work for the schools."

CHAPTER II.

WE have already said that it was neither our intention or wish to make this a narrative of Oxford life. It has been done often, sometimes excellently well, leaving little to be desired—each writer taking, as is but natural and fair, his own point of view and setting his palette according to his own scale of colouring. Unless some special aspect is to be developed, educational, religious, muscular, but little is gained by selecting an University as the scene of a history such as this, and accordingly we do not wish to introduce the venerable city more often than the course of our story actually demands.

College life is very monotonous—after all but a second edition of school life in a more elaborate binding. There are lectures public and private, examinations, and the round of amusements varying according to the season and weather. Then again there are the quarrels, friendships, and rivalries of boyhood transferred to a slightly more advanced age; add the element of unlimited "tick" and the resemblance is complete. But our hero had reached a period where all these elements make or mar but little of the character, accepting them only as ornamental accessories, not as the principal aims of college life. His reading occupied nearly all his time, constitutionals and the maintainance of a regular correspondence with Edith taking up the rest of his leisure. Of his cousin he did not see very much; with Cyril, idleness had apparently become a system, and it really was wonderful to see how consistently he applied himself thereto. He received the news of John's engagement with the same lazy laugh with which he had greeted his changed habits.

"I am afraid, my good cousin, you are in the right way to be spoiled. You are neither virtuous nor industrious by nature, as of course you know, and now if you intend going in for that line you will be sinning against the dictates of your nature. It's a mistake changing your *rôle* as you are doing, but you were always headstrong."

"Don't be a fool, Cyril," was the polite reply, "·and if you must talk, tell me what you have been doing all this ' long ?' "

"Doing ? why boring myself and every-one else, cultivating my family affections I suppose. I went home at first intending to be virtuous and dull, and fortifying

myself with a box of cigars from Hudson's.
But 'pon my life there was no enduring
my father. I think he's the veriest old
bore I ever came near; I beg your pardon
by-the-bye, I forgot he is your uncle.
Well, the old gentleman wanted to know
towards what branch of the Civil Service
my inclinations lay, and whether I had
commenced any special course of study,
which might prove serviceable to my future
career. On which I told him that I had
no inclinations at all in any direction,
and as for my mind it was neither made
up nor likely to be, and that I thought
one line of life about as good as another.
Then he got angry, and called me an
incorrigible trifler and a bad son, said I
should bring his grey hairs—he hasn't
got many by-the-bye—and all that kind
of thing, and abused me in good set
diplomatic terms.

"And then I told him that I didn't wish

to quarrel with him or anyone else, and that on the whole I thought I knew my own business, and would he give me a checque for £50 as I wished to go abroad. No, he'd be—well, not blessed if he would. I told him his language was shocking, and that really he ought to know better than get in a passion. Then I went to my mother and explained matters, and told her that the anxiety and wear and tear of college life completely unnerved me, and that I wanted change. And then she called me a poor dear child, and blessed me and quoted something from Solomon, only she just transposed the proverb, and then she gave me £30, and then she fell asleep as she always does after a scene. Do you know I rather like my mother, she is original and quaint. Well, after all this I went abroad, and I regret to say got stumped out at Homburg, where after winning frightfully for a time,

my system broke down and left me with
nil plus a deficiency. Now wasn't that
beastly ? And then I had to write to the
paternal, to remind him that if he had
given me what I asked this would never
have happened, and that if he would send
me the where withal to pay my hotel bill,
I was perfectly ready to play the part
of the returned Prodigal.

"By-the-bye, I wonder what the sequel
to that story was, I expect he couldn't
stand the cold veal on the third day, and
went back to the pigs, or dogs. I don't
suppose West Indian pickles were thought
of then. However, to return to your
humble servant, I duly received a letter
of advice which I burned, and a letter of
credit with which I squared my account
and hastened home again, very pale and
penitent. But, oh, that fatted calf! what
an indigestible beast he is ! I had to sit
and listen to long parental lectures on

Diplomacy and International Law, with
marginal notes of my worthy father's
personal recollections and the like; I don't
know how I survived it. However, I took
to hard reading for a while as an alter-
native, to which, of course, the old gentleman couldn't object; after a time I found
an amusement which exactly suited me,
combining occupation, mental improvement, recreation and mischief, all in one.
We happened to have a new clerical young
man, or curate in our parish, the very
facsimile of a boiled bull-dog in appearance. You know I don't like the breed,
so I was quite ready for anything which
should turn up. I had not to wait
long.

"At first I could see no difference in
his demeanour from that of any other
member of his tribe. He came often to
our house of an evening, when he talked
mediæval rubbish, drank gallons of tea,

and consumed mountains of toast. Of course, I drew him out considerably, and teased him till he was nearly wild—you know they mustn't swear—but after a time the tremendous fact dawned upon me that the creature was in love—yes—and more than that, in love with my sister Annie—yes—and still more than that even, that my sister Annie was in love with him of the eruptive countenance and the coat-tails. Do you know, for a minute I was actually surprised—I was indeed. Annie is rather a nice little thing, she gushes somewhat; but, still not so bad for a woman. And to think that she should fancy herself in love with a spotted-faced animal in Oxford shoes and coat-tails. Oh, ye gods and little fishes, what was to be done? She went in head over heels for Puseyism, got up when we were all in bed, fasted when we ate, stood up when we all knelt at church, and all that style of thing. She left off crinoline for a day, but that was too much for all our nerves, hers included, and she speedily resumed her wonted appearance.

" Then she took to working markers, and stoles, and reading little red-edged books with pictures of lean saints, making faces at each other as if they had been taking medicine. At last she went the whole animal and began to teach at school, and stay behind in the vestry after service. At this stage I interposed. The loving swain manifested *his* affection by blushings, stutterings, stammerings, and gaspings like a fish out of water. He would come of an evening and sit gazing at my goose of a sister, letting his tea trickle down his waistcoat, and, finally, upsetting his saucer with a crash.

" Now it so chanced that the worthy curate had a somewhat remarkable name, Jeremiah R. Dash, and it also chanced that once upon a time, in an idle moment, I had amused myself at the Union here, by glancing over a little red-hot pamphlet on the subject of Clerical Celibacy, with the same signature attached to it. In this *brochure*, the marriage of the clergy was pronounced sinful, and those in orders who ventured upon a wife were denounced as traitors, perjured, idolators, and other such sweet terms. The date was about five years back, soon after the worthy curate's ordination, I expect. As soon as I saw that the initials corresponded, I knew I had the game in my own hands. So when matters were ripe, I boldly attacked the gentleman, and asked whether I was right in supposing he had an affection for my sister Annie. With much circumlocution, he replied that such was the case.

" ' Then how,' " I asked, ' am I to reconcile your statement with the opinions

you so decidedly put forward in this
pamphlet? Which am I to believe?' You
should have seen him; he was sea-green
from suppressed emotion, or bile, or some
thing. I'll be bound he wished he had
never learned to write. That unlucky
pamphlet—I have no doubt he thought
it hidden in oblivion, and here it turned
up at the most unlucky time.

"Well, he began to stammer out about
modified opinions, longer experience, and
the like; but I rose to the occasion, and
became as it were a model of outraged
and indignant innocence. I told him his
conduct was heartless, unworthy a gentleman and clergyman, that only his cloth—
I nearly said coat-tails—protected him
from personal castigation, and, finally, I
demanded as some compensation that he
should resign his curacy at once, and
leave the place. What could he do?
He was frightened out of his wits,

attempted apologies to which I would not listen, and in the end did as I insisted."

"And your sister?" enquired John, as his cousin paused.

"Showed her good sense by first falling out of love with her curate in petticoats, and then, while on a visit, falling *in* love again this time with a fellow, to whom she is now engaged. So there you have the whole history of my Long Vacation and all its adventures, and here am I at the end of it neither richer, nor poorer, nor better, nor worse that I know of."

"I'll tell you what, old fellow," said John, laying his hand on his cousin's shoulder, "I suppose my own reformation is too scant to allow me to preach, but upon my life, it is a shame to see a clever fellow like you idle away time, chances, everything, as you do. If you would only, for once in your life, be in earnest, you might succeed in anything you took up."

"Cousin John," replied Cyril, more gravely than he was wont, "you are like the tailless fox. What suits you will not suit me. I neither hope, fear, believe, nor care much; certainly, not enough to bestir myself about anything. We shall see which of us will be better off twenty years hence."

CHAPTER III.

TO another of our friends also had this particular Long Vacation brought its own adventures, namely, to the little Puseyite, Edgar Purcell, and although he is not very intimately connected with our story, the said adventure must be related for the sake of its consequences. Purcell was an orphan left under the guardianship of a spinster aunt, and the family adviser, an old-fashioned lawyer, who had very little to do with his ward beyond investing his capital in the elegant simplicity of the three per cents and other such security as seemed undeniable. By the provisions of his father's will, the principal could not

be touched until Edgar attained the age
of twenty-five, in the meantime, however,
an allowance of five hundred a year was
to be paid to him while at College, to be
supplemented with another three hundred
on his attaining his twenty-first year.
So it will be easily seen that our young
friend already was in receipt of a handsome income, and would one day become
owner of some three or four thousand a
year.

Never, perhaps, did rich ward cause
his guardians so little anxiety in money
matters; neither at school nor at college
did he manifest any of those extravagant
habits which are the enrichment of knaves
and the delight of fools—he lived as a
gentleman and nothing more.   He delighted not in the company of grooms and
stable followers, a pet Skye terrier was
the only dog he kept; his tailor's bills
were, for Oxford, absurdly small; cigars

and tobacco he eschewed, cards he abo-
minated. Here indeed was a model ward!
What more could an anxious guardian
require, than a young man who kept his
signature for the benefit of his corres-
pondents, abhorred the tribes of Israel,
and never " backed " anything in his life,
not even the favourite for the Derby.
And, to do him justice, Mr. Twisden had
such perfect confidence in his young ward
and such perfect knowledge of his money
affairs, that he troubled his head very
little about him, contenting himself with
asking him up to town once a year to
overlook his statement of accounts and
eat an excellent dinner at the 'London,'
for which I am afraid Purcell cared remarkably little, and thought rather a bore
than otherwise. When I say, therefore,
that the female guardian, Miss Griselda
Flynt, never heard her nephew's name
mentioned without an ominous shake of

the head, it will at once be surmised that there must have been some deep and mysterious reason for this distrust and suspicion. What was it? housemaids? Oh, dear, no! nothing of the kind; for in the first place, all her female staff might have been descendants of the "Loathely Ladye," or the witches of Macbeth, and besides this she knew Edgar was a very Joseph. Drink? By no means; the driest of Ports and nuttiest of Sherrys were but as ditch-water to him, and as for brandy or the subtle whisky, they were almost unknown.

We have seen that horses, dogs, and cards were not his weaknesses; what then could it be? In a word then, and that a monosyllable, it was—monks. The lad had a bee in his bonnet, call it a drone rather, and that drone continually buzzing the refrain, "Be a monk, be a monk, be a monk." We no not exaggerate, reader,

but speak the words of truth and soberness
when we say that the poor good and
deluded little mortal had most firm hold
of the idea, that the best use he could
make of his large fortune was to invoke a
gothic architect, build a monastery, and
therein immure himself as Brother Mary
Joseph, or any other fanciful nomenclature
you like to select. Had he any grievous
burden on his mind, you will ask—any
hideous deed to bury, any past to atone?
Certainly not that we are aware of;
nothing greater, we should fancy, than
eating apricot jam on a Friday with too
much relish, or falling asleep during a
sermon of the Rev. T. Marbecke's; nevertheless, as Providence had given him an
excellent appetite, affectionate disposition,
and sufficiently intelligent mind, he
thought it his duty to be wiser than
Providence, and render all these blessings
of no avail by becoming that strange

compound of ignorance and idleness, a pseudo-monk.

As a coward, unable to face the troubles and difficulties of life, cuts the Gordian knot and his own throat at once, so our little friend, fearing the dangers and seductions of the world, thought to escape them in the quiet of a monastic cell. But then we must remember this was to be an Anglican not a real monastery. You see there are monks and monks. There would be just a delicious flavour of the world about this, enough to render the life piquante and agreeable; there would be the charm of being quite unlike anyone else, of morally standing on your head while others were content with their feet; there would be the excitement of continual squabbling with bishops, of inhibitions, of partial mobbing and amateur martyrdom, of severe leading articles, indignant questions in Parliament, and, perhaps, even actions at law—at the least, proceedings before a magistrate, upon kidnapping accusations. Add to all this an air of mediæval sonpambulism, thick with incense, dim with stained glass, faint with perfumed flowers ; add the attractions to vain minds of a peculiar garb, a luscious form of devotion, the romantic interest of fair ladies, and the general bewilderment of the world, and you see that there was something sufficiently attractive to a young, unripe, unsettled mind, anxious to do good, but seeing no other means of carrying salvation to the masses than the bare feet and knotted girdle of a monk.

The design was one of those extravagancies which are unassailable by reason, because the mind of the designer has long ago refused to listen to or accept reason. But, unfortunately, his aunt, Miss Flynt, was one of those hard, impenetrable creatures, who, sure of their own convictions, and the ground on which they stand, could not make allowance for feeling or fancy, and imagined that continual hammering upon one point must in time produce some result. In every letter, or interview with her nephew, therefore, the great monastic question was debated with a persistency which only excited corresponding opposition. Furiously Low Church herself, the good lady saw no better way to her purpose than fierce and indiscriminate abuse of all her nephew held most dear — his personal friends and advisers, his opinions and practices.

Possessed of an angelic temper, Edgar was, with all his foibles, too good a fellow to quarrel with his aunt, but meanwhile steadily held to his original purpose of being ordained a clergyman at the proper age, and carrying out the monastic scheme when he should come into possession of his property.

To this, of course, nothing but remonstrance and advice could be opposed, and to escape from this it was that Purcell started off on a walking tour by himself, in the Long Vacation. His intention was to visit some of the most remarkable and *prononcée* churches in the Midland counties, to store his mind possibly with the various methods by which the Church service may be rendered unintelligible; and as he was obliged to go through the usual formula of business with his guardian he selected London as his starting point.

The customary dinner at the "London" duly came off, where they had adjourned from Mr. Twisden's chambers in the Temple hard by. After dinner, when they were seated in a private cabinet discussing their wine—the senior slowly quaffing and swallowing his, as though it

were a religious ceremony, and the ward
playing with his glass to the intense secret
annoyance of his host. Mr. Twisden
drew a letter from his pocket, and in
slow and measured accents began a little
speech.

"I do not think, my dear Edgar, since
I undertook the responsible, and, I may
say, onerous duties of guardian to you,
that our mutual relationship has ever been
disturbed by any—I will not say disagree-
ment—but collision. I am open to cor-
rection if my statement is incorrect."

"I am sure, Sir," exclaimed his ward,
upsetting his wine in his eagerness, "you
have been immensely kind, and I only hope
I have not been very troublesome. I
certainly have tried to understand all I can
about mortgages, and stock, and consols
and all that, but I am afraid I am not very
bright at that style of thing."

"Well, well, well, that is travelling out

of the record somewhat, as we lawyers
say. I was scarcely intending to refer to
that, but simply to impress upon you the
fact that as such a perfect agreement between those standing in our respective
positions is unusual, so it is desirable that
it should be maintained to the end. You
were going to say that for your part you
intend it—allow me to anticipate you.
Now, here I hold in my hand," and with
much deliberation he proceeded to unfold
and flatten the document, " a letter from
your respected aunt, and my co-guardian,
Miss Griselda Flynt. It refers to a subject upon which she has been in communication with me previously, I may say on
many occasions, a subject on which she
feels deeply, and one in which she now
asks my interference with you. I see you
are about to speak, let me again anticipate
you. Yes, the subject is that of your
avowed intention of employing the pro-

perty of which you will enter into possession on your twenty-fifth birthday, in
founding what you are pleased to call a
monastery. Excuse me—one moment—
it is not my intention to wound your feelings, but I speak as a lawyer, and of
course can only recognise what the law
recognises, and to such degree as the law
recognises. Now the law does not recognise monastic institutions, and the church
as established by law in these realms does
not recognise them, therefore, you see, as
a lawyer, an English subject, and as a
member of the Protestant establishment,
I cannot use any other term in referring to
your intention. You would say they exist
de facto and the law connives at them—
excuse my anticipating you once more.
That, my dear Sir, is a very different thing
from a recognition *de jure*. Such establishments exist, because the law is not put in
force against them; but there are statutes,

nevertheless, which I could quote if necessary, which may be put in force against
them any hour. Therefore, they are illegal,
Sir, illegal, illegal, illegal. Now, strictly
speaking, your intentions respecting the disposal of your property after you are your
own master are no concern to me. My
interest in your estate is supposed to cease
on the day on which you attain your
twenty-fifth year, because although in the
eyes of the law you became a man on
your attaining your majority, by your
father's special arrangement as duly expressed in his last will and testament, you
will not possess the power of doing as
you will with your property until you are
the age of twenty-five. After that day,
therefore, if you choose to cast your
money into the Red Sea, or into the Dead
Sea, I can do nothing to prevent you;
and strictly speaking I have nothing to do
with your intentions respecting its future

disposal, so that I am assured it is neither
treasonable nor in any way contravening
the majesty of the law and the peace of
the realm. Therefore, understand me, I
only speak as a friend, a title I believe I
may claim, when I ask whether this purpose of yours be in your ideas irrevocable ?"

Edgar, who had all this while been
fretting and fuming like a hound in the
leash, now burst in.

"I dare say it all seems very foolish
and wild to you and my aunt, Sir, and I
know I am young and all that, and don't
know much about money investments and
so on; but this resolve of mine is a real
genuine determination, and nothing will
move me from it. I should like to give
you my reasons, if you will allow me."

"Thank you, my dear Edgar," replied
his guardian, hastily, "but I should very
much prefer your not doing so, if it is

quite the same to you. Allow me to
remark also, that if you hold a wine glass
upside down the contents are apt to run
out; you looked surprised when it happened, so I thought I might call your attention to the fact. Don't apologise.
Now to return. If I give you any advice
now, or express an opinion, you will understand that I still speak only as a friend.
You say your purpose is irrevocable. Excuse me if I say this is a mistake; the
past is, the future is not, irrevocable.
You will say that no circumstances which
can arise will prevail upon you to change
your mind. Excuse me if I say that at
two and twenty, which is now your age,
I prefer backing—to use a vulgar expression—backing circumstances against your
resolution. I know all you will say and
respect you, but such is the case. You
have three years yet before you, and at
your age three years may effect much. I

do not wish to reason with you, because any arguments you might bring forward would not be grounded on facts, which are the only things I recognise, but fancies with which I have nothing to do. I only ask one thing of you, and that I think you will allow I have right to do. I ask you to promise me as a gentleman that you will not bind yourself either by promise, oath, or any other engagement to carry out this idea of yours. Will you do this, Mr. Purcell?"

"Yes, Sir, I both can and will; the more so, because you have treated me like a reasonable being. I know you neither approve nor like my resolution to found a monastery, but as you say, when I come of age, I have the right to do as I please with my own. I know also that nothing on earth can ever change my present ideas, and therefore I don't mind making you the promise you ask of me, and I will keep it faithfully. Of course there must be some differences of opinion between men on such points as these, but if you will only let me, I could give you some very good reasons, for what I mean to do."

"Do you know I should prefer your ringing for coffee, my young friend, if you will not have any more wine. I dare say you will think," continued the old lawyer, placing his hand on the young man's shoulder, "you will think us lawyers little better than infidels. But you must not quarrel with your father's old friend, because he thinks God can be better served without a shorn head and bare feet than with, and because he has more confidence in the force of circumstances and experience, than he has in the steadfastness of purpose of a very young man. And now, if you please, we understand each other and can drink our coffee in peace."

Oh, wise old lawyer, in less than three months from that day, did thoughts of love rise in the breast of the would-be monk.

CHAPTER IV.

OUR young adventurer started forthwith
upon his pilgrimage—little believing
it to be one—of Love. His ideas of
pedestrian touring were like most of his
other ideas, of a somewhat feminine and
luxurious type, and did not give much
promise for those days when it would be
his fate to travel bare-footed. A gentle
walk of ten, or at the most fifteen miles,
relieved by many rests, and halts, and
generally finished by a resort to the nearest
railway station, when taken into conjunc-
tion with good hotels, comfortable beds,
and excellent dinners—Fridays excepted—
cannot be called an unpleasant style of

pilgrimage.   However, the frequent visits
to churches of promising aspect, the
" doing" cathedrals, and poreing over the
remains of abbeys and monastic ruins gave
an agreeable religious flavour, and kept the
main object of his tour constantly before
him.   As he went, he meditated on the
good old days gone by, and longed for
the time when it should be his to restore
them again.   Where another would have
paused to admire the rich and varied
landscape of woodland and champaign, or
traced the windings of the silvery stream,
he only saw an excellent site for a priory
or monastery, and wondered to what order
it had belonged in time past.   A village,
couched low among the trees with all its
quaint variety of gable and thatch, cottage
and farm buildings, hall or rectory, was
simply to him a parish possessing a church,
where the rubric was or was not observed,
where the service was choral or otherwise,

where the incumbent was a " Catholic minded man," or an old-fashioned parson. Oh, for those good old days when priests spake with authority and the laity bowed the head and worshipped, when churches were thronged with eager and devout congregations who had not heard of pews, and grouped themselves so picturesquely; those good days when the bells were always ringing for mass, or vespers, or compline, and there was no *Times* in which to insert angry letters complaining of the nuisance—the nuisance indeed of a bell properly blessed and duly christened ! those good days when people were always ready to ask a blessing, and some wandering monk or venerable priest was ever ready to reply " Benedicite" incontinently; when there were no railways, Government inspectors of schools, dissent, free thinking, arithmetical bishops and Protestant establishments, but England was a charmed spot, all stained glass, holy water, monkery, priesthood, and ritualism; where people believed what they were told, and either did no wrong or else confessed it like good Catholics and started square again.

Ah, yes, very puerile and absurd was it not? Altogether opposed to the spirit of the age, and mere impossible and ridiculous aspirations. It was so truly, and yet not this alone. Silly, and unreal, and useless as the lad's wishes were, yet there was a certain title in them to respect. He was in earnest, this little one, with all his crude ideas and desires. He looked about him and saw a flood of trouble, and sorrow, and crime, surging and boiling up all around, and yet he did not turn away either in despair or disgust, and decline to wet his shoes by approaching nearer—but was ready to fall to and sweep back the advancing waves of misery and sin with his own little mop; wretched little imple-

ment it is true, but still the best he knew
of and one he fully believed in.   We must
recognise his earnestness while we laugh
at his follies; we must give him credit for
some unselfishness, even while we ridicule
the soap-bubble schemes to him so full of
reality and life.   At an age when other
young men would have few thoughts
beyond their horses, and dogs, and guns,
this fair young enthusiast was ready to
devote himself to what appeared to him the
highest, purest, holiest life possible for
man to enter.   It was his misfortune that
his idea of the Deity was not that of our
Father to whom we may appeal as children,
but that of Seeva the Destroyer whose
wrath must be deprecated and evaded by
human sacrifices; it was his misfortune
and the fault of his emasculated teachers
that he was unable to recognise the
Divine voice speaking unerringly in the
dictates of the human heart and the

yearnings of the human affections. And
so the good little man passed on his way
musing as he went; until he came to the
fair town of Malvern and its lovely range
of hills, and there as he looked down on
the goodly land he resolved to stay, and
accordingly sent his luggage to the Foley
Arms, and followed in due course of time.

As he lingered over the excellent dinner
in which Severn salmon and stewed
lampern formed no unsavoury items, he
began to reflect that his Long Vacation
ramble was nearly at an end, and that in
three or four weeks he should once more
have to return to Oxford again. In about
eighteen months from that time he should
be ordained, in three years the height of
his ambition would be obtained, his utmost
desires accomplished, and he should be
the founder of a monastery and the first
monk of the English Church since " that
unfortunate Reformation."

Such thoughts were too high and swelling for the coffee room of the Foley Arms—the mountain, or at least hill-top alone was worthy of them, and thither accordingly he resolved to adjourn, and hold high converse with his soul. The Malvern hills possess, it must be confessed, certain advantages which to a practical man almost atone for their desperately *picnicish* aspect and reality. They command an extensive prospect without the trouble of an ascent, they need no guides, and the possibility of neck breaking is limited in the extreme, actually requiring the concurrence of the neck in question. *Du reste*, they are hopelessly cockney, and resemble a magnified Hampstead Hill on a Sunday afternoon, all through the summer months. If any reader should wish to really enjoy Malvern Hills, he is hereby advised and admonished to ascend them either on a wintry day with snow on the ground, or at least with the clouds flying low. The glimpses of landscape seen through the cloud rift are very fine and beautiful with a weird attraction of their own, and he will meet in all probability no tourists. Edgar Purcell, however, was too much engrossed in his own thoughts to care very much either for the view, or the chance tourists he might encounter. Had he known, perhaps, that the Birmingham Lodge of Perpetually Cemented Bricks had selected that day for their " outing," and Malvern for the *locale*, perhaps he might have deferred his ascent until the morrow. But of this he was not aware, and accordingly off he started.

Past the stands of patient donkeys and noisy boys, past St. Anne's Well, with its delicious cold spring, the taste of which even a trumpery bazaar of Tunbridge and Spa rubbish cannot destroy, or the crowds

of holiday makers defile; past the camera
obscura and photographic gallery, where
strut and scream two lovely peacocks
who pass their lives in evading the sacri-
legious assaults of donkey boys and other
juveniles; past turning after turning,
point after point, until his breath began
to come short and quick, his legs to feel as
though each step were accompanied by
a blow on the shin from an iron bar, and
in short, nature began to prompt him to
sit down, take rest and admire the fair
scene beneath. And fair enough in all
conscience it is; if Gloucestershire and
Worcestershire cannot lay claim to the
picturesque and varied beauties of Devon,
Monmouth, or North Wales, yet they
afford as fine a specimen of rich pasturage,
fertile corn-fields, and laden orchards as
England contains. Within a semicircle of
thirty miles the eye wanders over a succession of fair meadow lands, broken up

and interspersed by clumps of stately trees
or long lines of orchards.   Here and there,
unfortunately but too rarely, the river is
seen, while Gloucester and Cheltenham on
one side, and Worcester on the other, embracing between them Pershore, Tewkes-
bury, Evesham and Malvern, with their
abbeys and grand old churches, add the
human element to the fair view.

The evening on which Purcell sat
looking down upon the prospect beneath,
was one specially favourable. The sun
had set some little while, leaving the
horizon still ablaze with that mellowed
richness of colouring which forms his
after-glow. "Down in the west upon the
ocean floor," crouched a great cloud bank
of purple grey, luminous with streaks of
the fierce russet red and orange tawny
which lay behind it and overtopped it, to
tremble and quiver and pass in its turn
into sweet primrose shades, which had

pure green light in them until the base
and bank of richer hues stole off and lost
themselves by imperceptible degrees in
the calm grey-blue canopy above, already
sprinkled with the coming stars. And all
this was seen through that tender inex-
pressibly lovely vaporous haze which the
golden autumn alone possesses and which
constitutes one of its chiefest charms. There
was no one in sight, and Edgar, albeit his
romance was mainly of a limited and
mediæval character, could not but stop
and admire the beautiful view. He sat
down on a projecting ledge of rock, near
to a turn in the path which hid all above
him, and as he idly pulled at the short
grass and harebells which grew by, his
thoughts gradually passed back into their
old channel—the monastery.

He had not quite made up his mind
what Order he should revive, and it needed
some consideration. There were the

Carmelites to begin with, picturesque enough in their snuff-brown robe and scapular and bare feet, but then they were horribly austere and never ate meat. Then again the Benedictines, all in black, were taking, but they were mainly reputed for their prosecution of learning; perhaps they had a constant system of classical and theological examinations at work, and, though he should not mind reading St. Thomas Aquinas in the solitude of his cell, undergoing an examination on the Summa Theologia before a board of monastic examiners was quite another thing. Nor should he like the idea of perpetual silence. "Brother, we must die," was of course very true and proper, but somewhat monotonous, especially after college life. But then there were those dear picturesque Dominicans, with their white flannel robes—he had seen one once in London and wished to ask his blessing,

only was afraid—what could be nicer? Of
course they would wash and always look
clean, and besides he had heard flannel
was the best wear for summer and winter.
Then, too, all Dominicans were specially
given to the Fine Arts, and he ran over a
list of beatified Frari whose works he had
seen. He had a great taste for illumination and book-marker making, and had
several times held and washed the pencils
of the artists engaged in painting some
Oxford church. Yes, this certainly was
his vocation, the Dominican order and
Christian art, and he began to conjure up
a fair picture of himself and sundry other
brothers, Ignatius and Cyprian, and
Hilarion and Francis, living together in
some secluded spot and passing the time
sweetly between paint-pots, amateur
gardening, singing vespers, and eating
soup maigre and boiled cabbage to the

sound of Brother Peter reading aloud the Confessions of St. Augustine.

He had just travelled as far into the future as the death of the first Prior, and the possibility that he—yes, he—might be chosen successor, and was trying to frame an inaugural address to deliver in solemn chapter, when he was suddenly brought back to the nineteenth century by the sound of an oath which made him shiver, followed by a shriek—a female shriek, which made him jump to his feet. We might, if we chose, keep our readers in suspense at this critical moment by entering into conjectures, speculations, and the like; but, as we wish to avoid all mystery, and as really this adventure will prove a mere trifle after all, and will need no blue fire to give it effect, we prefer being plain and straight-forward, and stating as succinctly as may be exactly what the would-be monk saw, on turning

the corner of rock which had sheltered
him. In the centre of the rather narrow
path stood a young lady, who had apparently been sketching, for a small camp-
stool lay overturned close by, together
with a tin colour-box, and in her hand
was a small sketch-book, for the possession of which she was struggling with as
ill-looking a rascal as ever walked from
Newgate dock. Two others of the same
type stood by, whose coarse bull necks,
close cropped hair, brutal features, and
general hang-dog look would have marked
them out as Birmingham roughs, even had
not their gaudy red scarves denoted their
belonging to the Birmingham Lodge of the
Perpetually Cemented Bricks.

Purcell saw all this in a moment, and,
with the courage of a Paladin, rose to the
situation and rushed to the rescue. He
could plainly perceive that the men were
half intoxicated, and I do his prowess no

injustice when I add that he saw it with pleasure, as promising an easier encounter. He was not a fighting man, in truth, and though at the bottom no more a coward than any other young fellow of his age, he would most certainly have preferred, had the quarrel been his own, putting up with some amount of abuse rather than engage those Birmingham roughs single-handed. However, there was no choice, a woman was concerned, and, boxer or no boxer, he dashed in. Science he knew none; he had a vague hazy idea that the left hand was reserved for dealing, and the right for warding, blows, but he was in far too great excitement to put this small atom of boxiana into effectual practice.

Fortunately, the nature of the ground favoured his attack, which was as sudden as if he had dropped from the clouds. The young lady and her assailant had approached the edge of the path, which in that particular spot was not only narrow, but on the verge of one of the few steep places on the hill, the ground falling rapidly and abruptly, and ending in a thicket of furze. Swift as lightning, Purcell flung himself upon the rascal who grasped the sketch-book, and before he was even seen, delivered a couple of such very hearty blows upon his head as to make him slip and roll down the steep incline, with a rapidity which promised a speedy arrival at Malvern. The furze bushes, however, stopped his downward course, and there he lay for long insensible from the blow and fall, until the sensation of having been turned into a pin-cushion or human hedgehog at length brought him to.

The lady, thus released, made use of her liberty to run up the hill at no small speed, raising her voice and invoking

" papa " as she went, which brought about
succour, as we shall presently see. There
were then left Brick No. 2 and Brick No.
8, who had by this time somewhat recovered from their first surprise, and now
saw in their Heaven-descended opponent
simply a young man of slight stature and
no particular muscular developement.
Having their favourite odds on their side,
they drew up in order of battle, and, in
strict accordance with Homeric precedent, proceeded to hold a colloquy with
the enemy. Their command of language
was neither great nor varied, its monotony,
however, was atoned for by its highly
condensed nature, consisting mainly of
strongly flavoured adjectives and condemnatory participles. Edgar, not exactly
appreciating the beauties of Birmingham
diction, cut it short by informing them
they were a couple of rascals. On this
they requested him to " come out of that,"

and, on his declining the invitation, Brick
No. 2 followed it up by a blow, which, to
his great surprise, and I may add Edgar's
also, was parried and returned. Then
commenced a brisk encounter between
science tipsy, on the one hand, and
ignorance excited and energetic, on the
other. Brick No. 3, to do him justice,
felt so confident in the prowess of his
companion as to abstain from the combat,
contenting himself with dancing round
hideously, and making the air resound
with encouragements and threats which
could scarcely be distinguished.

We do not possess science enough
to distinguish the several rounds of
this battle-royal, but will content ourselves with the result to either side.
After about three minutes fighting,
Perpetual Cemented Brick No. 2 had
not been down, but nevertheless one eye
had temporarily closed business, and the

blood was flowing freely from a cut on the
cheek. Also he felt that he was too far in
liquor to be his own master, and that he
was fighting wildly. Edgar, on the other
hand, was as fresh as a lark, although he
also had received a blow on one eye which
scarcely improved its beauty or utility,
and having fallen heavily once, he felt as
though a very large bee was buzzing an
endless accompaniment obligato inside his
head. But even supposing Brick No. 2
vanquished, it was more than doubtful
whether Brick No. 3 would not prove too
much for him. At this moment, however,
victory was rendered secure by the mar-
vellously sudden arrival of succour. Most
strange succour, too. For first of all
there flew through the air with the
certainty and rapidity of a boomerang, a
huge leathern telescope case, which struck
on the head, and then clung around the
neck of Brick No. 8, thereby spoiling a

well-aimed blow at our little friend's remaining eye, next with a rush and a roar like that of an angry lion, came the owner of the said case, an incredibly active little old gentleman, who commenced laying about him on all sides with the great telescope itself. Lenses, it is true, flew about in all directions, but the body of the instrument was left, and with this did the new warrior deliver such sturdy blows as speedily to convert defeat into rout, for in utter dismay fled the Perpetually Cemented Bricks, leaving behind them the gaudy red scarves by which in their struggles they had nearly been strangled. They could fight with men indeed, but with optical and philosophical demons who employed Admiralty telescopes as weapons of offence, and laid about them with the strength and rapidity of a steam thrashing machine, no science could cope successfully. So they fled and left the field to the victors,

not even pausing to look for, or pick up, their
fallen comrade, Brick No. 1, who indeed
by this time was painfully wending his
way to Malvern, execrating sketch-books,
furze-bushes, and brisk little champions in
straw hats.

Last of all arrived on the field of battle
she who was its cause, bearing in her hand
an ivory-headed Malacca cane, and looking
as she advanced very much like a Norse
Valkyr, or Chooser of the slain.   Then
they all looked at each other, and burst
into a laugh.

CHAPTER V.

AND now, at length, Purcell had leisure
and opportunity to observe, both his
unexpected succour, and the young lady
who had been the cause of the battle. To
begin with the latter as gallantry commands. She was a fascinating little bru-
nette of eighteen or thereabouts, with a
clear warm complexion, now doubly flushed
with running and excitement, large dark
eyes, in which shone a mischievous life,
and a delicate little pursed up mouth, now
brimming over with suppressed laughter.
Her dark brown hair, cut short like a
boy's and pushed behind her small rosy
ears, was crowned by a coquettish little

straw hat and a bunch of scarlet feathers; she had on a dress of some light material with a jacket admirably calculated to display her figure to advantage; dainty little bronze kid *bottines* completed her costume, for her kid gauntlets had been pulled off in the struggle for the book, and lay, all trampled, in the path. It was a pleasant little face and form to gaze upon, a charming compound of good looks, good humour and good breeding, with just that amount of wilfulness and vivacity which gave piquancy to the whole. You saw in a moment that she was an only daughter and a spoilt pet; one who generally had her own way, but was none the worse for it. Edgar Purcell was scarcely a judge and connoiseur of female looks; but he—even he, unexperienced—felt that it was a goodly face to gaze upon, and a perilous.

The knight of the telescope, now reduced to shattered lenses and battered brass, was a short and thin little gentleman of perhaps some sixty years, whose trim erect figure, bronzed complexion and close cut grey moustache revealed at a glance the old military man. He had lively, restless, good-humoured grey eyes which sparkled and danced merrily under his bushy eyebrows, and a nervous way of tugging at his moustache, first on one side, then on the other, which gave him the appearance of perpetual motion. With the exception of a broad dome-shaped Panama hat, there was nothing specially remarkable in his costume, though his clothes were of severe military cut and his boots of the brightest.

" Ha," exclaimed he, pushing his broad brimmed straw hat to the back of his head, and wiping his forehead with a great snuff-coloured Bandana, " ha, sharp work while it lasted, upon my word. A very pretty affair, and very prettily managed. Sir," as he turned to Purcell, "I have not the least idea who you are, or whence you come, but give me leave to say that I am delighted to make your acquaintance, and think myself much honoured in doing so. The way you let fly at that rascally smoke-coloured Birmingham jackanapes in the pink rag—which by-the-bye, I see he has left behind him—was worthy of Cribb and Molyneux, and takes me back to my young days. It does, Sir, on the word of an officer and a gentleman. My name, Sir, is Harding—Major Harding—once of the 20th, and I shall be glad to know yours, that I may know whose hand I have the honour of shaking, and whom I am to thank for his pluck and courage."

All this while he had been working Edgar's hand up and down like a pump handle, until that worthy had hardly any breath to reply.

" Really, Sir, you thank me more than I deserve, it is rather I who should thank you for coming down to my assistance. I am sure I am most happy to be of use. My name is Purcell, Sir, Edgar Purcell, and I am only a visitor in Malvern."

" Mr. Purcell, I am delighted to know you, and can only say that it shall not be my fault if we are not excellent friends. Purcell is a name, I know very well—very well, indeed. My best friend and chum, when I was about your age, was a Purcell, Jack Purcell of the 31st; he exchanged into the 20th to be with me."

" That must have been my father," said Edgar laughing, " he was in the 20th, Captain Purcell; and now I remember to have heard him speak of his friend, Captain Harding. He sold out when he married and I am his son."

" God bless my soul !" said, or rather shouted the Major, " I never heard of anything so extraordinary in all my life; never, never. If any one had told me that one day I should meet Jack Purcell's son on this disgusting little hill, punching the heads of Birmingham pin-makers in red scarves, I should have said it was a lie; I should, Sir. Where's Myrtle—Myrtle, I say."

"Here I am, papa," replied that young lady, "I have been listening all the while, and waiting for you to introduce me to my champion. I am sure I don't know how I can thank you enough, Mr. Purcell, for rescuing me from those horrible men. I don't know what I should have done without you, and I only hope you are not injured by their violence."

She made her little speech with such perfect self-command as to set Edgar at his ease, although not much used to face young ladies; certainly not with an eye which he felt was putting forth prismatic effects of colour preparatory to total darkness. And so he shook hands like the honest true-hearted young fellow he was really, and hoped "the rascals had not hurt Miss Harding before he came up."

"Look here," said the little lady, holding out for inspection the daintiest little hand and arm, on the wrist of which was visible a broad red mark where the clumsy fingers of the Birmingham pin-maker had rudely grasped it, "the nasty monster caught hold of me, oh! so tight, when he tried to snatch my book away, but I hit him as hard as I could, great thumps, with my other hand."

"I don't think that would be very hard, Miss Purcell," remarked Edgar, quaking afterwards at his own temerity.

"Oh, you don't know what I can do, when I am very angry I feel quite strong."

"Ah, indeed!" interjected the Major, "I can tell you, you don't know half what

Myrtle is capable of; she rules me I can tell you, I never have my own way for a moment."

"Never mind, my dear old pater, you know you are all the better for it. A soldier ought to be able to obey orders. And now I think of it—there you are standing without your hat like a bad boy, and to-night I shall have you screaming out with neuralgia and ringing up the whole house. Put your hat on directly, Sir, and come home quietly, for I am sure we have had excitement enough for one day. And, oh good gracious me, pater! do look at Mr. Purcell's eye. I never saw anything so awful in my life. How could you say there was nothing the matter? Why it is black and blue, and I know you are in horrible pain. Oh, please come home with us, and Betty, the nurse, will put it all right for you."

"I'll tell you what, Sir," burst in the

Major, who had been waiting his opportunity, and meanwhile picking up some of the *disjecta membra* of his telescope, "that girl speaks right, and you must do as she says, I always do—and 'pon my honour, I find she is right in the end. Now look here, Mr. Purcell, I am a plain old man and always speak my mind, it is a way I caught, soldiering. I liked you before I knew you were your father's son, and now I know who you are, I like you better. So there. And another thing. If you don't instantly have your traps sent round to our house and come and stay with us this very minute, I shall say, Sir, your conduct is shabby and unworthy Jack Purcell's son. If you are half as good a fellow as your father, you'll do as I tell you, and as Myrtle tells you. He always did. No, nonsense now—I am not accustomed to be contradicted, except by Miss Mischief, there. You have been

fighting under my colours, and are bound
to obey your commanding officer. Myrtle,
my love, why don't you add your word ?"

" It isn't necessary, papa; of course
Mr. Purcell goes home with us, and is
doctored by us and stays with us, and
what is more we will all start off directly ;
for I have had quite enough of Malvern
Hills, and I don't want to have Betty
coming out with a lantern after you. It
is no use saying a word, Mr. Purcell;
papa was quite right, I always have my own
way, and always mean to. Are you sure
you can see your road ? Because if not
papa shall give you his arm. Major, why
don't you look after your recruit ?"

It was no use protesting and refusing.
Edgar found that the invitation was given
and meant with so much cordiality and
sincerity, that he could not evade it without positive rudeness and hurting the
feelings of his newly found friends. So

after a feeble defence soon relinquished, he submitted at discretion and was walked off by the Major, who, acting on his daughter's suggestion, would insist that support and guidance were necessary under the circumstances.

"And now," said he, as they proceeded from the field of battle, "that's what I call a model engagement. First the skirmishers encounter, that's Myrtle—then comes up the infantry hand to hand, that's you, you know—then follows a terrific cannonade, and last of all a cavalry charge sweeps the enemy away in utter disorder. Quite according to Cocker."

CHAPTER VI.

A PONY-CARRIAGE, lingering late for chance customers, soon conveyed the party to a pretty little cottage *orné*, in that part of Malvern called the Link.

"You must know, Mr. Purcell," remarked Myrtle, as she led the way into the house, "that we are only birds of passage here. We have contracted a habit of moving about, and never stay longer in any place than we find agreeable. Papa thinks he is campaigning again, and so I humour his whim, don't I, papa?"

"You must not believe all she says," was the answer addressed to Purcell, "she tells more fibs than any woman I ever met, and that is saying a great deal. The truth is, Myrtle has vagabondising tendencies, and likes playing at gipsies, as she calls it, and so I humour her whim. I believe she would like to go about with a real tent and three-legged pot, steal poultry too, for all I know."

" I should think you would find this style of gipsying more comfortable, Miss Harding," said Purcell, with a laugh, as they entered the elegant drawing-room, replete with all the pretty little nic-nacs and costly trifles which form part of the poetry of female existence.

And certainly nothing could have a more inviting aspect than the pretty apartment, with its handful of bright fire in the grate, not unwelcome even on an autumnal evening, its half drawn curtains just revealing glimpses of the not yet extinguished western sky, and its round

table duly spread with fair white cloth,
and all the equipage and accompaniments
of that most fascinating meal—tea. While
he was admiring the room and its pictures,
the Major, who had already despatched
a servant for Purcell's baggage from the
Foley Arms, commenced shouting out for
Betty; and presently, obedient to the
summons, Betty came. Betty was the
tallest, ugliest, most silent and composed
specimen of her sex that it is possible to
imagine. She stood nearly five feet eleven,
was bony and angular in proportion, possessed a face which looked as if it were
carved out of some very hard and knotted
wood, and as though in the process of
carving the graver's tool had slipped
often and chipped stray pieces out. She
wore a severely starched cap on her head,
which looked as though it had tried to
develope into a bonnet, but had failed
half way; over her shoulders was drawn

an Indian handkerchief, pinned in front
with a great gold pin like a skewer; there
was an entire absence of crinoline about
her, and, on the whole, she resembled a
very bad imitation of an ugly woman made
by an awkward man.

The Major, who began a fussy explanation of their adventures, was put aside
with the grim remark, "Too late for
you, you'll be ill." Then she bore down
on Purcell, and grasping his hands between her bony hands, with an energy and
vice-like force which would have rendered
her invaluable to a dentist, gazed for a
moment upon his eye. "Veal," was all
she said, and then retired; soon reap-
pearing with a large veal cutlet and a
bundle of rags.

"Oh, but am I really to have that mass
of meat on me? I think I should almost
prefer the eye as it is; at least, I cannot
think of intruding myself upon you in

such a condition. Let me go to my bed-room, Major; yes, indeed, if you please, I shall not be a fit sight for Miss Harding."

To which Betty replied oracularly, " Nonsense !" And Myrtle also put in her word,

" Nonsense, Mr. Purcell, we shall allow nothing of the kind. The idea of your sitting alone moping in your room; I never heard such a thing in my life. Oh, if it's your appearance you mind, we will manage that. Please sit down in papa's arm-chair ; now, Betty, the cutlet and rags." And in a moment, before he knew what he was about, Betty's strong hands had pushed him into the chair, applied the raw meat and bound it down with linen rag; while, to crown all, Myrtle herself had removed a pretty silk handkerchief from her neck, and bound it round his head with her own fair hands. " There,

Mr. Purcell, you'll do now, I think; but you must keep quite quiet, and not waggle your head about. We have invested you with the badge and ribbon of the cutlet for distinguished valour; and very, very much obliged we are, too, for your courage and kindness."

"And have you no order of merit for me, my love?" enquired the Major. "I think the charge of the Light Brigade should not be passed over unrecognised."

"There, then, Major, and there, and there!" responded the bounteous maiden, showering down kisses on the veteran, until that ungrateful Edgar almost desired to change places, and would have purchased the promotion yea with half a dozen black eyes, if he had possessed them to blacken.

A black eye and a veal cutlet, reader, are neither sightly nor romantic elements,

they have not been treated of in any Art
of Love that I am aware of. We don't
hear of Achilles or Hector, or Sir Laun-
celot, or Galahad coming back from the
wars with a dark aureola of extravasated
blood round their dexter or sinister eyes;
and yet it is noteworthy how great effects
may spring from causes insignificant and
unsavoury. Cupid's arrows are not always
made of lance-wood, and feathered and
tipped duly, any missile does equally well
for that young rogue.

Certainly, had Purcell been inclined to
make much of his position, there was
nothing to hinder, all to help, him; his
host's precautions were endless—would he
sit on an easy chair or lie on the sofa?
would he not have a pillow for his head?
did the lamp hurt his eyes? &c., &c.,
And when Myrtle herself placed a pillow
under his head, a foot-stool to his feet,
and a cup of fragrant tea in his hand, his

wonder and amazement reached the climax,
and he felt inclined to ask some one to
pinch him to test the reality of his
existence.

Remember, my friends, who read this,
that it was almost his first introduction to
the amenities of female society. Other
young men had sisters, cousins, and lady
friends to laugh with, talk with, and get
shaped and moulded by. Other young
men when at home danced, rode, croqueted
with their sisters' friends and their own.
But all this belonged to a life which was
unknown to Edgar Purcell; his aunt,
Miss Griselda Flynt, and one or two
maiden ladies who visited her, were the
only females he could include among his
acquaintances, if I except an elderly
Sister of Mercy, old enough, indeed, to be
a Grandmother of Mercy, and—Lizzie
Burton. But then—oh, how different,
was this airy, fairy little Myrtle

from the blonde Lizzie, in her tumbled
and soiled muslins, Palais Royal jewellery,
and not always tidy hair—she whom men
called the Burton filly, and winked and
laughed about! Besides, too, Lizzie had
long ago been banished from his heart by
Marbecke's counsels and his own good
sense. He had seen and heard what he
could no longer close eyes and ears to,
and knew that she was about as likely to
become, or wish to become, a Sister of
Mercy, as she was to become Queen of
England. St. Shallabala had utterly
triumphed over the dangerous Lizzie—
would she over this new opponent? Time
will show. At all events, it was really very
pleasant to sit in an arm-chair, watching
the nimblest little fingers in the world as
they flew over the keys of the piano, and
listening to Miss Myrtle's bright cheery
voice as she sang gay *barcarolles*, and
wandered into the old English ballads

which the Major loved, or professed to love.

"Are you fond of music, Mr. Purcell? do your sisters sing?" enquired the little songstress, whirling round on the piano-stool with a rapidity which caused all her ribbons and tails to flutter.

"I am very fond indeed of music, I like it better than anything, I think; and unfortunately I have no sisters, so I very seldom hear any singing."

"No sisters! Now I should like to know whether you are really glad or sorry, some gentlemen don't care much for sisters, they say they are a bore, have to squire them about, and all that sort of thing. I know some who think ladies' society a nuisance—now do you? Tell me candidly; forget my being a young lady, and tell me honestly as one man to another."

We may remark, by way of marginal

note, that the Major had fallen asleep, uttering every now and then a screech like a door turning on a rusty hinge. Edgar found that a *tête-à-tête*, was not so alarming as he should have thought.

"I think there must either be something wanting, or something wrong in a man who does not like and appreciate female—ladies' society, Miss Harding. Not that I am a good judge, for I have had little enough all my life. I have always lived with a maiden aunt, an elderly lady, and have mixed very little in the world."

"How very unpleasant!" remarked the candid Myrtle, with a little grimace, "I mean how horridly dull. Is your aunt nice? You don't mind my asking, do you?"

"Not in the least. Well, she is very kind in her way, a very sterling woman; but of course she has some peculiar ideas."

"Oh, I know; I hate sterling people, they are always contradicting and laying down the law, and doing all kinds of unpleasant things because it is right. And I hate sterling old ladies in particular, they wear drab silk dresses, and little black shawls, and poke bonnets, and such hard thick gloves—all ends—like rhinoceros skin or hide. And then they are very rich, and drive about in queer old-fashioned carriages; and call everything nice wicked, and everything nasty duty. I daresay they are dreadfully good, but I know they are dreadfully odious too. Now is your aunt anything like that?"

"A little, I must confess; but, as you say, she is very good, and has high ideas of duty, and acts up to what she thinks right. We differ very much on some points—religious points I mean."

"Oh!" responded the young lady,

with a queer little look, "what is she then?"

"Well, she belongs to the extreme Low Church party, almost dissenting, in fact; I should scarcely call her a Churchwoman at all, for I know sometimes she goes to a Wesleyan chapel to hear a favourite preacher."

Edgar dropped his voice, and spoke low, as though he were describing the abomination of desolation standing where it ought not. But Myrtle was undismayed.

"After that then, I shall fall in your estimation, I fear, when I tell you that when papa and I were abroad, I used to make him take me to the Roman Catholic churches for service. It is true there was what they called English service in a drawing-room at the Embassy; but it was horrid, you could not help thinking of balls, and valses, and polkas all the time you were saying your prayers; and as for the clergyman, I don't, and never will, believe he was a real one. He had great bushy, purple-looking whiskers, all shiny and greasy, I know he dyed them; and a horrid great red nose, all on one side, and then he was all rings and studs and watch-chain; and a shocking glutton; and, oh, Mr. Purcell! what do you think?" And she made a little pause. "I am sure one day I saw him tipsy."

"Oh, I know," rejoined Purcell, mournfully, "those foreign chaplains are a very indifferent set of men generally, not at all Catholic in their ideas, or in the least rubrical. It is very sad. But, Miss Harding, I think you were quite right to go to the Catholic places of worship; they are the only real churches abroad, all our places are mere schismatical conventicles, in fact, without any authority. The bishops ought not to permit them."

"Oughtn't they? I thought they were all right, because the consuls and ambassadors always went. But, as I said, I went to the Roman Catholic churches because they were not so stuffy, and people did not go to stare and quiz each other; and then there was the beautiful music, and of course you need not listen to the sermon unless you like."

"Oh I am so glad you like the real Catholic service, I think it is the most beautiful in the world—the old true service in fact."

"I'm not by any means sure I should like it always. I prefer our own in England because I like to know what it is all about. But their music is so beautiful. Do you know this?"

She turned again to the piano, and in a low hushed voice began one of the litanies of which the Catholic Church makes such frequent use. Edgar listened in rapture.

"I know it well, I know it well," he exclaimed, when Myrtle had finished the few phrases she remembered. "I have heard it often at the Oratory in London. I often go there for a treat."

"Do you really?" said Myrtle, in some surprise, "you must either be very fond of music indeed or—very religious." Her guest blushed. "What I mean is, you seem to feel and think very much about these things, more than most young men do. You don't mind my saying so, do you?"

"I don't mind anything you say," with a deeper blush than ever. "I cannot call myself very religious. But it is only natural I should think of those things, because I am to be a clergyman."

"Are you indeed?" asked Myrtle, with open-eyed surprise, "I did not know that.

How absurd I am! Why, how could I know it, when I did not know you three hours ago! And do you like the idea? Is it your own wish, or is it all arranged for you?"

"It has always been my choice and the wish of my life," replied Edgar enthusiastically.

He would have added more, but just then the Major gave a deeper screech than usual, and woke with a start, exclaiming,

"No more currie, thank you, no more currie, Colonel," to the great delight of his daughter.

"Why, you dear old sleepy papa, you have been snoring away as usual. Do you call these your company manners? Nice treatment of a guest, indeed. I can see Mr. Purcell is horribly offended. Come, Major, sit up and behave pretty."

"Don't be absurd, child, don't be absurd. I haven't been asleep, as you very well know, and as for snoring I couldn't do it if I tried. I have heard every word you said—you two. Come, Purcell, I hope Myrtle has managed to amuse you while I was—resting. Now, my love, do you know, I think it is time for Betty to come in."

"That means it is time for me to go to bed, you naughty papa. Well, well, be it as you wish."

She rang the bell, and in a minute or so Betty entered and went through a formula which was repeated nightly. In her hands she bore a tray, containing a bottle of Madeira, ditto of rum, ditto of lime juice, a jug of cold water, a lemon, some sugar, and lastly a box of Manilla cheroots. In perfect silence, and with great solemnity she proceeded to compound and mix the various ingredients with a dexterity which spoke of long practice. When the mystic brewing was complete, a wine-glassful was poured out and handed to Myrtle, who having tasted it, pronounced it 'right.' Upon which, Betty, having gravely shaken hands with her master, and wished him "good night," retired, carrying away her tray. The next act of the drama was Myrtle's who selected with much skill a choice cheroot, which, having lit, she presented to her father with a kiss. She would have done the same for Purcell— omitting the salute of course—had he not declared his inability to enjoy the proffered luxury. Then with a cordial handshake she withdrew, and left the Major and his guest together.

"I am sorry you don't smoke, Purcell," began the veteran, "but I daresay you won't mind keeping an old man company over his cigar. Taste that mixture; we used to call it in the Punjaub the 20th's night-cap; though, for the matter of that, I think it was pretty often a day cap too.

Good, isn't it—and just weak enough to make a pleasant drink in summer. That woman, Betty, is a jewel in her way. She has saved my life twice, as I consider. She was the wife of my orderly, and nursed me through a sharp bout of jungle fever in 18—, and then brought me round again after a tuzzle I had with a tiger, which left me scarcely a whole bone in my body. That woman, Sir, is one of nature's ladies, and what I call a real Sister of Mercy. And now, my dear lad, I am heartily glad to have your father's son under my roof, which you will just consider as your home as long as you please." And the good-hearted soldier stretched out his bony hand, and shook Edgar's warmly. "What do you think of doing in life, Sir, hay? Shall you follow your father's profession? Though you are almost too old I fancy."

"My intentions are quite the other way,

Major, I hope to be ordained in another year or so."

"The devil—I should say, indeed! A clergyman, hay? Well, well, a fine profession too and one I respect. Though, as you say, the very opposite from that I have the honour to belong to. We kill men's bodies, and you cure their souls— hay? And it is your own wish it seems? Well that is all as it should be, if you like it. I suppose you mean to buy a fat living and settle down and marry—hay? A fine life, Sir, a fine life, and one in which a man may do very much good if he pleases."

"You are right, Major, I mean to do my best; but I shall not buy a living— of course, I do not mean to condemn those who think differently, but to me it seems like the sin of Simony."

"Oh, ho, young Sir! you are all for promotion by merit and no purchase, are you? Well, I know, there are many of

you young men who think so both in the
Army and the Church; but you'll find it
don't pay, it don't work, Sir, that's
where it is. Money will always rise to
the top, and I don't see why it should
not as long as there's birth and brains
to back it. I know those French fellows
promote from the ranks — and deuced
good soldiers they make by-the-bye, but
then they are French after all you see.
But that won't do in England, Sir, or
in Her Majesty's forces, Sir. Let me ask
you how you should like to see your
parish clerk promoted from the ranks and
made a parson? Pooh! don't tell me—
the thing's absurd!"

"Ah, but there's the subdiaconate for
those classes, you know. We hope to see
that revived in a short time, and I have
no doubt that all parish clerks — if they
must exist, and I can't see they are
necessary—will be ordained acolytes or

subdeacons.   That would be very nice,
you know."

"Why bless my soul, Sir," exclaimed
the astonished Major, "what on earth is
all this? First you say that parish clerks
are not necessary—and who is to say
'Amen,' I should like to know? and
then you want to revolutionize the Church
and ordain them, and make them the Lord
knows what! I can't get to the bottom of
you youngsters now-a-days. You are all
for raising the masses, and educating the
people, and cultivating the intellect of the
lower orders and playing Old Gooseberry
altogether. It won't work I tell you—it
won't work. Why look at the masses, as
you call them. Sweet specimens we saw
to-day—those Birmingham pin-makers in
their red rags—who can't let a young lady
walk on those hills up yonder without
assaulting her. Wretched *canaille*, I should
just like to charge in amongst them with a

good stout horsewhip—a sword would be
honouring them too far. I'd educate
them." And the Major snorted, and
looked very warlike indeed.

"But don't you think, Sir, that the
present low and degraded state of the
masses proves the want of education—of
sound Church education, I mean."

"Pooh!" interjected the Major.

"Now, it will be very different when
the great monastic orders are revived
again—as they will be soon. Then they
will once more be the brothers, and
stewards, and teachers of the poor; and
we shall have no more work-houses or
Government schools, but all education
will be in the hands of the Church and
the monks, as it should be."

During this speech the Major's movements had been perpetual. He wriggled
in his chair, he tugged at his moustache,
he patted his bald head, and puffed at

his cigar, until, at last, flinging the
stump away with indescribable viciousness
as though aimed at some visionary monk,
he burst forth,

"God bless my soul, Sir! Monks!
stewards! why they're not fit to be
stewards on board a steamer. I never in
all my life heard of such ideas as you
have got hold of—never in all my life.
Look here, if I listen to any more of this
I shall go cracked or something, and shall
have to call Betty up. Monks for school-
masters—good Lord! what next? Come,
my lad, come we'll go to bed, I think,
and sleep it all off. No, don't apologise—
I like a man to speak his mind, though
I may not agree with him. Besides, as
you grow older you'll grow wiser, that is
one thing. There, my boy, there's your
room, so good-night, and God bless you
—and bring you to your senses," added
he, when he was out of hearing.

CHAPTER VII.

BOTH the Major and his daughter were early risers—the former being in the habit of smoking a cheroot in the garden before breakfast whenever the weather permitted. On the morning after the battle of Malvern Hill, the day dawned bright and warm, and accordingly the good man was enabled to enjoy his favourite luxury. He had not been long in the garden, walking up and down among the beds of china asters and bright geraniums, and switching off an occasional dead blossom with his Malacca cane, before Myrtle came tripping down the path to meet him, blowing kisses as she advanced, and looking more charming than ever in her fresh muslin dress and scarlet Garibaldi blouse.

"And now, my dear old papa," began she when the morning salutations were over, " I want you to tell me all about our guest. How you like him, and all that. I heard you ' God bless you' him when you parted last night, and I know that always means that you are in a good humour and like the person you are speaking to ; but then as he shut his door you said something I couldn't catch, and gave a great snort as you do when you are put out. What did it all mean ? Tell me, directly, like a good Major."

"You little eaves-dropper," said her delighted father, " what business have you to be awake at such a time ? I'll be bound you were sitting up reading some idiotic trash or other. Well, if you must know, I like Jack Purcell's son very much—he's a very good lad and an honest lad, but he has some of the queerest notions I ever heard of in all my life. There's one comfort, however, as I told him, as he grows older he'll get wiser."

" You rude old papa ! Fancy telling a guest that. That was because I was not there to look after your company manners. Well, but what are these notions you think so odd ? I'll be bound, Major, you didn't understand him."

" No—nor would any other sensible man, my dear. Notions; oh, all about parish clerks, and acolytes, and priests, and monks, and the Lord knows what besides. Such things are not in my way, you know. He's a good lad enough, and I like him; but for all that, if he is to be a clergyman, the sooner he empties his brain of all his monks and nuns the better. Look here, my little girl, we must make things pleasant for him while he stays. I dare say he has only been reading and muddling his brain as those Oxford men do. We will try and see what a little of your bright society will do for him. Just fancy Jack Purcell's son talking about monks—monkeys more likely. Look there, my dear, there he is, let us go to him."

In answer to his host's enquiries, Edgar assured him that he had never had a better night, and that Betty had paid him an early visit in his bed-room to inspect the state of his eye, which she pronounced favourable.

" She is a good creature is Betty," said the Major, " and she knows more than half the M.D.'s in the kingdom. Talk of your hydropaths and homœopaths —they are a pack of asses, Sir, asses compared to my Betty, here."

" Papa thinks Betty infallible, Mr. Purcell," said Myrtle, looking up from her employment of pouring out tea. "I think he consults her about every step he takes in life—what waistcoat he shall wear, what he shall have for dinner, and how he shall invest his money. Come, papa, now be honest, did you not have her down to look at the bay mare before you bought her? I think it was her advice which decided you to take her."

"And if I did, Miss, what then? She knows the points of a horse better than most men, I can tell you. I wish you had half the practical knowledge of life that Betty has."

"That means, I suppose, you want me to know how to make puddings, pack coats without crumpling, and see that your collars and shirts are starched properly. Why, my dearest old papa, I might as well be my own great grandmother. Now, Mr. Purcell," said the pouting beauty, "what do you say? Do you think I should be one bit the better for being like dear old Betty?"

"Certainly not in personal appearance, Miss Harding," was the ready answer, "I can't say I think the exchange would be a fair one there. And as for other things, I should say that you each knew what was best for your station."

"There, papa, you see you must retire from the field. Look—here's the post-bag to console you. Please be quick, and see if there's anything for me."

"I hate the very sight of that bag, Myrtle," said her father, "it never brings anything but ill luck, or, at least, letters to answer." He opened the bag, and began to peruse the one letter it contained; presently flinging it down, and muttering something which sounded so much like "jam," that his daughter pushed the preserve towards his side of the table; but he didn't want the jam in the least. "I beg your pardon, my dear, I am sure. But didn't I say I hated the sight of the bag. I had made up my mind to be quiet to-day, and here is a letter from Travers and Son, begging me to see them at Cheltenham. That rascally lawsuit, it's the plague of my life! Purcell, whatever you do, take my advice, and don't go to law; there is no amount of money worth gaining or preserving by a lawsuit. Now, here am I, who have, Heaven knows, enough to satisfy my simple wants and keep Myrtle in gloves and rubbish—here am I dragged head and shoulders into what is called a friendly suit, because some fool of a cousin I never saw chooses to die and leave his money to me. However, needs must when the d——, I mean the lawyers, drive, so go I must. Myrtle, my love, ring for Betty and tell her to

look in Bradshaw. I'll start at once, by
the first train, and be back in time for
dinner. Just give me another cup of tea.
Do you think you can manage to amuse
Mr. Purcell? Purcell, my boy, I must
leave you in Myrtle's hands for the day;
I daresay you'll get along without quarrelling; or if you do I'll forgive you, for,
'pon my honour, I think a little quarrelling
and contradiction would do her no harm,
she always gets her way now."

For about ten minutes wild confusion
reigned, until the omnipotent Betty arrived
with a laconic utterance of, " Train at
10·15, carriage at the door, great-coat and
shawl because of night fogs. Dinner at
6·30 for 4 o'clock train."

Then the Major disappeared, after a
shower of kisses from Myrtle, who followed him to the gates and stood waving
her handkerchief, until he was out of
sight.

"Now, Mr. Purcell, you are my guest, and so I must be very good and proper, and polite, and you must be very good and amusable. And we won't quarrel if we can manage to avoid it. Now what shall we do? Are you horsey and dog-gey? because if so, there's the stable with the one horse we have brought down with us, and fat old Carlo, the pointer. You shake your head; I thought all gentlemen liked loafing about in the stables after breakfast—don't be shocked at my slang, I know I ought not to say 'loaf,' papa would pull me up for it. Well, do you care very much for litera-ture, Hallam's Middle Ages and all that? because if so, there's papa's little study, where he goes to sleep, and all kinds of horrible dry books in it, and I will take you there if you wish, and leave you until lunch time, and have the house kept quite quiet. You shake your head again. Well, then, I'll tell you what, you must put up with me for a companion, and as I am going to be dreadfully busy, you must help me. How will that do ?"

" I should like it better than anything," responded Edgar, when the voluble little maiden paused at last, " let us begin at once. What are you going to do, and how shall I help you ?"

" First of all, I will take you round the garden and show you all my favourite flowers; then I have the bouquets to make up for the drawing-room and the study; do you know papa always likes one in his room ? and then let me see, oh, I know, if you are very good, I'll make you a green shade for the dreadful eye you got in my defence. You were very brave and I thank you very much. I like brave men."

" Do you know," said Edgar, earnestly,

" you have repaid me ten times over
whatever little I did. I only wish I had
to do it again."

" Now that is what I call very ungallant.
You want me to be stopped by those
horrible men again—and why, I should
like to know ?"

" To have the pleasure of doing something for you, to be of use in any way to
you," replied Edgar, who was now head
and shoulders in, and had quite forgotten
Marbecke and monasticism for the moment.

" Well, if you want to be of use, I'll
find some more peaceful employment for
you, Mr. Purcell. I don't like those adventures too often, although that had a
pleasant ending. I am sure I was horribly frightened ; did not I look so ? Come
be honest and tell me."

" You looked very—" began the youth
and paused.

"Very what?"

"Very beautiful, I thought," replied he boldly.

Reader, you must attribute his rapid development to the veal cutlet.

"Now that is what I call unfair; I ask you for truth and you give me a compliment. If you do that again, I will not make you your green shade. Now, please, if you are quite ready we will go into the garden, and you shall carry the basket for my flowers."

And so the two descended to the lawn. It was a pretty old fashioned piece of ground, full of quaint old world flowers, and not yet attacked by the hand of the reforming ornamental gardener. There were square beds, and round beds, and oblong beds, and beds which looked like a problem of Euclid done in gaudy flowers. And in and about all these moved Miss Myrtle cutting China asters, and geraniums,

and fuschias, and mignionette, and helio-
trope and Michaelmas daisies at her own
sweet will. And obediently did Edgar
follow, receiving the great bunches which
the liberal maiden plucked, and thrilling
and blushing as their fingers met in contact. It was very pleasant work indeed,
and quite new to him. Monks had gardens
it is true, but then they didn't have Myrtle
to walk in them.

"Now let us come and sit down in the
shade, and make up the bouquets," said
that young lady, when the basket was full
to overflowing. And they sat down accordingly, close together, with the flowers
between them, which was a very convenient
arrangement Edgar thought. He began
idly to put a few together.

"Oh, what taste you have, Mr. Purcell!"
exclaimed Myrtle, looking up from her
work, "how ever do you manage to
arrange your flowers so well? I can't

manage mine at all. There—" and as she spoke, she upset the great heap of variegated blossoms she had been labouring over.

"Oh, what a shame to undo your work; I thought it lovely! I don't care about artificial arrangements. Now, do try yours again," and he handed her some fresh flowers.

"No, not now. Yours have put me out of conceit with my powers. How did you learn to put up flowers like that?"

"I generally make up all the bouquets for the altar at St. George's—that's a church in Oxford, where I go usually."

"Oh, that's how you do it, is it?" exclaimed Myrtle, suddenly remembering the supposed monastic tendencies of her guest. "I suppose it is a very High Church place then. Are you very high?"

And she looked innocently at him, as

though her inquiry related to his bodily stature.

"I suppose I am what is called High Church, but I only call myself a Church-man, Miss Harding. I think that the Church of England's real views, are what is styled High, and so I try to follow them out."

"Ah, yes," was the somewhat hesi-tating response, "but is it not very diffi-cult to find out all about it? I am sure if any one were to ask me, I couldn't say quite what I was; of course you know I am confirmed and so on, but I mean there are so many good people Low Church, and so many good people High Church, that I should think as long as they are good it doesn't matter much."

"Ah, but we must go by what the Church says."

"Well, but what does she say? Nearly all the clergymen say that in their sermons, but I think they mean we are to go by what *they* say. *L'état c'est moi*, you know."

"But we find the Church's true views in the rubrics and formularies if we only look. And then there is tradition and Catholic antiquity to refer to, and the usage of other Catholic Churches."

"But, good gracious me, Mr. Purcell, you don't want to make us all do as those French and Italians do abroad, do you? Why what would be the good of the Reformation, and Cranmer, Ridley, and Latimer, and all the Martyrs."

"I dare say they were very good men in their way; but after all, their notions of church-teaching were very narrow —very narrow indeed. I often doubt whether that Reformation has done any good at all. There are so many infidels and sceptics now."

"I dare say there were just as many

before, only they did not dare speak out
plainly for fear of being burnt. But, of
course, you must know best because you
have studied all these things at Oxford, I
suppose. I am sure I cannot think how you
are able to study and read so much."

"Oh, but I assure you I don't know
half what I ought. I shall have to read
very much more before I am ordained. It
is of course only natural for me to think
about all this, as I am to be a priest—a
clergyman you know," observing Myrtle's
little look of surprise.

"Well I am sure I hope you will like
it, and be very happy. It is a great
responsibility, I suppose. But after all, I
don't see if a clergyman does his duty
why he should fret as some do because
people are wicked. You know, you can't
make people good if they won't be so.
And, do you know, I don't think people
are so very bad after all. I am sure

everyone is very good to me, very much more than I deserve, I am sure, for sometimes I am very cross when I am put out. Papa says I am spoilt."

"I am sure I don't think so," was the gallant rejoinder.

"Ah, but you don't know me enough yet. If we were to quarrel you would see how cross I should be."

"How do you look when you are cross, Miss Harding?"

"Oh horrible, I can tell you. I frown very much—like this."

And she tried to knit her smooth white brows with the semblance of a scowl, but failed egregiously, only looking more charming than ever.

"I don't think I should be frightened at that," said Edgar undismayed, "and then you'll never frown at me, will you?"

"Perhaps not, but then I must always have my own way. So mind. Now look here, Mr. Purcell, to begin. When you are a clergyman, I hope you are not going to be horribly severe and abuse everybody, and cut off your whiskers, and wear long coats, and never call on your friends, and preach against dancing. Shall you dance?"

"I can't say I think a clergyman ought to dance. How should you like now to listen to a sermon from your clerical partner of the night before?"

"Why, if he danced well and preached well, I should like him all the better. I don't see why doing one should prevent your doing the other. At all events, you need not dance on Saturday night. Still I know some people think differently, so I wont hold out about the dancing. But shall you never come to see your friends, or shall you give them up altogether?"

"Oh, Miss Harding, I am sure I hope we shall always remain friends whatever

I am. Of course my time will be more taken up then than it is now."

"Ah—that is a polite way of saying you don't mean to come near us. Well then I'll tell you what I shall do. Papa always does as I tell him, so I shall make him come with me and we will pay you a visit at your smoky old Oxford and see what you are doing. However, that is in the future, isn't it? And now we have done the flowers I think we will go and put them in the vases and then I'll make your green shade."

And so that happy day passed by, and the Major came home, and so, too, several other happy days passed on and on until Edgar began to feel quite at home at Link Cottage, and woke up with a start one morning at the discovery of two things; that it was time for him to return to Oxford, and that he was simply in love with Myrtle Harding. It was a terrible

fact to discover, the more so as he tried
to disguise it from himself as long as possible, by employment of gentle euphemisms
and circumlocutions. It was a friendship
—no, it was a Platonic affection—no, it
was only the christian affection with which
a good he-Catholic might regard a good
she-Catholic. St. Jerome had written
letters to female saints ; one of St. John's
epistles was to the ' elect lady whom he
loved in the truth.' But then, unfortu-
natly, Myrtle was not the least like a
female saint or even a Port Royal devout,
and some commentators hold that that
epistle was simply addressed to the Church.
However all this might be, we can only
say that the bright green shade made by
Myrtle's hands, after it had accomplished
its mission, found an honourable resting
place in Edgar's desk, and was often
gazed upon with more intensity than such
articles usually are, or this particular shade

deserved, and that the monastic scheme about this time became enveloped in a kind of hazy cloud or fog, which rendered its outlines very indistinct. It was not abandoned; certainly not — oh, by no means. Indeed, every now and again, Edgar would sit down and try to realize some of its details; the building, the habit the offices, the diet, and yet strange to say, a piquante little figure in white muslin, scarlet Garibaldi, and hair cut short, was always intruding itself in the oddest way. Waltzing down the cloister, making little *moues* at the boiled peas and brown bread, singing "Wapping old stairs" in chapel, instead of "Ora pro nobis," and reading the "Idylls of the King" to all the brothers in solemn chapter assembled. Do what he would, he could not expel this fantastic vision from the cloister; in fact the chances are that the fantastic vision would have the best of it, and perhaps end in annihilating the cloister and its inhabitants. At length the day of departure came, and sorrowfully Edgar went to assist Myrtle pick the few flowers which October frosts had spared.

"The last time," he said.

"I hate that 'last time!'" exclaimed Myrtle, who was scarcely as vivacious as usual. "It is a horrid word, and always comes when one is very happy. Never mind; though you are going away, I suppose you do not mean to quite forget us altogether, when you are in that smokey Oxford."

"Forget? No, indeed! I am sure I shall never forget dear old Malvern, and Link Cottage and this happy fortnight."

"Ah, you only say that to be polite," replied Myrtle with ready inconsistency, "you men go about so much, and see so many people that one puts the other out of your heads."

"Not out of mine, I assure you. I have not so many friends, or even acquaintances, that I am likely to forget you and my father's friend."

"Ah, how strangely things happen. How little we expected when we came to Malvern to make this acquaintance; only a fortnight ago, and I am sure it seems as though we had known each other for years. Now mind, you are to be sure and remember all I have told you, and not go and get gloomy ideas again among your books and colleges, and churches and stupid old fogies. Remember what papa told you the other night, that the best men were always the most cheerful, and that the best religion was to try and find out the good in the world, and not sit down and cry over what we can't help!" She held up her finger with mock solemnity, perhaps to conceal what she really felt.

"Ah, Myrtle," said the enamoured youth, forgetting all restraints of prudence, "if you were always at my side I should never be gloomy or despondent."

"But then you see I can't be, and I am sure I should not wish to be in that gloomy old Oxford, and it wouldn't be at all proper if I did wish it. So you see you must be good and remember my words."

"Give me something to remember them by. Oh, please now, you can't think how I should treasure it, what care I would take of it! oh, do now, Myrtle!"

"You mustn't call me Myrtle, Mr. Purcell. It is very rude and I won't allow it. You ought to remember my words without any *souvenir* at all, and I think you very absurd. Well, what shall it be then, if you will be so ridiculous? Here, this will do," and she stooped and picked a little branch of fern which grew close by. " Do you know what this is called ?"

" No."

" It is called after me, the Myrtle fern. So take it, and when you are getting gloomy and dismal, you must look at it and say, ' Myrtle—I mean Miss Harding —would be very angry with me if she could see me now.' And then you will get cheerful again. Now please don't squeeze my hand so hard, and there is nothing to thank me for—and oh, good gracious, here is Betty come to say the carriage is at the door."

Now we humbly put it to the reader to say whether, in his opinion, the asking for and reception of a *gage d'amour* or even *d'amitié* is an usual act for a would-be monk ; and why also after Edgar's departure Myrtle found it necessary to have a good cry, and then to bathe her eyes with Eau de Cologne ?

CHAPTER VIII.

A YEAR had passed away since John's engagement, and the Long Vacation was drawing near. The two cousins had breakfasted together in Cyril's luxurious rooms, and were now reposing after their labours. The host was in his favourite rocking-chair, smoking cigarettes and sipping very strong black coffee after a Turkish fashion, which was his last new whim. He seemed to take a lazy pleasure in watching the spiral curls of delicate blue smoke, as they writhed and twisted away from his lips like beautiful shadowy snakes.

John was seated astride on a chair, a favourite attitude of his, with his head reclining on his crossed arms, and his strong brown hands hanging loose. He was not handsome, it is true, but there was for all that a nameless charm about his face, hard to account for. His features were strong and emphatic, betokening resolution and decision. His fine dark blue eyes, the best point in his face, were singularly truthful, though they had a strange dreamy onward look as though gazing at something beyond the horizon. A great mass of hair, silky in texture and lion-like in colour, was always nodding forward over his forehead, and as often was sent back with an impatient toss. There was something manly and noble in his appearance, but for all that something indescribably saddening. Some men carry their fate in their faces—if so, John Fordyce was not destined to be happy in the future.

Philosopher Cyril was laying down the law in his usual quiet indifferent manner.

"You may take my word for it, Jack, you are mistaken. No man was ever yet the better for worrying and fretting. It is true, taken at the best, life is a huge nuisance, but then we certainly don't improve it by bothering about things entirely out of our reach. Now, to me, it is simply incomprehensible that you who might, to use a metaphor, live on strawberries and peaches, delicious fruit which need no mastication or digestion, should prefer wasting your time in trying to crack those horrible Brazil nuts, called religious and moral difficulties. I call such a line of action immoral. Besides, what does it matter?"

"Not much to you, Cyril, perhaps; but

when a man is to become a clergyman, he ought to try to the best of his powers, to understand such matters."

"Ah, that is another of your delusions. By-the-bye, just look at that last puff, three perfect rings of smoke in succession, I am improving. Let me see, where was I? Oh, delusions; you think that to teach it is necessary to understand. That is a fallacy, congregations don't want to be taught. They are not like fish out of water, fainting and gasping and dying for knowledge. They want to be let alone judiciously and decorously. Religious life moves in a circle, and always returns to its starting point. It has its storms and calms, its whirlwinds and stagnations, its revivals and its dead seasons, but it is just the same at the end as it was in the beginning. Religious opinions are all traceable to stomach and digestion; High Churchmen have weak digestions, Low Churchmen are bilious and given to liver complaint."

At this juncture the door opened, and Burke put in his head.

"I say, old fellow, give a man some breakfast, I have been kept the last half hour by Marbecke's jawing!"

"You'll find something there, if you don't mind the trouble of looking for it. There's some salmon by the fire in the little room and an omelette. Shout for what you want, and don't break my favourite coffee-cups if you can help it, I know you are clumsy enough."

"You have just come in time, Burke, to hear Ponsonby's last. He has defined religion as good eating and good digestion. What do you think of that?"

"Well, they are both forms of good living, aren't they? By-the-bye, perhaps that's the reason why all those charitable societies are always having such jolly good

feeds.   I never thought of that before.
At all events, Pon, you practise what you
preach, this omelette is first rate—Hinton,
I suppose? I shouldn't like to have to
pay your bills, young man."

"And I am sure I shouldn't either,"
was the quiet answer, "but then I
don't intend to, and so it does not
matter."

"That's as may be," said John, with
a laugh, "there are two sides to that
question."

"Heads I win, tails you lose, that's how
Ponsonby looks at it; he is the coolest
fish out."

"Go on, go on, both of you, I rather
like it.   Eat a man's breakfast and
abuse him the while, it gives a zest and
helps digestion.   Defend me from you,
good people, you always cast mud at your
neighbour.   Now here is my cousin,
John Fordyce, a converted character, and

all that kind of thing, who is always grizzling because he isn't an archangel, or something else full of wings. He tells me that I have no moral principles; and you, little monkey, you most junior of junior partners, you small worshipper of the golden calf declare I have no honesty! As if I had the bad taste to pretend to one or the other. I am a child of Nature, that's all."

"Then it's a great pity Nature does not bring up her children better," remarked a deep voice outside the open door, and in another moment Maxwell's tall form entered the room.

"Ah, now I shall shut up, three against one is too long odds for me. I am very glad to see you, and if it isn't too late for breakfast, perhaps you'll sit down and see whether that gorging vessel Burke has left anything."

"Thank you, no, I breakfasted," pull-

ing out his watch, "two hours ago, and
have had a long walk since."

"Oh, oh, I forgot I was addressing a
muscular christian."

"Well, no one can accuse you of being
either one or the other," remarked Burke,
who was fond of Maxwell, and always
ready to defend him when attacked.
"Some men are christian without being
muscular, and some muscular without
being christian; but upon my life, Pon,
you are neither."

Burke said it so gravely that all the
others laughed, Cyril the most.

"At least, Maxwell, you can bear wit-
ness to my forgiveness of injuries. These
two have pommelled me the whole morning. Do sit down, there's a good fellow,
nothing is so irritating to an idle man
as to see an energetic one looking ready
to storm the Malakoff single-handed."

"I didn't know I looked so warlike.

Well, I will sit for one minute while I tell you all what I came about. Fordyce, do you remember our projecting a reading excursion together for some vacation?"

John roused and shook himself.

"Yes, rather, and I have wished for it ever since, though something has always happened to prevent it."

"Well, I don't think anything need prevent it's coming off this Long Vacation. I have some writing to do, and shall be glad to get away to some quiet place to do it in. So there is the opportunity you have longed for, John. Now if any of your friends like to join forces with us, so much the better. Purcell has already asked to do so."

"What? Purcell, the most rigid of High Churchmen?" asked Cyril, with a laugh. "But how came it about? Have you given him satisfactory proofs of or-

thodoxy? Did he send Marbecke to
catechise you, or do you think he
comes as a secret emissary of the Pro-
paganda, hoping to convert you and your
pupil at one fell swoop?"

"Well, I own I was surprised at his
application; but I fancy I am 'taken
on trust.' He certainly expressed a faint
hope that I might find it convenient
to go within easy distance of choral
service and rubrical observances; but I
would not pledge myself until I knew of
whom the party would consist."

"Well, if you care to be plagued with
me, Maxwell," said Cyril, "I really think
I should like to go. I think reading
parties a great mistake, and never knew
of one where the men didn't hate each
other ever after; but for all that I don't
wish to be much at home this 'long,'
and as I can't go abroad, perhaps, on
the whole I could not do better than

join. There's only one point—I am not the least particular, but I do humbly trust that you don't intend going quite out of the limits of civilization. I don't care about my fellow-creatures, but I do care for creature comforts."

"My dear and most philosophical Mr. Cyril Ponsonby, be at ease on that point. It is quite necessary for me to be within reach, if not of choral service, at least of a railway station, a post-office and various other accompaniments of civilization. I think all unnecessary 'roughing' a great mistake, and appreciate a comfortable bed as much as any one."

"I suppose I am not swell enough to run in such a classical team, am I, Mr. Maxwell?" asked Burke in dolorous tones.

"Come and welcome, my good fellow, on the same conditions as every one else, a fair proportion of work to play."

"Oh, I'm on for that," was the young

gentleman's rather slangy rejoinder, "you know it's just the kind of thing to please the governor, it looks so respectable and all that.   You won't mind my having Sir Roger down, shall you ?"

"Sir Roger being a horse, I presume—certainly not. I shall be proud of his company. And now then the great question is where shall we go ? I am open to suggestions."

John thought of Wales ; Charlie Burke declared Cornwall would be "awfully jolly ;" and Cyril vacillated between the site of the Garden of Eden, or failing that the summit of Chimborazo. When pressed, he declared that all places were alike to him, and that he only stipulated for the neighbourhood of a library and a good tobacconist, unheeding the objections of his friends that neither Armenia nor Mexico were likely to supply these. At length, after much patience, Maxwell interposed.

"To tell the truth, I had a place in my mind already, only I wanted to see whether any of you would suggest something better. It will suit you, Fordyce; for it is on the sea and with beautiful scenery. It will suit you, Burke; for it is where I believe the horses are particularly good, and the downs will give you good galloping ground. It will suit Purcell; for the railway will convey him to at least a couple of very extreme churches which have been the subject of litigation; and lastly, I think even you, Ponsonby, will be tolerably well suited, as Llan-y-morfa is large enough for a library, and as for your idol, tobacco, I suppose you can get that from London. For my own part, it is all I can desire; comfortable, but dull and soothing to the spirits. And now—is it agreed?"

"Agreed *nem. con.*," was echoed on all sides.

And so the Welsh project was fairly started, and five men differing in character, ideas and aims, resolved to live together for the space of two months, with such friendliness as only Englishmen are capable of under the circumstances. Soon after this, John and Burke took their departure to their various lectures. Maxwell lingered behind, and after a few trifling remarks, addressed Ponsonby.

"I don't think I can be accused often of presuming upon my cloth—as the term goes—so I hope you will not take amiss what I am going to say, Ponsonby."

"I am not very likely to do so, I fancy, you know I am for freedom in everything —speech first of all."

"Ah, you think so I am sure. But I have often found those who were the most eager advocates of free speech, did not care for it when applied to themselves. However, I have a message unto thee, O cap-

tain, which I will deliver. I know that
as Fordyce's cousin and friend you see
him often, and are, perhaps, as intimate
with him as anyone. Now it cannot have
escaped you that his religious opinions
have been much shaken of late—in fact
that he is rapidly becoming very unsettled." Maxwell paused, and Cyril replied
quietly.

".Well, you know, religion and its fluctuations, whether towards my doxy or
thy doxy do not trouble me very much.
I do not know that I am a particularly
irreligious man, but all this discussion and
quibbling seems to me an unnecessary
trouble. However, I have noticed what
you say."

" And you thought ?"—

" Well, to be candid, I thought it was
your doing, Mr. Maxwell."

"Then God forgive you so false a
thought ! Whatever my own private opin-

ions may be, I am not the man wilfully to
shake the faith of another, or seek to influence it unduly. I have had long talks
with John, of whom I really am very fond,
but beyond replying to his questions, and
trying to meet such objections as could be
met fairly, I have not made or meddled in
the matter. Perhaps you will think I
speak professionally, when I say that I
look upon human faith as something more
than a matter of sentiment or opinion.
However, I will come to what I had to
say. Is it too much to ask of you not to
try to upset your cousin further? You
know you have a careless, light way of
treating religious subjects, which is very
much like throwing lucifer matches among
tow. You cannot tell how much mischief
you may do—unintentionally of course—
but still irreparable. And now that we
shall all be living together, I trust that you
will try to restrain those random sallies of

wit which may do John so much harm.
I have spoken plainly, because I thought
it best."

"And I can quite appreciate your
motives, believe me. Possibly I may be
careless on what seem to you important
subjects; but at least I know how to hold
my tongue, and you may depend on my
discretion."

"Thank you much," replied Maxwell,
"now you have relieved me of my fears.
And nothing seems in the way of our passing a pleasant time together. Good-bye."

"So I am the wolf," laughed Cyril to
himself, "who wants to gobble up the
pretty little lamb. Why what good would
it do me if John were to turn Mahomedan?
Bah, what does it matter?" And he lit a
fresh cigarette.

CHAPTER IX.

IN the last chapter, we stated the fact that our hero's religious opinions had become what is called unsettled. Let us see how this came to pass in the space of one year. At the death of his friend Brydges, he was an amiable heathen, how comes he now to be a heterodox christian? That is worth inquiry. Those three hundred and odd days, uneventful in themselves, had a fateful power of character-building in them for John Fordyce. They had changed him from a fine healthy animal with latent capabilities, into a man of well exercised and disciplined powers, hard-working and God-fearing. There might be university honours and victories yet in store for him, but let him gain never so many triumphs in the fields of thought and study, his hardest, greatest victory had already been won—his greatest enemy laid low. It had not been without cost and labour. The habits of regularity and self-discipline are not acquired without trouble and many an inward rebellion by one who has hitherto given way to every idle impulse. Maxwell, who acted as a true friend at this juncture, was of the greatest service in bringing his cool quiet head and mature judgment to bear upon John's impetuous nature. But for him he would have gone to extremes, and taken on his shoulders a burden far greater than he could have borne.

But in advising the alteration of certain habits, the cultivation of others, and the submitting to various rules and principles,

he was careful to suggest only just so
much as was really necessary and desirable. Attendance at chapel, regularity
at lectures, fixed hours for study, curtail-
ment of certain expenses; here was
nothing which might not be done without
special notice or remark. And so,
although John's religion did not take
the Ornamental line and blossom into
red-edged and gold-crossed prayer-books;
or fill his rooms with triptychs, candles,
sentimental German engravings; nor the
Synagogic line to the multiplication of
reports of the Pongo Conversion Society
and the apocalyptic lectures of the Rev.
Boanerges Reveal, yet it was patent to
all that Fordyce was an altered man.
Don't suppose, good reader, that he gave
up all amusements or became a self-
contemplating ascetic. Possessing a
handsome allowance, he saw no reason
why, after discharge of duty, he should

not enjoy himself in the manner of his age and time. He cricketed, and rode, and kept his own outrigger skiff as before. If he did not frequent the billiard rooms as often as he once had done, I think it was because he gave the sum he used to spend there to Maxwell, who acted as his almoner. Some men would have joined a Guild or Brotherhood, taught in a night-school, or visited the sick. John did none of these, being satisfied with the brother-hood of all his fellow-men, and not seeing the "help" or comfort to be found in a select little clicque devoted to mediæval observances and quasi-religious prattle. And as to undergraduate amateur parish work, Maxwell informed him, with much truth, that both to visitor and visited it usually resulted in more harm than good, and that the best mission for him was to do his duty to those by whom he was surrounded.

He received his friends to wine as usual; but it was soon known that those who wished to continue friends with him, must be rather more discriminating in the style and subjects of discourse than in the old days. He never preached, improved the occasion, or referred to the former times. He did not give his "experiences," or turn himself inside out for the inspection of his friends, but for all that he was a changed man.

"But his religion, his creed, his shibboleth? You take a delight in telling us what he was not, Mr. Author, your photographs are all negatives; cannot you give us a positive also?"

For my own part, I believe in this plan as the best. Nothing is more difficult or unsatisfactory to give than the positive side of a man's religious conviction. Extract all the negatives and accept the residuum. Certainly, from John's training and early life nothing else but a negative could ensue. He was baptized a member of the Church of England, that was an incontrovertible fact, but about that Church he knew nothing. He was, in fact, an amiable heathen—Zulu if you like—only a member of the Christian church, and entitled to its privileges.

And so it was but natural that his awakened conscience, and quickened moral feeling should lead him to consider that church in which he found himself. That was the first step. Again, whereas in old times the animal part of his nature had had undue play, now there was a danger of the preponderance of the spiritual. Hitherto, the scales of his life had been overweighted on one side—he now tried to right himself by over-weighting the other, and in consequence nearly lost his balance altogether. Heart

must form the equipoise between body
and soul. Who was to guide him ?

Mr. Crammer, who at this time was his
tutor, would have been charmed to tell
him all about the differential calculus, or
investigate the theory of æsthetics, as
exhibited (*a*) in Greek (*b*) in German
dramas. But when it came to such a
question as : "What must I hold and
believe to be saved?" he could only
babble feebly about the judicious moderation of the Church of England, and the
great danger of excitement. Fordyce
asked for bread, the well-meaning little
man handed him a fair specimen of the
old red sandstone, and accompanied his
gift with remarks upon aërolites. Good
food for ostriches, scarcely for humanity.

There was Marbecke, it is true ; but
that worthy priest always began by de-
manding a perfect unquestioning obedience

and assent from his pupil, his "penitent,"
he would call him, and an entire belief in
his own infallibility.   Two points which
John felt might better be demanded in
Rome than in England.   Besides, his
hard, dry, obstinate, unyielding nature was
the very last to attract a man in John's
position.   At first he tried to satisfy his
craving hunger by swallowing doctrine
without examining it.   But the food, so
administered, neither warmed nor nourished
the body, being indigested.   Moreover,
this diet such as it was, was soon stopped
by   the   puzzling   question,   "What
dishes   does   the   Church   of   England
allow?"   Puzzling   to   him,   reader,
of course not to you or respectable
people.

"Well," you will say, "that was easy
to determine—to continue your culinary
simile—by looking in the bill of fare, the
Formularies and Articles."

But he *did* look, and, whether from the foreign language in which they were written, or from his own density of perception, he was quite unable to find out any but the most simple plain viands. He found that each guest read and interpreted the *carte* differently; then generally each selected his own favourite, or, if he could not find it, called some other by that name and then vowed it *was* in the *carte*. He found that many never looked at the bill of fare, but ate at random—that some said all dishes were to be found at the Church's banquet, if you only knew where to look; others that many viands were actually noxious and indigestible, and ought to be expurgated. So the end was frequent disputes and quarrels, and the unhappy *carte* being flung at the head of some guest. He found, moreover, that the acerbity of these quarrels was in inverse ratio to the importance of the subject in question, and that the "infinitely little" was never so surely reached as when the 'welkin' rang with the anile shrieks and execrations of the combatants. Some, indeed, never seemed happy unless they were inditing "a letter to the Rev. A B C," or "a rejoinder to &c., &c.," or "a few last words respecting &c., &c. ;" the femininity of the whole affair peeping out in the struggle for those "last words," and the general determination not to be convinced displayed on both sides.

Wearied, hungry, unsatisfied and perplexed, he stole apart from the din of quarrelsome diners, and mused sadly.

"Where and how may I learn the truth ? how know what the Church of England holds, and whether she hold that aright ? Is there no certainty, no assurance ? is all to be vague and shadowy and unsettled ? Does any party represent and embrace the Church? Can I learn the whole truth from any one section, be its pretences what they may? Must I not go deeper and farther for the final great truth, underlying and pervading in various degrees all these isolated expressions of it. There must be a Church and that Church must be universal; can any National Church then express and contain that great body of truth enshrined in the whole? How is it that scarcely two of the clergy agree upon all these vital points? How is it that they argue differently— come to opposite conclusions—and each maintain so stoutly the absolute truth of their own conclusions?"

And then he took himself and his troubles to his friend Maxwell.

"You told me not to take a difficulty to another for solution, until I had first thoroughly tried my own powers upon it. Now I come to you. Here is my difficulty, and after a thorough grapple with it, it has thrown me. You know I am to be a clergyman. Now I have many doubts, not as to religion in general, but as to the doctrines of the Church of England. Again I am perplexed at the amount of authority which exists in any National Church. Can faith be determined like national character and government by the boundaries of seas, or mountain chains? Or, if so, when those boundaries are enlarged by conquest or lapse of time, is faith to change and alter too? Vital, necessary Faith, Christian Faith must be as universal and extensive as Heaven above us, as comprehensive and eternally One, as God over all. I believe in such a Catholic Faith as that, and in its infallibility; but I cannot see that it is or can be limited to any national branch or section."

Maxwell smiled gravely and replied :

"To whom have you been talking lately, John Fordyce?"

"I had some talk the other day with Mr. Marbecke, quite accidentally. And he was pointing out the difference between the Catholic Church, and the Roman, Greek and Anglican branches of it."

"How did he define the Catholic Church?"

"He limited it to those three branches I have mentioned, and regretted the want of inter-communion among them."

"Alas, the theological learning of some good men seems confined to a Statute of limitations in a religious sense. First cousins to the Pharisees of old, they delight in taking away the key of Heaven into their own special keeping. John, what did the Great Master say to the blind man?"

"'Dost thou believe on the son of God?'"

" And Paul to the gaoler ?"

" ' Believe on the Lord Jesus Christ, and thou shalt be saved.' "

" If then Christ and his apostles had no severer test than this, though, mind you, here is much in little ; what right have we pigmies to narrow and limit the conditions of salvation by our private shibboleths. No, John, thus far at least I may help you and give you comfort. Do you remember the text, ' If any man will do His will, he shall know the doctrine whether it be of God ?' Look in your Bible and follow its precepts, and remember faith comes by practice. Before you encounter the difficulties of national churches and national creeds—things of human institution—study and get well by heart the Church of Divine Institution, and the Creed of Christ's teaching, which you will find in Scripture ; and remember, study simply as a man desirous of the truth, not as an intending clergyman anxious to discover the Anglican Church in the Gospels and Epistles. After that we will go farther as we may."

Was it strange that John felt comfort?

CHAPTER X.

IT had rained for twenty-four hours in the little sea-side town of Llan-y-morfa, and there appeared every probability of its raining for at least twenty-four hours more. The streets were deserted, the gutters mere swamps, the very houses had a sodden appearance, the water-pipes were as busy as they could be, and choked and gurgled in chorus. A few discontented shopkeepers stood listlessly under cover of their doors, with bovine stolidity gazing upon the dreary scene; a few cross-grained faces were to be seen peering over the blinds of private houses; babies at nursery windows crowed and danced, as they watched the bubbles and sticks and straws hurrying down the flooded gutters; and down on the beach the sea kept up a continuous moan and sigh like a creature in pain, while it lashed itself up into a more foamy mist until you could scarcely distinguish earth, water and air—but all seemed merged and mingled into one.

Three men, a donkey and a dog, stood long at the Market Cross, possibly waiting for something to happen; when their patience was exhausted they retired— the men, I mean, not the quadrupeds— to the "Goat and Compasses," evidently expecting a change of circumstances would follow the change of scene.

Left to themselves, the dog suddenly woke up from a semi-comatose condition and bit his companion, the donkey, without apparent reason. The donkey, scarcely resenting this insult, responded

with a long bray, and then both animals
settled down again into their former state
of despondency. They were at length
rewarded for their patience, for theirs
were the only eyes to behold that marvel
at Llan-y-morfa, the advent of a stranger.
An altogether wonderful stranger, too,
who appeared to care nothing for the
rain; who even seemed unconscious of
it, so tranquilly and calmly did he pursue
his way under the very questionable
shelter of a very questionable and out-
landish pea-green umbrella of the smallest
in size and the newest in shape. He
was a young man of slight but graceful
figure, well dressed in a suit of light
materials, from the pockets of which
flowed little streams of water. In his
mouth he held a cigar, from which he
puffed long, delicate spirals of smoke.
Straight down the long High Street he
went, until he came to the Market Cross

and Town Hall, and there he stopped. Well, he might. Much credit is due to the architect, who, sixty years ago, erected the said Town Hall, inasmuch after great expenditure of thought, money and material, he succeeded in producing a building incapable of affording the slightest instruction, pleasure, or profit to any one.

Some men blunder upon a happy arrangement by mere lucky chance; sometimes beauty of material, or prodigality of expenditure redeem a building from utter ugliness and contempt. Not so at Llan-y-morfa. The architect had employed Portland stone, and might as well have used mud, or lath and plaster for all the effect it produced. Consistent dullness, utter frigidity, had been his aim, and in this, at least, he had been successful. The guide book "of the period" described it as "of just

and correct proportions, and majestic out-
line, possessing a classic grandeur which
could not fail to strike the intelligent
observer." It did strike the observer
accordingly, and struck him generally
with dismay, to think that so much
money should have been wasted upon a
Gorgonised mass of frigid absurdity and
dullness. The basement consisted of a
rusticated arcade, wherein the good,
sound Portland stone had, with much
labour and expense, been made to assume the appearance of rotten pumice.
In front projected a portico, the columns
of which were apparently formed of alter-
nate layers of stilton and cheddar cheeses,
blossoming at the top with florid somethings resembling Bath chaps and pigs'
faces. Above all, a pediment with its
due proportion of metope and triglyph
and guilloche, and egg and arrow mouldings, formed a stage for the display of

certain bulky soup tureens, emblematic of civic hospitality, which was further typified by the ropes of onions, turnips, carrots and celery pendant between the windows.

To show at once the thorough respectable heathenism of the thing, the pediment was filled with a bas-relief of Neptune, clad in nothing particular but a helmet and a sword, offering in the handsomest manner to Britannia a broiled bloater, which he extended on a toasting-fork of large dimensions. Apparently overcome, either by his generosity, or the strong flavour of the gift, she reclined pensively upon a shield like a dish-cover, and seemed in some doubt as to whether she might receive the advances of the marine deity. The overgrown poodle, which did duty for the British lion, apparently had no such scruples, inasmuch as he was performing "down charge" at Neptune's feet. Above all, a plethoric, frantic, and scantily-draped female, with a mail-horn at her mouth, swam through the air, and doubtless with the best intentions, amused herself with pelting the group beneath with oranges and lemons, of which she had a large store in a cornucopia. Thus was represented and allegorised "the Union of Britannia with the Ocean," and the abundant plenty resulting there-from.

Before this triumph of art and archi-tecture, the stranger with the green umbrella paused in silent awe. He then turned round and faced the market-place, with an expression of calm despair which was infinitely touching. Evidently the donkey felt it so, for he immediately brayed loud and long a second time, thus rousing and bringing out his master from the "Goat and Compasses." Upon which the stranger began to flourish his umbrella, thereby intimating a desire to parley.

"My dear friend," enquired he, as the man slouched up, "can you tell me whether this is a deserted city?   Does any one take the trouble to live here?   For I have now been in it half an hour, and seen no one man, woman, or child."

Thus addressed, the man shifted from one leg to the other, hitched up his trousers, scratched his head, and having by this process collected his ideas, replied,

This here's Llan-y-morfa New Town."

"Then what can Llan something old town be like!" mentally ejaculated the stranger.   "Of that I am aware, my dear Sir, but does anybody reside in this delightful place—human beings, I mean?"

"This here's Llan-y-morfa New Town," responded the man unmoved, "and a mort of people come here in race week; other times it's pretty much as you see."

"Does it always rain like this?"

"Bless your heart, no. Sometimes on, sometimes off like. It *do* rain now, sure*ly*, and no doubt about it. You was a coming to lodge here, m'appen, Sir; if so, I can show you to a nice clean place hard by, name of Evans, David Evans, general dealer, licensed to sell tea, coffee, pepper, tobacco, and snuff, yes, *and* snuff," repeated he, as if this were the chief inducement.

"My dear Sir, a thousand thanks for your most obliging offer, which I much regret previous engagements will not permit me to accept. I am now in search of the house over which Mrs. Markham presides—I have no doubt with much grace—where I expect to find the friends and companions of my youth, if they have not yet committed suicide or murdered

each other. Can you inform me where
this may happen to be ?"

" Oh, Mother Markham's, is it ? Yes—
she gets all the quality gents, got four
there already—and you are going there,
are you ?"

" Such is my desire, my friend."

" Well, if you go down there straight as
you can go, first to the right, you will see
a white cottage facing the beach ; that's
Markham's."

" Nothing could be plainer than your
direction ; with your permission, therefore,
I will follow it up."

And he turned to go.

" You'll remember a poor man, y'r
honour, this wet day, won't you ?"

" Certainly, certainly, my dear Sir; I
shall have much pleasure in remembering
you."

" I mean I should like to drink your
honour's health," rejoined the man,

thinking how very stupid the stranger must be.

" To that also there can be no objection —at your own expense; indeed, I may say I feel much gratified at the attention from a total stranger. Good morning, my dear Sir."

And lighting a fresh cigar, and shouldering the green umbrella, he walked off in the direction of the beach. So the foiled native consoled himself by kicking his donkey in the ribs, and returning to the " Goat and Compasses."

A few steps brought our friend in the light suit to a long low two-storied white house, with a pretty green verandah, and external staircase, like that of a Swiss cottage. From one of the open French windows projected a pair of legs, the feet of which were shod with red Morocco slippers. With a chance oyster-shell from the beach, the stranger took aim and succeeded in knocking off one of the slippers aforesaid, which fell into a puddle of rain. From the window proceeded an exclamation I will not quote, the legs were withdrawn, and a jolly red face thrust out, on which followed a shout of, "By Jove! here's Ponsonby come at last."

In a few minutes more Cyril was in the centre of a group of his friends who constituted the reading party, getting no small amount of "chaff" for his personal appearance.

"It's all very well for you fellows to laugh, but the part of Jupiter Pluvius isn't nice to act. Why, my dear Maxwell, this place must be the abomination of desolation standing where it ought not. No fly nor omnibus at the station, no human beings in the streets, a donkey, a dog and a man—I designedly put him last—are all I have seen. What do you do with yourselves ? Does anything ever happen ?"

"Oh, it's awfully jolly," replied Burke, who had just fetched up his slipper, "lots of riding, boating, fishing, and all that, you know. It does not always rain like this."

"Come, I won't have you cry out before you are hurt, Ponsonby," said Maxwell, "we have specially reserved the most luxurious bed-room for you, and as Mrs. Markham has taken up the idea that you are a 'young gentleman who is rather delicate,' you may expect abundance of attention. We have each made some delightful discovery. Burke has found out splendid stabling for his horse, Purcell a charming old thirteenth century church close by, and some æsthetical young ladies also, I believe—don't blush, Purcell, you know it's true; and you, John, what was your find? Oh, the nearness of the post-office, wasn't it, and the delights of two posts a-day?"

And there was a general laugh at Fordyce, who was in that stage of love when a letter given and received per diem is an absolute necessity.

"Oh, well, if all is *couleur de rose*, as you say, I dare say if I wait something will happen to me also. In the meantime, perhaps, some of you good people will furnish me with apparel, unless you wish me to go about like an ancient Roman in a sheet. I suppose my luggage will come somehow from the station where I left it; there's one comfort, it can't run away, and there certainly is no one to steal it. My opinion is that we are the only human beings in the place."

CHAPTER XI.

CYRIL'S unknown friend was perfectly correct in his statement that it did not always rain at Llan-y-morfa. The day after his arrival dawned bright and warm, so that even that confirmed cynic, when he looked out on a two mile bay of smooth, firm, golden sand, bounded on either hand by a huge mountainous promontory, was obliged to confess to himself that Maxwell might have selected a worse locality. He did not acknowledge this at the breakfast table.

"Now, look here," was his greeting, "if any of you good people can give me a rational description of this place Llang something and its attractions, I shall be obliged. Only don't gush, please. I can't stand gushing, and I can't stand the picturesque. So if you gush I shall go back to bed."

"As I think I am the least likely to be charged with 'gushing,' as you call it, perhaps I had better become your guide-book," answered Maxwell. "Let me tell you that Llan-y-morfa is extremely dull; but then it is the mitigated dullness of utter stagnation, not the miserable dullness of a third rate English bathing place, where everyone is trying to be lively and failing. No, there is neither parade, nor spa, nor band, nor assembly rooms, nor any other resorts of that nature. But to console you, there are mountains, and lakes, and the sea; good climbing, fishing, and bathing. What more would you have?"

"Oh yes, I know. Please don't toss

your beard, and look at me in that 'I
pause for a reply' manner; since I am
here I mean to be very good and muscular,
and hard-reading, and generally virtuous.
At the same time I have a private opinion,
you know, about mountains, and I think
them a horrible mistake and a horrible
nuisance. Why on earth couldn't Nature
be content to lie flat, instead of bumping
up in hillocks like a school apple-pie? It
is a waste of energy on her part; I think
a mountain always means—to me at least
—a great deal of fatigue and a great deal
of perspiration, and all for nothing but to
be a few feet nearer the sky than some
other Tom fool. Why not say you have
been up there, as Sheridan advised his son
about the mine? People tell so many lies
themselves, that they dare not find you out."

But his harangue was interrupted by
Charlie Burke, who, taking him to the
open window made him crane his neck

round the corner, to look at a great mass
some twelve or fifteen miles off.

"Do you see that, Ponsonby?

"Certainly—quite enough, thank you,
if it's all the same to you I will go on with
my breakfast.   Well, what is that?"

"That's Carnedd Llewelyn."

"I have no objection I am sure.   But
what has the gentleman with the Welsh
name to do with me, or I with him?"

"You'll have to go up him some of
these days.   I have been; we all have
been, and you will go too.   He is a
glorious fellow, and only one hundred and
fifteen feet less than Snowdon."

Cyril looked appealingly to Maxwell; but
he only laughed and said,

"You will find it best to give in, Burke
has gone mad about the mountains and
makes us do as he likes to the peril of our
necks.   Never mind, Burke, I take it out
of you of a morning, my boy, do I not?"

"Indeed and you do, Mr. Maxwell, I never knew what a hardworking fellow I was until I came down here. I shall have to change my mind, and go in for honours with the rest of the 'swells' I think. Now you look here, Pon," to Ponsonby, "I am going to take you as my private pupil in athletics and that sort of thing, and I'll undertake to turn you out in such form that your people won't know you; and so in earnest of our compact, if you hand me your cigar case, I'll smoke a weed, mine are all gone and your taste is the same as mine. I am going out to look at Sir Roger."

"I'll come too," replied Cyril, to every one's amazement, especially Maxwell, who declared, with a laugh, that Burke had certainly been taking lessons of Mr. Rarey, and had cast a spell over the languid Cyril. But as the reader may suppose, that young gentleman had his reasons.

"My dear Burke," he said, as they were walking down together to the stables, where the much vaunted Sir Roger was kept, "you are not clever, you know. I don't mean to be personal or offensive, but that is the fact. Nevertheless, I think you can see straight before your nose about as well as any other man I know of. Now you have been down here for the last ten days and have been about with my good cousin, so you can answer a simple question about him. What on earth makes him as gloomy as he is? I can't quite see my way clear to it. He is not generally a down-hearted fellow, and I know he is not over-anxious about his class, and though he is in love, that need not make him so like a gloomy Gorilla," finished Cyril, by way of a simile. "Now do you know whether anything is up?"

"Well, you know," replied Burke, not

over lucidly, "the question is not what I know, you know, but whether Fordyce would like me to tell you, you see what I mean ?"

" I see you're a long-eared ass," mentally ejaculated Cyril; but outwardly he only said, "quite right, oh, my beloved Burke! quite right. At the same time displaying a caution I admire and respect. But suppose I were to relieve your mind by saying that Maxwell has already told me what he knows, I suppose you would have no objection to do the same."

"" Oh, you know, dash it all, that alters the question altogether. Of course I don't know much, but you shall have that much. It is all about some religious botheration old Fordyce is in. You know he has gone in for that line ever since Brydges' death; he seems to think he had something to do with it—though how he could help it if the pony chose to bolt when Brydges was driving, I don't know —and what with religion, and what with his class, and what with being in love, and what with his going to be a parson, he seems in no end of a stew and as lively as a fish out of water. So that is all I know, and I should have told you at once, only I thought that as John Fordyce had not told you himself, perhaps he didn't want you to know."

"And having disposed of this matter, perhaps you can help me in one more, if there be no mystery in it; may I enquire what is up with Edgar Purcell, that he too should be absent and *distrait*, and given more than usually to blushing? Has he run away with a Sister of Mercy, and is afraid to meet old Marbecke, or what is it?"

"Oh, Purcell?" shouted the unreserved youth, "it's the jolliest lark in the world;

he is spooney, awfully spooney, about some girl he met last Long; and now he's in no end of a stew because he thinks parsons ought not to marry, and does not know what to do?"

"Has he asked the young lady in question her opinion upon the subject?"

"Why, no; that is the lark. I believe he had made up his mind to throw old Marbecke and all his nonsense over, and actually went down to Malvern to look the girl up, and when he got there the cupboard was bare, or at least she and her father had gone, and he could not get their address. So he is in a hole, you see."

"Upon my honour, I have fallen on a nice nest of cheerful lovers," observed Cyril, contemplatively. "And you, my son, are your tender affections engaged; have you any amatory or religious troubles to confide to me? if so, open your heart, and unburden your bosom, I am ready to hearken."

"Not I," said jolly little Burke, "that isn't my line, old fellow. I trust in God, and keep my powder dry, you know. Time enough for that ten years hence, when I settle down and imitate the governor; but your C. B. does not see things in that light yet. Here we are at the stable, come and have a look at Sir Roger."

And accordingly that noble animal was admired and slapped, and "come overed," much to his own and his master's content.

The little company very soon shook down into their several places; each having his special predilection and occupation, besides the idea of reading which had brought them all together. Maxwell, in addition to the magazine and review work to which he generally gave his spare moments, was briskly engaged upon a large work on certain matters of Church History.

As his mornings were taken up by his reading with the young men, and the afternoons given up to some ramble or excursion, the evening was the only time at his disposal for his private work—occasionally prolonged far into the night after his pupils had retired and all was still. John and Cyril both devoted many hours to their necessary work for " Greats," either alone, together, or with Maxwell. In the afternoons they generally joined the rest of the circle in fishing and boating, or gave themselves up to sturdy Charlie Burke, to be guided up some mountain which he had previously explored. In the evening, when the day's work was all over, John would lounge down to the beach *solus*, and smoke moodily and thoughtfully.

He was very grave and constrained

now; not as ready for a joke as usual, silent and rather melancholy. All the rest felt that some shadow was over him, and even Maxwell, who knew its cause, could effect but little to cheer him.

"It's no use talking, now, Maxwell," he would reply, "when all is settled you shall know. But I have a knot to untie, and my hands alone can do it. I must decide on my future before I leave this, and when I have I will tell you."

And Maxwell would answer him,

"You know best, John, my boy, you know best. If you want help or advice, here is such as I have to give; but, as you say, I don't quite know what good it will do you; but if you want a friend, here he is always ready for you, never better pleased than when you use him."

Charlie Burke and Edgar Purcell were both goaded on by Maxwell to get through a respectable amount of work, and then sought their relaxation each in his special way; the former in long gallops on his beloved horse, in fishing—nearly always unsuccessfully—for trout, in boating and in mountain excursions on which he generally lost his way.

Purcell was decidedly "spooney," as Burke phrased it, being not only in the agonies of love, but of indecision also. In the year which had passed since the memorable battle of Malvern Hills, and his acquaintance with Myrtle, many and various thoughts had been revolving in his breast. On his return to Oxford, it was not long before Marbecke gained nearly his old ascendancy over him. The word "nearly" is inserted advisedly; for whereas before, every thought and fancy and wish had been offered up to the gaze and inspection of his spiritual director, now the recesses of his heart held one little sacred

chamber, into which the eyes of his grand
inquisitor were not permitted to peep.
And there was enshrined the name of
" Myrtle." No word, no allusion ever
fell from him which could reveal the
Malvern adventure to the austere Marbecke. He confessed his sins, but this
he thought was no sin. He spoke of plans
for the future; but on this point he had
no fixed plans, only uncertain hopes—and
hopes he need not refer to. But then
how about celibacy and monasticism?
Ah, there was the rub! He could not
be a monk and marry Myrtle Harding.
That was certain; but was it absolutely
necessary that he should become a monk?
Was his call to be the first English monk
since " that unhappy Reformation " so
very clear? was the scheme so feasible
as it once had seemed? was he so indu-
bitably fitted to encounter the difficulties
which beset the founder or restorer of

a system? Mark you, his ideas respecting
his ordination had altered not one jot.
He would still in any case be ordained,
with this difference. Celibacy no longer
appeared an absolutely necessary part of
the priestly life. Every day he saw and
heard of leaders of the Tractarian party
who were married men. Every day he
saw instances of pert young curates who
had rapturously upheld the superiority
of celibacy, and lamented "Alas, my
brother!" when any poor wight was
deluded into matrimony, succumb to the
same fatal influence themselves. What
was he to say then? If Marbecke yet
was unmarried, might it not be—first,
that he cared for no woman, or, secondly,
that no woman cared for him. Possibly
to play Abelard to the Heloise of Sisters
Mary, Catherine, or Theresa suited him
better. Certainly they treated him with
a reverence and awe mingled with affec-

tionate adoration, which few wives could be brought to render.

Such and such like thoughts passed though Edgar's mind, now raising him to the clouds, and now casting him to the ground, until at length he resolved to rush down to Malvern, try his fate, and leave all minor points to arrange themselves. With what success the reader has learnt. He found Link Cottage "empty, swept and garnished," with a bill of "To let," the Major having departed six months before, and no one being able to give him certain information of his whereabouts. What was left the unhappy youth after this but to tear his clothes, cast dust on his head, and return to Oxford tenanted by seven devils, by name; Doubt, Despair, Irresolution, Regret, Peevishness, Self-accusation and Hopeless Love, which accordingly after a fashion he did, and actually brought

his houseful of devils down to Llan-y-
morfa.

To turn from John and Purcell to the
philosophical Cyril is like stepping from
a volcano to an iceberg. He was neither
in love nor doubt, and accepted facts with
his usual cool indifference, mildly grumbling at nature occasionally for the amount
of boredom she made him undergo. He
worked, it is true, and worked hard also.
Maxwell saw to that; but it was neither
very steady nor regular, and would be
broken by intervals when a sofa, a
cigar and novel constituted, he declared,
his whole idea of existence. When this
fit was on him, it was no use teasing
or baiting him; he was immoveable
and impenetrable, having a lazy retort
for every sarcasm launched at him,
until his friends gave him up in despair and let him have his own way.
After one of these fits he would say to

himself during the intervals of smoking,

"This will not do, you know. You are getting idle, Cyril, idle, and with you idleness means mischief. Don't you know that Shaitan always finds a nice little piece of work for all pairs of hands he may find idle? Pon my honour he'll have to look you up soon."

CHAPTER XII.

MRS. EVANS had taken Cyril specially under her charge, believing him to be delicate and weakly. Many were the little messes and particular dishes prepared for her favourite, " who was so gentle and sleepy like," and much care did the good woman take of her self-chosen pet and nursling. The softest pillows, the most comfortable easy chair; the night-cap of eggflip; the early draught of rum and milk; all these were the lot of Cyril Ponsonby: purchased for him by a pale, interesting face, a languid air, a gentle smile, and a civil if not animated manner of speech.

One afternoon he had complained of

headache, and employed it as an excuse for staying at home in the general sitting room, while the others went out for a sail. He was lying on the sofa reading and yawning when the hostess entered softly.

"I have brought you my salts, Mr. Ponsonby, I heard you say you had a nasty headache, and they're what I always use myself when I has them. I hope we didn't disturb you last night, Sir? Did you sleep well?"

"I slept the sleep of the just, I am happy to say, Mrs. Evans. I always do sleep well. In fact I prefer to sleep well and therefore do so. But how disturb— what was to disturb me?"

"Oh, Sir, nothing much. Only when you are delicate like, a slight thing will stir a body up and put you about. Yes, indeed. Why, Sir, my niece came late last night—not unlooked for, quite, because I had written to bid her come. Not that I expected her to come in the middle of the night, a knocking me and Evans out of bed and bringing my heart into my mouth; I was that frightened you might have knocked me down with a feather. I thought it was a wreck a knocking and calling Evans down to his duty."

"But may I ask how your niece came to arrive so late?"

"Oh, Sir, it was along of them nasty engines breaking down between here and Chester. Yes, sure they did, and kept her waiting and shivering in the middle of the night, which isn't at all proper for a young female, let alone one respectably brought up to be a doing of. But, however, she has caught no cold, that's one mercy. But here I am standing talking to you when your poor head's a'aching, and I ought to be up to the Old Town. If you want anything while I'm out, Sir, Lucy shall bring it you, for our Mary

Anne's got a bad tooth and that cross that I sent her off to bed as soon as I saw her face."

And so Mrs. Evans talked herself away, and in a brief while Cyril saw her sturdy form trudging up the rocky point on which the Old Town was situated. Left to himself he yawned, attempted to read, yawned again, and finally thought he wanted something. That something could have been easily procured by adjourning to his bedroom adjacent, being simply a glass of water. And such, under ordinary circumstances, would have been his course of proceeding. For some reason, however, he did not so to-day, but rang the bell instead. In a minute or so he heard a light step, and in answer to his "come in," there entered Mrs. Evans' niece, a young girl of about eighteen or nineteen.

Lucy Stainer was one of those charming *blondes*, of whom you read so often in novels, and meet so seldom in life, especially humble life. An elegant, well set up figure, surmounted by a small delicate head, rather pale complexion, dark violet purple eyes, slightly sensuous mouth, and long wavy, not curly, hair, half gold, half auburn; this certainly is a rare combination, and yet it only does scant justice to Lucy Stainer. That she was conscious of her charms is only true, what beautiful woman is not? but at the same time, no one could be more modest and quiet in her manner. She moved about with a gentle grace, and at the same time had an air of languor which became her well. Her great blue eyes opened to the full when she saw Cyril's reclining figure, and she paused to know his wants. He made an unwonted exertion and sat up.

"Upon my honour, I am ashamed to have troubled you, I thought Mrs. Evans was in; I have not an idea whom I have the pleasure of addressing?"

"Pray don't apologise, Sir; my name is Lucy Stainer, and I am Mrs. Evans' niece. She is out, and as the servant is ill, I came in her place. Can I do anything for you?"

"I really could not think of troubling you, Miss Stainer. Yes, you must be the niece who arrived late last night; some accident, I think; I do so hope you are none the worse for the fright, you do not look very strong—pale, you know."

"I always look so, I believe, Sir, it's the work, and the late hours I'm obliged to keep. But is there—"

"Late hours! ah, I am very sorry to hear that. I am somewhat an invalid myself, and know how trying they are. You spoke of work, will you excuse me if I ask of what nature?"

"I am apprenticed to a milliner in

Chester, and live with her since my parents died. I am an orphan now, and Aunt Sarah is my only relation. She is very kind to me, and I come here every summer for my holidays."

"What a charming arrangement, and what a good woman your aunt is—it must be nice to be so good—she is very kind to me also, far more than I deserve. But if your hours are so late, do you not find your work a little wearisome, Miss Stainer? I don't think you can care much about it."

"Indeed no, Sir, it's fidgetty work, at best, and sometimes I am sorry I ever chose it. But there are so few things a poor girl can do, and I thought I should like it better than being a lady's-maid. I suppose I shall get used to it."

"I don't think you ever will," replied Cyril, gently reclining his head on the sofa-pillow, and looking at her through his half shut eyes, "I am sure you do not look fitted to be either a milliner or a lady's-maid. Lady's-maid, indeed! dependant upon the whims of some a—a—minion of fashion."

He was at a loss for a wind up, and so threw in this phrase, culled from the halfpenny literature of the day.

"That was it; I had read so much of the airs fine ladies give themselves, that I thought I should like to be more independent."

"Oh, you are a great reader, are you? Please don't go yet, you cannot think how soothing a little talk is to my poor aching head; and what kind of books do you prefer?"

Lucy smiled as she replied,

"I don't much care for history, or that sort of serious books, Sir; but I do enjoy a novel when I can get one from the library. It is such a change after sitting stitch, stitch, stitch, all day long; it seems like taking one into another world. I often sit up an hour or so instead of going to bed, to finish some tale."

"Ah, I see our tastes are the same. I am a tremendous novel reader, and, like you, I read them to get away from the hard, matter-of-fact world I find around me, and forget my troubles." And he looked very melancholy and romantic indeed. "Tell me some you have read, perhaps I know them too."

"Oh, I can scarcely remember them, there are so many, and sometimes one puts the other out of my head." And she ran through a long list of the usual type, ending however with 'Lady Audley's Secret,' "and I was just in that when Aunt wrote to me to come here, and I was just coming to the most interesting part, and then I had to put it away, and pack."

"If that has caused your grief, Miss Stainer, I can soon remove it, for I happen to have it here amongst the books

I brought, so, if it can afford you one moment's amusement, I beg you will take it or any other book I have."

"I am sure, Sir, you are very kind," said Lucy, the colour flushing up in her pale cheeks with pleasure, "very kind indeed; but I could not think of such a liberty as to borrow one of your books; and, besides, what would Aunt say?"

"My dear child," said Cyril, in the most paternal manner, "I scarcely think it desirable or necessary for your dear good Aunt to know anything about it. Not, mind you, that there is any possible harm in it, or I should be the last person to advise you. But, you know, old-fashioned people have their own ideas even about the most innocent things, and it is as well, therefore, to respect and humour them. As for the books, my own mother and sisters read them, so there can be no reason why you should not.

Take them when you like, and either
return them when you see me, or
keep them in your room until convenient.
Ah, there is your kind aunt coming back,
I see; how industrious she is. There is
the second volume. You can't think how
much good a chat with you has done me.
Good-bye till we meet again." The door
closed, and Cyril sat upright on his sofa,
looking round the room. " Yes; there *is*
a wonderful dispensation of events; there
really is. I was murmuring against
Fortune for permitting me to be so bored
in this abominable Welsh place, and here
she sends me a jewel of the first water. I
was beginning to say ' *toujours perdrix,*'
and she pops a truffle into my mouth.
Lucy—a sweet little name, and a sweet
little owner, a beam to lighten my darkness. Oh, *lux beata!* Cyril, my good
fellow, you may be idle, your enemies say
you are; you may be listless, your ene-

mies say that also ; but you are benevolent
—it is a way you have—and here is a
fitting case for your benevolence. Feed
the hungry, give drink to the thirsty,
succour the destitute—why so I will,
and this shall be the object of my charity."

Which was but a fantastical way of
expressing his desire to amuse himself.
As yet he meant no harm, certainly not,
he never did mean any harm—only somehow he did it in the end. As he would
say, " things happened." And as he had
not the slightest idea of resisting any
temptation which arose, the chances were
that his whim and fancy of the moment
would always carry him along in triumph.
He was indolently selfish, a type common,
and the more dangerous, because not
openly repulsive. And so commenced, in
thoughtlessness on one side, and unsus-
pecting innocence on the other—the old,
old game, so often played, so often fatal

to one, if not both. If Hell be mainly paved with good intentions, surely some part, some vestibule, let us say, is paved with no intentions at all. There is a '*tertium quid*' between meaning well and meaning ill—meaning nothing—and sometimes it is the most dangerous.

So passed the time at Llan-y-morfa.

CHAPTER XIII.

THE sun had gone down all golden
in a sea of crimson and silver; a
fog cloud was creeping out seaward, and
a chilly night beginning to make itself
felt. Yet still John Fordyce continued
to pace up and down upon the sea-shore
of Llan-y-morfa. Crash, crash, crash he
tramped along among shingle and pebbles,
and sand, and sea-weed, now pausing to
watch some boisterous wave expend its
strength and dissipate itself in creamy
froth upon the beach, now making ducks
and drakes with a chance smooth flake
of stone or slate, now picking up and
trifling with a long ribbon of seaweed,

and ever puffing away half moodily, half
carelessly at his short ' clay.'

There is no better place for thought
than the sea-side. The changeless and
yet ever changeful accompaniment of the
waves harmonises with every melody or
discord which the human heart can frame.
In whatever mood a man may be, he
will find sympathy by the sea; that is,
he will be able to extract from its
murmurs the exact tone he wishes to
hear.

So at least thought John, as he strode
up and down by himself. Far away to
the right a line of gas-lamps marked the
fashionable quarter of Llan-y-morfa. To
the left, one pale glimmering light denoted some signal station; while shore-
ward in gradual, though constant
march, rose the purple downs, from
which the keen wind I mentioned came
pouring down. The sunset colour faded

from the sky, leaving only as it were its echo on the horizon, where pale cinnamon hues and tender green were barred with long level reaches of darker purple floating off to the upper grey cloud bank. One of those subtle harmonies of delicate colour which a careless or vulgar mind utterly ignores, but which form half the pleasures of life to more cultivated minds.

Presently there appears a small speck of glowing light, which reveals itself as the tip of a cigar in the mouth of the Rev. A. Maxwell.

"John, my boy, I thought I should find you here. I have left those three in-doors and came down for a saunter and a talk."

"Glad I am you came. I had just made up my mind to speak to you, and would rather do so here in the open air than in the house."

"Is it treason, then, my dear boy, or do you fear pretty little Lucy's ears?"

"No treason, at least, but something sufficiently serious. Maxwell, you have known of my religious doubts and scruples for long, have you not?"

"Yes, John, known and respected both you and them. If I have not—"

"You were going to say, if you have not taken a more active part in advice and suggestion it was because I did not seek it? If I did not so, you will know it was from no distrust or coldness. I am not one who can easily lay bare the inner mysteries of my soul, and talk of them as men do of the weather. To me they seem too awful and sacred. And so in silence, and I may say mental solitude, I have 'eaten my heart.' But I knew that when my mind was fully made up, I might safely come to

you for your open, unbiassed opinion
of the decision I had arrived at."

"You are right, John. And is that
time come?"

"It is. I have now carefully reviewed
my religious faith as in the presence of
my Maker, and the result is that I
cannot take orders in the Church of
England."

"I cannot say I am altogether unpre-
pared for this. Months ago, when you
first mentioned your doubts and difficulties to me, I foresaw they might end thus.
I recognised your case as one in which
very little external help could be given.
It was not a hesitation between England
and Rome, or a mere technical difficulty,
or a matter of authority and rubrics. It
was just a question, the solution of which
could come from one source only." And he
raised his hat reverently. "To interpose
between you and your Maker seemed to

me sacrilege, and I forbore accordingly. If you remember, I referred you to the Scripture as your best guide and to that, as I take it, you have gone. As long as you can justify your decision to your conscience, I cannot say a word. Still I should like to know, if you do not mind, the process by which you have reached this determination."

"You shall—as well at least as I can describe my own feelings. As you advised, I endeavoured to approach the subject in an unbiassed manner, as a Christian but not as a Church of England man, or as an intending clergyman. For what I know, I have kept these ideas distinct and separate, and can honestly say that I have not looked in the Scriptures to discover any favourite system of mine own. Well, the Church of God indeed I found, a kingdom broad, infinite, catholic as declared by Christ. This Catholic Church, indeed, I

recognize as divine and infallible, as worthy
of an All-wise and All-merciful Creator.
But in it I see no such dogmatic teaching
as men have engrafted on the simple
doctrines of Christ. To me it appears to
depend solely on the recognition of Christ's
mission and the sincere imitation of his
example. In his teaching, I recognise
none of those doctrines and quibbles
which have convulsed Christendom. I see
universal love and charity, meekness, self-
denial and good works upheld as necessary,
and I see mere legal ceremonialism, narrow
mindedness and exclusiveness denounced.
It is a Faith which the simplest may grasp,
believe and carry into practise, but alas! its
very simplicity seems to have made it
distasteful to men after the first burst of
enthusiasm was past. With the necessity
of some organisation appears to have
come the rise of sacerdotalism, of priestly
power, of dogmatic teaching, and ulti-

mately of the substitution of an elaborate
system of rites and ceremonies burden-
some as the old Judæan law. The Church
of God seems to me to have gradually
been narrowed and narrowed until the
monstrous end is reached, that all who
do not accept a creed consisting of human
propositions and deductions are excluded
from salvation.

"Maxwell, it is this human interference
in the Divine which revolts me. I feel
God's voice speaking to me within my
conscience. I recognise His voice speaking
through the pages of Scripture, I recognise
the teaching of Christ in the gospels; and
all this is to me simple, intelligible, all-
holy. What right, then, has any man
made like myself to say to me, 'Unless
you believe this or that you cannot be
saved?' Where can you find Christ's
promise that any particular set of men
should have the power to draw up infal-

lible dogmas and creeds? And if they claim Christ's parting promise that He would be with them even to the end of the world, how can this honestly be made to mean more than that presence of his within the heart of every faithful follower, how can it be made a ground for claiming his prerogatives, and acting as his vice-gerents? To a clergyman, as a messenger of good tidings, in God's name, as a minister of Christ's teaching, as one who has professionally studied Holy writ, I will at all times listen gladly, but when he claims powers of binding and loosing spiritually, of narrowing the path of life, and declaring who is and who is not saved, then and there we part.

" So then, though I fully and thankfully acknowledge that Catholic Church, of which all who love God and Christ are members, I do not, and cannot recog-nise the infallibility of any section or branch, however high sounding its title. To me they are mere human economical systems; embracing, indeed, the great central truth, but overlaying it with much that is unnecessary and undesirable.

"I fully believe that the Churches of England, Rome, &c., are paths to salvation; but then I believe as much of any dissenting congregation you can name. Religion, in a word, is a matter between God and our conscience, and no man has the right or power to interfere or dictate whatever may be the conclusions to which his brother may honestly come. I have laid the matter before my God, and have asked His guidance. I accept, therefore, the conclusions to which I have come with all humility.

"With regard to the Church of England, while fully recognising the fact of salvation being attainable by her, her position appears to me almost inexplicable.

Her very existence seems one long, and not always dignified, compromise between Church and State, between Catholicism and Protestantism, between Authority and Reason. Comprising within her pale a party bordering on Romanism, a second dissenting in all but name, and a third who carry their doctrines to the verge of scepticism—all alike appeal to the same Formularies and Articles of Faith, all alike claim to be the true representative minds of the English Church. And yet this Church claims direct authority, upholds certain dogmatic teaching, applies tests to those without her pale, and brands them with the title of dissenters. How, with justice, deny to these men the right to secede from her, which she claimed so vigorously and applied so effectively to the Roman Catholic Church? Where draw the line and say, ' Thus far mayest thou reform, but no further.'

"What respect, what reverence and obedience can I pay to a Church which neither is able to give any certain ground of doctrine, believing it necessary to salvation, or to enforce discipline and uniformity, whether in teaching or practice upon her ministers and members? How—even were my ideas other than they are—how could I believe in a Church from whose pulpits you may hear the most contradictory and opposing doctrines maintained, and whose difference from Rome is far exceeded by that existing between her own parties and sects? No, Maxwell, if, as I said before, my ideas about the Church of Christ were not what I have described, a Minister of the English Church I could never be."

"God forbid you should do violence to your conscience. That I should be the last to advise. I am aware that by a process of jugglery rather too

often practised now, you might possibly
accept the Articles after a fashion, and
take orders, notwithstanding your ideas
and belief; but it must be by the sacrifice
of every principle of honesty and manly
honour, by closing your eyes lest you
should see light, and by a daily negation
of truth. No, your decision so far is right
and just, and as a Minister of the English
Church, and, I hope, an honest man, I
cannot gainsay it. Disappointed, of
course, I am; for in many points we
agree so heartily that I had entertained
hopes we might perhaps have worked together. But let that pass. I have listened
very carefully to all you have said, and
though I thoroughly sympathise, I do not
agree with all. I do not speak now for
argument's sake, or with the idea of con-
verting you, but simply because, reasoning
from the same premises, I arrive at a
rather different conclusion.

"I fully believe that the infallibility Christ spoke of refers to the universal body of believers, and not to what is technically called the Catholic Church, or to any national branch of it. I believe it points to the ultimate triumph of good over evil, and not to the invariable truth of any system of dogmatic teaching. Still for all that, though conscience alone is the highest guide of life, and the spiritual communion of the heart of man with his Maker, the highest religious act, man is so constituted that he requires some system and order for the external expression of his religion. Hence what we call Churches, which after all are but human efforts to crystallise and preserve certain doctrines contained in and held by the whole universal body, or Catholic Church, as we understand it. With the necessity of a human element come also the attendant dangers of prejudice, obstinacy, and mere ceremonialism. Like men regarding nature through variously coloured glasses, each set of men, each national church gives its own colouring to the broad doctrines of Christianity, and hence we get sectional teaching. With an exaggeration of that respect due to antiquity, we get traditional teaching with all its merits and defects. And from a somewhat one-sided view of the exceptional conduct of the Apostles and first Christians, we get sacerdotalism and ceremonialism.

"Still for all this, just as a precious jewel is safest in a casket, however poor and humble that casket may be, so the precious truths which Christ came to teach are enshrined even among the manifold errors and corruptions of human systems. And for this reason, those incongruities in the Church of England which distress you so, affect me not at all. I am able to preach Christ; I find in her sufficient of truth for salvation; I am content to leave to others subtle points and distinctions, doctrinal disputes and sectarian jealousies, and to embrace and stand by all that is broad and noble in her. I think that on the whole—compromised as she is—she reflects faithfully the mind of England, and as such I respect her. I think you regard her with somewhat of *animus;* perhaps, though, it is only natural."

"I may have expressed myself more bitterly than I feel. I meant only to denote the horror with which I look upon the idea of orders in my own case."

"Then there we are heartily agreed. As for other points, no possible good could come of argument between us. You are possessed of equal mental abilities with myself, you have studied the matter calmly, and in an unbiassed manner, and after prayerful consideration have arrived at conclusions from some of which I differ. Your conscience is satisfied, what then have I to do? It is not as if we differed upon a matter of fact and history, in which arguments brought forward by me might be of use. It is a matter of faith and opinion, and must be left to God to alter and solve. The history of God's dealings with Man is the history of Religion, that of Man's dealings with his fellow-men the history of intolerance. And now to another subject. Have you thought well of the result of all this?"

"Yes, indeed, thought till my heart is nearly sick and faint. I know well how disappointed and angry my father will be. You know the family living was to have been mine."

"I know it. It is a part of a vile

system altogether. Parents are very fond
of playing the part of Abraham, and offering up a sacrifice of their children. I
often think that mothers believe the
sacrifice of one son as a clergyman, against
his will, prevails to save the other sons in
the world who are a "little fast." However, this has nothing to do with your
case. Do you intend openly leaving the
Church of England?"

"Oh, no, far from it. Although I do
not care for her forms and ritual, they
would not be sufficient to keep me from
her worship. I suppose, after all, I shall
not be worse than many another layman
who calls himself a Churchman."

"True; half what is styled 'sound
Churchmanship' is simply a lazy acquiescence in certain forms and doctrines
which the 'Churchman' is too indifferent
to question or examine. Men of that type
prefer their food ready cooked, without

the trouble of selection. Often the best Churchman is the man who is content to shut his eyes tight, open his mouth wide, and swallow all placed therein by his spiritual cook."

"But in the very fact of my remaining a conforming member of the Church of England, and yet declining to become a minister, will be the great difficulty to my father. If I were to become a Dissenter or Roman Catholic, he would be more disposed to pardon me; but my position will appear to him inexplicable. However, I need not anticipate troubles which will come only too soon. I shall not tell him my determination until I am ready to leave college."

"Better so. I want you to do well in the schools, and so you had best avoid any domestic disturbances previous. Well, John, though I cannot say I am not grieved in some points, I can say that I am proud of you as an honest man, and one whom I hope always to call my friend. Shake hands, my boy, and remember however coldly the world and old acquaintances may regard you in the future, I shall never change or alter my affection for you."

And so, with a great hand-grip, the two men went in out of the cold night air.

CHAPTER XIV.

THE reading party at Llan-y-morfa came to an end, and the friends parted to meet again a little later at Oxford.

As the day of the examination drew near, John's time was more and more occupied by the work he still had to get through, which left him little leisure, save to write a few lines to Edith daily, and to take the constitutional on which Maxwell insisted. Cyril, however, was not to be disturbed from his usual listless mood. At night, it is true, he worked tremendously hard, harder than he cared to confess. But his days were spent as if no

such event as "Greats" were imminent.
He pronounced himself a waiter on Providence, and certainly sustained that character very well. Tutors remonstrated in
vain; he declared that his health did not
allow of hard work; he was not equal to
the exertion, and was prepared to take
the consequences.

One Sunday morning about a week
before the examination began, the two
cousins were seated at breakfast in
John's lodgings. The said lodgings
consisted of, perhaps, the ugliest room
which author or reader ever saw, or
imagined.

The sitting-room looked into a back
street, and its staring paper of grim
pattern, its rhubarb-coloured curtains, and
flaming, though ragged carpet, showed
that the landlady must really have studied
long to compress so much ugliness into a
space twelve feet square. Ornaments of

any kind there were none. An old-fashioned print of John Wesley in a little black
and gold frame hung over the fire place,
but that was all. Tables and chairs were
heaped with papers and books, pens and
writing materials were to be seen everywhere, and tidiness there was not. Cyril
had often joked his cousin about his
hideous lodgings, and John had as often
replied, that "they suited him." Cyril's,
I need scarcely say, were all that is delightful.

"I say, John," enquired Cyril after a
long pause as he flicked the ash off his
cigar, "do you care much about your
class, that you work so confoundedly
hard? It can't make much difference to
you."

"Difference? I don't know about that.
I shall be disappointed if I do badly in the
schools, I confess. And as for working
hard, I think every man is bound to do

his best and cultivate such powers as he has."

"I have a powerful amount of idleness in me, and think it right to cultivate that. So your work proceeds from abstract ideas of duty. Of all words I hate that most. It always means some disagreeable task which your adviser would not think of undertaking himself—a burden always fitted to a neighbour's shoulder. Now I go in for honours, simply because they will 'count' well in the life for which my infinitely wise father destines me—the Civil Service. But why you, who have no need to work, should choose to 'grind' like a nigger, I can't conceive."

"How do you mean I have no need to work?"

"Why, what will it matter to you as a parson whether you are a Pass or Class man? Who do you think of your congregation will care? The stupider a clergyman is the better, I think, as he is less likely to meddle in things which don't concern him."

"That I deny altogether. The wiser a clergyman is the better he knows his own business, and the better able he is to perform it. However, all your theories concern me little, as you will see when I tell you a piece of intelligence which you must know sooner or later. Mind, I do not wish it made generally known just yet. Cyril, I am not going to take orders."

Cyril, whose chair was tilted to an almost impossible angle, recovered his equilibrium and sat upright, genuine amaze on his face.

"Look here, you know, you musn't take my breath away in that manner, you really mustn't in the state of my nerves. You are not serious, you are trying a rise on me."

"My dear Cyril, I am perfectly serious, never more so in my life."

"Seriously deranged, you mean. And what possible combination of reasons can be strong enough to make you give up ease, comfort and £1,000 a year? What better chance have you in store?"

"Simply nothing. As for my reasons, I have religious scruples which prevent my taking orders."

"Good heavens! ye gods and little fishes! A man with, apparently, his full amount of faculties, in this nineteenth century talking about religious scruples, and weighing them against a good income! Why, man, I begin to be afraid you have a conscience!"

"Occasionally I think I have, cousin Cyril."

"Get rid of it by all means, my dear John; throw it overboard as the

most useless incumbrance you can have.
And in Oxford, too, of all places ! What
should a conscience do here ? Conscience
is always detrimental to a man's success
in the world; but at Oxford it is fatal.
That is the reason we have so many
comfortable dons. They are not troubled
that way, be sure of that. Then what on
earth do you think of doing, eh, my most
erratic cousin ?"

"Well, my plans are not yet made
up. Oh, I shall get on well enough,
I have no fear of that—Government
office—the Bar—anything."

"Ah ! that is the advantage of being
a rich man. After all, I suppose a
conscience is a mere *objet de luxe* like
truffles, or *pâté de foie gras ;* it certainly
is not a thing to run into debt for.
Well, each man knows his affairs best;
but your ideas strike me as slightly
crazy—if you will forgive the expression.

And what says the Reverend to this little game ?"

" 'The Reverend,' as you call him, has not yet been told by me. I am only waiting until this examination is over."

" Oh, you think a First will be a sop to Cerberus—if again you will pardon the expression. And Miss Masterman ?"

" Edith does not know," replied John, with a half sigh.

" Well, on the whole, I cannot say I envy you my dear, deluded, conscientious cousin. Rather than decline £1,000 a year, run the risk of infuriating a profitable parent and generally complicating matters, I would swallow all the tests, creeds, formulas, heresies and ' doxies' of every kind which have entered at any time into the heart of man. Why can't you do like other men and take your pill—as long as it is gilded—

without wry faces? I am like Theodore
Hook, and would sign thirty-nine, forty,
or forty thousand articles, at so much per
article, even including the quite unintelligible seventeenth."

"Come, come, my dear fellow, I know
it is your whim to make yourself out
worse than you really are. But that is
what I will never believe. You would not
take upon yourself the most serious
obligations and duties imaginable, without
the slightest intention of carrying them
out. You would not preach and teach
what you did not believe yourself, or enter
on a sacred office simply for the income
attached."

"My dear and most innocent cousin,
you being a guileless and most conscientious dove, think in your boundless
charity that all the rest of the world
resembles yourself. As for the clerical
duties, beyond going through a certain

amount of mechanical movement, very
much like military drill, preaching, marrying, &c., making friends with your
rich parishioners, dining with them and
keeping them in good humour, and dun-
ning the bishop to promote you to
something better; I am at a loss to see
what they are. Doctrine? Well, as no
two parsons seem quite to agree there, I
suppose, you might take your choice;
certainly the results are the same in all
cases. And, of course, as faith is so far
superior to sight, the less intelligence the
greater merit. Money is a thing we
know despised by all the clergy—in their
sermons—in which doubtless I should
follow them. Bah! John, the days are
gone for ever when parsons were looked
upon as something peculiarly sacred.
Isn't it St. Paul, who says something
about having 'treasure in earthen vessels?' Well, the treasure is gone, the

pots and pipkins remain. I think I should make just as good a crock as many another man who makes a noise in the world, and is run after by silly women and idiotic youths. Perhaps, if my purse were more elastic, my conscience were less so."

"Are you much dipped, old fellow?" asked John, in his kindly way.

"Last night, by way of amusement, I made a rough schedule of my debts. The state of things stands thus: My governor allows me exactly £200 per annum, a ridiculous sum, which possibly might pay my tailor, certainly no one else. This your good father and my most reverend uncle has kindly supplemented with £150, total per annum, £350; total allowance in three and a half years about £1,230. Now, for many reasons, it was more convenient and pleasant for me to live at the rate of £800 per annum than the former sum. And so, with that adaptability of mind which is my chief merit, I did so. Now observe, three and a half years at £800 a year, amounts exactly, if I am right, to £2,800. Deduct £1,230, and you have a residue of £1,570; to that add a cautionary margin say of £230, and you have a grand result of £1,800, which, as far as I can see, represents my total indebtedness in Oxford and elsewhere. You are shocked, I perceive, but without reason. You walk by sight, I by faith. Something will happen, and if not—something else. 'Am I not ashamed?' you ask. 'Not in the least,' I respond. 'Does it make me uncomfortable?' 'Certainly not.' 'Do I know how to pay it?' 'I neither know nor care.' I tell you my faith is sufficient to fill that mustard-pot yonder, and I never allow trifles to disturb me. And now, if you will be so good as to look out of window, and tell me who that may be knocking at the door, you will oblige your affectionate cousin."

" Hulloh ! it's Maxwell. Whatever can bring him here at this time in the day." He had scarcely finished speaking when the door was thrown open, admitting their visitor, who looked pale and excited.

" I am very glad I have found you both in, very glad indeed, for I am come upon a rather serious errand."

" Is it to ask me to preach the University sermon, or to say you are made Provost of St. Wilfrid's ?" enquired Cyril.

" No, no, Cyril, I want you to be serious. No laughing now. I have just had a letter from the Rev. Arthur Bigman of Llan-y-morfa. What's the matter now, Ponsonby ?"

For that young gentleman had ejaculated a word which rhymed with " jam," and dropped his cigar.

" Matter ? simply that I have burned my finger with the ash of my cigar. Well, go on. What does the giant say ?"

" Very bad news. You both remember Mrs. Markham's pretty little niece, Lucy Stainer ?"

" Yes," and " yes," was the reply.

" She has left Llan-y-morfa, suddenly; run away, and left no trace behind."

" Good God ! how shocking," exclaimed John. " Do you mean she has run away with, or to any one ?"

" So it is supposed. What else could she have gone for ? Mrs. Markham was only too indulgent to her, and they had no quarrel of any kind."

" Do they suspect any one ?" asked Cyril, " surely they must have some clue ?"

" There are suspicions about, I am sorry to say; but there appears no certain ground to act upon."

" Why do you say 'you are sorry ?' "
asked both cousins in a breath.

" Because Bigman, in a manner, which
I think unjustifiable, points to the fact
of her having left so soon after our departure as suspicious. It is not so much
the suspicion itself, as the ungenerous
way in which it is expressed which angers
me."

" Do you mean, Maxwell, that he ac-
cuses any of us ?" asked John, indignantly.

" He certainly begs of me to demand
a denial, on oath, from my four pupils,
that they were connected with this painful business. By a wonderful effort of
charity, he does not include me."

" The fellow must be an idiot, as well as
an ungentlemanly beast," remarked Cyril.
" The man who would do such an act
would not hesitate to deny it, of course."

" I certainly do not mean to humiliate

both myself and you by requiring an oath
of any one of you. Your word as christian and honourable gentlemen is sufficient. Had I thought any of you capable
of such an act, I should neither have
asked, nor accepted, your companionship
to Llan-y-morfa. I may rely on you both
in this, I know."

"You have my solemn denial," replied
John.

"And mine," added Cyril, "and I
would beg to suggest to the Rev. Arthur
Bigman, that his suspicions, as well as
his charity, had better begin at home.
Spite of his ministrations, I dare say
Llan-y-morfa is not immaculate."

"It certainly is a very sad affair. Poor
little girl, she was such a bright gay little
maid, that one never thought of the possibility of so sad a fate. I sincerely trust
she may be found and reclaimed. I shall
write a few lines to her aunt as well as

to Bigman. Well, good morning to you
both. Now my errand is done, I will be
off."

About three weeks after this, appeared
that fatal list which was to carry triumph
or disappointment, exultation or woe to
many a heart. Charlie Burke, who was
only a Pass man, had received his Testa-
mur long before, and celebrated the fact
with the most gorgeous and festive wine
ever known at St. Margaret's. Nor were
our other friends altogether unsuccessful;
for in Classis I, we may read the name of
Fordyce, Johannes; in Classis II, of
Ponsonby, Cyrillus; while the asterisk
prefixed to Purcell, Arthurus, in Classis
IV, denotes that he has obtained an
" honorary fourth."

CHAPTER XV.

TO pass his examination in what is called the Second School, and to assume his bachelor's gown and title was got over by our hero as quickly as possible; accordingly at the end of the October term he was ready to bid farewell to his Oxford life. His mind was by this time fully prepared for the opposition he might expect at home. However, he wisely resolved to declare his intentions respecting the Church *vivâ voce*, and so only communicated the fact of his good degree to his father and Edith.

The head of his college was the first

to hear of his change of plans. It is the etiquette to pay a visit to him upon taking the degree and finally leaving college. Accordingly, John duly waited on Dr. Field. A little, active, bustling, round-about man was he, of excellent temper, although brusque and odd in manner. He had received too many sugar-plums from the Church not to admire her as a mother, and defend her system against all impugners. He had an unlimited belief in the power of money, and used to say that the best way of curing a man of heresy was to give him a good living.

He was standing in front of the fire when Fordyce was shewn in, and immediately placing his hands under his coat-tails, he mounted upon the fender-stool, along which. he walked up and down after the manner of a parrot, his head on one side, and his coat-tails, grasped in one hand, vibrating up and down.

"How do you do, Sir," he commenced, with a scowl which was meant for a smile, only the bushy eybrows intercepted it, "how do you do, Mr. Fordyce? Sit down, Sir, sit down. A very praiseworthy career, Sir, very much so, indeed, and I congratulate you."

The reader must be good enough to imagine each sentence "let off" like a cracker, and accompanied with a defiant jerk of the head, which seemed to say, "Just you contradict me, now, I should like to see you."

John thanked him for his kindness, and informed him that he was about to leave.

"Oh! dear me, Sir, you are in a great hurry, it seems. Yes, Sir, your career has been very praiseworthy on the whole. I didn't expect it. To tell you the truth, Sir, I thought at first you were a fool. Fast, you know, fast, fast, fast !" John regretted the fact that his early conduct had been very reprehensible. " Quite true, young man, quite true, Sir. Never mind now, let bygones be bygones. I dare say you will do very well, perhaps rise high in the Church. Your father—friend of mine—has told me of his plans for you, and I very much approve. When are we to be ordained, eh ?"

" To tell the truth, Dr. Field, my views on certain subjects have so changed, that I do not intend to take orders."

" Oh ! dear me, Sir !" exclaimed the little Doctor, for a moment shaken from his perch but instantly remounting; " oh ! dear me ! this—will—never—do, never do—at all, Sir. I don't understand this, young man—no, not at all. I should think you are silly, young man, eh? What are you, then, eh? A Mormon, a Methodist, a Mahomedan, a Monophysite, eh? This will never do. What business have you with any views at all, eh? Answer me that, Sir! Views—fiddlesticks!"

"I suppose, Sir, it would be desirable to have some views if I am to be a clergyman."

"Don't be ribald, Sir! I won't be insulted—no, not by the King! This, you know, is all very extraordinary, and quite irregular. There's no precedent for it, no precedent. You're an atheist, Sir, you're a fool, Sir, and I won't allow it. As long as you are in *statu pupilari* at St. Margaret's, I stand to you in the light of a father. I'm not sure but what the statutes would bear me out in giving you personal chastisement, and I should like to do it. Now you sit down and tell me quietly, if you can, what your objections are."

"They are these, Sir, as shortly as I can put them. I cannot undertake to preach and maintain, as necessary to salvation, doctrines which I cannot believe myself. I cannot force myself to believe the Articles which the Church of England binds her ministers to; and I do not think that doctrines and creeds drawn up by any man or assemblage of men, have the slightest power over the consciences of other men, and therefore I cannot become a clergyman."

"So foolish and brainhot a young man, in all my life never did I see," responded the Doctor, growing almost poetical in his indignation. "Here is a young man comes to college, plays the fool, then turns round and takes an excellent degree, and then, just as he ought to be ordained, and succeed in time to a living of eleven hundred a year—eleven hundred pounds a year, Sir—what does this young man do? Flies straight in the face of Providence, and because of some romantic silly ideas, refuses it. Ah, you have been in bad company, Sir, I can plainly perceive—don't you deny it. I will not be insulted and contradicted, Sir!" John had not said a word.

"A young man who talks about views and conscience is lost, Sir, lost! Young men should do as their elders and betters have done. Why, Sir, Andrews and Bramhall, and Jeremy Diddler—I mean, Taylor —have been priests before you; and you flout, and turn up your nose at English orders, forsooth! Conscience, indeed! do you think I should be a rector and the head of a house if I had talked about my conscience? Bah, Sir! get along with you. A knave I can away with, a fool I cannot abide!"

What was to be done in such a case? The conversation had not once turned upon any vital point at issue, and the little doctor's well meant, but rapid attacks did not allow John a moment for calm statements or defence. He rose at length to go, and thanking him for his kindness, regretted that his determination should have caused him so much annoyance.

"Annoyance, Sir? Yes, Sir. No, Sir, none at all; don't you flatter yourself you can annoy me with your nonsense. Eh? Who can help being annoyed at seeing a young man of promise and ability turning up his nose at the Church, and taking to preaching on a sugar-barrel, and singing hymns through his nose. There, go along, Sir, you are laughing, I can plainly perceive. So indecorous a young man I never have seen. Now, good-bye, and try to come to your senses.

Stay, here is a copy of my book on the 'Philosophy of the Very-Everything; with a Postscript, confuting Dr. Schlang-abad's Remarks on Infinite Nothingness.' Read that, and don't talk any more non-sense."

And now, a hand-to-hand encounter having taken place, and the heavy artillery of the enemy having been employed to no purpose, it remained to be seen what might be effected by following up the enemy, and pursuing him with a brisk cavalry charge. Dr. Field, despite all his eccentricities, was simply one of the kindest little men in the universe. He delighted in uttering tremendous diatribes and phillippics of the most terrifying description, and at the same time would not for worlds have hurt a hair of the head of him whom he was delivering over to the infernal deities.

The poorer scholars of his college

experienced his fatherly kindness, and had reason to bless his memory when he departed this life. Hating poverty himself, and esteeming the Church Establishment as a vast Pagoda tree, planted for all her good children to shake, conduct such as John's was completely inexplicable, and though the good little gentleman would not himself have committed an unworthy or dishonourable action for any sum, nothing made him so angry as to hear others talk about conscience and scruples.

Accordingly, the head of St. Margaret's penned the following despatch to the Rev. H. Fordyce, which was posted just in time to anticipate John's arrival, and warn his father of the state of the case.

" My dear Fordyce.

" As you know, I have very small opinion of the young men of the present day.

They have degenerated since the time that
we were undergraduates. They talk about
'scruples' and 'ideas,' and have 'views'
and 'sympathies.' We knew none of this
trash and were the better for it. However, to come to the point, there is some
good in most of them, and your boy is
not bad as far as he goes. He has just
come out a very good First, and reflects
honour on his college. In our days this
would have been sufficient, and he would
have been ordained as a matter of course,
and settled down quietly. But all is
changed now. He has, it appears, taken
up some of those diabolical German views
which are so popular. What he means I
cannot say; but certainly he talks of unsettled views, scruples about ordination
and the like. I have talked the matter
over to him calmly and dispassionately,
and placed the true Church of England
view before him; but like all young men

he wont listen to reason. Now take my
advice—the advice of one who has had
considerable experience in dealing with
youngsters, and with some very queer
specimens too. A weak notion becomes
strengthened into a firm resolve by opposition.

"If a man takes it into his head to
stand upon one leg, let him : after a time
he becomes tired and uses the twain
nature gave him. But if you pull and
haul him about, and try to force the
other leg to the ground, what does he
then ? Why, of course, he puts out all
his muscular force, learns to balance himself, *stans pede in uno*, and very possibly
in the struggle thrusts you in the mire.
Your son now wishes to stand on one leg.
Be advised by me, and let him, until he is
tired of that eccentricity. He is a lad of
sense, and after a time will come to his
right mind. If I were you I should let

him go among all the rascally Dissenters I could find without restraint. After a time he will sicken of the society of such illiterates ; men whose English has no quality, and whose Latin is destitute of quantity. He will be glad enough then to return to the bosom of the Church. Now to other matters.

"I heard a very good joke, which is now going through the Common-rooms, about P. and the Whigs; but it is too long to write, so you must come up and hear it. If you want some more of that dry Port I can get it for you, at the same price as the last, 72s. Good-bye."

"Yours ever,

"EDWARD FIELD."

When this was despatched, the head of St Margaret's thought he had done the business. The letter was subtle, diplomatic, admonitory, and contained a thorough diagnosis of the case. Alas! that the effects should have been so far from what the writer desired.

The unhappy missive arrived in the post-bag at breakfast in company with the "Standard," and a few begging letters. After duly examining the seal, handwriting and post-mark, and speculating whence they might come, as is the manner in the country where the arrival of a letter is regarded as a solemn event, the Rector opened, held the epistle at arm's length, and proceeded to study it with stertorous breathing and occasional snorts and grunts.

He was not quick to comprehend anything, the orifice of his mind being so small as to allow but of a small stream entering at a time; but at length the fact that John declined being ordained stood potent before him, coupled with a supposition of his own—speedily transformed into a decided conviction—that he had become a Dissenter. Can I—no, I feel altogether the futility of any attempt to describe the wrath of the Rector. Niagara, volcanic eruptions, and earthquakes stand undescribed, and for the same reason so must the "divine" anger of the Incumbent of Easimore—words could not express and depict it.

I am informed, on the best authority, that from a change in the formation of the larynx and epiglottis consequent upon presentation to a living, the superior clergy cannot utter any exclamations of greater strength than 'Yea' and 'Nay.' As it was, therefore, I am only warranted in applying the term "strong" perhaps—very strong language to the exclamations which escaped the Rector. A domestic storm reigned around. Bells were rung, doors slammed, and the servants something-elsed which rhymes,

besides being called pig-headed idiots
and gaping owls.

All agreed they never had seen master
so rampagious before—no, not when a
church-rate was refused, or Jim threw
down the bay mare. And in such a
storm wind, with the thermometer at
spirit boil and the barometer at stormy,
with the drum and cone signal flying,
John arrived with his heart very low
indeed. In a moment he saw how things
were going, though, not being aware of
Dr. Field's letter, he was at some loss
to conjecture the cause of so great a
disturbance; but the grim nod of his
father when they met, warned him to
expect the worst and speedy breaking
of the storm. Dinner passed in ominous
silence. A few attempts at news im-
parting on John's part were received with
"strangled whistles" of impatience and
contempt, nor met with any reply. As

soon as the decanters and fruit were placed, after filling and drinking a great bumper of port and giving two or three preparatory coughs, Mr. Fordyce suddenly produced Dr. Field's letter and tossed it over the table to his son.

" Read that, and tell me what you have to say to it."

He complied, and in a moment the cause of the paternal ire became manifest.

" Dr. Field had no business to write this, Sir, even were it less absurd than it is. Why need he interfere between me and my father, or anticipate what I was about to tell you myself? This very night I intended to inform you of the change of my opinions."

" I didn't ask for any fine language, Sir, I asked you what you had to say to that. I want to hear the truth, if you know how to tell it, which I very much doubt. Now then, tell me in one word, is Dr. Field right in stating that you refuse to be ordained?"

"Yes, Sir."

"Yes, Sir!" mimicked the father, "and you sit there, you sneaking hound, you rascally liar, you, and dare tell me so, when you know it can be concealed no longer. You dare look me in the face and confess to what should make you blush to say. I knew it was true. I felt convinced months back that there was something wrong; that you had some disgraceful nonsense in your head. You have been cheating and deceiving me all these years past—all your life, perhaps. I am ashamed of you, and disgusted with you. I thought once you were a manly young fellow, of whom I might be proud, and now I see you are a methodistical canting rogue!"

Oh, how the uneasy blood flushed up

to John's face and then suddenly retreated, leaving his cheeks ashy pale! Have *you* ever been called a liar? Do you know what that keenest agony is? It is, perhaps, the sharpest anguish a man can bear. Worse than a blow, far worse, it is a blow on the heart, which stops its pulsation for a moment, and makes a man experience a moral death. But then, if you have so felt, you could at least shake off the unworthy name, you could answer in words of flame, and confound the accuser. And so a great throng of words came up tumultuously to John's lips, and struggled to free themselves. But one, and only one thought repressed them, " He is my father, I must bear it."

" Father," he replied, as calmly as he could, " I know you must be very disappointed, very angry at what you have just learnt. I know my resolution must

seem very strange—perhaps very wrong,
to you—but I only want you to hear me
calmly, and then say whether I could act
otherwise. I have suffered deeply, I
assure you, and do feel most keenly for
the disappointment I am causing you."

"Look here, Sir," was the fierce reply,
"when I want any of your fair speeches
and excuses I will tell you. I never yet
knew a coward and liar who could not
find plenty to say for himself. Remember, I am not a man to be trifled with.
When I pass my word, you never knew
me to fail or alter my mind. Now it
seems to me that you have taken some
confounded foolish ideas into your head.
You want me to hear them 'calmly,' as
you say. I'll do no such thing. I'm not
going to listen to you, or any other young
fool talking Jacobin rubbish. I don't
understand anything about what you call
duty and scruples. Your duty towards

God and your father ought to teach you to have nothing to do with that kind of thing. When I was young, there was nothing of the kind. What my father told me to do, I did and never asked questions, and you had better do the same. You know perfectly well that I mean you to be ordained, and take this living. Now all young men are fools, I know, and I suppose you are like the rest. But I am willing to forget all the nonsense you have talked, and burn this letter, if you agree to my wish and do your duty. But by the Lord who made me, if you *will* be obstinate and a fool, I will have nothing more to do with you. Out of this house you shall go, and I will never see or speak to you again as long as I live, or forgive you when I die. Your fathers were good men, who did their duty to Church and State and led a sensible life. If you choose to be a knave and a fool you shall be no son of mine. I won't have an infernal Dissenter for my son, I can tell you. And now you know my mind which I shall not change." And having thus spoken he leant back in his chair, with his fierce little grey eyes fixed on the plaster ornaments of the ceiling.

And all this while John sat pale and mute. He kept his temper, but by a terrible effort. He speaks at last, but hoarsely —each word tearing its way out by force.

"If I were to think for a thousand years I should not alter my mind, father. If I were to consider for ever, my conscience would not allow me to do as you wish. I respect the Church of England, but I do not believe all its doctrines, and will not bind myself to its articles. I will not teach to others, what I do not believe or think necessary. In all else I will be your obedient son—with everything else I am ready to comply, but in this I may not and cannot please you. Do not let us quarrel for this, father—I am your only son—there are only us two." He rose and leaned with one hand on the table, bending forward to see whether there was any hope. But the iron, grim face turned to him dispelled all idea of pardon or grace.

" You, my son? No, indeed, young Sir, not now. You have made your choice, and *I* will keep you to it. If I have to adopt a beggar out of the streets, you, at least, shall never have a penny of mine. I forbid your ever coming to this house again, I forbid your speaking to me again. I have nothing more to do with you, and dis-own you. Go, and starve, and rot, and take my curse with you. Go to your Dissenters and infidels, and cast in your lot with 'them—I don't care. And don't think when you are in trouble to come to me and work on my feelings. I have none

for you.   As for money, your mother's
money I can't keep from you—worse luck.
Go and squander it with drunkards and
harlots, as you did mine years back.   By
heaven, you were more a man then than
now with your lies and scruples.   There,
go, and never darken my doors again!"

How vain to remonstrate!   The Reverend gentleman was right when he said he
never changed his mind when once resolved.   Unmoved, he listened to John's
entreaties, and then rang the bell and
ordered the servant to "show that
gentleman out and never admit him again."

And thus from the gates of Eden was
thrust the rebellious, disobedient one into
outer darkness—physical at least.   But
as for the Rector of Easimore, he reposed
in the depths of his easy-chair, and easy
conscience until bedtime.   Then he had
his usual night-cap, said his usual prayers,
went to bed and slept sound.

CHAPTER XVI.

TO the ordinary mind, there would appear no reason why our worthy friend Cyril should not have returned, directly the October term was over, to the delights of the paternal roof tree. Be this as it may, the fact is that the brief letter which announced his degree, contianed also a request for twenty pounds, and an intimation that important business would detain him in London for perhaps a week, but that he certainly should arrive at the Lindens on Christmas Eve.

The dinner hour at the Lindens was six, but the French clock in the drawing-room had chimed a quarter past eight, which was its way of denoting a quarter to seven, and yet dinner had not been announced. The Ponsonby family were grouped about, waiting with more or less impatience for Cyril who had not arrived. As it was only a family gathering, Mrs. Ponsonby had not on the cap of ceremony, compared by some kind friend to Noah's Ark with the embarkation of the insects; being adorned simply with a chaste *coiffure* of ribbon, lace, cherries and butterflies. The young ladies also were in somewhat dowdy silks, accompanied by the second best crinolines, those that had long lost their proper circular shape from much and undue pressure.

"I shall wait no longer, Mrs. Ponsonby," at length exclaims the master of the house, returning his watch to his pocket with a jerk. "I consider Cyril's unpunctuality as a very marked disrespect to the head of the family, one to which

I am not accustomed. Ring the bell,
Annie."

" Dear papa, do just wait a wee bit
longer, the poor fellow will be so horribly
tired and cold."

" A wretched waste of time : you
young people have no notion of its value.
When I was head of the Rag Bag Department, the punctuality with which all business was transacted was proverbial. I
regulated all the clocks by my own watch,
and hence there was a fixed standard to
go by."

Charlotte, the philosopher, is reminded
of Charles V., and is just unfolding a
quotation from Prescott, when her
mamma yawns in a manner indicative of
speech.

" Very true, my dear, I wish we were
more punctual. I always tell Horace,
' Punctuality breeds contempt,' no, not
that; what do I mean, dear ?" to Annie.

"'Punctuality is the thief of time,' mamma, isn't it?"

"Yes, my child, something like that."

"Mrs. Ponsonby," says her spouse, with his head on one side, like a bird about to peck, "if you have only inconsequent and ridiculous nonsense to utter, it would be better, I think, to remain silent. Annie, when you have finished miserable attempts at jocularity, perhaps you will ring the bell. I never joke."

Just as the signal for dinner was given, the sound of a carriage was heard, and amid considerable noise of bumping of luggage, Cyril, the unpunctual, entered the room. His father had taken up a Roman parent attitude in front of the fire; Annie ran to meet him, and Mrs. Ponsonby was sufficiently roused to give furtive twitches to her cap, until it threatened to come off altogether, at the same time plaintively drawling to her eldest daughter,

"Charlotte, how do I look?"

Cyril was one of those delightfully cool people who are never disconcerted. No combination of circumstances could put him out, no frowns shake him from his imperturbability.

"Ah," was his quiet remark, "your clock's a little fast, I fancy. How do, Sir? how do you do, mother? I hope you are better. Well, girls; don't squeeze my hand off, Annie. Let me see, I suppose it's the proper thing to wish merry Christmas, and all that kind of thing. Imagine it done, please. And will somebody give me five shillings to pay the fly man? I daresay he expects to be paid."

The paternal purse was produced with a growl.

"If you had possessed the forethought to tell us you should not be here to dinner,

Cyril, we need not have waited an hour and a half for you."

"Dear me, Sir! really I am very sorry. You see I am never quite sure of my time, and I have had my dinner, as it happens."

"Ah, my dear child," replied Mrs. Ponsonby, "I wish you would remember 'one stitch in nine saves time.' However, better late than never. And here is dinner, I declare."

Of the Ponsonby *cuisine* the less said the better. Mr. Ponsonby considered himself a *bon vivant* of the first order; a harmless enough delusion had he only been concerned, but when it came to considering his guests as fellow *bon vivants*, it became quite another matter. A flavour of candle-grease pervaded all, as though the cook had put the last finishing touches with the kitchen-snuffers.

It was a Barmecide's feast, at which

the hungry and disappointed guest wandered from dish to dish in search of something to feed upon, finding only indigestion and nausea served up under various names. And the wines also! The host was one of those who indulge in curious old tawny Ports at 20s., very superior old crusted at 36s., and magnificent ruby Beeswing at 40s.; and then his Amontillado Sherries, his Clos Vougeot, his Mümm and Clicquot! Ay di mi! what lies the man would tell about them, though he knew that his guests knew they were lies! Solomon must have been thinking of wine-buying when he wrote "It is naught, it is naught, saith the buyer; but when he is gone his own way, then he boasteth."

The dinner was originally so bad, that the extra ninety minutes had scarcely made it worse. Mr. Ponsonby was unsuspicious; his digestion was excellent,

and although he was silent—appeared
in a good humour. He had received a
letter that morning which had caused
him to drive over to the D—— Station
in great haste, and had only returned
in time to dress for dinner. Still
it was evident that whatever had happened, had been of a pleasant nature.
Had it been otherwise, Mrs. Ponsonby
would have suffered. When dessert was
on the table, he filled his own glass,
and pushing the bottle to his son, remarked,

"Help yourself, my boy, there's a glass
of wine you won't get every day."

Cyril inwardly hoped not; but he
slowly sipped, frowned, and raising his
glass to the light inspected it with his
head on one side, after the approved
manner.

"Yes," said he, after a pause, in a
deeply emotional voice, "yes."

It was very simple, but told well with his father, notwithstanding. One of Cyril's maxims was "never lie unless necessary, but then lie deep."

"You are a good judge, Cyril, for a youngster. Taste, like wine, needs age to mature it."

During the short time that the ladies stayed, the conversation turned mainly upon Cyril's recent achievement in the schools, and although he knew his father to be deeply annoyed and disappointed about his failing to obtain a First—to his great surprise—no reproaches, no anger, no sarcastic queries and remarks.

"So much the better," thought he. "I shouldn't have cared much if the old boy had cut up rough; but as he must soon know of my debts, it is better he should take it pleasantly."

At length the ladies rose and departed, and then, having closed the door carefully, Mr. Ponsonby turned his chair round to the bright fire which blazed on the hearth, and opened fire upon his son.

"You will scarcely guess, Cyril, where I have been to-day."

"In that case, Sir, I think I'll not try."

"Well, I will tell you at once. I have been over to Easimore—by request, special request—and I was petrified—yes, petrified, Sir, at what I saw and heard!"

Cyril raised his eyebrows, and muttered something about it's being "deuced unpleasant I should think," and then waited further information.

"Of all the incomprehensible young fools, I think your cousin John must be about the greatest, the densest, the most self-willed."

"Oh, ah, now I see where you are,

Sir. I had forgotten all about John's affairs. Has Blue-beard cut up rough? If so, he would be an unpleasant person to deal with."

" I'll tell you what, my boy, you must speak rather more respectfully of your uncle—you will find you have chuse if you play your cards well, I can tell you. I received a letter from Fordyce, begging me to go over at once—to lose no time. Naturally perceiving the matter to be of importance, I started immediately. No words will depict my amazement when I learnt what had happened. Fordyce was like a raving lion. I never saw a man in such a fury in all my life, when he came to speak of the matter. Of course *you* know of your cousin's madness—his insensate folly ?"

" You mean his going in for Methodism, or something of that kind—well, I fancy I knew as soon as anyone."

" Well, *now* you have to hear the sequel. On his return home, I suppose an *éclaircissement* took place ; Fordyce insisted on his ordination, and when John refused, turned him out of doors—disowned him, Sir !"

" What ?" exclaimed Cyril, " do you mean literally and actually, or only as a figure of speech ?"

" I mean that at the present moment, John Fordyce is disowned by his father, cut out of his will, and has simply that pittance, his mother's settlement, to live on."

" Well, all I can say is that they are the most wonderful father and son I ever heard of. I am deuced sorry for John, though after all he must be an awful fool to bring matters to such a pass."

" Well, but hear me out, Cyril, I have not done yet. You have been made the subject of a most handsome proposal to-day—"

"Of marriage, Sir? I am open to anything of that kind which combines style, beauty, and money."

"Don't be absurd—no—not of marriage—unless you can be married to a good fat living."

"A *what*, Sir! I begin to be afraid you are not unpetrified yet."

"Now just listen to me quietly. Fordyce is so mad at his disappointment that he is resolved to punish John how he can. In a word, if you choose to take orders you may be Rector in his stead—that is as soon as all the Church formularies will allow, and I *do* hope you will not be such a fool as to refuse such a wonderful, unexpected chance."

"Good gad, Sir!" exclaimed Cyril thoroughly serious, "do you mean what you say?"

"I do, every word, my son. His plan is this. The living is worth just £1,100 a-year. As long as he lives £400 is to be deducted and paid to him. This leaves £700 to deal with. Now, until you are in priest's orders, of course there must be a curate as *locum tenens* to keep the place warm for you. Many a man will jump at £100 a-year, thus leaving you exactly £600 per annum until his death, after which you will have the full income—I only wish I had such a chance offered me. Nor is this all. Fordyce is, as you know, a man of private means; he has, I think, about £600 a-year of his own—more for all I know—on this and the £400 from the living he will live snugly enough at Bath, or Brighton, or some of those places. Now he did not in so many words say that you would have this at his death, but he *did* say that his son should not have a penny, and that it would depend upon the behaviour of others how he remembered them. Accept his offer,

Cyril, and you are a made man; refuse it, and you are a greater fool than your cousin. But, I think I know you too well for that."

"You have no scruples of conscience, Sir, I suppose."

"Conscience be, hem—I mean this is not a case for any such, and for heaven's sake don't *you* begin to talk about them."

"Well, Sir, you know, of course, your opinion eases my mind. I'll sleep on it and give you my decision to-morrow."

His decision was in fact already made as both he and his father knew, but it looked more decent to act thus deliberately. In a few weeks, the name of Cyril Ponsonby was on the Bishop of A——'s list of Candidates for Orders.

CHAPTER XVII.

THERE is no point in which the tyranny of society over the individual is more felt than in matters of religion. Not simply the intolerance of the clergy towards recalcitrant members of their flocks, or to members of their own profession, but of society in general towards its members.

Political opinion no longer disturbs the peace of nations, and endangers the life or liberty of citizens as it once was wont. But it may be questioned, whether the religious liberty of which we are so proud is really as extensive as we imagine. It is true that pains and penalties are no longer judicially imposed as of old for variations of religious thought from the orthodox standard, but society undoubtedly has a Star Chamber of its own, whence it issues sentence of *peine forte et dure* against those who have presumed to differ from its authority. The liberty and independence of thought which we claim for ourselves, we are very loath to extend to our neighbours. And it will generally be found that the indignation with which we regard any denial of a doctrine, or set of doctrines, is in inverse ratio to our comprehension of them. We have received them mechanically without examination, and finding them suit our case fairly well, are angry if another presumes to examine and dismiss them as untenable. Thus, while the general principles of Christianity, those doctrines in which all churches agree, are comparatively neglected, the little shibboleths which separate church from church are vigorously maintained; though the inner meaning and spirit of a doctrine is almost forgotten, the phrase which is its shell is vigorously fought for.

We may know absolutely nothing of the religious life of our friend or neighbour, and as long as he professes the same creed as ourselves, may care less. Let him, however, change that creed never so conscientiously, and forthwith we feel annoyed and suspicious. Any man who has been converted from Romanism to Protestantism, or *vice versâ*, must know the distrust with which he is regarded by his old colleagues, the injury he is supposed to have inflicted on them, the withdrawal of sympathy which immediately follows, and the barrier which is interposed. And yet, beyond the fact of occasionally attending the same place of worship, there need have been no religious connection or

sympathy existing between them.   Indeed,
it will generally be found that those really
least concerned and interested in the religious change of their friend or neighbour
are the first to resent it as a personal
injury.   Accept the authoritative decision
of the world, or that section which forms
your world, and whether conscientiously
or not, you are safe.   Traverse the same,
never so conscientiously, and you will
have to pay the penalty of esteeming a
pure conscience a higher and nobler possession than outward obedience and inward
revolt.

An age in which there is so much religious discussion and controversy must,
primâ facie, appear a religious age.   And
yet, when we look closer and test the
spirit and actions of the present day,
there seems no reason for believing there
is more vital faith, more Christianity existing now than in any other age.   That

there is more civilisation, less open and undisguised vice prevalent, may be granted readily—but that we are nearer the type of Christianity, as taught by Christ, cannot be proved or maintained. The vices of each age vary with the circumstances of the age. As the inflammatory disorders of the past generation seem to have given way to the group of nervous maladies under which the present generation now suffers, so is it with the mental disorders we term vices. Perhaps, in no age was there so much noisy discussion and angry asseveration mingled with so much real doubt and perplexity. The trumpets are blown loud and long, but neither hearer nor blower knows what the signal means.

All this John Fordyce was beginning to realize in his own person, and to discover that while errors of action are readily pardoned by the world, errors of faith—that is, against the faith of society —are deadly sins. While he was simply a fornicator and drunkard, he was very well received in the world, but when he became a Dissenter from the Established Church, he lost caste immediately. Stunned and confused, he left his father's presence. His father's anger and harsh words had cut him to the heart; although I cannot say that the paternal curse had much effect. John believed the Registry of Heaven had other work to do than to record and ratify the curses of angry old gentlemen. To have merited it by filial disobedience would have been sad indeed; but as it was, he felt he could not accuse himself of that. Half mechanically he mounted his horse, and gave a few directions as to the disposition of his belongings, much to the amazement of the servants, who could not understand the state of things. Then he slowly turned away, and rode over to

Arlington, putting up and spending a sleepless night at an hotel there.

From that sleepless night, however, arose this one determination, that he would lose no time in seeing Edith and telling her all that had happened. It would be a great blow, a terrible disappointment to her, he felt sure. Still, surely her good sense and upright feeling must tell her that he had acted rightly. She had no direct interest in his opinions as his father had, and therefore was not likely to be prejudiced or biassed. Surely she would respect conscientious scruples, and the resolve to suffer for the right. Still, if—. But that was impossible. And yet—well if it did change her affection for him—why then, God help him! Poor John!

On his arrival at the Hall, he heard that Mr. and Mrs. Masterman were out on a visit, and only Edith at home; a fact which did not cause him much regret.

Their interview would be subject to no interruptions. In a few minutes, Edith was in his arms, hiding her blushing face upon his shoulder and murmuring,

"Oh, my darling, my darling! how glad I am to have you back again once more! It has seemed so long."

"Not longer than it did to me, my Edith."

"Ah, but you have had your reading and books, and all that to think of, while I have only had to count the days until you came. And, oh! how proud I am of you, John! I can never make too much of you. A First, a real First! You know I always said I was sure that you could get nothing less, if they were fair."

"You must pardon me, my darling, if I thought others might not think as well of me as you did. If you had been one of the Examiners now—"

"Why, I think I should have wanted a new class invented to put you in all by yourself. You see I am always right about you, and so I ought to be, for don't I know and think about you more than anyone else? Do you know, John, you are looking pale and ill? you have been working too hard and knocked yourself up, Sir. Never mind, I shall become your physician and soon put you right again. Papa was speaking of you only yesterday, and wondering when you would be here. When did you come?"

"Yesterday from Oxford."

"And rode over from Easimore this morning?"

"No, from Arlington; I slept there last night."

"John, you silly old thing, you are dreaming! You look as grave as an owl, and say you slept at Arlington. Why, where's your father then? He

is not at Arlington, I know. I think
your First has turned your head."

"My darling Edith, if I look grave,
it is because I feel so—because I have
something very serious to tell you—because something very dreadful has happened!"

He tried to speak calmly, but it alarmed
Edith terribly.

"Oh! my love, my love, tell me at
once—is it very dreadful indeed—is it
death?"

"No, Edith, try and compose yourself—not death; something between my
father and me. He is very angry with
me, more so than I had thought possible;
he has turned me out of doors, disowned
mé, and, Edith—I can scarce tell you—
he has cursed me—yes, me—his own son!"

"Oh! John, John! what are you saying? It cannot be true, I cannot believe
it!"

"My dearest, it is only too true. I left the Rectory last night, never to return."

Edith withdrew her arm from John's for a moment, as she sat down.

"But what can be the reason of all this? What made him act thus? I know Mr. Fordyce is passionate; but this—oh! it is too horrible! John, what is it—what have you done?"

"Do not turn against me, my Edith, it is nothing I have done. It is because I will not do something against my conscience; I have refused to be ordained."

Edith looked up with a quick glance of fear.

"Oh, John, what has come to you? What is the meaning of all this? Why have you refused to become a clergyman? I thought that was all settled. I do not understand this."

"My dearest, I am shocked to pain you thus; but you must know all. My views on religious subjects have changed so, that I cannot become a Minister of the Church of England."

"Have you become a Catholic?" was the immediate question. Women can only understand leaving England for Rome.

"A Catholic? No, my dear Edith, no indeed—not if you mean a Roman Catholic. Nevertheless I cannot think of being ordained. My conscience would not allow me."

"John, this is the most dreadful blow I have ever received, and from you, too. I can scarce believe it, now. What has done this—has made you change, I mean? How long have you thought of all this?"

"For months, Edith, for months my doubts have been silently growing, until some weeks ago I came to this resolution."

" For months, John ? And you never told me, never told any of us, but left us to make so many plans for the future. Oh, John ! it was wrong—it was cruel to your father, and to me, and to all of us."

" God knows, Edith, I did not mean it for cruelty. I acted as I thought was for the best—to save you needless pain. What good could have resulted had you known my doubts months ago ?"

" Why, perhaps, we might have persuaded you. Have you spoken to any one and asked their advice ?"

" Yes, to several. All good and wise men. They have talked the matter over with me, but I have not been able to see it in their way."

" And don't you think you may change your mind again, John, now you have done so once ?"

" Speaking humanly, I believe it to be

impossible that I should alter the views I now hold."

"But what are you then, John? I can understand a man's becoming a Catholic, though I think it very horrid and shocking, worshipping graven images, and kneeling to a wafer and confession, and that. But you do not say what you mean to be."

"A christian, Edith, I hope, even though the member of no sect or party. I do not blame all those who think differently, and act as they think right; but I claim that for myself also, when I say that I can never be a clergyman of the Church of England. My dearest, surely you would not have me dishonest—you would not have me believe one thing and teach another. I know you too well, I hope."

"I am sure I don't know what to say, John, I never thought it possible you could become a Dissenter, or Atheist, or whatever you are. There are so many parties in the Church of England, and so many good men in them all, that it seems strange you cannot be like others and choose your party and keep to it. I don't know what papa will say."

It was in vain John explained and modified, and tried again and again to state his position. At length he said, " My darling, surely this will not alter your feelings for me, you do not love me less because I am not an orthodox Churchman; I have suffered very much, surely you will not add this grief to me. What difference can it make to two loving hearts ? I shall not try to influence or shake your faith. I shall be the same John to you I was before."

But Edith was reserved, and would only answer, " I must not answer you, John, until I know what papa thinks. I love you very, very much, as you know ; but he must be my guide in such a matter as this. Were it poverty or anything of that kind it would be different, but faith is a very serious thing, though you may not think so."

What the Squire's opinion on the subject was, may be gathered from the following letter, which was handed to him as he sat at breakfast next morning.

"Dear Sir,

" I have learnt with considerable surprise the nature of the disclosure which you made to my daughter yesterday, and the fact of your having quitted the Established Church of this country, to embrace doctrines, which, however disguised, are called atheistic by all honest men. You must have been perfectly aware of my views on such subjects. As I am informed then, that your faith has been sapped for some months, I can only attribute your silence to an unworthy desire to entangle matters, and avoid the consequences which you were aware must follow your infidelity. Under the circumstances, therefore, I am perfectly justified in reconsidering your engagement to my daughter, and with her full concurrence beg to state that it must be regarded as though it had never existed. I am happy to say that all members of my family have ever been loyal to the Church and State, as by law established—the union with one who appears to respect neither would be contrary to our tradition, and could only be attended with consequences undesirable and disastrous.

"My daughter encloses a few lines to show the unanimity of our sentiments, which, I may also remark, will under no circumstances be altered.

"I have the honour to be,

"Your obedient servant,

"EVERARD MASTERMAN."

Enclosed, was an open note in these words :

"Dear Mr. Fordyce,

"I write by papa's permission and advice to assure you that our engagement must be regarded as terminated. I could never marry any one who was not a Churchman, whatever my feelings for him may have been. I trust that in time you will see the error you have committed, and seek pardon where alone it may be found.

"Believe me, yours sincerely,

"EDITH MASTERMAN."

"P.S. Please to return me my letters."

Upon which, John packed up a few articles and left Arlington for London.

CHAPTER XVIII.

WHAT mysterious power is there in London that attracts to it men in trouble, sorrow, and those whose homes once broken up are free to wander where inclination leads them ?

It is because whether a sufferer desires to hide, to nurse, or attempt to escape his grief, there is no place in which this may be better effected than the great metropolis. Next to Sahara, there is no solitude like that of London. On entering it, a man almost ceases to exist individually—he is swamped and swallowed up as in a great ocean, he is lost in the boundless crowd, always changing, surging, moving onwards. He ceases from being what he was before, and becomes simply an atom, an unit in an aggregate of three millions. He is no longer a man, but a cypher. In London you need know no one; you may remain unknown to all; satisfy the very commonest and most customary requirements of nature and human law, and your nothingness, your solitude, are at once conceded to you. Tithe your anise and cummin, the rest is your own.

You may live next door, to within a few inches of a murderer, a philosopher, a black-leg, a poet, and perhaps never know it. You move in your groove, he in his and never meet.

Tragedies, comedies, farces, melodramas are enacted daily, hourly, almost within hearing—only a few bricks, a little partition separate you, and you need never know it. Why should you? Look at the faces of those you meet in the streets, stand at

the window and watch the bye-passers.
Every face a puzzle, a mystery, a locked
door of which the key is lost to you.
Grave or gay, laughing or agonized, they
pass in an endless stream ; sometimes an
index to inward thoughts, oftener a mask
drawn over hidden sores. Who are they ?
Whence do they come ? Whither are they
going ? What vain questions, destined
never to be answered—perhaps in their
right time, and when least expected.

Reader, have you ever gazed on faces
thus, and wondered whether among the
passing stream there might be one which,
in time to come, should have a fateful
power over you ? Is it not strange, that
in a white face rapidly whirled by us in a
carriage, as we tramp along in the mud,
we may have gazed on the countenance of
one, who, some years hence, shall control
all our life, our dearest friend of a friendship yet unborn ; our cherished wife of a

bond yet untied; our murderer may be of
a hate yet unknown? How little can we
tell, how vain our guesses and conjectures
must ever be. We stand like men on a
desert island rock, around us and beneath
us an unknown, surging, ever moving
ocean, whose waters we can neither guage,
fathom, control, nor resist. And so at last
we plunge in and try our little powers,
and go to meet our fate be it what it may;
to be landed by some chance wave on a
smiling, blooming land of happiness and
affluence; to be dashed by some chance
wave on the shores of the land of Death.

Has the reader ever slept, and dreamed
he was constantly ascending pathless mountains in pursuit of something—he knew
not what—which as constantly eluded his
grasp and mocked his efforts? If so,
he will remember the weary, unsatisfied
longing, the hungry desire, which marked
that dream, he will recal the inward im-

pulse which seemed to drive him a
wanderer into space, a pursuer of an
endless guest, a traveller through infinity
to a bourne shadowy, unreal, and invisible.   A dream such as this may
proceed from over-anxiety, over-work,
or physical derangement.   There is,
however, to some—those who have ever
suffered from it will recognise it even
in these faint outlines—a condition of life
in which this terrible dream becomes a
still more terrible reality.   Whether it
proceed from mental or physical causes,
or a combination of both, the agony of a
fierce unsatisfied longing after some unreal, unattainable object, unsettling the
life, etiolating the powers, destroying the
affections, and at length sapping the mind,
comes to visit some sufferers.

They feel a thirst which no draughts
can slake, a hunger no food can satisfy;
in crowds they feel alone, alone they

are ever in the presence of the shadowy object of their vain pursuit and longing. There is no feeling more awful than this death in life, this unresting, unceasing, sonnambule-like walking of the spirit. It is the reverse of the legend, and Frankenstein pursues his monster—his own phantom creation.

The world around sees and recognises nothing more than a disordered abnormal condition of the physical system. The scientific probe deeper, as they think, and attribute it to some favourite theory of predisposing causes. The sufferer only knows, that like the sharp sword in the scabbard, it is gradually wearing him out, and that unless in mercy some relief be afforded, death alone can end the vain longing which seems to swell his heart to bursting.

Let him attempt to describe this feeling to his dearest friend, and most probably

he is met with an unthinking laugh, or
unmeaning piece of advice. He is unintelligible, and speaks in a language and of
things which the world cannot understand.
His medical adviser orders change of air,
but the sufferer carries that within him
which poisons every atmosphere, which
robs the sky of its colour, the sun of its
warmth, the flowers of their beauty, the
sea of its freshness—which reduces the
world to a pathless desert, over which
he ranges, unresting, unsatisfied, until the
curse of existence is removed, and his
wanderings ended by the hand of Death.
There are no statistics of broken hearts,
my friends, nor do we know what torture-
chambers are hidden away deep in the
bosoms of those around us. We do not
hear their cries and groans, for the walls
are very thick. We do not see the
writhings and contortions of despair, for
a smile masks all. But hearts break

around us unknown, and friends die daily at our sides, and we walk with corpses which have but the semblance of living men. If only the inarticulate groans of the weary and miserable, who lie up and down in our great cities, hidden with their griefs, could once be rendered audible, no human ears could endure it and live.

Now and then, like a broken lute, some oppressed heart utters one dying wail, and passes into silence. We hear it, and wonder for a while, but there is not much time to listen, and the voices in our own hearts are too clamorous to let us hearken long. And so we all learn of our own experience the truth of those words, " The heart knoweth its own bitterness, and a stranger doth not intermeddle with his joy."

It may perhaps be thought that John Fordyce was utterly cast down and crushed by this second blow which had

come upon him so unexpectedly; but it
was not so. Stunned he certainly was,
crushed he was not. The sudden termination of long cherished hopes could
not but cause him poignant grief, and
yet he was able to see that the realisation
of those hopes would possibly have caused
him greater disappointment. The fact
was, he now recognised for the first time
that he had all along taken a mistaken
estimate of Edith's character, had viewed
her through the highly coloured glasses
of his own imagination, and clothed her
in ideal virtues and graces which did
not of right belong to her. It had not
been that amiable delusion of lovers,
which often enables them to see beauty
in green eyes, tow-coloured hair, or
upturned nose; it was more than this,
for it saw what really did not exist.
His Edith had appeared large and noble-
minded, generous, impulsive, affectionate;

but Miss Masterman now turned out to be quite of the ordinary type of Eve's daughters, incapable of independent thought or action, fettered by the chains of conventionality and solely guided by the society in which she lived. What that acknowledged, she recognised—what that disallowed, she rejected—as long as her friends moved on smoothly in the beaten track, all was well and they had the benefit of her society; but let them only strike out a path for themselves, and she discovered that they could no longer be fellow-travellers.

The greater portion of womankind is cast in this conservative mould, and for some purposes, perhaps, it is as well; but it is not for this type that men feel they could lay down their lives and hopes, and John's nature was of that impetuous kind that knows no medium between feasting and starving. He awoke

from his dream, found his idol dashed
to pieces at his feet, and at once recognised the poor materials of which it had
been composed, and which to his dazzled
eyes once had possessed the brightness
of gold. Sad though he felt, he could
not but acknowledge that Edith could
never have been a help-mate to him in
the truest sense of the word.

Accordingly he wrote a few farewell
lines, quiet, but dignified, and complied
with her request that her letters might
be returned. To her father, he wrote
a short and rather curt note, fully ac-
quiescing in the desire he had expressed
for the discontinuance of any intercourse
for the future. Perhaps Edith was not
so very much to blame. Like most young
ladies, she idolised what is called " the
cloth," and looked upon marriage with a
clergyman as the *summum bonum*. Per-
chance she had yet to discover that the cowl

does not always make the monk, that
the cloth is occasionally better than the
body which it covers, that it is possible
to marry a Reverend gentleman and not
be completely happy, and that at the best
they are remarkably like ordinary mortals in their foibles and failings. Be this
as it may, she had set her heart on
wedding not simply John Fordyce, but
the Rector of Easimore. When, therefore, she discovered that these two were
not to be obtained in the same person,
she at once decided that John was not
for her. Again, how could she marry
a renegade from the church—in fact a
dissenter? There was something revolting
in the very idea, it was altogether against
the proprieties and not to be thought
of. And so with a half sigh John was
dismissed, with the specious plea that one
who had changed his faith in religion would
be very likely to change it in love also.

Before leaving Arlington, John had sent his address in town to his father, together with a list of a few things which he desired to be forwarded to him. He received in reply a brief letter from his father's lawyer, in which he was informed that all should be sent as he wished, moreover, that the principal of his mother's property had been paid into Messrs. A, B, and C, in his name and under his sole control; moreover, that Mr. Fordyce wished him to understand that this was all he had to look to, as from his will he would find himself excluded; lastly, that all further communication was declined. And about a few weeks after this came a letter from his cousin, which together with its answer, I subjoin.

" My dear John,
"I wish myself to be the first to convey to you a piece of news, which,

whoever may be your informant, will, I have no doubt, cause you some surprise. Very soon after Christmas, and the most unhappy misunderstanding with your father, I received a message from him stating his desire to see me. It cannot surprise you more to learn, than it did me to receive the offer he then made me. It was nothing less than that I should occupy the place in his plans for Easimore which you had formerly filled. A proposition so generous and uncalled for, coming, moreover, from so near a relative, naturally demanded my best consideration, although his impetuosity did not leave much time for deliberation. And now, my dear cousin, it is with the full knowledge of the generosity of your character, and your inability to mistake or attribute motives, that I write to say that I do not feel justified in refusing an offer which has so many advantages. Such a chance may never occur to me again, and though my thoughts have certainly never yet been specially turned to the Church, yet as my views are large and broad, and my nature adaptable, I do not doubt my ultimate success. Did I feel that I should in any way stand in your light by thus acting, nothing would induce me to accept this living; and, indeed, even now I shall not feel quite at ease until you write me a few lines to say that you still believe me, your affectionate cousin,

"CYRIL PONSONBY."

Thus under the guidance of the late Secretary of the Rag Bag office wrote Cyril.

And John replied,

" My dear Cyril,
"I should indeed be unjust were I to be angry or hurt at your accept-

ing what I voluntarily rejected. After that rejection, I can only desire to see the living occupied by one who would endeavour to fulfil its duties to the best of his power. If you mean to do so, of course all is well, and you alone can be judge of this. At the same time, it would be untrue in me to say that I think you are fitted for the clerical life, as I cannot forget certain conversations we have had and the opinions you expressed therein. However, at least I have learnt neither to judge others harshly, nor to attribute motives rashly, and so wishing you all success and happiness, can sincerely sign myself, as your affectionate cousin.

"JOHN FORDYCE."

"*Ite missa est*," ejaculated John, as he finished and sealed his epistle, and so, doubtless, he thought.

Solitary lodgings in a small back street

in the neighbourhood of Bedford Row, beloved of lawyers, are not over cheerful at the best of times; but when their occupant is in bad spirits, has his own troubles and but little else to employ his time, their effect is found to be terribly depressing. In this situation, John Fordyce now found himself. With regard to the actual means of existence, he certainly was in no want. He possessed a small, but certain, income of about two hundred a year; away from Oxford, amply sufficient for a man of simple tastes and few wants. Had he been so inclined, he might with some little management, have contrived to see enough of London "life" on this sum, and gone the dreary round of "amusements and recreations;" but to what purpose, if he took not with him the faculty of being entertained? or, had his bias been in a High Church direction, he might have enjoyed religious dissipation enough, attached himself as pet layman to some special church clicque, and gone the round of re-openings, consecrations, and other "interesting ceremonies;" where doctrine, ritualism, and cold collation, are found united. He might have become thuribler, banner-bearer, acolyte— what not, and suffered amateur martyrdom at the hands of irate and protesting mobs. However, as we have seen, John's fancies did not lie in this direction, nor were his devotional tendencies dependent upon millinery, upholstery, and posture-making. Nor did he at all incline to the brotherly love of Exeter Hall.

He had written, soon after his arrival in London, to his friend Maxwell, asking his advice respecting the occupation of his time. He stated how great his desire was for active work for the benefit of his fellow-men, and yet how far off any opening seemed. His principles made

him equally obnoxious to High and Low
Churchmen, and yet he could not but feel
that there was a sphere of work open to a
layman, from which great good might
result.   Part of Maxwell's reply was as
follows.

"I deeply regret, my dear fellow, my
utter inability to assist you at the present
juncture, when you say you most need it.
I have undertaken to travel abroad for the
next year with Lord ——'s son, as my
companion and pupil. The offer was
made me in such a manner as rendered
refusal almost impossible, and I accepted
it the more readily, as I saw in it a way
—perhaps the only way—of realising a
prospect I have long had before me, which
some day I hope to detail to you.

"What you say about fruitful work is
true and good.   Man needs it for himself,
for the development and perfection of his
own nature.   I do not think you so poor

a Christian as to suppose you would take
up hard work for the souls and bodies of
others, as a reparation for the share you
may have had in the moral death of poor
Brydges, though I am aware there are some
who would actually recommend it as a penance. We wretched little mortals are too
fond of having transactions, as it were,
and settling accounts with the Divine, who
is quite able to work without us, if necessary. To believe that Brydges either
does or will suffer eternally for errors
you did not try to check, is to take a view
of Divine mercy of which, I think, you are
incapable.

"Work then, not penitentially with a
reference to the past, but hopefully looking
on to the future, and your own self-
development. 'But how?' you ask.
Have you the patience to wait for my
return to England? If so, take my advice, and spend that time in travelling,

studying the while both men and manners, and, if you will, such books as lay down the principles of political and social economy—books, the children of facts, and destined themselves to reproduce more glorious facts. Believe me, your time will not be wasted. Return with body and mind refreshed and invigorated, stored with useful knowledge and experience, your heart full of hope; come thus, and I say we will join hand in hand in the work there is to do—aye, and, please God, will do it, too."

And in a few days after the receipt of this letter, John Fordyce began to make arrangements for his travels; caring little whither his wandering steps were turned.

END OF THE SECOND VOLUME.

BEYOND THE CHURCH.

"The shadow cloaked from head to foot,
Who keeps the keys of all the Creeds."

IN MEMORIAM.

IN THREE VOLUMES.

VOL. III.

LONDON:
HURST AND BLACKETT, PUBLISHERS,
SUCCESSORS TO HENRY COLBURN,
13, GREAT MARLBOROUGH STREET.
1866.

CHAPTER I.

"JOHN! John! Why, bless the boy, he's deaf! John Fordyce, I say. Stop man, are you deaf, or cracked?"

The speaker wss a pleasant rosy-gilled man of about fifty; a clergyman of the Church of England by his attire—one comfortably beneficed, and consequently conservative by his look of satisfaction; and better than all, a thoroughly kind-hearted, amiable man, by his open brow and beaming smile. He was in fact the Rev. Alfred Royd, rector of a wealthy London parish, and godfather to John Fordyce, being an old friend of his father. And at the time we introduce him to our readers, he was taking his usual morning constitutional in the Square of Bloomsbury—habit by which he sharpened a very excellent natural appetite for breakfast. And as he walked along with his head well thrown back, a pleasant smile on his face, one hand behind him, and the other grasping a handsome ebony cane, he became conscious of a figure before him which he seemed to recognize. A free use of his gold-rimmed eye-glass, put the recognition beyond doubt; and in a moment afterwards, in answer to his genial greetings, John turned round, and on his side recognised his old friend and godfather. He showed a face so white and ghastly, as to astonish and shock the good Rector.

"Why, my boy, are these the fruits of your reading and your honours? It is time you had done with Oxford, I think, for I can scarcely recognize you. You

want a run with the hounds, man, as soon
as this frost gives, that's what will do you
good. How's your father, and how come·
you in town just now?"

"Oh, I am well enough," replied John
indirectly, "well enough, but jaded and
tired—nothing to hurt. Will you give me
some breakfast, Mr. Royd? and I will tell
you all my news."

"Will I? Why to be sure I will; that's
exactly what I meant to do. Come along,
my dear boy, I know it is waiting for us,
and to tell the truth I am quite ready for
it."

Then taking John's arm, and looking
nearer at him, he perceived that he was
disturbed and in grief about something,
and so kindly forbore to question him
further, but hurried him to the cozy well-
warmed study of his house, which was
close by in the Square.

There, broiled fish and ham and sau-

B 2

sages and eggs awaited them, and to these
the Rector at least did full justice; both
for himself and his guest too. He had
great faith in good living, which he regarded as the medicament of all human
evils. To give him his due, though a
gourmand, he was not selfish, and willingly
dispensed to others the good things he so
much enjoyed himself. By an odd freak
of nature, his heart was centralizing in his
stomach; but it was a heart still, and one
that beat for others too, to such an extent even, as to sometimes cause indigestion to the circumjacent regions. So he
chatted merrily, and helped liberally,
though his silent guest seemed scarcely to
appreciate the good Westphalia Ham and
Oxford sausages, and actually rejected the
buttered toast and marmalade. At length
the Rector pushed his chair back, crossed
his well-shaped legs, took a pinch of snuff
and opened fire.

"John, my boy, what is the matter? I can see something is wrong, you know. You have not disagreed with your father, have you?"

"I have not disagreed with my father," repeated John, mechanically, "but I have no longer a father to disagree with."

"The boy is certainly mad," thought the Rector, with some feelings of alarm, "he can't have been drinking, he's left that off, I know; besides, it's too early. It's brain-fever coming on. Come, come, John," continued he to his godson, "you are not yourself to-day. Your over-work has been too much for you, you must have a rest and be quiet. I say, take care of the cloth."

This appeal was made, not on behalf of the clerical body, as may at first appear, but of the fair linen covering of the breakfast-table, which John, in utter abstraction and forgetfulness, was piercing and stabbing with his fork. Then he rose with a jerk.

"I can't stand this any more. I had hoped you knew it—you must soon, so why not now. My father has cast me off and disowned me because I won't be ordained !"

Royd's ruddy face lost every vestige of colour, as he gasped out,

"Good God! John! it's not true— say it's not true—I can't believe you. I was afraid you had quarrelled, but nothing like this. Turned you out of doors? Good heavens! Why how came that about? It can't be true !"

"It's as true, nevertheless, as I stand before you. It all happened about ten days, or a fortnight ago, I can't remember. I have been thinking over it for months, and meant to tell him, but that kind-hearted fool, Dr. Field, thought it necessary to interfere, and wrote a letter which set my father in a flame; and when I said it was true, and that I would not take orders, he cursed me and told me to leave his house—I was no longer his son!"

"You said you would not be ordained? Why, John, this is more wonderful to me than the other news! What am I to hear of next? I knew nothing of all this. When did this idea come into your head? For God's sake tell me what you *do* mean!"

There was a spice of bitterness in the tone in which good Mr. Royd spoke to his godson. Depths lower than he had dreamed of seemed to open out. Was it possible that John Fordyce was one of that class who are popularly described as "flying in the face of Providence?" Mr. Royd was a zealous upholder of the Establishment, but then the Establishment reciprocated and

was a zealous upholder of Mr. Royd.
Any one, therefore, who, having good
prospects, declined to " enter the
Church," appeared to him guilty of suicide.

"I know you will be amazed and
shocked. I know you will agree with
my father, and perhaps have nothing
more to do with me; but I cannot
help it. I cannot swallow down my
doubts and difficulties, and say to my
mind, 'don't think' to keep my friends'
good opinion—no, nor my father's either.
I have thought about it for months and
months, and the fact is, I cannot take
orders. I don't believe in the Church
of England. No, you need not start,
for I am not a Romanist, nor likely
to become one. What I mean is, I do
not see what claim she has over me ;
I do not believe her doctrines as far
as I can discover what they are, nor

will I undertake to preach and uphold them !"

" The Church of your fathers, young man, the Church of your fathers !" said Royd, in his Sunday voice.

" What, this present Church of England and her teaching ? I should like you to prove that. Of course she uses the same places and forms of worship that she did in the days of my fathers, but every fifty years makes a difference in her doctrines and teaching. If our fore-fathers and those before us had stifled the voice of conscience and stuck to the Church of *their* fathers there would have been no Reformation, mind you."

" Ah, but that was a return to first principles—to the ages of primitive simplicity."

" Do you mean the first three centuries ? I think you will find corruption already rooted there. First principles are what I seek; but I seek for them in the words of the great Teacher, Christ. What he pronounced essential, I will accept and bow to; but I refuse to accept as such the human corruptions and interpolations of later ages."

"Then you altogether reject the Catholic Church?"

"I can scarcely find two who agree in their ideas of what the Catholic Church is. The Roman Catholic says his is the only true Catholic Church, and excludes all the rest of the world. A Protestant says that the aggregate of 'orthodox' Protestant sects make up the Catholic Church, and exclude all Romanists and Greeks. The High Church clicque have their special shibboleth and test. I would regard it as embracing all Christians alike who worship one Father, and accept Christ's promises and imitate his example.

That is the Catholic Church I accept
and believe in. National Churches, like
National Governments, are useful as representing the agreement in main points
of the majority.

"But when men come forward with the
chains of tests and articles, and would
limit faith, and define and dogmatise on
mystery, then I shrink back and cannot
take orders, or pledge myself to such a
system. God's voice, speaking in my conscience, tells me what is necessary for my
salvation, and that does not include the
Athanasian creed. National Churches,
whatever the authority they may assume,
can only give human ideas and speculation
about eternal truths."

"John, John, where did you learn all
these German views of yours? You make
me perfectly shudder."

"I learned them on my knees, Sir, and
when studying my Bible. Whether they be

German or no, I neither know nor care. Truth is truth whatever form it bears, or name it carries. I know nothing of German views, or doctrines as such. But I find that while I was a mere heathen and cared nothing about religion, no one was shocked, or said a word; since I have begun to try, and think, and act aright, all my friends reproach me. I knew I should shock you, but now you see why I cannot be ordained."

But, no. Mr. Royd could only see a recalcitrant godson who held German views, and refused a most excellent living. He began to see also that mere invective and reproach would not bring back this wandering sheep to the fold. " Let us see," quoth he to himself, " whether a few drops of ' *oleum gammonicum* ' will grease the rusty cranks and wheels, and make the machine work kindly." Then aloud, " I am sure, quite sure, my dear boy, that you mean all you say, and I respect and admire your conscientiousness. I am only afraid you may do something on the spur of the moment which you will regret afterwards. You know St. Paul and the copy-book both bid us to do nothing rashly. Let us understand each other. You say that you have no leanings to Rome, but you object to the Articles. Is it to the idea of religious tests?"

" I do not see the utility of religious tests. Religion lies between the human conscience and the Deity."

" Why pray would you abolish them?"

" Because I do not recognise the right which any set of men have to dogmatise to their fellows, and limit salvation to the recognition and belief of certain Articles. Beyond the most simple and primitive articles of faith, I do not see how we can safely venture. When the ' Church ' begins to define and dogmatise, and explain mysteries, then I say she is as faith-less as Thomas, when he wanted to place his fingers in the print of the nails. And when the Church, or any corporation calling itself a Church, begins to enforce her peculiar notions on her members, then I say she places a yoke on men's shoulders too heavy to be borne."

"But, my dear boy, do you mean to say that you would deliberately reject all the judgments, authority, and teaching of the Church, which has come down to us from the Apostles' times, and is, as I think, embodied in the Church of England?"

"I find no promise of infallibility to the Church of England, or any other Church —save that the gates of Hell shall not prevail against her, which, as I take it, means that the power of good will finally prevail over that of evil. Therefore, I cannot give unlimited assent to the de-

cisions and dictates of any set of men,
however good and wise. I don't see that
what we call wisdom has much to do with
salvation, nor does Christ seem to insist
upon it. There are wise and good men
of all countries and times and faiths; but,
however much they may differ in religion,
I find them agreeing in loving God and
each other. I must then decline to give
assent to what I cannot understand or
see. If my heart and intention be right,
God will show me all I want for salvation."

"And to what, young man, do you
think such doubts, such opinions, must
lead?"

"To God, I hope," was the quiet answer. "Look here, I can't say 'yes' and
think 'no.' It is a defect in my education,
perhaps. And as my doubts are here,
unsought, I must let them work out their
answer. It would be criminal, as I think,

to crush them, and then undertake duties
and responsibilities, and give pledges I
neither understand, believe, nor approve."

There was silence for a few minutes.
John looked straight out of the window
into vacancy, his host built a little *crom-
lech* of dry toast, and then crushed it with
a well-aimed blow of his fork.   But to his
mental eye those were no mere scattered
pieces of toast—infidels, sceptics, ideolo-
gists, of all ages lay writhing before him.
At length he began again.

"From what I can see, my dear John,
your objections are to Church authority
on dogmatic points.   Well, now, I won't
argue about them, but I want to ask you
one question : do you think you are wise
to permit your ideas on those matters to
interfere with your ordination, and cut
you off from a sphere of great utility ?
We want earnest fellows like you."

Oh, Mr. Royd ! surely the *oleum gammo-*

nicum was uncorked here! "To work and Christianise the masses; and here, for a whim, you hold back and refuse to labour. Again, you must belong to some Church, you will find difficulties and discrepancies in all; nor do I think you would find orders anywhere so easy as in the Church of England. She allows great latitude of opinion on certain points, and includes all classes, from those who are Dissenters in all but name, to those whom only a narrow line separates from Romanism. You might go further and fare worse. You see all these men, holding such different shades of opinion, are able to sign the Articles on taking a living. So, you see, the case is this. By letting these scruples stand in the way of your ordination, you are cut off from doing much good which would otherwise be in your power. You give up all, and gain nothing. Try to forget it all—try to forget it all—

regard it as a snare of the devil to hinder you from the good you might do. I am sure Bishops A and B would say so."

" My dear Mr. Royd, I would as soon take your advice as that of any of the bishops on the bench—nay, sooner, for you are, I know, in the habit of meaning what you say; but I can't burke my doubts and smother them that way. I don't believe my ministry would be helped by my commencing it with a lie, nor do I see that my only way of utility is in taking orders. But even were this not so, even if a state of apparent idleness were the result of my holding these views, I could not change. A man cannot change and alter his belief as he pleases. You don't believe transubstantiation, do you, Mr. Royd ?

" I ? Good heavens ! certainly not. You don't mean to end your catalogue of what you don't believe, by declaring your faith in that?"

"No, indeed; but to a Romanist your not holding transubstantiation is as inexplicable and deadly a heresy as my views are to you. You could not undertake to believe it for any sum which might be offered. No; nor can I undertake to change my views for any livings, or to please any one."

"I don't doubt your sincerity, my dear boy, for a single moment; but, oh, all this is such a sad disappointment to me. I cannot understand it. Talking with you is like wrestling with a shadow. I suppose I am growing old-fashioned, and my ideas do not fall in with the age. If you had come and said 'I am a Romanist, or an Atheist, or even a Dissenter,' I could, at least, have understood what you meant; but there is nothing definite in what you say, no

c 2

'ism' in it at all; it seems to start from nothing and lead nowhere. I can't understand it, and even now scarcely believe it; so if you have been playing with me, say you are joking, my boy, and end my trouble."

"Would to God I could, my dear, kind old friend, or rather thank God I cannot. No, indeed, I am in sober earnest at last. I have wasted too much time to joke now. I know well enough what I am doing, that I must expect all my friends to be against me, and that I shall be accused of conceit, self-will, obstinacy. I am glad, at least, they cannot accuse me of self-interested motives."

"Well, well, promise me one thing, come and stay a week with me, my boy, before you go away." John had briefly mentioned his plans. "You will be heartily welcome, as you very

well know.   Perhaps we may see matters
more clearly—who knows ?   Now you
will not refuse your old friend and godfather this one thing ?"

"Let it be as you wish.   I will defer
my going for a week, but I do not think I
shall change my mind."   Nor did he.

Argument, persuasion, entreaty; entreaty, persuasion, argument, all in vain.
Pearson, Paley, Harold, Browne, Tomline, all in vain.   Endless talk, endless
discussion, isms and doxies rampant,
" alarums, excursions"—what ! all in vain ?
Yes, all to no avail.   Yet the Rector had
gone cunningly to work.   He knew the
connection of mind and matter, of faith
and feasting.   Tawny old port at 80s.
per dozen, he thought would be enough
to convert the most rampant Dissenter.
Creeds should come on with the *entrées* and
be discussed over dessert.   Who can convert
a hungry man, unless, indeed, his dinner

depends on his conversion? High feeding must make a high Churchman, that is in the Rector's old-fashioned interpretation of that term.

Most mental maladies are traceable to disordered digestion. Therefore, in Mr. Royd's eyes, the greatest heretics were simply men whose biliary or digestive organs had departed from their proper normal condition. Arius probably had liver complaint, Eutyches dyspepsia, Macedonius jaundice. They neglected their dinners, and so fell into heresy. Why, he, Mr. Royd, had never been troubled with scruples or doubts, and what had been the bulwarks which kept his orthodoxy straight and his Churchmanship upright? A pint of port, ditto claret, with salmon, venison and oysters *ad lib.* So he tried all upon poor John, mentally praying "Let digestion wait on appetite and *faith* on both."

But as we have said without success.
At the end of three weeks, John Fordyce
remained precisely where he was before.
He read all he was told to read; he
listened to all that was said; he thought
on all arguments produced, and remained
still of his old opinion. Strange that
where Mr. Royd so clearly saw white
he could only perceive black; strange that
what to his eyes appeared sable, should
shine so brightly white to the Rector's
vision! But so it was, and his good
friend had to give him up in despair.

"My dear John," at last he said, "I
see it is of no use. I must leave you in
better and wiser hands. I don't pretend
to understand you, or any of the young
men of the present day; all is changed
now. We used to hunt and enjoy our
glass of wine and cigar, and say our
prayers and worship God and serve the
King, and what more would a sensible

man wish for? There were good men
too in those days, I can tell you, honest,
God-fearing men, who did as much real
work as any of you young fellows. But
bless your heart, we never had doubts or
scruples, they never occurred to us, we
were too busy. And you young fellows
now are quite a different set; all talk and
theories and universal knowledge which
bears no fruit. Well, God bless you, my
boy! I can't think any ill of you. You
are in earnest if you are headstrong. Go
on in your own way—I suppose you must
at least. I think you will find out your mistake, though I have not much hopes for a
man who has read Tomline and yet does
not see his way clear. Good-bye, my
poor boy, good-bye. I shall not be surprised at hearing you have become a Catholic abroad. These are topsy-turvey days
now, and one scarce knows what to do in
them."

The good Mr. Royd sat silent and sad long after his godson had departed. He was very fond of him, and very sorry for him, and looked upon him as lost. At length he rang the bell for the cook, and in reply to her enquiries about dinner, murmured softly,

"Just a ptarmigan if you can get one, Mary, and a little clear soup and a pudding; and, Mary, you may try that stuffing of oysters you spoke of. Ah, poor boy, poor boy!"

CHAPTER II.

AND so John Fordyce went abroad on his travels—a new Childe Harold on a new pilgimage. Whither, my dear reader, by your good leave we will not follow him. A dry catalogue of places visited, compilation from Murray and Bradshaw, would but slightly interest or instruct; a random sketch, vaguely outlined, of places never seen by the author would fatigue rather more. It is not everyone, who, with Moore's fairy power, can summon up dreams of the golden East from the guide books of the period. And after all it was men and manners he went to study, more than to admire

scenery or do the picturesque. Like
Shaitan, he wandered " to and fro," if not
" seeking whom he might devour," yet
seeking pasture on which his mind might
feed. With him he took such books as
Maxwell had advised. Books treating
on political and social economy—entering
into educational and sanitary subjects—
books which might supply him at once
with facts, and principles founded on those
facts. Like the Lady of Shalott, he felt
" half sick of shadows," he pined to get
forth from the limbo of theories and
doxies, to breathe the pure air of Nature,
to look upon the world external, and
listen in silence to the lesson she had to
teach him. Here was an Alma Mater
indeed, one whose warm open bosom
was ready to welcome and receive him as
a child, and to her unerring voice was
he ready to give that ready, cheerful im-
plicit obedience, which the dogmatic de-

mands of men could not wring from him.
And side by side with this great form of
Nature stood the figure of Science, her
exponent—supplementing her teaching and
declaring to all her mysteries, leading the
enquirer on by steps steady and sure,
however gradual, to those heights the
utmost of which is but the footstool of the
throne of God. And the more John studied, the clearer he saw how that Science
is the friend of Religion, and not the an-
tagonist which selfish priests would make
it. He saw how intimate and necessary
is their connection, each perfecting the
other, each satisfying some want or ener-
gising some power of man.

He saw, moreover, how Faith, which
leads to godliness, is of no age, or country, or system—and that superstition, and
unfaith, and intolerance are of all. He
saw how the first bright memories of the
face of the Divine become gradually

blurred and obscured by the clouds of human prejudice and error. How, as if conscious of their own decadence, men began to demand human mediators between themselves and the Almighty, and to enter into transactions about their souls. How, after a while, man arrogated to himself the powers of the Divine, and then, Saturn-like the old religions devoured their own children.

Lastly, he saw how, by a silent subtle movement thrilling throughout the world, a new spirit of religion arose in which there was more of God and less of man— in which men no longer speculated about the Divine nature, or dogmatised about the doctrines of their own selection, but were content to worship God's perfection, accept his revelations to their conscience, and imitate His nature by their love to one another. He looked forward, and saw religion no longer a matter of mechanical

transaction of certain hebdomadal duties;
no longer a mere Sunday parade of the laity
to listen submissively to the stammering
orders of their clerical drill-masters. He
saw a time when the oracle should speak
loud and clear to the instruction, and not
the confusion of those who approached it.
But most important of all, he perceived
how that a man, desirous of benefitting
the lower orders, must commence by improving their social and sanitary condition,
before preaching heavenly truths to their
minds, and that Science must be the
pioneer of Christianity.

And so, encouraged and refreshed by
what he had seen and learned, he prepared
to retrace his steps, and commence at
home such work as he might.

Whenever he determined upon making
any lengthened stay, he duly forwarded
his fresh address to his lawyers, and
through this means received, among

others, the following letters during his absence of more than two years. The first reached him about fifteen months after his first leaving England.

Letter No. 1. From Edgar Purcell to John Fordyce.

"My dear Fordyce,

"I am writing now in but small hopes of this letter duly reaching you, although your lawyers have promised to send it on to your next address. How long it is since we have seen each other, and how many strange events have happened in that interval! Were I not so bad a correspondent myself, I should feel inclined to reproach you for not keeping me duly posted as to the incidents of your travel. However, I suppose I can scarcely do that, as this happens to be my first epistle to you since your departure. I may, perhaps, excuse myself

by informing you that you are the first
of my old Oxford friends to whom I have
yet written, to give the news of the most
important event of my life—my marriage.
I know how amazed you will be when
you get as far as this—prepare to be still
more so, when I tell you my wife is no less
a person than that Miss Harding about
whom you used to tease me at Oxford,
and when we were all together at Llan-y-
morfa. It has all come about in a wonderful way, and, as I do not know when
I may see you again, I will endeavour to
give you some account.

"You know all about my Malvern
adventures; and how I made the acquaintance of Miss—the *late* Miss Harding, and her papa, Major Harding, so I
need not repeat it now. She had made
a very great impression upon me by the
time of my return to Oxford, and I was
rendered very uncomfortable by the

struggle between my affections and my conscience. You remember what my views were respecting celibacy of the clergy, and also my ideas about founding a monastery. Well, of course, Marbecke, whom you never liked, but who was very kind to me, bore me out and encouraged me in those views. But the difficulty of the matter was that I found my own ideas had changed very considerably, and I no longer quite saw my way clear as to the absolute necessity of celibacy, or the desirability of founding a monastery and becoming a monk. Still, when a man has expressed himself strongly on any point, he does not like afterwards to go back from his word, and confess he did not know his own mind—at all events, I did not. However, after bearing all this for a long while, I decided, just before we went to Llan-y-morfa, to run down to Malvern again, and see the Hardings, that I might be quite sure of my own feelings, and learn whether they were reciprocated, which, of course, would have settled the question.

"I was doomed to disappointment. When I arrived, I found that Major Harding and his daughter had left their cottage, and, indeed, Malvern ; nor could I get any information as to their destination. This, of course, brought affairs to a standstill, and very much threw me out. However, I tried to persuade myself that all was for the best, and I should do better as a celibate clergyman.

"Then came my ordination. Marbecke had been most kind, and had got for me a very nice curacy with a friend of his, the Rev. H. Travers, a very good Churchman, and great ritualist and celebrated preacher. The name of his living was Affcolmbe. I wish I could say as much for his character, as I can for his principles and Church-

manship; but he was a most dictatorial
person, and had views about passive
obedience which, to his curate, were very
trying. Marbecke had told him I needed
guiding and ' forming,' but I do not see
what incessantly contradicting and snubbing me had to do with that, or that
personal discourtesy was necessary.   I
daresay that I was to some degree in
fault, but still, as I am conscious of a
great desire to learn, and do my duty, 1
think a few occasional kind words would
have encouraged me and given me heart
for my labours.   The church and its
services were all I could wish, and I am
sure Travers must have spent large sums
from his private means upon both.   However, unfortunately, his dictatorial and
ungenial manner had rendered him most
unpopular in the parish, and I soon saw
how possible it is to do a good action in
such a way as to produce bad effects.   In

spite of all the money he spent upon the poor and the schools, he was heartily disliked, which was, perhaps, the reason he so seldom stayed long at Affcolmbe. While I was curate, he was seldom there for more than a few days together, accepting frequent invitations to preach all over England, and acting as confessor to some of the various sisterhoods.

" In his absence, I was always under the *espionage* of a couple of spinster ladies, associates of some sisterhood, who resided in the parish, and did more to set it by the ears through their injudicious interference and constant tale-bearing, than I have leisure to tell you. On his return, there was always something which went wrong, some complaint made, some objection to bring forward.

" At last, I really grew weary of my life, for though I could not help admiring the sincerity and hard labours of Travers, my spirit was nearly broken by over-work and frequent snubbings. I had made up my mind to leave when my year was up, and had begun to think again of my monastic plan, when something occurred which altered all my plans.

" The hall had remained untenanted all the time of my curacy, and, on enquiry, I was told it belonged to a Mr. Vyvyan, who had come into it recently and never resided. About seven months ago, I heard that the family were in residence again, and you may imagine my surprise on recognising in Mr. Vyvyan and his daughter, my old friend Major Harding and Miss Myrtle. I then remembered that he had been engaged in a lawsuit for some property when I knew him at Malvern, and having been successful, had been obliged to adopt the surname of the cousin from whom the estate came. He had been travelling abroad for his rheumatism, and had only just returned. His welcome to me was most friendly; and it only needed one glance at his daughter to revive all my old feelings of affection, which, from what I now see was a mistaken notion of duty, I had repressed so long. I carefully and conscientiously studied the question of clerical celibacy, and came to the conclusion that Scripture, the early Church, and the Church of England, throw no obstacles in the way of such of her clergy as choose to marry.

"As soon as I saw my way clear, I explained my feelings, first to the Major, and then with his consent to his daughter, with what result I leave you to guess, when I say that within three months she was good enough to become my wife. The only drawback to my entire happiness, was the uncalled for anger with which my news was received by Marbecke and my Rector, Travers. I had not interfered with their convictions, nor did my marriage make the slightest difference to them. I certainly thought it hard, therefore, for Marbecke to write and warn me of the fate of him who put his hand to the plough and drew back; informing me also that he feared he had been deceived in his estimation of my character. My Rector simply informed me that it was fortunate the termination of my curacy was at hand, as he did not like married curates or their wives, and thought that no acceptable work could be done save by women bound by holy vows of celibacy.

" I was heartily glad to leave Affcolmbe for the old cottage at Malvern, and am now waiting until I can purchase a small living and settle down. I still dislike the system of purchase, but as it is destined to outlive me, must bow to it if I wish to do any work. Do not think from all this, that my Church principles are in the least changed. Although, however, I still think as I used—save as to celibacy—I hope I am less obstinate in proposing my own views, and more tolerant of the ideas and prejudices of those who sincerely differ from me. And now I have written so much, that I have only time to add how delighted both I and my wife, who sends her kindest regards, shall be to see you on your return, and that I am always

" Your sincere friend,

" EDGAR PURCELL."

Letter 2. From Messrs. Hunt and Ferret, Lincoln's Inn Fields, to John Fordyce :

" Dear Sir,

" We regret to say that it is our

unpleasant duty to inform you of the death of the Rev. H. E. C. Fordyce, late Rector of Easimore, our much respected client. It took place on the 2nd ult. at Bath, where he had been resident since his resignation of the living of Easimore, and was immediately caused by a seizure of an apoplectic character, as we have learned from his physician, Dr. Choke. Having been officially present at the reading of the will of the deceased, dated Christmas, we may inform you that the whole of his estate, personal and real, is devised to his nephew, the Rev. Cyril Ponsonby, Rector of Easimore, to the entire exclusion, we regret to add, of yourself. In consideration of the long period of time for which our firm has been honoured with the confidence of your family, we have felt it our duty to communicate this intelligence to you personally, instead of

to Messrs. Pescud and Pobjoy, your legal
advisers.

"We have the honour to be,
      "Dear Sir,
            "Your obedient servants,
                  "HUNT & FERRET."

Letter 3. From Cyril Ponsonby to John
Fordyce :

"My dear John,

"Although we have had no personal
correspondence since the time of your
departure for the continent, and the unhappy misunderstanding which led to it,
I hope I may say that there is no ill-
will or quarrel between us. Indeed, for
my part, I can in all truth declare that
I have never quarrelled with any one in
my life, and that you are the last person
with whom I should think it possible. I
may have felt some disappointment at

the manner in which you received my letter, announcing my acceptance of your poor father's most generous offer. I may have thought that your answer displayed a want of confidence in my sincerity, which scarcely did credit to my real nature. However, the peculiarity of our relative positions was a sufficient excuse for this, even had not the sacred nature of my calling taught me to forgive such insinuations wounding to my vanity. It is, therefore, with the feelings of an affectionate relation that I once more have to communicate an important event in my life, on which I hope I may claim your congratulations, although the feelings with which you learn my news may be of a mingled character.

"In telling you of my marriage, and that Miss Masterman is the object of my choice, I know that I shall cause you much surprise. Such is the case.

I had not been long in orders, before I felt how much my celibate state crippled my utility as a clergyman. On looking around for a help-meet, it was impossible not to be struck with admiration of the qualities of Miss Masterman, a feeling which only increased with knowledge and opportunity. After waiting a fitting period, to assure myself of the permanent nature of my feelings, I proposed, was accepted, and am now what I hope one day to see you—a happily married man. I am quite in earnest when I say that a good wife would be, under the circumstances, the best possible thing for you, and give you a hold on life nothing else can.

"I sincerely trust that you do not intend prolonging your continental sojourn indefinitely, and that there is some hope of seeing you back in England again. If it would not revive painful feelings too much, I need not say how acceptable a visit from you would be to me and my wife, or that Easimore Rectory will ever be ready to receive you and make you welcome. You will find many alterations—we call them improvements—since your poor father's time; but it will always be our endeavour to preserve the old, hospitable spirit of the place. And now with all kind wishes, in which Mrs. Ponsonby begs to unite,

" I am, my dear John,

" Your affectionate cousin,

" CYRIL PONSONBY."

And this was Letter 4. From the Rev. Allan Maxwell:

" My dear John Fordyce,

" I wonder where this will find your restless wandering self. From the accounts of your lawyers—if they be not polite lies—you are flitting up and down like the dove of old, finding no rest for the sole of your foot. Do you ever mean to come back to the Ark whence you started, and if so, how, when, and where? Perhaps you will retort that it was my advice which started you on your travels. True, my son, but I did not intend their being indefinite in duration. Nevertheless, good John, I have all faith in you, and know that if you tarry it is with a reason; and yet I write to say that if you have no other call, I have a need of you—a work for you to do in your own way, at your own time, unlimited and unfettered by any restrictions. I cannot in a letter tell you all the particulars of my situation, or of the exact nature of the work I reserve for you. Thus much you can know. Turn back to the date of my letter,

yes, 'The Rectory, St. Lazarus, Marbury.' That is my residence, my dear
John, that is my Rectory, and when
you next see me, you will see, and, I
hope, reverence a beneficed clergyman;
a portly Rector, a stalled ox.

"Open your eyes wide at the idea of
my being an incumbent, wider at my
being no longer a Fellow of St. Catherine's, widest of all at my living being
the gift of a peer! And so to tantalise
you, I will give you no more details.
Ah! how glad I shall be if you
come; would that for 'if' I might write
'when.' I have need of some friend,
'like-minded,' with whom to discuss
matters and hold council. I am hard
at work, combatting, sometimes with
success, sometimes with loss and failure,
the forces of evil in a manufacturing
town.

"Happily I am not a *doctrinaire*, or

theorist. I am sufficiently elastic, and take my knock down blows only as incentives to fresh exertions. For, oh! my dear John, the most pitiably ludicrous sight, is that of a clerical *doctrinaire* tinkering up the holes in his pet theory when the water runs through. And of pet theories we have just now enough and to spare. Talkee, talkee, by yards, gallons, tons; acrid, washy, heavy stuff, inducing indigestion, somnolence, night-mare. We have just had a clerical congress in the nearest Cathedral town, which people believe will effect great things.

" For my part, to believe that the clergy will redress grievances they admit, requires an amount of faith which I possess not. Bakers do not generally complain of the high price of bread. There, however, we all appeared mounted each on his favourite hobby, and there we executed various gambadoes and caprioles in a circle. There, too, was a *grand écuyer* in the person of a Right Reverend to keep us all in order, and restrain our hobbies when they became rampagious. And the hobbies themselves? Hacks and screws all, scarce one sound in wind and limb. Broken-kneed, sand-cracked, spavinned, bolters, crib-biters, roarers. They were only fit for Jack Atcheler's. But here I am getting horsey, and most unclerical.

" It is well to laugh now, but I could almost have wept to see some hundreds of us priests and levites gathered together, with the best of intentions, to confess that all was not quite as it should be, and then to discuss and listen to so many plans of how not to do it. Oh, those hobbies! those hobbies! I hear their neighings in my ears yet. ' *Et tu Brute!*' sayest thou? I fear I am not much better than my neighbours. Let me confess it in deadly

F

secresy. I have a pet theory—I have a
fixed idea, and I know of an infallible way
of regenerating the world. Do you ask ?
It is in *cocoa*—Theobroma, food for the
gods. If only my people would drink
that instead of gin, which isn't even gin,
but adulterated, methylated spirit. However, enough for a while. You see I had
half an hour to spare, and have been
letting off the steam to you. And now in
all sober earnest, if your heart is as mine,
and you desire to do some useful work for
your fellow-creatures, no amateur dab-
bling, but honest hard work, come to
Marbury, and join with me in what I have
in hand. I know you, and can honestly
say that I shall be glad and proud of my
helper. You know that when I say a
thing, I mean it, and will believe me
when I sign myself,

" Ever your affectionate friend,

" ALLAN MAXWELL."

" At last," said John, when he had
read the last of these letters, delivered to
him at various times in his wanderings,
" and now, good bye to the old life, and
welcome what Fate has in store for me.
I left England broken and shattered in
hope, and I return with hopes renewed.
I am to begin to work now after these
years. What will the work be, I wonder
—will it last? And when will the end
be ?"

CHAPTER III.

WITHIN one week after the receipt of Allan Maxwell's letter, John, embrowned and bearded from his wanderings abroad, landed in Southampton, and speedily found his way to Marbury. It was one of those great midland manufacturing towns, where the atmosphere is darkened with smoke, redolent of hot oil, and resonant with an incessant clang, clicking, and buzz of the unwearying iron steam monsters. For miles about, the water is blackened with foul ooze and slimy out-pourings from the mill-yards, the earth is parched and burnt and sapless, the vegetation is stunted, and over all hangs the dark canopy of smoke, lowering and sullen. A wilderness of small stunted houses, ill-drained, ill-lighted, ill-ventilated, and arranged in what, by little mockery, were styled, " gardens," " courts," and " yards," interspersed here and there with the staring, hundred-eyed factories, with their monstrous high walls and great gates, constituted the town.

It was a gloomy place, a sullen place, a place to rouse feelings of despair at first sight. To a stranger, the first idea was one of wonder how any human beings could voluntarily choose to live there—how they could make it a home, and marry, and gather families around them, and cultivate all the amenities of life under conditions so monstrous and unnatural. And yet such was the case. In that busy, teeming, smoke-stained town, life went on no other than in the country, which is styled innocent. For good or ill, for mutual help or mutual hatred, for the cultivation of the divine, or the base, part of human nature, there was room there, in the crowded city as in the open fields, as in every place whereon the eye of God looks down. And here, while sentimental ladies and gentlemen are compassing sea and land to make one proselyte of some interesting negro, or delightful Zulu—a process which generally results in adding drunkeness and hypocrisy to the indigenous vices of the native; here, in the very midst, are to be found those who are the real heathens of these days—British born brothers and sisters, under the same rule and dominion as ourselves, whose chief misfortune is, that in possessing white, and not black, skins, they have no claim upon us.

Here you will find religion, not cor-rupted, but non-existent, morality and self-restraint almost unknown, and the choice lying between the Deism of the shrewder minds, and the pure and simple heathendom of the coarser. View man simply as a "forked animal," and you have him thus in the lower orders of such a town as Marbury—an animal whose only idea is that of the necessary struggle for existence, and the gratification of such appetites as he has in common with the brutes. Its birth ushering in an unlovely round of dreary monotonous work, commenced with the very earliest years, when happier children are playing round their mothers' knees, and terminated only when the withered hands are too feeble, and the dried-up frame too broken to toil longer; a few intervals of frantic dissipation and coarse indulgence, marking such a special event as a birth or marriage. Death—and all is told. A hopeless journey over a dreary barren desert, leading nowhere.

Such is life among the lower orders of
our great cities in this Christian land,
where the gospel of Christ is nominally
the religion of the country. All honour,
therefore, to the "few" stout-hearted
labourers, whatever their creed, whatever
their various crotchets and whims, who
are found willing to live and labour among
them, to let in some faint gleams of light
into these dark corners, and carry some
few crumbs of comfort to the souls who
are too far gone to know that they are
starving. For the work, other things
set aside, is no light one, from the very
fact that, although we can see somewhat
of their outward appearance and life—
within, their feelings and wishes and
desires, those hidden springs of action,
are as great and complete a mystery to
us as if they spoke a foreign tongue and
inhabited some island in the Pacific.

They have to be studied, these English

heathens; yes, and they will amply repay the study, too. For after all, they are men and women, wild and tangled as their life may seem to us, children of the same father, and sharers of the same salvation. Yes, and in those dark corners and noisome places will be found growing oftentimes the fairest flowers, such is the wonderful economy of nature. Spite of all disadvantages, of the pestilent condition of life into which they are forced, the true noble soul will be found shining out all the brighter for its dark surroundings.

After some little time expended in vain enquiries and fruitless wanderings, John managed to discover the whereabouts of St. Lazarus, which lay, as he expected, in the very lowest quarter of the town, in a district which told an unmistakeable tale of extreme poverty.

It was at some little distance from the mill-quarter, and its population consisted

chiefly of labourers, bricklayers, costermongers, and petty hucksters. Every
tenth house seemed a beer-shop or gin-
palace, whose gaudy splendour was more
apparent from the mean and squalid
tenements by which it was surrounded.
Ears, nose, and eyes were all equally
outraged and offended in a passage
through the district of St. Lazarus. Think,
dear reader, what a residence in it must
have been like to educated gentlemen,
daintily brought up! Yet here, in the
very heart and thickest of the neighbourhood had Maxwell chosen to take
up his quarters, having let the proper
rectory which stood in the fashionable
part of the town. The house he inhabited
as such, was a large old-fashioned building,
erected in those days when men built to
last, and not to let. Its chief merit, in
Maxwell's eyes, had been, next to its
central position, the fact of its possessing

a large number of apartments, two of
them of considerable size. This was the
more fortunate, as, in addition to the
ordinary sitting-room — in his case, it
might have been called an extraordinary
one—he was enabled to combine in miniature, a dispensary, hospital, and school-
room under one roof, at a considerable
saving of expense and labour. One large
room he had kept for the general sitting-
room, where nearly all business was
transacted, and here it was that John
found him.

The same confusion and chaotic disorder,
which had been so pre-eminent at Oxford,
reigned here also, only on a much extended
scale. A specimen of everything which
the house contained was to be found
there, each where least expected, for no
" scout " was there, to attempt to bring in
order and method, and Maxwell had his
own way undisturbed.

As John's arrival had been unheralded by any warning letter, the more welcome and hearty was the greeting of the two friends, once more united. The endless questions, referring to old times and old Oxford acquaintances, may be imagined, interrupted as anything like conversation was by the frequent calls upon the "Rector's" time and patience. At length, however, with the hour of dinner, business decreased, until Maxwell and his guest were able to sit down together in peace.

"And now let us have a talk."

So saying, Maxwell proceeded to tilt his uncompromising Windsor chair to a sufficiently dangerous angle, to move a small round table, on which was a bottle of claret in honour of his guest, until it stood between them, and then with eyes half closed to await the questions with which John was surcharged.

"To begin then at the very beginning. How came you here? What made you leave Oxford? How do you like your new style of life?"

"Nay, softly. It would need Cerberus himself, 'three gentlemen at once,' to reply to all your three questions at the same time. To tantalize you I might answer your first, by referring you to the London and North Western Railway, which brought me with 'my ox and my ass and everything that is mine' into this place. But I will be merciful, and taking your two enquiries as one, will explain how I came to quit Oxford for Marbury. I left Oxford because I was no longer 'of' it. I found that my desires and hopes and aims were in opposition to the spirit of the place, were antagonistic in nearly all, and as the mouse in company of elephants must not hope to wage war successfully with them, so it was better for the said mouse to come and live among his fellow mice. No, John, you know pretty well what was my desire and aim in my Oxford life; it was only when I found that was to a great extent unattainable, that I began to open my eyes to the fact of there being other spheres of utility ready for me."

"But you of all men, Maxwell, seemed suited for the work of a Fellow."

"You mean I had fair abilities and a sufficiently candid spirit to permit freedom of opinion."

"Well, yes. The presence of one such mind among others—if I may say it—of grosser calibre, could not but work good. 'A little leaven,' you know.

"Yes, true enough. But put the leaven in clay and what then? You can make nothing of utterly incongruous materials. But observe, I do not wish for a moment to insinuate a word against the general body. Let it have its due. It desires good, doubtless, and would do much to effect what it conceives to be such. But my idea of good was so utterly different from that of those by whom I was surrounded, that I soon perceived the inutility of the struggle.

"The aim of the governing body was to keep those entrusted to their charge in certain fixed and regulated grooves, not to be transgressed. Anything like independent thought and enquiry was to be repressed. Liberty of opinion was regarded with dislike and mistrust; most of all to be crushed was the idea that a man might lawfully try and examine the grounds on which his faith stood. Now I never have valued highly the lazy acquiescence in certain tests and formulas which goes by the name of orthodoxy. Those persons who clamour most loudly for the retention of such

'orthodox' tests, are generally utterly
unable to give you a good reason for
their meaning or existence. I respect
Christ's injunction to search the Scriptures, and His Apostles' to 'prove all
things, and be ready to give a reason
for the faith which is in us,' more than
I do the assertion that you must believe
such and such doctrines because the
Church teaches them. In the one I
recognise the spirit of freedom, in the
other of bond-service.

"Now, with these opinions, and without
an official position to cover them, what
could follow but confusion and discom-
fiture? In my college, at least, it was
'Athanasius against the world,' with this
disadvantage, that Athanasius was the
heterodox and the world the orthodox.
I had certainly an influence over the
few who were my pupils; but it threatened
to become the very thing I most ab-

horred—a clicque. Better anything than
that, thought I. Just then, when my
mind and heart were yearning after that
great, toiling, and suffering world, which
lies outside the Oxford world, came Lord
——'s offer to me to travel with his son.
To make a long story short, I accepted
it, on the condition that instead of any
other remuneration, he should give me
the first small town living in his gift
which fell vacant. A few weeks after
my return, my predecessor in this cure
died, and so you behold me Rector of St.
Lazarus.

"And now, John, if your desire for
work holds good, and your heart is still
with me, let us join hands and go about
that which God gives us to do. I warn
you, expect nothing easy, fanciful, or
romantic. You will have to labour among
disease, filth, abject poverty, and all that
offends the outward senses. You will

meet with revolting crime, unutterable shame, and complete recklessness. You will meet with indifference, opposition, ingratitude, deceit and dislike. The most terrible knowledge and practice of evil in the very youngest, practical atheism and heathenism all around, rooted prejudice, and repeated disappointment when you begin to hope, you must be prepared for. Now, if your heart faints at this, you can still pause and turn back; but if not, give me your hand, and let me welcome you as brother and fellow-soldier."

You can guess John's reply.

"Well, then, now that is settled, we will go into some details, if you please, to give you an idea of your future work. At the same time, remember, I am only suggesting what I have found best, not dictating Median or Persian laws. In the first place, I have made it my aim to be severely practical, and to exclude all that looked like mere theorising.

" Practical utility and reasonable results are what I strive for and aim at. I was so convinced of the utter inability of a house-to-house visitation, to cope with the wants of this place—even if it were in itself a desirable thing, which I doubt—that I reserve my visiting entirely for such cases of illness and distress, where there is reason to expect a visit may be useful or desirable. Anything like patronage or enforced visitation, I need scarcely say I do not think of or practise. A few words in sickness are infinitely more valuable than many preachments in health, when the strong sense of physical power and enjoyment must always, in an uneducated mind, overweigh any merely spiritual considerations. I have offered encouragement rather than opposition to workers of all

creeds who desired to come and help,
laying before them the system I approved,
but throwing no obstacles in the way of
any they preferred.

" So far from harm resulting, I find
nothing but unmixed good; and though
naturally I have a prejudice in favour of
the Church of England, when that mani-
festly cannot be had, I prefer any form
of Christianity to heathendom. So I am
on excellent terms with ' schismatics ' of
all kinds, yea, even the Roman Catholic
priest is civil when we meet. As for
purely spiritual instruction, the opportunities are, I need scarcely say, very few.
I give my people two short, sharp sermons
on the Sunday, practical, as far as I can
make them, with allusions to passing
events, and I make the Sunday services
as short and simple as I can—no æstheti-
cism or decorative upholstery. Then, as
for the school—that is where I want

assistance from you—there will be the boys' school daily, there is no Sunday-school to weary the unfortunate children, but they simply meet and come to church, and all the winter there is a night-school. In both of these you may be of great service, and will thus free other hands for other work. Lastly, there is a small dispensary in this house, where a good doctor, a friend of mine, attends once a day; and, crowning glory of all, a Working-man's Club, where I generally manage to look in of an evening. The management is entirely in the hands of the working classes, with a paid accountant and with me for general adviser. And there, I think you have the main part of my scheme. All such matters as coal and clothing clubs, savings-banks, and such, I have tried to make non-parochial, as I think a feeling of citizenship is more valuable than mere parochial ideas. In a

short time, you will find that to be a good
worker, you must be a bit of a doctor,
lawyer, carpenter, builder, gardener,
schoolmaster, chemist, and possess a
good wholesome love for honest vaga-
bondage."

" Come, at all events," said John, " my
travels these last three years have taught
me the last.   I am glad to see your system
does not include compulsory cocoa—that
I could not have undertaken to swallow."

" Ah, that will come in time with increased wisdom," was the reply.

CHAPTER IV.

" JOHN," said Maxwell, as they were seated one morning at the breakfast table, " an eligible opportunity now offers for you to become acquainted with clerical work in this city."

" What do you mean ?"

" Why, to-night is one of our ' Clerical Association Meeting' nights, to which I am going and may, if you like, introduce you as a stranger guest. I advise you to avail yourself of the chance of going behind the scenes and examining the machinery."

" What is it like ? A convocation in miniature, I suppose."

"It is a shame of me to laugh at my cloth, I own," replied Maxwell, laughing nevertheless, "but you know we must prefer truth to Plato. To be candid then, it equals, if not surpasses the august model, by exhibiting the maximum of talk with the minimum of result. The mountain is continually in labour, great roarings are heard, and lo ! the most ridiculous of ' mures.' In one point, however, we are in advance of Convocation."

"And that ?"

"We provide refreshments."

"Maxwell, that decides me, I shall go. By the bye, the fact of refreshments goes to prove the truth of a remark made by some cynical writer, that the clerical mind has one strong point of resemblance to the feminine, its love for tea and talk."

"I say, young fellow," replied his host, "if I laugh at the cloth myself I don't mean to allow you that privilege. Let

me tell you that if we talk it is with the
best intentions, and when we agree, our
'unanimity is wonderful.' Seriously,
however, the idea of occasional clerical
gatherings, wherein to compare notes of
our various modes of work, the difficulties
we encounter, suggestions for improvement, and matters of that kind, is an
excellent one. If we make ourselves
ridiculous rather than mutually useful,
that is because there is some error in our
way of setting to work. But even take
it at the lowest, the mere fact of a dozen
men engaged in the same work, but bringing to it every possible variety of mental
condition and temperament cannot fail to
do good. It rubs the rust off which
gathers so quickly upon a solitary worker;
to a certain extent there is some encouragement, selfish perhaps, in finding
others struggling under the same difficulties which beset us, and if we only

related the facts which had come under our observation, instead of airing the theories which generally have no basis, we should be much improved. Nevertheless, such as it is, I always make a point of attending, just to show that however great a heretic and radical my brothers may think me, at least I am a friendly one."

"But what is your vocation?" asked John, "what kind of business do you transact when you meet?"

"I will tell you. The society, which includes all the beneficed clergy, and the curates introduced by them, meets alternately at the houses of its members, once a month. Tea, toast and muffins are 'exhibited' with more or less success—after which there is prayer, and then the subject for discussion is introduced by the host of the evening, and afterwards worried to death by the guests. When we have talked ourselves hoarse, and trotted out all our several hobbies to the opposite poles of thought, we congratulate one another upon our harmonious evening, 'and so to bed, mighty content.'"

"What is the subject for to-night?" asked John.

"'The best method of employing female agency in parochial work,' a subject which, you will find, is well adapted for displaying the various theories of the society. Then I may expect you at seven?"

"Yes, certainly; I shall be very pleased. I suppose there are no masonic ceremonies, hot pokers, &c., are there?"

"Go off to your work, you scoffer!"

At seven o'clock precisely, Maxwell and our hero knocked at the door of the Rev. H. Summerly, who was to be the host of that evening; and at 7·1, to employ railway parlance, the portly butler of the Reverend gentleman admitted them to the drawing-room. Now the Rev. H. Summerly, although the Rector of a very large and desperately poverty-stricken parish, was a wealthy, and, I may add, a good man. His large private income was expended liberally among the sick and destitute.

So much for his heart; as for his head, perhaps the less said the better. Supposing he had occasion to advertise in the columns of some clerical paper, he would have described himself as "an Incumbent of sound but not extreme views." As such, therefore, I suppose, we must accept him. His motto was "*In medio tutissimus ibis*," and his anxiety to avoid giving offence so great, as to lead him to qualify every assertion with a possible negation, which in the end reduced it to *nil.* He held the balance

of doctrinal opinion and practise with
so even a hand, that it was hard to
say which scale had the best. Thus,
in his church, his seats were low and
open, but they were all reserved. The
pulpit and reading-desk equalled each
other in height; the communion-table
was covered with a rich velvet cover
and had an alms-dish set upon it, but
there were no lights or embroidery.
His sermons, which averaged twenty-
five minutes, were intended to prove
that on the whole, perhaps it was nicer
to be moral than immoral. If he used
any technical term which was capable
of party interpretation, he carefully explained it down until it meant nothing.
He read prayers in a suggestive manner,
as not asking for any particular blessing
or virtue, but hinting that it might be
as well. And so the Rev. H. Summerly
managed to jog through life, doing good,

doubtless, in his own way, sufficiently popular, but neither much trusted or respected. He was to open the discussion of that evening.

I must confess that the dispensing the good things with which his hospitable table was crowded, was far more in his way. There was a kind of agreeable fiction kept up among the members of the Clerical Association, that the refreshment part of the evening was something extra and unlooked for. So the etiquette was to express a gentle surprise at the sight of the tea equipage, as though nothing were further from the clerical mind than the thought of muffins and toast. At the same time, it must be confessed that reverend members would have looked somewhat blank had the host confined them to the " feast of reason " alone, and commenced the subject without the introduction of the cup which cheers but not inebriates. And so, in time, member after member dropped in, to the number of fourteen or fifteen; and the host " thought there was some slight refreshment waiting in the next room— should they go in ?" No objection was raised, and they migrated accordingly.

There was the Rev. H. Summerly and Maxwell, to begin with, and there was a little Mr. Green, curate to Mr. Summerly, who certainly was of Carlyle's opinion as to the golden nature of silence, using his mouth for mastication and deglutition only. Next came an orthodox Churchman, of " high, but not extreme, tendencies," the Rev. Edward Forbes by name, a great advocate for ritual observances, yet carefully fighting shy of the developments of the young Puseyite party. He liked plenty of music in church, but not Gregorian, and he indulged in candles on the altar, only he never lighted them. He was a portly, rosy, middle-aged man, of pleasant manners and good temper.

A High Churchman of a very different kind was the Rev. Thomas Gordon, the most advanced of all advanced High Churchmen. Indeed, to some he seemed to have advanced completely out of the pale of the English Church altogether, and to be more Catholic than the Roman Catholics themselves. There was no ritual ceremony he was not "up to," no observance he did not observe, no legal loop-hole through which he could not wriggle. He was the object of most unfeigned dislike to his parish, and of terror to his bishop, whom, he openly stated, could only claim his obedience as long as his commands were based upon the practice of the Holy Catholic Church, of which, of course, he, the Rev. T. Gordon, was the sole competent judge. By some marvellous gift, he seemed aware of just the very doctrines and practices which would be most odious to his parishioners, and chose them as his chief standing-points.

By this means, he kept his parish in a kind of controversial vapour-bath, which must have done much to promote the reign of peace and good-will, he was supposed to preach. However, his sermons referred to no such common ideas as peace and good-will, but were generally upon some disputed point, as Auricular confession or Extreme unction. Perhaps this mattered less, as they were obscure in style and unintelligible in delivery, plainness of speech not being a gift which the Rev. T. Gordon thought worthy of cultivation. He was the *enfant terrible* of the Association, as he was in the habit of speaking his mind with a freedom which regarded not the feelings of his neighbours.

Perhaps the next most noteworthy man was the Rev. Henry Warricker, the very opposite of the gentleman last named. He was the leading man of the Low Church, or Evangelical party in the town, and the most popular preacher and speaker they possessed. He was the author of that remarkable course of sermons upon the Interjections of Scripture, "Ah! and Oh!" as well as of another course upon " A, An, and The, as used by the Patriarchs." His researches into apocalyptic and prophetic marvels were truly wonderful, although his facts were scarcely those of history or his dates of chronology. His manner was unctuous, flowing, and discursive; however, spite of his egotism and unfortunate predeliction for clap-trap and maudlin religious sentimentality, he was a gentleman, and in earnest about his work. There were several others, all representatives of various church parties and schools, whose characters and opinions will best be shown by their speeches.

After the good things provided by their bounteous host had been duly discussed, an adjournment to the next room was proposed, and after reading prayers, the Rev. H. Summerly stood up with a beaming face to introduce the subject for discussion.

" It had fallen to his lot," he began, " to place before them, and make a few remarks upon the subject chosen for that evening's consideration. A most charming and interesting subject, he was sure, and one reflecting equal honour upon the head and heart of the clerical brother who had suggested it. Female agency in parochial work was one of those vital points which could neither be dismissed altogether, nor treated in a light and careless manner. He felt quite sure that all his clerical brethren recognised fully its importance, and were prepared to give it that careful consideration which it deserved. He had considerable diffidence in bringing forward his own ideas upon the subject, when he saw before him so many better qualified to treat upon it. In fact, he was there rather as a pupil than a teacher, and felt more inclined to benefit by the experience of others than obtrude his own poor thoughts. At the same time, it appeared that there were several methods of employing that assistance which was placed at their disposal by charitable ladies, and of course each clerical brother had a right to his own opinion.

"He had no doubt but that there was good in all of them, and would suggest that each should keep to that which he found best suited to his own circumstances. Some might think otherwise, and he was sure that he was far from wishing to force his ideas upon them.

His earnest hope was that brotherly (and sisterly) love might continue."

The reverend gentleman was then about to sit down, when a long, lean, gaunt figure, which looked all coat-tail, nose and spectacles, and rejoiced in the name of the Rev. Richard Barnard, rose and suggested that it would be agreeable to the Association if their host would give some account of his practice in this matter. Upon which, with a gentle sigh, Mr. Summerly arose once more.

" Oh certainly, nothing would give him more pleasure. In dealing with the delicate question of female help, his aim had always been to avoid extremes. By which he was far from wishing to cast blame on those who thought otherwise. Certain ladies—he preferred them middle aged— were good enough to assist him in the parish work. Their efforts were chiefly directed towards the sick and the schools ;

of course under his supervision. They
distributed tracts of an inoffensive nature,
and he believed had a Dorcas society, over
which his wife was good enough to pre-
side.   Once a month they met at the
Parsonage for a little refreshment—just
tea and cake you know—and afterwards
there was edifying conversation, and a
little prayer.   Of course, he was not suggesting this as a model, it was his humble
practise, and he should most gladly adopt
any better."

Upon which, up rose the Rev. Thomas
Gordon.   "He regretted having to differ
from his Reverend Brother in every particular.   He had said that there were several
ways of employing female agency, and that
all had their advantages.   He denied this.
Their Reverend Brother had said that each
was at liberty to use that he thought best.
He denied this also.   There was but one
way recognised by the Catholic Church, and

as Catholic priests that was the only way
they were at liberty to adopt. His Clerical
Brothers knew what he meant, if they
didn't like it he couldn't help that, he was
there to speak his mind. That Catholic
method was Sisterhoods — Sisterhoods
bound by vows of celibacy, poverty and
obedience, marked by a special dress and
bound by a special rule. That was the
Catholic plan, and that was the plan pursued in his own parish of St. Dionysius."
And then he proceeded to descant at
length upon its excellencies and recom-
mendations, dwelling specially upon those
details which he knew were most offensive
to his audience. The works they were
chiefly employed at were baking the wafers
for Communion, washing the linen, and
scrubbing the Altar steps, embroidering,
illuminating and text painting, saying
the breviary offices, visiting the sick,
&c., &c., and ministering to the needs of

the clergy. His Reverend brethren might laugh ; he dared say the Catholic system seemed unpalatable to them, but he cared not for the opinion of men." He finished with a series of quotations from the Fathers in support of his position.

When he ceased there was a little pause of dismay, which was broken by the uprising of a nervous abstracted clerical brother, who, near-sighted and very deaf, usually sat in one corner, and alternately rubbed his spectacles and sucked his knuckles. He had a habit of forgetting the topic of discussion as he very soon proved. His quiet mumbling was diversified by sniffs, and ineffectual dives into his capacious pockets for his handkerchief, which he always forgot.

" He had discovered," he began, " in the course of his reading something which, he believed, would very much interest his clerical brethren. It appeared that in the time of St. Basil, the Christians were in the habit of duplicating the amen at the end of their prayers. Thus, " Amen, Amen." Now to his mind this corresponded exactly with the modern custom of crying, ' hear, hear,' and he had no doubt—"

But here the Rev. Edward Forbes rose to order.

" He thought their Reverend Brother had wandered slightly from the subject, and that his remarks had better be reserved for another occasion."

Upon which the Reverend Brother afore-said, sat down on his neighbour's hat and sniffed softly. Business was resumed by the Rev. Henry Warricker.

" It was impossible to conceive a more truly interesting problem to the enlight-ened christian mind, than the best way of employing that aid which our Christian sisters were so ready to proffer. What should we do without woman, fair woman,

whose ready wit, untiring energy and un-
selfish devotion, were ever ready to aid, to
succour and to cherish. He rejoiced that
this Reformed Protestant Church of England, in common with our Reformed brethren on the continent, had seen fit to abro-
gate and nullify that detestable enormity
of the Popish faith, the celibacy of her
clergy. In this enlightened and truly
Protestant land, there were happily no
priests with a yoke on their shoulders
harder than they could bear."

Here the Rev. Thomas Gordon uprose,
bristling with a call to order.

"He begged to observe, that however
little Mr. Warricker might value it, he
could not escape from the position and
privilege of being a Priest of the Catholic
Church. For his part, he did not recognize the Protestant Establishment. Celibacy was the voice of Catholic tradition."

Upon which, sweetly smiling, Mr. Warricker resumed,

"He was very sorry if he had offended his brother. Scripture, as delivered by the apostle Paul, cautioned us against offending the weak brethren, and he would endeavour so to do. As for the word priest: he was aware that that section which amused itself by masquerading in the cast off rags of the harlot of Rome, delighted in assuming the title of priest. But Protestants neither recognised the name nor the power."

The Reverend host, smelling danger, rose to suggest "that Brother Warricker had, perhaps, in his laudable zeal, wandered slightly from the point. It is true Michelet had written a book called 'Priests and Women,' but the subject of discussion was the latter, not the former. St. Paul also remarked that we were all priests, therefore the two

Reverend gentlemen were both right."

Again the Rev. Henry Warricker resumed. "He should not have referred to the subject, only he remembered the warning against those false teachers who were prone to creep into houses and lead captive silly women. Now this was exactly fulfilled by the pernicious teaching of the Confessional, a doctrine which no truly pious Bible Christian could hold." And in this strain did he continue for some while to the confusion of his auditors.

The Reverend gentleman with the spectacles and coat-tails then arose, and unfolded various paradoxes which were his delight. He rejoiced to see so many various opinions, because, to his mind, that was the surest proof of unanimity; for it was impossible to have unanimity without free expression of opinion. He had been unable to organize a regular Sisterhood in his own parish, but had instituted a secret one called the " Mystic Sisterhood of Dogmatic Theology, or the little family of St. Theresa." The advantages were very great, as it appeared to him. He had endeavoured to counteract the principal failings of women—talk and dress. They were bound to keep silence six hours out of the twenty-four, and were only allowed a limited range of subjects for conversation. With regard to dress, they dispensed with that altogether." In answer to a querist, the Reverend gentleman proceeded to explain, that he meant that the Sisters did not use those sinful contrivances called hoops, or, he believed, crinolines. He habitually treated them with much reserve, and kept them at a distance which, to his mind, was very valuable, as inspiring confidence.

" They met once a fortnight, and each

had a dogma of Mystic Theology given her to meditate upon for an hour daily. They were bound to keep their special dogma secret from the rest of the sisterhood. Then they all meditated for an hour in silence before the altar. When two sisters met in public, they had a sign and countersign. The first said "Saint The," and the other added "resa." The exoterics did not understand, as it sounded like a sneeze. He thought this was very valuable."

When this very practical plan had been duly discussed, the Rev. Alfred Chambers rose to make a few remarks. "He had no doubt that what he had to say would appear very old-fashioned and out of date, but he was not ashamed of it for that. He believed that the best female help in a parish was that given by a clergyman's wife, and he should like to see every one of his clerical brethren a married man. He thanked God that he had a good wife, who, for fifteen years, had done in his parish the work of three curates."

Some one then rose to observe, that excellent as that idea was, it was not generally feasible. A man could only have one wife, and yet there were many candidates—he meant for work, not wedlock—in every parish. What was to be done with the spinsters?

This no one could solve, and the discussion languished until the host rose to observe that he should be glad to have a few words from their Reverend Brother Maxwell, who had not yet spoken.

So urged, Maxwell arose and remarked " that he was, comparatively speaking, such a novice, that he had waited to learn the opinions of his elders. The case seemed simple enough to him. If a true-hearted woman desired real useful work, he did not see how vows, sisterhoods, or dresses could aid her much, whereas, he saw very clearly how they could and did minister to the spirit of vanity, exclusiveness, and mère *dilettante* work. The only vow such a woman needed, was that of her baptism; the only sisterhood, that which she had in common with every daughter of Eve; the only dress, the consciousness of her own good purpose and the garb of purity.

"As for work, there seemed plenty to be done in school teaching, sick visiting, and reformatory work. But the great necessity was to find those who would take it up as real work for the love of Christ, and not a mere playing at nunnery. It should be studied as a business—thus, in visiting the sick, the best works on the subject should be read, and their maxims carried out. In school teaching, the lady-teachers should always submit to the regulations of the schoolmistress. And, again, the greatest tact was necessary to be observed in general visiting, for often-times visitors, with the best intentions, really gave great offence to the poor by reckless intrusion at meal-time, indiscriminate tract-giving, or uncalled for advice and interference."

When Maxwell had concluded, the host, who perceived threatening symptoms on the part of the Rev. Thomas Gordon, hastened to close the meeting by the proposition of the following resolution, which was carried unanimously.

" That the Clerical Association fully recognises the importance and value of female parochial agency, and its need in this city; and pledges itself to employ it when and as desirable."

The meeting then broke up, after the absent-minded clerical brother had proposed, as the subject for discussion next

time, "The Influence of Infinite Ab-
stractions on a System of Dogmatic
Theology."

"How do you feel, my son?" enquired
Maxwell, on their return.

"As if I had supped on feathers and
oyster-shells, and had indigestion."

CHAPTER V.

"WELL, John, and what is your candid opinion of the deliberations of the Clerical Association?"

"I am more convinced than ever of the truth of Oxenstiern's remark to his son, 'With how little wisdom the world is governed.'"

"I am afraid you are right; the only question is, is it governed at all? Government means, I presume, direction and restraint, but it is hard to see how these little clerical concourses either direct or restrain any one. However, after all, our practice is not so bad as our theories. Half the crude and ridiculous ideas you

H 2

heard ventilated last night will never become anything more. The act of speaking and debating to us clergy, is merely the letting off of steam—like an engine's screech, we drag our burdens along, neither better nor worse for our occasional whistling. And yet, all our friends fully and entirely believe in the wisdom of their theories and suggestions, and, for my part, I rather envy them that *naïve* frankness and charming power of belief. You will laugh, Master John, but I often look back with a kind of envy to my 'salad' days, when I was a gushing young undergraduate, and believed so implicitly that A and B and C were the real lights of the High Church world, and their dicta infallible. In those days, we always had some new article of faith, which, like Moses' rod, devoured its predecessors. We were ready to regenerate the world, on an average once a week, and were always discovering some new lubricating substance which was to grease the rusty machinery of the universe, and make its wheels move gaily to the measure we approved.

"Now it was chasubles and dalmatics, now it was choral service and Gregorians. After a while, celibacy and brotherhoods came into fashion. Then we went off at a tangent for soup-kitchens and public baths. I don't quite remember how these were to have the real High Church flavour imparted, for at first sight they seemed to smack too much of muscularity. And then, too, our innocent little predilections and partizanships and triumphs. What rejoicings and verbal fireworks there would be when Bishop A read the Communion Service looking east instead of south; what shoutings of joy when a doubtful passage in a sermon by Archdeacon B

was discovered, which might be tortured
to hint at seven sacraments! Then the
fluctuations between hope and fear!
Some bishop was beguiled into ordain-
ing or confirming with a real, veritable,
pastoral staff, held for him by a meek
curate; up went the thermometer to
fever heat and all was hopeful. The
Evangelicals couldn't resist such a de-
monstration as that. But, perhaps, the
next week the same unlucky prelate
attended a meeting of the Church Missionary Society, or held up one finger
when he should have extended three;
then we hid our faces in shame and
despair.

"Very childish and ridiculous those
days—were they not? Altogether absurd
our ecstacies and our longings? Granted.
But, at least, there was much of the freshness and confiding simplicity of youth,
and we were in earnest. Of course, our

blunder was mistaking means, sometimes
questionable means, for ends. At least,
all my young High Church follies have
taught me to endure, with tenderness and respect, those fancies and foibles
of my brothers in the work in which I
cannot believe. It is only when I see
really vital issues staked upon the ' infinitely little,' that I feel bound to protest.
If the Reverend Y. Z. goes into ecstacies
because he has bearded and defeated his
bishop in the matter of incense, and calls
me to rejoice with him, *Que voulez-vous?*
I care very little for his gum benzoin, it
is true, and can only see a bald-headed
man turning ' wheels' of delight about a
trifle, but I can joy in his joy natheless.
And so, when the Reverend Z. Y. reports to me the enormous success of the
M auxiliary branch of the Pongo Mission
Fund, I respect his spirit of earnestness
and rejoice with him. The ' sheep' which

our neighbour has recovered, may seem an
unpleasant woolly brute to us; but for
all that we must not decline his invitation
to merriment."

"I think I agree with nearly all you
say, Maxwell, the more easily, perhaps,
because I am scarcely called on to put it
in practice. For all that, it would be as
well if your Clerical Association would
arrive at some definite conclusion from
the subject of debate, instead of echoing it
like an address upon the royal speech at
the opening of Parliament."

"Well, I don't know; unless we were
prepared to act upon it, which, of course,
we are not. We always end by 'recognising the necessity or importance of'
something or other. It is a form of words
very soothing to the mind, 'The Emperor
recognises the French Republic,' you
know."

"Some day you will find a Buonaparte

among you who will reply, it ' is as clear as the sun at mid-day.' But, seriously, I should like to know your real ideas of female parochial work."

"If you will be ready in a couple of hours' time, you shall see, not my ideas, but my practice, in the matter."

"What do you mean?"

"You shall come with me and pay a visit to the Phœbe, the deaconess of St. Lazarus, and, if you don't admire my system, I shall say you have no taste."

"But who is she, and what is she like, this said deaconess? Is she a Mother Superior, and am I to expect a figure robed in black, white or gray, girdled and rosaried? Will she give me her blessing at departure, and want me to go down on my knees?"

"You may expect what you like, but not one word shall you hear from me. I

shall send you packing if you make me
loiter over breakfast in this way. I ought
to have been off an hour ago. Now, mind,
at twelve, sharp."

And then the two friends separated for
their several occupations, meeting duly at
twelve, to start on their walk.

What was called the Rectory at St.
Lazarus, stood, as we have before observed,
in the very heart of the parish, surrounded
on all sides by the mean alleys, courts,
and yards, in which, for the most part,
the working class of Marbury resided.
The ground sloped gradually down to the
canal, which was protected with high
banks, so as actually to be raised above
the level of the fields on either hand.
Those houses which, to use a French term,
"gave on" these fields, were flooded in
the lower stories in winter time, and
unwholesome all the year round. When
fever visited Marbury, it always made its

appearance in the canal district, nor was it easily driven out. A few half-rotten summer-houses slowly dropped to decay on the banks, looking as if they had been stranded there after the Deluge, and forgotten ever since. But the gloomy nature of the place did not seem to affect the spirits of the poverty-stricken children whose playground it was, and who made the air resound with their shrill cries and noisy mirth. Skirting along this pleasant region, Maxwell led his friend into one of the long and comparatively broad streets which ran down to the canal, at the head of which stood the church.

Although less dismal than the water side, there was enough to offend the senses here. Life seemed to be carried on, for the most part, in the open air, possibly because the interiors were too unbearable for business purposes. Barrows of vegetables and coarse fish occupied the sides of the road, leaving but little passage for vehicles, while the groups of loquacious, not to say abusive, females clustered round each door, left equally little room for foot passengers. From the upper windows lounged others bare-headed and bare-armed, who· kept up a conversation and interchanged remarks with their friends below. The atmosphere was tainted with the heaps of foul refuse and garbage in the gutter, and not less was the air, polluted with the foul talk and hideous ribaldry which resounded on all sides.

"John," observed Maxwell gravely, as they made their way up the street, "depend upon it, the most wicked cities have always been those which were the worst built and ventilated and drained. When squalor and splendour jostle and elbow each other, crime is the result."

As he spoke, they turned into a second street, one side of which was occupied by

a blank wall. About half-way down, there
was a gate at which Maxwell knocked. As
they entered John conld not restrain a cry
of surprise. The high walls enclosed a large
court-yard, laid out in the old-fashioned
style, with a shrubbery on each side, and
a sun-dial in the centre. Facing the
entrance was a double flight of stone
steps, ornamented with great vases full of
flowers, and flanked by a couple of quaint
looking lions bearing shields between their
paws. The house itself was one of those
erections of dark red brick and stone,
which were the taste of the eighteenth
century, and have a peculiar charm for
all time. A deep porch, many lights of
small panes, projecting dormer windows,
and a long low roof were its principal
characteristics. It was called Mostyn Hall,
and had originally been the country residence of some wealthy squire. But Marbury had grown fast, and its aristocracy

emigrated to the upper town, so that now
it was embraced on all sides by the mean
buildings and squalid huts of the canal
district.

Maxwell paused to ask whether Mrs.
Harcourt was at home, and, on being
answered in the affirmative, was at once
ushered into the drawing-room. It was
a long, low, panelled apartment, with a
deep bay-window facing the door. The
floor, dark with age, and slippery with
much rubbing, was covered in the centre
with a Persian carpet. The curtains were
of some foreign material and pattern,
rich in colour and design. A few good
modern engravings in handsome frames
hung on the walls; there was abundance
of vases of flowers on brackets, and tables
and shelves, and the recessed book-case
was well supplied with a varied collection of books, in elegant and tasteful
bindings. At a writing-table, in front of

the bay-window, was seated a lady, apparently busily engaged in looking over a large mass of papers, whose varied and uncertain caligraphy and frequent blots betrayed them to be school exercises. As Maxwell was announced, she rose, and came to greet him with outstretched hand.

Mrs. Harcourt was very beautiful; so much so as to merit a few lines of description, especially as these pages have not erred in that way before. She was tall and slight in figure, and both stood and walked with dignity, and without stiffness, two points which we mention because rarely found in tall women. I have said she was beautiful, but, strange as it may seem, her beauty was not the first idea suggested by her face, that grew upon you afterwards; but when you first looked, you were more struck by the expression of perfect calm and composure

written on her features. It revealed the
presence of one who had through life
much occasion of self-reliance, and who
had accordingly acquired the habit of self-
control and independence. The brow was
no cold chiselled abstraction, hard and unyielding as marble, but showed benevolence in its broad sweep and intellect in
its height.

The small, delicately curved mouth,
though somewhat grave and determined,
had nothing of coldness or severity, and
occasionally relaxed into a quiet smile,
betokening a keen appreciation of humour,
and, perhaps, just a touch of satire. Her
complexion was of that clear pure olive
tint, which is rarely seen, save in an
Italian or Spaniard, and was rendered
the more remarkable by its contrast to
the dark violet colour of the very bright
eyes, which lit up and gave character to
the face. She wore her thick masses of

dark brown hair cut short and falling in clustering curls behind to the neck, just revealing the delicate, shell-tinted ears—the surest sign of blood and birth. She was dressed in a plain, but rich, grey silk dress, with much of black velvet about it, and the simple lace-collar was bound by a crimson ribbon, and fastened about the neck with a small enamel brooch of Eastern workmanship.

As you looked at her, you felt that you were in the presence of one accustomed to command and influence those with whom she came in contact. Before long, you knew that she was exercising an influence over *you*, and while drawing out your nature, and causing you to exhibit all your true colours, giving little or nothing in exchange. Hers was not a nature to be sounded and gauged at pleasure, the attempt merely revealed, not her depth, but the shallowness of your measure.

That Maxwell was a favourite, was very evident from the genial smile which broke over her face as she greeted him.

"Most reverend mother," began he, as they shook hands, "I have brought you a neophyte, who needs instruction in the mysteries of the good work."

"Most reverend father," responded she, "I rejoice to see you in your usual health and spirits, and I am also very glad to see you, Mr. Fordyce, neophyte or not."

"Ah, Mrs. Harcourt, always the same; there is the most pitiable lack of sentiment about you that I ever saw in any woman."

"How you can see what does not exist, Mr. Maxwell, I don't know. I suppose that is one of the advantages of being a man. You know very well that I agree with Moore, in dividing all things into matter-of-fact and matter-of-fudge."

"Now, you really are too bad. And all

this after I have led my friend Fordyce to expect a real Mother Superior, in scapular, hood and beads."

"That is not my fault, at least. If you choose to romance, I can't help it. Are you very disappointed, Mr. Fordyce?"

"A little, I confess; the outside of your house looks as if it contained nothing more than a choir of nuns."

"It is a whited sepulchre then; I am afraid the best part is outside. It is a surprise, is it not, finding such an old-world mansion in the heart of Marbury. I took to it as soon as I saw it, and decided to live here. I don't dislike the neighbourhood; in the first place, the contrast is pleasant, and in the second, I like to be near my work."

Just then a man-servant appeared to summon Maxwell away.

"Whose cow is dead now?" sighed he.

"I suppose some lynx-eyed parishioner has dogged my steps even here. Well, I suppose I must go ; but I shall come back—"

"To lunch," finished Mrs. Harcourt.

As the door closed upon the clergyman, she looked at John for a minute with a half puzzled air.

"What shall I do to amuse you, Mr. Fordyce? Are you willing to be useful?"

"Certainly," replied he, somewhat bewildered.

"Look here. Are you all right in your spelling? Don't look offended. It isn't Latin and Greek. If it were, I should not presume. But I know you University men are not generally at home in such a vulgar matter as English grammar and spelling."

"Will you try me?" asked John, with a smile. "It is true we didn't learn spel-

ling either at Eton or Oxford; but nevertheless, I think I am tolerably ' up' in it."

"Ah, that is right. Perhaps you will
be so good as to look over and correct
these school exercises. Only attend to
the grammar and spelling, if you please.
I must finish them by this evening, or
I would not trouble you; and we can
talk all the time if you like, Mr. Fordyce."

"How come you to know my name so
well, Mrs. Harcourt? I do not remember
ever having met you before."

"I know your name because I am a
woman; or in other words, because I am
curious. Although you do not remember
me, I have seen you several times about in
the parish under the guardianship of Mr.
Maxwell. And so you have come—I wish
this child would learn the difference between wich with a *t* and wich with an *h*—
and so you have come to help us put the

world of Marbury to rights." And she
gave him a keen look.

John was nettled, he did not know why.
He did not like *badinage* in what appeared
a very serious matter.

" Scarcely that, Mrs. Harcourt," he replied, " I have come to add my little mite
to the good work I find already going
on."

" That's modest. If your expectations
are as modest as your language, I should
think you would be gratified. How surprised you look. I shall begin to believe
Mr. Maxwell, and think you really expected to meet a Mother Superior here.
Do you think it wrong to laugh ?"

" Pray don't mistake me. I was only
speaking seriously upon what to me appears a very serious subject."

" Ah, Mr. Fordyce, you are no philosopher then, after all. Do you not remember what a wit says ? ' Let us hasten

to laugh at these things lest we should feel inclined to weep at them.' Do not mistake me. I feel the terrible nature of the work to be done as much as you or anyone—more than you, in fact, because I have been long at it. But one cannot for ever look upon the grave side, and the grotesque is always an element of the tragic. I suppose if I were a real Mother Superior I should discourse to you of the 'good work'—a phrase, by-the-bye, I was sorry to hear you use—and caution you against levity and relaxation, perhaps throwing in a little advice about a course of reading, &c. However, I am so far from it that I shall give you advice of a very carnal nature. Work as hard as you please, but walk well, live well, and sleep well. Don't grizzle over grave and abstruse books. The fiends which tormented St. Anthony came from over-study and indigestion.

" By-the-bye, you will always find a
strong meat luncheon here about one
o'clock to which you will be very welcome.
As, indeed, to any other kind of meal
during the day. Are you a horseman?
Yes? That's well, for there is a second
animal of mine that is always wanting
exercise. I will speak to John the groom,
and he shall have orders to have her
ready for you whenever you wish. No
thanks, I beg. I can see you still are a
little disappointed, and would have preferred my blessing and a rosary, perhaps.
You shall have the former before you go
perhaps. Seriously, do you know why
I advise you thus? I can remember a
young man who entered upon parochial
work—he was a clergyman—in a similar
spirit to yours, who poured out his
strength as it were for his people, and
scorned all precautions, all aid, all advice;
and what was the consequence? For

eleven months he did the work of three men and then died worn out.

"Now I should be sorry to see you waste your energies like that, and therefore take upon me to advise you in my homely way. And now as I hear Mr. Maxwell returning, and I think luncheon is ready, if you will give me those exercises we will go into the next room. Oh, Mr. Fordyce, look what you have done, you have put your pen through this word 'inconsequence,' spelt quite right, and have overlooked 'cow' spelt with a *k* and an *u*. I said you Oxford men didn't know how to spell."

"What's that about Oxford?" inquired Maxwell, as he entered.

"Mrs. Harcourt is abusing me for forgetting all else and listening to her discourse, Maxwell."

"No I am not, I am simply abusing you for undertaking what you could not

perform.   And now let us go to the
dining-room.   Come, Mr. Maxwell, your
arm."

The conversation during the meal was
lively enough—and John was content to
play a silent part, and listen to Mrs. Harcourt and his friend as they tilted in a
friendly way.   She did not pay much
attention to him, and was mainly occupied in asking various questions about
Polly this and James that, which seemed to refer to, and betrayed a great
knowledge of the work in the parish.
When they all rose, she dismissed them
in a perfectly free but graceful manner.

"Well, I think it is time for me to be
off to my work, and so, with your permission, I will say good morning.   Mr.
Fordyce, I hope we shall be very good
friends, and that you will use me in any
way.   Good bye, most Reverend Father,

God bless you both." And then the two friends departed.

" John," asked the elder, " what do you think of my Sister of Mercy ?"

" To be candid," replied he, after a pause, " I am almost more puzzled than pleased. There is something about her I scarcely can make out. A kind of levity, half bitter."

" Wait a while—wait a while, my son, before you judge. If ever there were a genuine true-hearted and noble-souled woman, Maud Harcourt is her name. You should see her as I have, and do, among the poor. Not only does no little practical detail of household work, or sick nursing appear strange to her, but her warm heart seems only equalled by her judgment and discretion. I have seen her with the young and old, and with the sick and the sinful, and the influence she has over all alike is to me wonderful. She is a good woman, John, and the 'God bless you!' she uttered, I valued as more than a mere conventional farewell."

" I have no doubt I shall like her better as I grow to understand her more. Her manner is strange, you will own."

" At first, perhaps. I find her spirits very unequal. At times she will be as depressed, as to-day she was lively. To tell the truth, hers is just the character to conceal deep feelings—perhaps deep sorrow under a mask of assumed cheerfulness. Doubtless she has had her troubles, which she strives to forget in her arduous labours of charity. She is quite young, however, not more than twenty-three, I should say."

" Who was Mr. Harcourt?"

" That I cannot say. She was a widow when I first came to Marbury."

CHAPTER VI.

JOHN FORDYCE soon became warmed and accustomed to his work, strange though it appeared at first. And yet this was mainly the consequence of Maxwell's good sense and judgment. He was a man who neither worked a willing horse to the death, nor, on the other hand, allowed his volunteers to become mere idle *dilettanti.*

" Don't undertake too much at first, my son," he had said to John, " but stick to your work, and don't be above doing it regularly. If you begin at a gallop, you will very soon be winded—for the race is trying, both to wind and limb."

He explained to his neophyte, as he

called him, that his undertaking certain
regular duties would be of great help, as
enabling him to employ, for other purposes, the money which had hitherto gone
to hirelings, who might now be promoted
to work John was not fitted for. And so
John came to have his stated hours at the
day-school, and in the winter at the night-
school, and refuge for the homeless, which
had been started in the district. Besides
this, there was a frequent attendance of
an evening at the Working Man's Club,
which, after a time, became popular, and
one of the institutions of the place.

Regular house-to-house visitation there
was none, and the sick were in more
experienced hands than his. But, as he
grew accustomed to the working-men, and
they to him, he would sometimes drop
into their houses of an evening, when he
had reason to think his visits might be
acceptable; and in this way he gained

more knowledge of their character, and feelings, and sympathies than he could in any other.

Certainly there was no romance in the life he led, or the work he did. Visiting among the poor of a town is altogether another matter from walking in and out of rustic cottages. A rustic cottage is generally a pretty sight, although God knows it may, and often does, contain as much vice, and misery, and poverty as any town hovel. Still, there is something picturesque and quaint about it, with its little garden and flowers and beehives. The rustic, moreover, is far more subservient and—after a fashion—civil than your town-bred workman. He is accustomed to bow to the parsonage and the great house, he is innately Conservative, and believes in a kind of divine right inherent in "the quality." Moreover, spite of Unions and poor laws, there is something

of the old patriarchal idea still lingering
about the relationship of farmer and labourer, and the two have never been
brought so sharply into opposition as have
master and hand. For all these reasons,
therefore, John Styles submits in a stolid,
bovine way to domiciliary visits from ladies
young and old, curates, *et hoc genus omne.*
He can't quite see what they want, and
would certainly prefer their not intruding
during his dinner-hour. Nor does he
read their tracts, which matters less, as
he would not understand them if he did.
Their money and their gifts in kind, he
and his "missus" accept, perhaps not
over gratefully, but then, have they been
bestowed with delicacy ?

On the whole, if the quality regard him
as a curious animal to be gazed at, or a
difficult problem to be solved, he lets
them—it amuses them and doesn't hurt
him. But your townsman is quite a

different case, and requires special treatment. He thinks, does this man, and generally with remarkable acuteness, respecting all those points which concern him. He has no belief at all in divine rights of any kind, and much prefers proofs and facts to assertions and theories. But, at the same time, while he maintains his own sturdy independence, he is quick enough to recognise the advantages which education and *savoir faire* give "the quality" over him. He is ready enough, too, to recognise and hold out the hand of fellowship to any one—a real man—who is striving manfully and earnestly for the amelioration of the working classes' condition; and, though he rejects charity, even under circumstances when it would be little less than life, he is willing to receive help such as one man may offer another. Once conquer the first repugnance with which you are apt to regard the proud independence of a 'hand,' and you soon grow to acknowledge and admire the spirit of honour and manly feeling which is his characteristic.

One day, as John was returning from his school work, he was waylaid by two ladies, who introduced themselves to him as fellow-labourers in the parish of St. Lazarus. The elder of the two, who might be about five and forty, was tall, thin, angular and yellow—a piece of parchment wrapped round a drumstick would perhaps give the best idea of her figure and complexion. She had an abrupt way of speaking in little jerks, and snapped out each word distinctly, as though giving a lesson in dictation. Her dress was remarkable for a certain precise neatness, the more noteworthy as its material and pattern were staring and obtrusive in the extreme. She rejoiced in hard contrasts of positive colours, and wore each article as if it were a separate protest against the fashion of the time.

On her arm, she bore a satchel full of books and papers, in one hand she carried a stout umbrella, the other grasped the arm of the lady, her companion. This companion was in all respects a contrast. She was short and stout, florid, with fair hair and light blue eyes, in manner she was exciteable and gushing, brimming over with words and feeling. She was one of those good people who take you by storm, and seem to be half a dozen rolled into one. She asked you questions and answered them herself, she despaired and revived, doubted and recovered confidence all in a minute. She never took a view of circumstances which was likely to be unpleasant to her, and wrested facts until they fell in with her theories. Her name was Mrs. Floss and she was a volunteer district visitor. Her friend's name was Mrs. Visor—Mrs. D. Visor as she was always careful to explain—and she was a great volunteer school teacher. The latter lady it was who commenced the attack.

"Mr. Fordyce, I think, in fact I may say, I know. I am glad to make your acquaintance, Sir, and glad to introduce you to a fellow-labourer my friend, Mrs. Floss. I am Mrs. Visor, Mrs. D. Visor, if you please, for there are other Visors in Marbury who are no connections. We are all accountants. My grandfather was one, my father was one, my brother is one and I am one, for I often help keep his books. So you see I was born and cradled among figures and fed upon facts, other people don't like figures and facts, I do." She ended with a jerk, and Mrs. Floss took up the tale.

"You know, Mr. Fordyce, it is so nice holding out the right hand of fellowship,

and all that, to one's fellow-workers in
this most delightful field of labour. There
is such encouragement and that sort of
thing, in finding others engaged in the
same troubles, and joys, and sorrows,
and all that, as you are yourself. And I
am sure, for my part, I always shall.
And do you find it somewhat trying at
first ? I did to the nerves and nose, because you see although vinaigrettes are
useful, you cannot always hold one to your
face, and drains and ill ventilation are
very much in the way, and how they live
through them, I am sure I don't know,
though use is everything; but then my
feelings are exciteable I own."

" Arabella Floss," said Mrs. D. Visor,
in grave tones, "that is what I am always
telling you. Keep yourself cool and calm,
and never allow yourself to be excited in
your work. You see, Mr. Fordyce, I
have a theory, and upon that I always

act. Are you Oxford or Cambridge, may I ask ?"

John modestly claimed the former University as his own.

" I am sorry for it," was the reply, " very sorry. Mathematics are not understood there, figures are not known, statistics are not studied. Now I live on figures, statistics are my food and drink," and, indeed, her appearance almost bore out this statement. " Bring up a child on tables, work him well with the four rules, let figures be the employment of his hours of study, and problems be the recreation of his idle hours, and that child, when he grows up, will recognize facts, and cope with facts. Do not tell me of fancy, I have nothing to do with it; figures and facts, figures and facts, I say. I might, indeed, alter Dr. Watts, and say, ' In figures, sums, and algebra, let my young hours be past.' Now, my friend here, Mrs. Floss, does not see things in this way. She indulges in fancy. I. don't."

"You know, Mr. Fordyce, it is not every one who has such a strong head as dear Mrs. Visor. And, indeed, though I should be the last person in the world to undervalue figures at school, I never could understand the Rule of Three myself, and as for calling it inverse—I call it plaguing—yet I don't see of what use they can be in visiting the poor, except to count up the number of their children; and, indeed, their recklessness and extravagance in that matter is most extraordinary—for I notice that the poorest people always have the largest families, as if it were out of contradiction on their part, though whether it's the parents, or the children's, I can't say, nor do I see how it is to be stopped."

"The increase of population, and the

ratio of that increase, like every thing else, is a matter for statistics," responded Mrs. Visor. " Give me a group of married couples," and she looked about as though she wanted them immediately, " and I will tell you exactly the number of children they will have in a given time, the number of males and females, the amount of sickness and health, and the ratio of deaths. Whatever does not come under statistics may be dismissed from the consideration of reasonable beings."

By this time, John, who had grown rather weary of his lecture, attempted to put in a word.

" I am sure it is very good of you two ladies to give up so much of your time and thoughts to the poor of this place. The work must be particularly hard for ladies, for some of the places are anything but agreeable. I suppose you know your *collaborateur*, Mrs. Harcourt ?"

A change came over both the countenances before him. " Oh !" said one lady, and " Ah !" exclaimed the other.

"Know Mrs. Harcourt !" repeated Mrs. D. Visor, austerely, " well—after a fashion —yes. You see, Mr. Fordyce, I have my own ideas, and as they are founded on facts I think I have a perfect right to them also. Now a worker is a worker in my eyes, and nothing more. Let myself be represented as a worker by A, Mrs. Floss by the letter B, and Mrs. Harcourt by C ; or reverse the order, if you please, and I want to know what is the difference between them. Nothing. Then why make a difference? I may not be rich and I may not be beautiful, not that I see much beauty there, but practical I am, and as a practical woman, protest against pretending to work. That's my idea."

Then Mrs. Floss—

"You see, Mr. Fordyce, I don't say a word against Mrs. Harcourt, nor would I for worlds; but I don't like mystery, and I don't see any need for it. Why not be friendly and hearty with fellow-workers, ready to hold out the hand of fellowship and all that, and for my part ever shall be; and I am sure though we make no fuss, or pretend to dine late, why not a hearty tea and a little bit of something hot for supper as friends should, engaged in the same work, just dropping in you know most welcome. As the great Dr. Johnson says, 'The feast of reason and the flowing bowl.' Then why not, Mr. Fordyce? That's what I want to know—why not?"

"Well, of course, that is very difficult for me to say," replied John, who had not the slightest idea of what the exact purport of the question was. "Mrs. Harcourt has always been very polite to me on the few occasions when we have met. I am sure she works indefatigably. I continually see her out in the district where she lives."

"Ah, well," responded Mrs. D. Visor, "if friendly offers are made and friendly offers are not accepted, there is only one course left for a practical woman to take, and as a practical woman I have taken it. I never quarrel, and I never have any words. I state facts, and if people can't see facts, that is their fault, not mine. I leave them to themselves. If I have figures and facts on my side, I don't care what fancies are opposed to me."

"Ah! you are so strong minded, Mrs. Visor," said her friend, "I wish I was, but I am not, so what is the use? But still my great desire is to be friendly with all the world, and when friendly advances are repulsed, feelings are wounded, and without any cause that I can see. For, if a person chooses to live bottled up in an

old house with walls like a convent, or a
prison, is that any reason why the rest
of the world should do so too? And what
is life, Mr. Fordyce, if you never meet
your fellow-creatures? You might as well
be a hermit at Vauxhall, or a Skylight,
and live at the top of Pompey's pillar.
Though I must say, that to my ideas
rich silks and velvets are altogether unbefitting a district visitor, let alone a
hermit and all that. And I am sure I
find, that what with babies and dirty
chairs and wet paint, and that sort of
thing, a gingham, or cotton, or at the
best a turned silk that won't do even for
candle light, is quite good enough. Well,
Mrs. Visor, we are keeping Mr. Fordyce,
and I for one must be moving on."

" One moment," said the arithmetical
lady. " You look pale and thin, Mr. Fordyce. Now take my advice, and don't
wait to get ill, but take the bull by the

horns at once. I have a most delightful
pill made up from my grandfather's pres-
cription. It is very simple, and ultimately unfailing in its effects, and it suits
all constitutions. The first night you
take one. If that has no effect, you double the dose, then double again, and
again in regular arithmetical proportion.
In time, you hit on the exact number
which suits you. The largest dose I ever
knew to be taken was thirty-two, but
that was taken by a gentleman of peculiar
constitution, upon whose death, which
took place not long after, the Registrar-
General made some interesting special
remarks. If you will allow me, I will
send my servant with a box to-night.
Good morning, good morning."

The promised box duly arrived, and, as
it contained sixty-four moderate sized
bolusses, John found them of great use,
in combination with a pea-shooter, where-

with to wage war against the cats of the neighbourhood. I am sorry to say, he had the hypocrisy to inform Mrs. D. Visor that he felt very much improved in health and spirits, and attributed it entirely to the valuable proportional pill.

Go where John would among the poor, but one account of Mrs. Harcourt's character and labours was given. All spoke in praise of her kindness, her generosity, her unwearied tenderness with the sick, and it was evident that her influence came far more from the manner in which her money was given, than from the gift itself. While other female visitors were rejected and threatened by the rougher members of the district, Mrs. Harcourt was permitted—nay, invited—to come, and moved when she would among the discordant elements, pure, calm, and resolute, like the lady in the rebel rout of " Comus." All kinds of work seemed to come to her

as a second nature. Sometimes he would
see her nursing a refractory baby in its
mother's absence, or attending to the
meanest and most toilsome household
duties. But, oftenest of all, he saw or
heard of her by the sick bed, displaying
a readiness, composure, and thorough
knowledge of her duties, which seemed
to indicate a long apprenticeship.

They never had leisure for more than
a few moments' conversation, when they
met by chance; but John always found
that the few words she uttered on these
occasions seemed deprived of their ordinary conventional meaning, and acting as
a spur and incentive to him throughout
the day. As she perceived that John
Fordyce's idea of work was no mere whim,
but the project and labour of a life, so did
she change her lively air of *badinage* with
which she had addressed him, for one more
in accordance with his feelings. And thus

it came, that the feeling of reserve, with which he had regarded her on their early interviews, gradually changed into one of deep and intense respect and admiration.

A chance incident made them even better acquainted. One afternoon, cold and dreary with the approach of winter, John was returning home, and happened to direct his course by the old-fashioned brick mansion where Maud Harcourt lived. As he passed, the open gates showed him a little group in the court-yard which arrested his attention, and caused him to approach nearer and enter. On the ground lay a little Italian organ-boy, whom, with his organ and monkey, he had seen about the streets only that morning, merry and laughing as he begged his way through Marbury. A waggon, turning a corner rapidly in the dusk of the evening, had knocked him down, run

over, and injured him mortally; and, as
he lay there, it was easy to see that his
life was to be numbered by minutes only.
Dusty, uncleanly, and uncouth, though
gentle in appearance, he lay extended on
a few soft cushions Maud had ordered
to be brought out, his head in her lap, one
travel and labour-stained hand grasped in
her soft fingers, while the other was feebly
feeling for the companion of his wanderings,
the little shrivel-faced monkey. The poor
little beast sat a short way off, his painfully human features wrinkled into an
expression, part of sorrow and part of
suspicion of the strange bystanders. It
was just that mingling of the grotesque,
which is never lacking to the tragic in this
life.

As the cold beads of perspiration
gathered on his swarthy brow, and the
tears stole quietly down his cheeks—for
he was too far gone to use the violent

lamentations of his race—he was murmuring in low broken tones, half to himself, half to the beautiful face of Maud bent over him compassionately. He seemed to be thinking about his home in Bergamo, and his old mother, who would never more prepare *risotte* or *polenta* for her hungry little lad. Then he was in the vineyards with his childish friends, whose names sounded so strangely in that foreign land. Then his thoughts turned to the hard *padrone*, in the Italian colony in London, and he murmured deprecations of the threats and blows with which he believed himself menaced; and, when at last his eye met the bright eye of the shivering monkey, all the dreadful reality came upon him, and with fresh tears he told his *scimia carissima*, that he should never go to Bergamo again, or eat *polenta*, or bathe in the lake, or play with the boys in the village; he should never see his old mother and little sister Francesca, but he must die in cold dark England and be buried where no one knew him. And then he turned his great dark eyes mournfully up to Maud, and asked her, in his broken English,

" Signora mia, tell me the true; do I die much fast, quick, quick?"

And she bent down and kissed him, and said in his own soft language, " Listen, Giuseppe, listen *caro fanciullo mio*. Il Santo Bambino Gesù will come and fetch you soon, and you will go home with Him, and presently he will bring your father and mother, and you will all be together, and never part. Heaven is larger than Bergamo and more beautiful, and there is no more work, and hard food, and cruel words, and blows, and there is no wicked *padrone* to beat you; and San Giuseppe will come and meet you, and lead you where you may lie down and rest."

"Oh, signorina mia, it is too beautiful. Oh, tell me is the holy Bambino coming for me soon? I am much tired and don't want to stay. Do you think Gesù speaks my language, because I cannot tell Him all I mean?"

"Gesù speaks Italian, *carino mio*, but he knows all you want without your telling him. What is it?" for then the child tried painfully to raise one hand to his neck.

"*Il medaglio benedeto, il medaglio di Santo Padre.*"

She put her hand down, and detached from his neck one of those little common medallions with the figure of St. Joseph, which Italian children often wear.

"Take it for poor Giuseppe," he whispered in faint tones, and smiled to see her place it round her own neck. Then she bent once more as she saw the end approach.

" Listen, *Pepino mio*, I will say a Pater and Ave, and you can join, il Santo Bambino is coming." She began in that Italianised Latin which Romish priests employ, but she had not proceeded far before a quiver and sigh showed that all was over with poor Giuseppe, and the soul of the wanderer had gone to that place " where the wicked cease from troubling and the weary are at rest." She pressed her lips solemnly to the dead boy's brow, and then covered it reverently with her handkerchief. As she looked up to give some order to her servants, she caught sight of John who stood by with the tears in his eyes.

" I am so glad you are here, Mr. Fordyce, for I am sure you will do what I want; you will so much oblige me if you will call on Father Mulligan, and tell him of this poor child's death, and say I will pay the expense of any funeral he thinks proper. Will you come in and talk it over?"

She saw the corpse deposited in one of the many unused rooms of the mansion, and then returned to John, whom she had left in the drawing-room.

"Poor child," she said, half unconsciously, and then checking herself, "yet why poor? Why do we always use that word in speaking of the dead, though they may be far happier than the living? They gain and we lose."

"Is it not because we know nothing of that state into which they have passed? Present and seen evils are better than the vague and shadowy."

"No, Mr. Fordyce, no," replied Maude with energy, "this life is at the mercy of man," and her beautiful lips curved with scorn, "but the rest is altogether in the mercy of God. The spark of life which has been imprisoned in man, returns to the bosom of God from which it emanated and is at peace. Death is the only thought which makes life tolerable."

The working of her face showed the violent emotion she felt, the more violent because ordinarily so repressed.

"But do you feel this, Mrs. Harcourt; I know some, wearied and sickened of life, find it as tedious as you say, but surely you have no cause."

"Oh, Mr. Fordyce, do you judge as shallowly as all the rest of those I meet? Do you think that quietness of demeanour proves happiness, or regularity of life, content? Or do you think me a *femme incomprise*, bidding for the sympathy which is the mere morbid craving of vanity?"

"No, indeed; I know and esteem your character far too highly to suspect it of anything so repulsive. I spoke more what I hoped than what I thought. If wishes could procure happiness, yours were beyond a doubt."

" I believe and thank you; it is not often or to any one I complain. Sometimes an event will happen which forces the wish away and makes the blood look out. It is a duty, I know, to make the most of life—but is that happiness? Life is a burden laid on our shoulders in a wisdom we can neither see nor fathom, and doubtless for a good end. Religion bids us bear our burden, but no religion can make us enjoy our burden."

"And yet," replied John, " there are times of enjoyment in the lives of all, times when in our measure, and according to our ideas, we are very happy."

" Yes, but they are gone before we can handle them. We most enjoy ourselves when we think and reflect least, and yet that should not be human enjoyment surely."

"You say only too truly there. The happiest time of my life was when, like a careless child, I never reflected, and let my will direct my actions. I am ashamed to confess it, but since my conscience has had due play, endless cares and anxieties have seemed to hem me round."

"Why are you working as you do now?" said Maude, adding afterwards, "do you mind the question?"

"From you—no, I have all too few who have any interest in me to mind any question you might put. My work is no work of penance, no supposed expiation for the past. I have a bad black past to look back on, and the ill I did then is past cure now. There was one whom I loved dearly, and yet held out no guiding or restraining hand to him. I led him astray into bad courses, and then saw him dashed down at my feet—dead—past help or cure from me. I am not so poor a christian as to think I can expiate my deeds and buy his pardon by any hard work of mine, though his memory always haunts me daily. No, I work simply from a sense of its being a duty in my particular position, and with my means and opportunities."

"And I work because I have a past I would forget if I could, and a future I cannot even look upon. Your motive is a death, mine is a life. Never mind my mysterious words, I am not usually mysterious, as you know. There is a bond between us, a bond of sorrow, as well as a bond of work. Let us be friends, Mr. Fordyce, if you will."

She held out her hand, which John grasped eagerly and warmly, as he said,

"I accept and welcome the bond, and all it brings."

And then in a minute or two more, after a few words relating to the business of Giuseppe's funeral, he turned and left Mrs. Harcourt, and passed away from the old mansion into the dark and dirty street which lay beyond the high brick walls. The old work to be done, the old burden to be taken up, the old war to wage. The chill damp air of the wintry streets, the muddy causeway and its pushing throngs; the costermongers' cries and children's shouts, all recalled him to himself. He was the same he had been an hour back—no change of circumstances had taken place—then why was he conscious of such a lightened feeling within? why did he feel as though he could meet any dangers, undergo any trials cheerfully? If no change had taken place in externals, a mighty up-heaving was commencing within. He began to perceive that the feelings of admiration and respect for Maud's character were beginning to mingle with a warmer sentiment. He did not call it love, he did not acknowledge or realize it as love—nay, he was scarcely aware how the subtle change was working.

But, nevertheless, the old feelings of passion with which he had once regarded Edith, were commencing to return again only far intensified, as became his natural character, and the very different object of affection. Edith had been one to love, Maud was one for whom to die. Edith he could have influenced and led ; Maud was one to command. The very strangeness of her distaste for life and the vehemence of her feelings were so many additional attractions. Her life had some great void in it —would it ever be his to fill it ? The chord of her life had in it a missing string —might he ever aspire to restore it and make sweet music ? And so, slowly at first and then rapidly by degrees did these thoughts arise in his heart, bringing with them thoughts of peace and hope for the future in which he had not indulged for long.

CHAPTER VII.

GIUSEPPE was buried, with John and Maud for mourners; his monkey was sent to the zoological gardens of Marbury, and his organ was deposited at the police-station, and all was over. Perhaps the poor mother at Bergamo continued to sit of an evening at the door of her cottage and wait for the boy's return. Doubtless, she often mused on the happy days in store, when Pepino should come back rich from that wonderful far-off Inghilterra, rich enough to buy a cow and a few goats, and live in a little cottage on the mountains with his old mother and little sister. But time passed on, and his fond mother never knew her favourite was lying in a corner of the cemetery of smoke-stained Marbury, and would never more return to see the vines, and olives, and pines, and cypresses of his fair Italian home.

Maud had a little iron cross put up to the young wanderer, and his grave was tended, by her orders, by the old gardener of the Catholic cemetery, who wondered at the interest which the rich heretic lady took in a poor Bergamese.

And so time passed; to "please some," to "try all." Maud was not one to permit her feelings to gain a mastery over her for long, and when next she met John Fordyce she wore her ordinary aspect; and her greeting, though warm and genial, had none of that burst of sympathy which had marked their last conversation. And John also managed to restrain the thoughts which were filling his heart from finding any outward expression beyond what prudence would suffer. He had decided that, let his heart prompt him as it might, he must allow some time to elapse before he made any declaration of his affection, and that time must be spent in a careful study of the woman of whom he felt more and more the influence.

A strange incident brought them again into intimate connection. John's evenings were usually passed at the Working-men's Club. At first, he had taken this up from a feeling of duty, in time it grew into a pleasure and relaxation. He found that he learned more of the working-man's real nature in an evening spent thus, than he could from volumes of reports, statistics, and formal visits. Here their nature showed out naturally and unstrained, and, as the management was mainly in their own hands, and the institution, once started, self-supporting—all were enabled to meet within its walls, without that restraint and sense of obligation which marks institutions burdened with a committee of the "quality," and a long subscription list. One evening, about ten o'clock, John Fordyce was returning from the club, and had just parted with one of the members at the corner of the street, when he thought he heard the sound of hasty steps following him. He took no particular notice, but passed on, and had nearly reached the street in which the Rectory stood, when he felt a light hand placed on his arm, and the bright lamplight, into which at that moment he passed, shone upon a figure at his side, a woman's. Thinking it was some poor wanderer of the night, he was about to pass on with a kindly word, when, at the sound of his voice, as he advised her to go to the Refuge to sleep, the woman, whoever she was, uttered a shrill cry.

" I thought it was; I thought I was not mistaken."

Something attracted John, and he stopped and turned, saying,

" Do you know me then, my poor girl?"

A dreadful pang came over him, lest it should be some shadow from the old past thrown across his path again— some ghost unlaid come to reproach him.

" Do you not know me, Mr. Fordyce; am I so changed as that?"

The words were spoken in a low broken voice; telling of much sorrow and agony and disappointment, but the voice itself was not unmusical nor was the accent uncultivated. The poor shadow of the night was clad in garments, showing a miserable compromise between utter poverty and that natural instinct for dress which woman has as long as she is woman. But they hung loosely and all too large for the shrunk form, and the wan pale face was only mocked by the gaudy attempt at flowers the bonnet bore.

The wan, pale face! Yes, was it possible that those sunken, tear-reddened eyes, that wistful mouth, that pinched brow belonged to pretty little Lucy Stainer, whom he remembered so well nearly four years back at Llan-y-morfa, and whom he had then thought too lady-like for her position? It was so; and now she had passed into a mere weary wandering shadow of the night, a shattered bark without a guide, drifting further and further out to destruction.

" Good God !" was all he could say, "good God! has it come to this, Lucy, my poor girl ?"

" What, are you not ashamed to speak to me ; to be seen with me ?" the girl burst out, half bitterly, half in real surprise.

" I thought it was you, but I scarce know what made me come up to you and stop you, except because I am weary of strangers, and the sight of you seemed to take me back to the old days. No, don't take my hand, you don't know what I've been."

John bent down with his air of grave courtesy to shake hands with her, as he would have done years back.

" I don't know, as you say, what you have been. I only know that I knew you some time ago, and you seem ill and in trouble now. Lucy, Lucy, for the sake of old times, you must let me help you. I cannot see you like this."

" Don't talk to me of old days, or old friends, or old places," said the girl fiercely. " What would old friends say to me now if they could see me ?"

" They would say what I do, my poor Lucy, that you are ill, and want care and attention, and they would do what I am about to do—take you where you will have it. Take my arm."

"Are you mad, Mr. Fordyce?" said Lucy starting back, "or do you mean to make me so? What have you, a respectable gentleman," she managed to throw ineffable scorn into these words, "to do with me; leave me and let me go on my way; our ways are not the same. I only wanted to look once on an old face, and ask a question or so about old friends."

"Look here, Lucy, I will answer what questions you like, but not here. I cannot and will not let you go. Listen to me, and I will tell you what I mean to do. I know a respectable couple where you can lodge for the night. They need know nothing about your history; they will ask no questions and will treat you kindly, for my sake and for yours. No, do not speak, for you must not refuse me this. To-morrow I will see you again, and speak about you to a lady who can and will do all that is best for you. You shake your head. Poor child! you do not know how kind and gentle she is, how well she will understand your troubles. And there is Mr. Maxwell, too, in this town, who will be ready to do all for you."

But it was no such easy matter to gain her consent; sometimes she seemed ready to relent, and then just as John thought his point was gained, the old stubborn look came back, and a fresh burst of objection arose. At length, after a solemn promise that neither Maxwell nor any of her home friends should be brought to see her without her consent, she agreed to John's plan, and prepared to accompany him to the place where she was to sleep. But with the quickened instinct of those in her condition, she felt that in her present state her being in John's company would only excite wonder and remark.

"Wait a moment," she said. In a minute her bonnet was snatched off her head, the flowers and gaudy ornaments twitched out, her shawl settled demurely; and a general alteration in her appearance effected, which was little short of marvellous, and betrayed a long acquaintance with the mysteries of millinery.

She was, however, neither particularly docile nor pliant. She walked along by John's side with a certain dogged resolution, although her feeble steps betrayed considerable bodily weakness. She made no reference to past days, save one apparently careless request to be informed of the fate and whereabouts of the members of the reading party at Llan-y-morfa. She did this, however, so naturally as not to arouse suspicion in John, who gave her the required information, and indeed tried to turn her thoughts to the old times, hoping they might have some softening effect. But after this, nothing but "yes" and "no" could be extracted from her, and her guide was not sorry when they reached her destination.

A few words, of rather apocryphal explanation, sufficed for the worthy couple, and the spare bed was immediately prepared for the tired wanderer whom their favourite John had brought. Whether they believed his story or no, I cannot say. But they certainly displayed the best of breeding, by maintaining the appearance of belief and asking no inconvenient questions. And so having seen Lucy Stainer safely housed, John once more started on his homeward path, musing on the strange fate which had brought her across his path, wondering also as to who her wronger had been.

CHAPTER VIII.

WHEN John Fordyce, according to his promise, visited Lucy Stainer on the morrow, he found that a great change had taken place. The night's rest, the company of the quiet old couple, who had been her hosts, and reflection, had soothed and calmed her, and she no longer displayed the hard indifference which had marked her demeanour over night. She was quiet and depressed, listened to all John had to say, and made no objection to the course he advised. She still stipulated that her friends should not yet be communicated with, and it was evident that her pride would keep her from making any advance to reconciliation, until she knew how it would be received. John, who felt the anomaly of his position as adviser to a young woman of her age and circumstances, pressed earnestly to be allowed to bring Mrs. Harcourt to her, and to this at last she consented.

The evening was cold and damp. Snow had fallen during the day, and the traffic of the thousand feet of Marbury had trampled and churned it into a vile, unlovely, blackened compound, which lay in heaps by the side of the pavement, as unlike the beauteous, glittering veil covering the country hedgerows as anything could well be. A few flakes were yet drifting along, giving promise of a heavy fall in the night. Down the dirty, smoke-stained High Street of the district, men and girls, the "hands" of the factory, were thronging home from their work, the

latter with their tawdry glass jewellery,
and print-frocks and shawls thrown over
their heads, all talking, laughing and
making the street resound with their
rough jokes and pleasantries. The music
halls and dancing saloons were beginning
to light up and prepare for their evening
guests, their bright gas illuminations con-
trasting strangely with the meagre oil-
lamps, or " dips," of the surrounding
houses. A few stragglers lounged at their
doors, hands in pocket, pipe in mouth,
interchanging rough greetings and sentences with long pauses between. But
the night was too inclement for prolonged
al fresco conversations, and one by one
they dropped off—some to their own
homes, some to the many public-houses
with which the neighbourhood teemed.
John received and returned a few nods
as he passed down the street, stopped
to say a few words to some of his friends,

and then turned down the lane with the
high walls which enclosed Mrs. Harcourt's
house.   He had not been in the house
since the day of the Italian boy's death.
Business seldom took him there, as they
frequently met during their respective
"rounds" of work, which rendered calling unnecessary.

He crossed the court-yard, and ascended
the flight of stone steps guarded by the
twain stone lions and their shields, who
looked to him to grin in not unfriendly
greeting.   The door was ajar, and a servant who, by chance, was in the hall,
admitted him without the formula of ringing, and, informing him that her mistress
was in the drawing-room, left him to an-
nounce himself.   He turned the handle,
and, as he entered, his eye fell on the
strangest and fairest picture he had seen
for long.   The lamp was turned down
low, and the only light in the room pro-

ceeded from the great fire, piled up high with logs of wood and coal, and blazing fiercely with intense heat and ruddy glare. In front of this, on a low cushion covered with a Persian mat, sat Maud. Her head resting on her hands and bent forward, as she directed her intent gaze upon the fire as though questioning its secrets. Her short clustering curls were thrown carelessly back from off her face, her eyes were bright—very bright, as though with tears—her colour was flushed and kindled into a deeper tint than usual, and reflected the bright light of the fire, mingled with its own rich crimson tints.

John had entered so softly that she did not hear him, and for a moment he stood in silent admiration of the beautiful creature before him. Then as she turned, he advanced with outstretched hand. She looked up half puzzled, to see his form emerge from the shadow of the door, and then her face lit up with a smile of welcome.

"I shall not make a stranger of you, Mr. Fordyce," she said, "nor shall I get up from my comfortable place. Come and sit down in that great easy chair, and tell me what news you bring from the outer world which makes you look so grave."

"You look so Eastern and picturesque on your divan, that it is difficult to believe we are in smoky Marbury, and that I have left the mills, and the sodden streets and the 'hands' outside. It is like a dream."

"My dream is at an end," replied Maud, as she rose and seated herself opposite him with the little table between, "dreams are too pleasant to last, and you have brought reality in with you. You look grave. What is it? Anything I can do?"

"Yes. Something you only can do.

You are right to bring me back to reality,
for though you say I came in with it on
my face, this luxurious air would soon
have made me a dreamer also. Well, I
will open my business. May I tell you a
tale of sorrow?"

"Surely, yes; I am not unaccustomed
to them, as you know."

"It is an old story, often told—repeated, God knows, every day. A story
where woman trusts and man deceives
and wrongs, where one is weak and the
other wicked, where one suffers and the
other goes free, and the world scouts
one and welcomes the other. Mrs. Harcourt, last night I met in the streets a
poor girl whom I knew some four years
back, when she was innocent and happy.
For several weeks she lived under the
same roof with me, for I and four friends
were on a reading party in Wales, and
lodged at her aunt's house. She came

to spend her holidays in Wales, she was a milliner's apprentice, and soon after our party left, she disappeared also, leaving no trace or clue behind. She has never been seen or heard of since, until by chance I met her last night. It was not a case in which I could do much, but what I could, I did, and took her to lodge at the Collyers until you could go and see her."

"Right, right, Mr. Fordyce, and in the name of my sex I thank you. I am glad you came to me to tell me, for I have a double sympathy with all such as women, and as women who have been wronged."

Her eyes shone with a noble indignation and her teeth were hard set, as she said these words.

"A woman, of course, can do so much more than any one else," replied John, "and yet how seldom does an outcast

receive the sympathy she needs so sorely,
I don't mean maudlin sentimentality, but
real sympathy."

"I know, I know, we are apt to be
too hard upon those of our sex who are
fallen. We cannot put ourselves in their
place and circumstances, and make allow-
ances for the temptations to which they
may have given way. But I feel such
have a special claim on me. Every woman whose shattered life I may in any
way repair or restore, is a step gained to
me. So you may command me to the
uttermost—what would you have me do?"

"I must leave that in great measure to
your own judgment. At present she objects to her friends being informed of her
present state and address—indeed, she
will not even allow me to tell Maxwell
who was one of our party. But it seems
to me, that with our help, she might be
set up in a way to get her own bread, as

she understands millinery I believe, and
then perhaps we can effect some reconciliation with her friends. What do you
say to that?"

"It shows your knowledge of the world,
Mr. Fordyce; her friends are far more
likely to forgive and recognise her when
they find her respectable and thriving,
than if she went to them penniless and
with never so much of penitence. Is she
ready to agree with any scheme of this
kind?"

"I think so; nay, I am sure a few
words from you would persuade her to
anything."

"And the betrayer?" asked Maude,
with bitterness. "He is beyond us, I
suppose. Is it not hard that a few
kind words and the expending a little
money which we cannot miss, may re-
cover this poor fallen girl, while the
more guilty party is out of our reach?

He will never know the ruin he has caused, he will never see the wreck he has made; doubtless he is going on his career, and is received and welcomed by the world, and no efforts of ours can make him feel or repent."

"As you say, he is out of our hands," said John, "but he is in far better hands than ours. I believe that for every ill deed men do, they receive their retribution in this life. We do not hear the judgment pronounced, or see the bolt fall; but sure I am that we are our own executioners, work out our own sentences, and carry our prison chambers within us."

"You rebuke my wishes of vengeance and punishment; you are right, and we will leave this unknown to his conscience. I suppose what you say is true and that we do carry our prisons within us, however gay the outward appearance may be.

After all, the Ducal Palace contained the Piombi as well as the council chamber. But what of those whose hearts were intended for palaces, and have been converted to prisons by the violence of others and no doings of their own—who are prisoners and not of hope, but of the world's cruelty."

"Ah, Mrs. Harcourt, what sympathy can be too great for such? There is not a day passes but I meet such sufferers as you speak of, whose sorrows have been caused by the injustice of others, and who bear their heavy burden, and even seem to smile under it—and I feel how utterly helpless one is in the presence of such a silent grief. Words are powerless."

"Do you know that old proverb, 'the burden is light on another man's shoulders?' We all have good advice for the sufferer, and each thinks himself worse off than his neighbour. I hope the converse of your theory is true, that wounds bring their own cure in this life when not self-inflicted."

"I am sure of it," said John, eagerly, "I am sure of it. I do not mean simply that time alleviates and heals; but I know that a grief which comes to us not of our own creation, after a while leads to a happiness we could not otherwise have enjoyed. The blow upon the heart which seems at the moment to paralyze and almost kill us, is succeeded by the flow of waters which only that blow could have set free. I find it in my daily work, and I find it in my daily life."

"Again what you say rebukes and teaches me," replied Maud gravely. "I am impatient, and sometimes too apt to cry out against fate. You woke me from a bitter reverie when you entered, and you give me heart to look forward instead of backward. You are a gentle schoolmaster," she added, with a faint smile.

"It is to one who needs no teaching, to one whose every act and word teaches, and convinces, and arouses."

"Do not praise me for what I do not deserve."

"It is your example which has given me courage and heart for the work I have undertaken. Thank God for the chance which has brought me here, and shown me one living down grief in good works. I always think, that however dark, and sad, and gloomy a life may be, the clouds must lift and clear, and let the sun shine. The night may have its doubts and sorrows, but the light comes with the day dawn. My night has been long, but I sometimes fancy I can see the glimmering of the dawn. We must wait, and with what patience we may."

"You have caught your friend Mr. Maxwell's tones of hope, Mr. Fordyce.

Generally we weak women have to cheer your sex, when you faint and grow disheartened. But you have reversed this, and make me ashamed of my distrust and doubts. It is well if we help one another in our several measures. Ah! Mr. Fordyce," added Maud, forcing a laugh, " confess now you did not approve of me at first—you thought me flippant, did you not? Not sufficiently grave and reserved?"

" I will confess that you did me great service by piqueing my self-conceit, and making me set to work in a real practical manner. I have to thank you for all."

" Even for the promised hot luncheons, which you never came to eat? You must either think me very unsociable, or be so yourself, for you partake of nothing but talk in my house. I shall insist upon your bringing Mr. Maxwell to tea some night, and if you like we will be proper and formal."

" I take that as my dismissal now then, for I feel anything but formal and proper at the present moment; and so, farewell. I shall leave Lucy Stainer in your hands with all confidence."

Nor did Maud betray John's trust. She was one of those energetic souls, who, when asked to do a thing, undertake and perform it while others are pondering its possibility. But then she well knew the materials and tools she had to work with, and understood their capacity, so that she never promised rashly. Next day she went at once to see Lucy Stainer, and by her good sense and grave, but kindly, manner, overruled all the objections and demurs that poor waif would have made to her schemes for her good."

Now Maud Harcourt's plan was this. She was just then attempting, on a small scale, what has since been carried out in full dimensions, a system which should improve the payment and sanitary condition of those poor creatures who minister to the requirements of fashion, the milliners' workwomen. By her exertions, a small body of *employées* had been mustered under a fully competent head, and, as none but good and experienced workers were admitted, not only was the rate of wages fair, but the amount of employment steadily increasing. By a little delicate *finesse* and withholding herself from any prominent position, she had contrived to get the "patronage" and support of some of the leading millowners' wives, and yet retain the detailed working and management in her own hands. In this little society, therefore, she proposed to find a place for poor Lucy, there to stay until some reconciliation with her family could be effected.

She spoke to her in her friendly tones, telling how that life is but a series of falls

and repentances, and that in the cheerful
acceptance of such means of recovery as
presented themselves, lay the only hope
against further falling; and that she could
best show her sorrow for the past by
working hard and struggling honestly for
the future. By her advice, Lucy allowed
Maxwell to be informed of the strange
circumstances which had brought her to
Marbury, and solicited his aid and advice
for her future course of life. In one
matter alone was she obdurate, and
neither would be moved from the resolution she had formed, nor give any
explanation of her purpose. In the most
respectful manner, she begged that she
might be allowed to go for two days
on a journey, promising faithfully to
return at the end of that time; but
declining to say where, or to whom, she
was going, or the object of her journey,
save that it was for no harm, and had no

dangerous connection with her past mode of life. Her earnestness left no room for doubting her repeated assertions, and, accordingly, although somewhat perplexed, neither Maxwell nor Maud Harcourt could withhold their consent, and she was let go, and furnished with the little sum she thought needful. If our readers have not already guessed her destination, we may, perhaps, be allowed to outstrip her, and anticipate her arrival.

CHAPTER IX.

REGARDLESS of the example and practice of the world, this veracious narrative has somewhat neglected the Rev. Cyril Ponsonby since the improvement of his fortunes, preferring to follow and abide with those less prosperous. It is time, however, for us to return to him, and give him some portion of our attention.

He might be, and, indeed, was, called by the world, a very lucky and prosperous man; to which the world generally added, "and one that thoroughly deserves his fortune." About this, perhaps, the reader has his own ideas. At the age of twenty-

eight, when most men are still fighting a
hard battle with life, and have little prospect of peace for some years to come,
Cyril was able to rest on his oars in quiet
security. He was in possession of a fine
living, a handsome private fortune, and a
ladylike, well-connected wife. If we put
the lady last, it is not of ungallantry, but
following the order in which our friend
Cyril estimated his own good fortunes.
And yet he could scarcely be called a
happy man. He had conformed to his
new position, certainly, and made a very
tolerable clergyman, as times go. No
scandal was ever associated with his
name, his theology was negative, and his
morality positive. Nor did he ever advance an opinion, or do a deed which
could bring his prudence into question.
On entering upon his living, he at once
showed his determination to continue in
the safe paths of his predecessor. Perhaps

thinking that the less active connection he had with his parish, the better it would be for both parties, he engaged the services of a curate.

Curates were then quoted at about £80 per annum, and the market was dull, the demand being chiefly for special articles, such as " sound Rubricians, and thorough Ritualists," "good barytone voices," and the like. However, our prudent friend offered the very liberal stipend of £100, with a cottage; and managed to secure an undoubted jewel, who devoted all his energies, heart and soul to the parish, and employed his spare time in " dragging up " his numerous and rapidly increasing progeny. Between him and his rector, there was not an atom of sympathy. Cyril addressed and treated him quite as a gentleman, but with a studied cold courtesy which was a continual " *Noli me tangere.*"

His checques were sent him quarterly, with precise regularity to the very day. In summer, fruit, vegetables and flowers found their way to the cottage—in winter, game and poultry. Six times in the year the Curate and his wife dined with the Rector and his wife, and met the doctor and *his* wife; and once a month, Edith's pretty pair of grey ponies conveyed her on a formal morning call upon Mrs. Curate. So you see, really the Rev. T. Jones had nothing to complain of in any way. At the same time he knew that the Rev. the Rector did not like him, and the Rev. the Rector knew that the curate did not like him, and so they were not cordial or friendly, but very polite and regardful of their respective positions. And their wives, as a matter of course, hated each other, as was natural and proper.

The poor old Rectory where the Rev.

Henry Everett Comberland Fordyce had sipped his glass of dry port so often, was changed and pulled about past all recognition. The old drawing-room had been converted into a study, the old study had become a smoking-room—of course it was not called so, you understand—and a splendid drawing-room and boudoir had been added on, and a new wing thrown out. The conservatory had been pulled down, shifted and altered, the gardens had been re-modelled and laid out in the most modern fashion. Cyril cared little for riding, but he had the stables freshly arranged and furnished with all his coachman thought necessary for the advantage of his guests, if not for his own pleasure.

In the same way, although he seldom or never went near his schools, he took care to procure and pay well a very magnificent specimen of a certificated

Government master, who came charged
to the muzzle with useful (and other)
knowledge, and brought a wife who
could play the organ in church. So if
idle himself, Cyril, at least, had his
work done by deputy. He had begun
by preaching his own sermons, clever,
frigid little sermons, which reached to
a kind of "half believe," and balanced
the advantages and sacrifices of a moral
life so exactly, as to leave the hearer
in doubt which was to be preferred. But
after a while he wearied of the uncon-
genial task, and contracted privately with
one of those ingenious gentry who are
to stupid clergymen what *perruquiers* are
to bald men, for a supply of short and
unemotional discourses, free from all extreme views and offensively pointed appli-
cations, and then he commenced firing
blank cartridge. He hated his work,
for he knew he was a hypocrite and in-

truder, and ever feared that the world must see it also. He was not a happy man, for he scorned the platitudes of the life he had to lead; the "small beer" chronicles which he had undertaken to keep. He saw now how for a savoury mess of pottage in a gilded bason, he had sacrificed the life of intellectual energy he might have lived, for one which can only be tolerable to the man who has his heart in it. He saw how, in the very wantonness of his *insouciance*, he had married a woman who cared little for him, and whose romantic ideas had all faded away in presence of reality.

Their nursery stood empty—an annoyance to Cyril, but the secret cause of intense regret to Edith, who tried to escape her reflections in the round of such amusements and dissipations as their side of the country offered. Cyril was a listless, politely indifferent husband, caring little about anything as long as his own comforts were attended to, and the social obligations duly observed. He found that half his pleasure in life had vanished with his accession of riches. He had been far happier in debt. Hudson's Regalias and Trabucos tasted no better than cheap Manillas now they were paid for on delivery, and although he took far more wine than was good for his sedentary life, it is very doubtful whether he enjoyed the splendid old wines his predecessor had stored, as he had once relished an Oxford wine merchant's "magnificent dry crusted Port" drunk on credit as long as its price.

His days were passed in the perusal of the newspapers, and such periodicals and novels as came in Mudie's weekly parcel, the smoking an immense number of his favourite cigars, and occasional constitutional rides which his doctor advised.

Every now and then he would utterly weary of the dullness of his existence, and start off, sometimes alone, sometimes with Edith, for Brighton or London. In the autumn, his delicate appearance always served as an excuse for two or three months on the Continent; he would have liked to go *en garçon*, but made up for the presence of his wife by dropping the remnant of his clerical attire and going in mufti. And such was his life.

Now it so chanced that about this period, the Right Reverend the Lord Bishop of Arlington having done nothing particular to make himself notable for many years, thought that he would make a sensation by dying, which he accordingly proceeded to do. As of course the quality of bishop, "Low" or "High" depends upon the Whig or Tory Government of the day, and at that time the Liberals happened to be in power, the

reverend gentleman who succeeded to the
See, belonged to the former party. He
was a young man, that is about forty,
and possessed of great energy and resolution, determined to make up for his
predecessor's failings.

After he had been for some time resident
in his palace, the idea of a diocesan tour
occurred to his episcopal brain, and like
most of his other ideas, was speedily
carried into practice. Having communicated his desire to his clergy generally,
and found that it met with their high
approbation, he proceeded to throw himself upon their hospitality, and claim one
night's lodging of each, expressly stipu-
lating that he wished to be received
simply as a fellow-clergyman, without any
pomp, parade or expense.

The idea took mightily, being chiefly
helped on by the clergywomen, to whom
the idea of a real live bishop as occupant

of the best bedroom was an irresistable attraction. Accordingly his lordship found
no lack of hospitality, and indeed had
oftener than not to rebuke his hosts for
excess. Poor man! perhaps of all his
many episcopal and apostolic labours, this
was the most weighty. Let the reader
but once peruse the circular of an adver-
tising, cheap wine merchant, and remember
and lay to heart the fact that the clergy
are the main consumers of the "magni-
cent, old, crusted Port, at 36s.," the
"Amontillado character sherries at 30s.,"
and the "luscious malmsey Madeiras, at
28s.," to this let him add the courteous
entreaties of hospitable clerical helpmates
proud of placing their choicest *entrées*
before a Lord Spiritual and taking no
refusal, and let him finish with the after
dinner declarations of orthodoxy, protestations of over-work and such histories of all
parochial grievances, and then imagine the

state of the good prelate's digestion,
physical and mental, on his return to the
palace and his *placens uxor*. Surely if
any man might, he could exclaim " I die
daily," and most surely in the secret
depths of his heart did he resolve that
such a perilous missionary enterprise
should never be his again.

Among the first to respond to the Episcopal offer was Cyril; desirous of standing
well in the diocess, and well aware that he
was better able than most of his brother
clergy to entertain their spiritual head in
a worthy and dignified manner. So when
a gracious reply to his invitation was returned, and a day appointed for his lordship's visit, he issued his sovereign man-
date that no expense should be spared, or
trouble omitted to render the thing . a
success. The programme of the visit was
arranged thus.

The Bishop was to arrive on a Tuesday

evening, in time for a quiet "family" dinner. On the Wednesday he would go to hold a confirmation in a neighbouring town, and return in the evening for the grand entertainment, to which all the neighbouring clergy and magnates were bidden—leaving early on the following morning. Edith fully coöperated with her lord and master in his hospitable ideas, and they both were determined to show the diocess that its youngest incumbent, at least, knew how to live well, and practised the virtue of charity. I am sorry to record that the Rev. T. Jones was not included in the invitations issued, for either dinner—a piece of bad taste on Cyril's part, which was inexcusable, because a blunder in policy and manners, as he afterwards found. But with this exception, all was as it should have been. To say that the wines and cookery were excellent and of the finest quality, would be to gild refined

gold—the united forces of Masterman
Park and Easimore Rectory were enough
to guarantee that.

In due time, the barouche and pair of
bays drove over with Edith to the D——
Station to receive the Episcopal body, accompanied by the waggonette to receive
the Episcopal luggage. I am afraid the
good Bishop fell somewhat in the estimation of the servants' hall, when the said
luggage proved to consist of one small port-
manteau and a bag, the latter supposed
to contain the wonderful lawn sleeves which
ladies admire so much. However, although he came not habited in mitre,
rochet, pallium, cope and pastoral staff,
and riding a white mule, yet at least he
was a real bishop after all, clad in the
combination of infantine and anile garments which the Church of England ap-
proves and delights in.

His hat, if shabby and dusty, was looped

up and had a charming cockade, his apron was there, and so were the episcopal legs clothed in the proper gaiters, and, perhaps, the air of sublimity appertaining to the dress only piquantly. enlivened the air of mystery which environed the man. He was a charming man, this bishop. There was he, chatting and laughing, and joking with Edith as though those lips had never uttered charges, addresses and sermons, and patting her favourite Skye terrier with the same hand which was supposed to wield the pastoral staff, and really indited the pastoral letters. But he was practical, too, he travelled with a great dispatch box, bursting open with letters and papers, took notes as he went along, and carried on a correspondence all through his route which might have puzzled a Briareus to conduct. And he liked to go into the church and the schools, when time allowed, and would ask questions about the average attendance at the two places, which sometimes puzzled the incumbents to answer.

Nothing could have been more charming and simple than the family dinner on the first evening; only that it is difficult to connect St. Paul with wax-lights, Palestine soup, turbot and sparkling Hock, you might have imagined you saw him visiting old Mnason of Crete in a friendly way, or Apollos dining with Aquilla and Priscilla. The parents on both sides had been invited, and duly came. Mr. Masterman and his handsome wife well representing the grand old squirearchy, while Mr. Ponsonby was no bad specimen of the courtier of the old school; his wife could be said to represent nothing particular, but amiable and harmless idiotcy, but that she did thoroughly.

And now you see why Mr. and Mrs.
Jones were omitted—neither could be
asked without the other, and together
they would have made the table ill-
balanced, whereas a neighbouring friendly
Honourable and Reverend gentleman kept
it as it should be. Mr. Jones had given
way to a foolish, but not inexcusable,
piece of pique, on perceiving his exclusion
from the episcopal presence, and gone
out for the day—which really placed a
weapon in his enemy's hands, enabling
him to regret the absence of the worthy
curate whom he had not invited.

However, things went off charmingly,
and, as the good Prelate took his chamber-
candlestick and went up to his luxurious
room, he blessed Providence for providing
an Established Church in England, and
making him a bishop in it. For almost
the first time since he had begun his rash
tour, he slept well, undisturbed by indi-

gestion, nor did he need his customary camomile pill, with which he always provided himself.

Why did not his visit end there? oh, why? For Cyril's sake, we mean, not the Bishop's. Alas, Cyril! Nemesis had marked thee long, and now was her time to strike; the word had gone forth, and the Furies mustered in dread conclave over that fatal roof-tree. The morn dawned bright; but the little cloud, no bigger than a man's hand, was beginning to rise above the horizon. The day began ill, it was but a trifle, but still it would have been far better avoided. Before the Bishop's arrival, Cyril had gone through a form, observed in many pious households on Saturday night, and had duly "dressed" the rooms. That is to say, the highly flavoured sensation novels of the day were removed from the bookstands of the drawing-room, and their places filled up with

"Half-hours in Capernaum," "Travels in Mesopotamia," "Babblings in Babylon," and such other works of Oriental travel as combined the theology of a Simeon and the topography of a Murray.

Then these were "top-dressed" with others of a general and inoffensive nature, to give a desirable, natural appearance. So in the study the "Westminster," "Fortnightly," and other reviews of a strong nature and Tübingen character retired, vice "Edinburgh," "Quarterly," &c., promoted; a few Whig political works and tractates lay amiably side by side with the pamphlets and productions of the Evangelical school. The shelves were well filled and very tidy—not too tidy, you understand, which would have been suspicious—but enough to suggest the careful and methodical habits of a diligent student. So far so good. But, oh, my dear, clever Cyril, why stop there? why not carry the reforming hand still farther? Is it not the duty of a bishop to oversee and look upon and scrutinise things? Might not his very name have taught thee thus much? But the Fates would have it so.

We have duly chronicled the change of the old Rector's old study into a smoking-room, and the erection of a grand new library. The old room still retained its name, and was called variously the master's room, or the little study. In it would Cyril spend his morning hours; there were kept his choice cigars, his Eastern pipes, his jars of Turkish tobacco. There also were to be found many of the yellow-papered productions of MM. Jules Janin, Georges Sand, and other such instructors of French youth and French morality. No guest ever came here; those who smoked had to smoke on the lawn, and as the domestics had not the French

tongue, Cyril saw no reason for concealing
or restricting that wide range of study,
which was to give him the knowledge of
men and manners so desirable for a clergyman.

Now what reasonable man could have
supposed it likely for the Bishop to find
his way in here? Why on that morning
of all others should he wake early instead
of dosing on pleasantly until eight of the
clock, as was his wont? Why, after
turning and tossing for long should he
be seized with a desire to rise and be-
take himself to his correspondence? And
why, oh why, most of all, should he miss
his way and blunder into this clerical,
Bluebeard closet—this chamber of hor-
rors? Alas! no good genius, no shrewd
domestic headed him back and put him
in the right way. He entered, and perceiving all the appointments of a study
writing-table there thought all was right.

Still the smell of Cyril's last Regalia could not but strike on even Episcopal nostrils, and he shook his head sadly.

"A pity, a great pity; a bad example for others!" But then he was charitable, and did not call tobacco "a gorging fiend," mentally adding, "he's very young." But again his roving eye fell on one after another of those deadly chrome yellow *feuilletons*, and though, to do his Lordship justice, he was perfectly innocent of their contents, he knew well enough that they were of a character which no clergyman, to say nothing of an honest man, should read. The titles and authors' names were quite enough—Janin, Sand, Dumas. Good gracious, what was the world coming to? And to make matters worse, and as if to leave no doubt at all, there was his own letter appointing the time of his visit sticking out as a marker from one of the yellowest!

Then the Lord Bishop grew very angry indeed, and turned very red, nor did he summon up Cyril's youth to plead excuse. He would depart from the sulphurous apartment as soon as possible; but he would leave a mark which should appeal to Cyril's conscience. You cannot, bishop or no, reprove your host for his choice of novels, discovered by you accidentally, but you can show your disgust at his conduct. And so, with his own Episcopal hands, he tore the sulphurous romance through its flimsy pages, and placed upon it conspicuously his own letter with his signature, "James Arlington," uppermost, as though to say, "I deliver this as my act and deed," and then he turned away and forgot all about his letters.

At breakfast he was a little short, contradicted Cyril twice, and several times spoke of the desirability of young

clergymen giving up secular and unprofit-
able habits and luxuries. However, as
pâté de Périgord, cold ham, omelettes, and
stewed kidneys did not come under any of
these heads, no one's appetite was the
worse.

As there really happened to be a
parochial matter in which his opinion
was desired, he accompanied his host to
the study, the real study this time; and
after a little while seemed to get into his
usual *suave* vein. He spoke of his pleasure
at his cordial reception among his clergy,
and was dwelling upon his desire never
to intercept their routine by his visits.

"I always like, Mr. Ponsonby, to see
something of the parish working, for who
knows but what I may learn a hint? I
like to be present at any interview they
may have with their poor people, for I
know that sometimes cases will arise when
another judgment may be of use. So if

any applicants come to you, I hope you will neither send them away on my account, nor me on theirs."

And now came the time for the practice of this. "The bearings of this observation lies in the application of it," said Mr. Bunsby. Alas, alas! the "bearings of it" were heavy on Cyril.

At that moment a stupid, new footman, Nemesis causing the other experienced one to gossip in the stables at that moment, knocked at the study door, and said,

"Please, Sir, here's a woman wishes to speak to you."

Had Cyril been alone, he would have answered without hesitation, "Send her to Mr. Jones, the curate."

But could he do so in his bishop's presence? Never. He scowled at John Thomas, while the Bishop pleasantly said,

"Come, Mr. Ponsonby, you won't turn

me out, or shall I think you practice auricular confession, and that will never do, you know. Show her in, show her in, my man."

Let us remark, *en passant*, upon the topography of this study, destined to be far more fatal to Cyril than ever the secrets of that other chamber. It communicated with the hall by a passage from the back door, and by this parishioners and such visitors were admitted. Another door, however, opened into Edith's boudoir, but as this had been insufficient to prevent sounds from penetrating thither, a second door had been added. When both were closed, nothing could be heard in the boudoir; when, however, the second door was by chance left open, every word could be distinguished. And now careless John Thomas, on his passage through the boudoir, shut the inner door of the study, but left this fatal portal on the jar in the room where Edith was at work.

He then went to the last act of his share in the tragic drama where he was an unconscious performer, and returned ushering in at the parochial door a veiled woman. Then having duly placed the fuse to the mine, and the light to the fuse, he retired—thinking what a promising, active, young fellow he was.

The woman threw up her veil, and disclosed the pale, but determined, face of Lucy Stainer! There was no flurry or excitement about her, her manner was perfectly composed, and though the occasional twitchings of her face showed the intensity of her feelings, her voice did not shake nor falter, nor betray any symptoms of fear.

She took no notice of the Bishop, but kept her cold scornful gaze upon Cyril Ponsonby. And he? When she entered

he was standing with his back to the fireplace, full face towards her, and as she
raised her veil, and he recognised his
visitor, he turned that deadly green white
which dark complexions change to under
sudden emotions. He set his teeth firm,
and placed his hand on his heart to still
those great thumps it was striking within
his chest; and a sick trembling came
over him, and for a moment he felt giddy.
He had been very clever and cunning,
but he knew he could not weather this
storm. The fox was trapped, and in his
own earth too. Then he looked up, and
tried to frown. Useless. His emotion
had not escaped the notice of his visitor,
or of his guest. The Bishop who had
called up a beaming good-humoured smile,
ready for the supposed parishioner, was
puzzled at Cyril's silence, and looked up
at his host's face. Struck by what he
saw written there he was about to en-

quire, with alarm, whether he felt ill, when a second thought made him look once more from him to the " parishioner," and he sat down in silence. Then Lucy took a step forward, and began to speak.

" Ah ! your face tells the tale without words. You recognise me, although I am changed. You know the girl whom you wronged so cruelly, and deserted, and left to starve, or die, for all you knew or cared. Oh, how you change and tremble ! what ! are you afraid of *me* now—of *me*, whom it was so easy to forsake ?"

But Cyril burst in upon her speech. " You must be mad, woman, to speak like that. My Lord, you will not pay any attention to the abuse of this poor creature. Her state is quite evident."

" Indeed you are right, Mr. Ponsonby," replied the Bishop, in tones of marked sarcasm, " and anything less resembling madness, I never saw. As to the attention I pay, that must depend upon circumstances."

"My Lord, if you are his Lordship the Bishop I was told was here, I ask you to hear me a minute. I will not detain you long; nor, though I confess I have gone astray, will I say a word which your ears should not hear. I am not come here to quarrel or abuse, and I ask you to judge between me and that wicked man there, clergyman though he is now."

"Pardon me, my Lord," again interposed Cyril in his agony, "but really your Lordship must see the impropriety of listening to the insinuations of such a woman as she confesses herself to be."

"And pardon me, Mr. Ponsonby, if I request that you will permit me to be the best judge of my own conduct. I acknowledge, Sir, you are my host, and can prevent my listening to this poor woman in your house, but as your Bishop, it is my right and duty to receive all complaints which may be made against my clergy; whether you would prefer my hearing this here or at the Palace, you may decide. My poor woman, I am ready to listen to what you have to say, speak it without fear. But remember that it is one of God's ministers you are speaking of, and think how great a sin a lie would be—one too, sure to be discovered."

"My Lord Bishop," replied Lucy in her quiet monotonous tones, by which she endeavoured to conceal her emotion, "though I am a sinner, God knows I am a penitent sinner, and would not tell a lie on any account. I did not come here to complain to you, Sir—my Lord, I mean— nor did I know when I came, that you were here. I came but to see Mr. Ponsonby there, and try whether his heart was utterly of stone, to tell him, in spite of all his wickedness, I have been brought to see my own sin in having listened to him years ago, and that now I have repented, and friends are helping me to lead a better life; I thought now he was a clergyman and a married man, he would have felt some pity and remorse for me, but it seems not, as he tries to prove me a liar and a madwoman."

"You say, years ago; am I to understand that Mr. Ponsonby was the cause of your fall; and, if so, can you state at what time, before or after his being ordained a clergyman?—stay, Mr. Ponsonby, if you please I will hear you presently."

And again he waved Cyril down.

"Oh, before, my Lord, before; God forbid he should be so bad as that! Four years ago, my Lord, I was an innocent girl, with no worse fault than having my head turned by a pack of silly novels. Mr. Ponsonby was staying with a reading

party at my Aunt's, and there he began
to flatter and deceive me, and at last I
was weak and wicked enough to run away,
as he wished me; and then—oh, when I
think of it, it makes me nearly mad!—he
left me six months after, ruined as I was
—ruined as I was, he left me without a
word or a line, only an envelope and a
twenty-pound note! I do not excuse
myself, my Lord, I was weak and wicked,
and truly do I repent it; but, oh, it was
cruel and heartless. And then he becomes
a clergyman!"

"My Lord," now burst in Cyril, white
and furious, "by this woman's own statement, the occurrence to which she refers
took place prior to my ordination, when I
was a layman, and under no authority.
With all respect for your Lordship, I
would submit that it is no part of your
duty to listen, nor of mine to answer
before you, to charges relating to

a time when I was not a clergyman."

" Shame, Mr. Ponsonby, shame !" replied the Bishop, with warmth, " shame upon your language, and your manner of speaking. I know my duty, Sir, better than you do your's, I fear. Let me tell you that your subterfuge avails you nothing. I know the date of your ordination well, and from this woman's statement, I perceive that your desertion of her was prior to your ordination but two or three months. I do not know when I have heard of anything more revolting; and your manner only adds double infamy to a bad deed."

" I cannot prevent your hard words, my Lord, but I must protest against your employment of knowledge gained in this way, and of events when I was neither under you or any other jurisdiction."

" Rest tranquil, Mr. Ponsonby," replied the Bishop, with intense sarcasm, " if you fear my 'employment' of the knowledge of your character I have gained. For the sake of the rest of my clergy, and for the moral tone of my diocess, it will be my duty to suppress it. My poor woman," he continued, turning to Lucy, "you have done quite right in telling me what you have done, and from my heart I pity you. If you came with any lingering feelings of affection for this—unhappy man, you must see yourself how utterly unworthy he is of it. If you came with any desire of retribution, I advise and exhort you to put these unholy desires away as unbefitting you, or any other child of Adam. You say you are penitent, and I believe you, and pray God may accept your penitence, and keep you evermore in the right way. God bless you, my girl, and have you in his guidance."

He rose as he finished speaking, and, without a word to Cyril, opened the door

for Lucy to pass through. Her tears had
been flowing freely at the Bishop's kind
words, but she obeyed him with a silent
courtsey, and departed. The Bishop did
not sit down again, but turned to Cyril,
who was leaning his head on his hands,
and never looking up.

"Mr. Ponsonby, I cannot express to
you how shocked I have been at what I
have heard; and not only at that, but at
your manner. All sins, duly repented of,
are forgiven, but to deny and excuse a sin
only aggravates it. I am well aware that
I can take no official cognizance of a sin
committed by you when a layman; but,
as your bishop and pastor, I must exhort
you to lay this matter very seriously to
heart, and make it the subject of your
prayers for pardon. You must excuse
me if I add that, under the circumstances,
I think it best to leave your house without
carrying out my first arrangements, or

keeping my engagement for to-night. What you may feel, I know not, but I confess I feel too acutely what I have heard, to play the part of guest any longer to one whose character has been revealed to me in the light in which yours has. I think it best to speak plainly. I will trouble you so far as to ask for a servant to fetch me a fly from the station, and will, on its arrival, proceed to the Confirmation alone."

Cyril made a few sullen apologies and deprecations, but to no avail, and within half an hour the Bishop of Arlington departed, sending his adieux to Edith by her husband, as he was too truthful to give a false excuse for his sudden departure. Now, if the reader will be so good as to remember that the inner door of the boudoir was open all this while, and that Edith had heard every word, he will at once imagine the manner

in which Mrs. Ponsonby received the excuses of her lord and master, and may
conceive the agreeable dialogue which
followed. Also, perhaps, he will exert
his mind a little further, and imagine the
behaviour of eight influential clergymen
and their wives invited to meet the Lord
Bishop of Arlington, when on arriving
they discovered that the said Lord Bishop
had departed quite suddenly without reason—that their host and hostess were in
the vilest of tempers with themselves, each
other and all mankind; and lastly, that in
the family party at the Rectory there
seemed not one dish, but a whole dinner
service of crockery down. Finally, if his
mind be equal to the effort, he may imagine what the Diocess of Arlington said
when the Rev. Cyril Ponsonby was excluded from the general invitation to the
grand reception at the Palace.

CHAPTER X.

LUCY STAINER returned from her journey to Easimore Rectory quiet and composed, and ready to accede with gratitude to any plans for her future which Maud should approve. As at this period she drops out of our history and is met with no more, we may take this opportunity of observing that her end was as satisfactory as could be desired. After she had been received as one of the workwomen on the system Maud had established, and had by her steadiness and diligence shown the reality of her repentance, Mrs. Harcourt wrote to her aunt in Wales to inform her of

Lucy's past history—her fall, her wanderings, her recovery. The warm-hearted Mrs. Markham had long since changed her wrath for sorrow, and eagerly embraced any chance of reconciliation. Ultimately, she decided upon moving to Marbury, and there living on the savings of her long and industrious life, and in this way were the aunt and niece reconciled and brought into relationship once more. The forgiveness of the one was as hearty as the penitence of the other, and perhaps their mutual affection was only increased by their troubles and separation.

Time passed on, and each day only served to deepen John's love for Maud. Nothing but his own diffidence of himself, and the doubt that he could ever win a creature so glorious kept him from declaring his affections. He looked back upon the far distant past of his life which

he now so much abhorred; he looked on
to his present humble condition, to his
blank future, and then exclaimed, "How
can I ask her to share my lot? how can
I ask her to become the wife of a poor,
obscure man, one who is glad to hide
himself and his sorrow in the work of
a great heathen town?"

And yet, if he at times despaired, at
times he ventured to hope. The work
they were both engaged in was self-
chosen, their thoughts and aspirations
were alike, their faith was the same,
nor did she despise him for the doubts
and difficulties he honestly confessed to.
Both had painful memories of the past,
both sought relief in practical work for
the good of their fellow-creatures. A
hundred circumstances brought them into frequent contact and interchange of
thought. Each had need of the other's
help and sympathy. Could any position,

then be more favourable than his? But the important question, the one John daily asked himself was, "Does she love me—is it possible for her to return my affection?"

And to this, no certain answer could he return. Narrowly as he watched her, he was unable to perceive in her bearing towards him more than a generous and sincere friendship would warrant. Sympathy, friendly behaviour, generous confidence, she offered—but love? Did she love him as he loved her? If you think John Fordyce a timid lover, a half-hearted suitor, good reader, remember that he had been once rejected, and that a man does not easily forget that. Remember that he was conscious of having made a mistake in his lady-love then, and was determined to be quite sure this time. He could wait.

One day he met his old acquaintances,

Mrs. D. Visor and Mrs. Floss. They were both returning from their day's visiting, and common courtesy forbad his passing them unnoticed, although they were no particular favourites of his. But even if courtesy would have allowed him to pass by, the two ladies would not.

"Well, I'm sure," began Mrs. Floss, "we thought you had quite cut us, Mr. Fordyce, although we are engaged in the same interesting work and all that. And I am sure that for my part if the cholera is coming as fast as they say, there is more need than ever that we should all be friendly and agreeable."

"Don't talk nonsense, Arabella Floss," interrupted Mrs. Visor, "I have told you again and again that cholera is a case of drains—a simple case of drains. Give me a town infected, and tell me the character of the drainage of the towns between the first which I call A, and Marbury, which

I will call B, and I can calculate to a
certainty the time in which cholera will
travel from A to B. And how are you
Mr. Fordyce? you look ill and anxious.
Why are you ill and anxious?"

"My looks belie me, Mrs. Visor, for I
am glad to say I am neither the one nor
the other. Perhaps I look hot, for I
have been hurrying from one place to
another."

"Never hurry," was the solemn reply,
"I never do. My actions are all based
upon exact calculation, which nothing
short of a miracle can disturb. You
know my hobby. Facts and figures—my
facts are stated by figures, my figures
guided by facts. That is the rule of life."

"Ah yes. It's all very well, Mr. Fordyce, is it not, for Mrs. Visor to talk
about figures like that. But my head
isn't a ready reckoner, nor ever was. I
try to love my neighbour, when he isn't

too disagreeable, and do as I would be done by. But there are people who won't be done pleasantly by, but turn up their nose and think every one else dirt. And that I don't like. Why not be friendly, eh, Mr. Fordyce?"

"I am sure, Mrs. Floss, I have no objection if you mean me—indeed, I always thought I was friendly."

"No, Mr. Fordyce, no. It's not you, I mean, it's a certain lady who shall be nameless. Now if you consider short hair like a boy's, and silks and velvets, and stuck up noses district visiting, I don't; no, nor high brick walls shutting people out."

"Mrs. Floss," responded John, "it would be idle of me to pretend to be ignorant of the lady you mean. Mrs. Harcourt is a lady from whom I have received the greatest kindness, and for whom I entertain the deepest respect; nor will I hear a word spoken against her in my presence. If, therefore, you have nothing else to say, you will allow me to wish you good morning."

He raised his hand to his hat, and was about to leave then, when Mrs. Visor, trembling with spite, put her hand on his arm and stopped him.

"Stay a moment, Mr. Fordyce, stay a moment, if you please. You spoke just now of Mrs. Harcourt as your friend. Now I like facts better than fancies, as you know, and am sorry to see a young man deluded by an artful, worthless woman. Yes, Mr. Fordyce, you may stamp and start if you please. And yes, Arabella Floss, you never knew what I heard last night. Perhaps I should not tell you now, but for the sake of this unfortunate young man. I have it on the best authority, Mr. Fordyce and

Arabella Floss, on the authority of a lady who knew her well, that this woman who calls herself Harcourt is in reality a Mrs. Armytage, that she is no widow but a divorced, bad wife, and that, for all I know, her husband is alive while she is carrying on her devilish cantrips here, the hypocrite!"

Thus far Mrs. D. Visor—but her facts were cut short by John, who, hoarse with passion, thrust her aside, informing her with more truth than politeness that she was a "miserable defamer." Then he strode off in a rage.

CHAPTER XI.

ALLAN MAXWELL was seated at his desk, diligently working at the rough notes of his next Sunday's sermon. Every now and then, he laid down his pen and whistled softly, drumming upon the table with his fingers; but he had not the slightest notion of time and tune, and only indulged in these musical exercises when his thoughts were far away. Suddenly the door was opened and closed with a bang, and John Fordyce entered, in a towering passion.

" ' Enter Zamiel in a flash of lightning !' Why, bless the boy ! what is up now ?"

" Up ?　Why, the foullest lie ever uttered by any tongue, man's or woman's either !"

" 'Pon my honour, then, I should like to hear it.　I have listened to so many in my time, and each seemed greater than the last.　What is the maximum ?"

" I'm not joking, Maxwell; now.　If it had been a man who told it me, I should have knocked him down on the spot."

" That is what is called the *argumentum ad hominem*, but more resembles the ' countercheck quarrelsome ' than the retort courteous," remarked the incorrigible Maxwell, " but tell me, what is the matter ?"

" The matter !　Why, I have just met those lying vipers, Mrs. Visor and Mrs. Floss."

" And not a word of sense did you hear from either, I'll engage."　This was *sotto voce.* " Well, and what had they to say ?"

" Do you know that they are going about with their false tongues defaming the noblest and best woman in the world—spitting out their poison at one whose shoes they are not fit to touch ?"

" That like all women, they are fond of gossip, I know, and, that like some, they are not regardful of truth, I know ; but, hyperbole aside, what have they told you, and whom have they defamed ?"

" I blush to repeat what that hatchet-faced lying viper said, but she dared to insinuate that Mau— Mrs. Harcourt had no right to that name, and that she is a *divorcée*, a dishonoured wife. Ah ! I have surprised you now, then ?"

" My good John, you have surprised me ; not with this particular intelligence, but with the fact of these women being aware of it, and talking of it openly."

" Do you mean to say, then, you knew this, and had heard it before; and have never told me ?"

" Why on earth should I, my dear lad ? It was no business of your's, or, for the matter of that, of mine, either."

" Bah ! You Scotch are as cold and cautious as stones."

" As you say, we are cautious—though how stones are cautious is more than I can say, unless the philosopher's stone be so—and it is just as well that some men should be cautious in this troublous world. Well, man, what now ? I told you I had heard this; I did not say I believed it."

" Believe it ! No honest man would do so for a minute, no one who is worthy of the name of man. Of course, you do not. But who told you, and how came these monstrous lies in circulation ? I should like to meet him."

"Her, more likely. If lie there be, in all probability it comes from a female source."

"If ! Good Heavens ! You don't mean to say there can be a moment's doubt ?"

"I mean to say this, John Fordyce, that there is some mystery about Mrs. Harcourt ; but that I do not believe her to blame, nay, believe her to be a spotless, good woman, and the victim of some mistake or persecution. It need not necessarily be a lie, you know, only a misapprehension or misstatement of facts."

"Then what you heard corresponds with the atrocious statement I have just told you. And what did you reply ?"

"My informant was a chance visitor to Marbury ; who, meeting Mrs.. Harcourt, recognised her as one she had

known as a Mrs. Armytage, and whom
she was aware had since been divorced.
The statement was free from any *animus*
or virulence, and I had hoped would not
have been repeated. I suppose the love
of tattling was too strong."

"But what remark did you make?
surely you denied the possibility of the
tale."

"My good John, do be reasonable.
When an eye-witness states a plain fact
which you cannot disprove, what is left
but to accept it? I told my informer
that I did not wish to dispute her statement, but that I felt quite convinced as
to Mrs. Harcourt's innocence, and that
on enquiry it would turn out that there
were circumstances extenuating the main
fact. Meanwhile, I said I could not
think of interfering in so delicate a
matter, and that as I had always found
Mrs. Harcourt, as she chooses to be

called, a virtuous, large-minded, charitable woman, as such I should always continue to treat her. If she be a sinner, I wish there were more such. And now, my dear fellow, I should like to know why this excitement? why this special interest? Who made you squire of dames in general, and of Mrs. Harcourt in particular?"

" Oh, Maxwell, Maxwell!" said his friend, "this is no trifle, no laughing matter to me. I love her—I love Maud Harcourt better than my life, I love her better than all the world contains."

Maxwell looked at him with genuine surprise, and put his hand upon his shoulder as one brother might to another.

" My poor John, my poor John!" was all he said, " and I never guessed it. Have you told her yet?"

"No, Maxwell, no. I have never yet summoned courage. I have longed to do so, but dared not. I have never quite ventured to hope, sometimes I have thought she liked me better than as a friend, and then I have despaired again when I thought how impossible it was for such a noble, peerless soul to care for such as I am. But now this is a blow like death to me."

He sat down and covered his face with his hands, nor did his friend break the silence for a minute or so. Then he said,

"I would not raise false hopes, my dear John; but still I see no cause for despair. The story is vague in the extreme. We neither of us believe her guilty for one moment, and even supposing the truth of the divorce question, her husband may since have died and set her free. Of your chances

with her, of course, I can say nothing,
you know them; but until we get the
truth you can do nothing. For heaven's
sake be careful, my dear fellow, and do
not entangle yourself in sorrows which
may be lifelong!"

Good advice, prudent advice as ever
was given. But then how easy to advise when the heart is not concerned,
how easy to lay down rules when no self-
action is required. John was on fire
for action. He burned to refute the
calumny, to try his fate and know his
destiny, and here was his friend advising
him to wait! Ask an earthquake to
pause, or the sea to stop!

He talked the matter over with Maxwell again and again, this way and that,
chafing against, yet forced to acknowledge his friend's cool, calm judgment.
He would give no pledge for his actions
immediate or future, he would not under-

take any special course of proceeding.
And so as time wore on, he gradually
lashed himself into a miserable state of
mad despair and uncertainty, and his
life became a burden.   He would not
permit Maxwell to take any steps to
ascertain the truth of what they had
heard, and at length ceased to utter
Maud's name at all.   His friend, unable to do anything, could only trust that
time would alter and clear the existing
state of things.   Interference and advice
were but ill-received, action was impossible; he could only wait and hope.

John and Maud seldom met, and then
only for a few minutes.   This was partly
chance and partly John's management.
He felt he could not trust himself in her
presence yet; he had not schooled himself
sufficiently, nor was he prepared to hang
his fate upon one word.   He felt that if
he were doomed to disappointment, it

would crush his very life; and so he dragged on from day to day in weary doubt.

One evening, he was in Maxwell's room looking for a book he wanted, when Allan, after learning its name, informed him that it was in the school library, adding,

"And I am sure I wish you would go and fetch it, because then you might also bring me my 'Cosmos,' which I left there by mistake."

John had really nothing to do, and so complied with his friend's request. At that hour the school and its library were generally closed; John felt some surprise, therefore, at seeing a light shining in the upper room where the books were kept. Far greater, however, was his amaze at finding Mrs. Harcourt seated at one of the round tables with a heap of exercises before her, occupied as he had first seen her, in revising and correcting them. His

heart began to beat uneasily, and his voice
was unsteady, as he greeted her with some
common-place remark.

"You have caught me, Mr. Fordyce, I
declare," she said with a laugh, "I have
no business here, I know. But I wanted
to have a few books to refer to for these
tiresome exercises, and so save myself the
trouble of taking them home. Do you
remember helping me the first time we
met?"

John thought he detected a slight
tremor in her voice as she said this.

"Remember! Indeed, yes; that was
a happy day I am not likely to forget."

"Ah, Mr. Fordyce, but I think you
have forgotten something I told you then.
I warned you not to overwork yourself,
not to get too anxious, not to wear yourself out. You remember now. But I am
sorry to say you are looking very much
worse than when you came; you look ill

and pale and haggard; will you never think of yourself and rest?"

"Oh, Mrs. Harcourt," replied John, who felt all his resolves fading in her presence, "it is not the work, it is not the work. I believe I have lost heart in it, and though, God knows, I am anxious enough, it is not for that. No—other thoughts have filled my heart now, and my labours here are merely mechanical.

*　　　*　　　*　　　*

"I sometimes wonder," he continued, and his voice had a tremulous tone, "whether this is always to continue— whether I am always to live this dreary solitary life, and let all my heart's best blood slowly ebb away in one monotonous stream. Is the past never to die to my memory? Am I always to stand alone, and never know the intense joy of sympathy? Must I always restrain my real inner feelings, and try to crush them with a ceaseless round of work. Such aspirations are the highest and holiest part of our nature, are they never to be fulfilled? I once thought that I loved, I once thought I was understood and loved again, and the awakening was bitter. I think now, after all my toil and sorrow, if only I could feel that I did not stand alone, that one generous heart could feel for me, and with me, and love me—then I could die happy, and know I had not lived quite in vain, that my life had not been quite dry and barren."

He leaned his head upon his arms, crossed upon the table as though forgetful of Maud's presence. His rough dark hair hung forward in masses over his forehead, already wrinkled and ploughed up. His powerful hands were nervously twined together, and the veins stood up in great knots.

The slightest touch in the world sufficed

to send an electric thrill through his whole
soul and body—to make his heart beat in
great plunges, to make his breath come
hot and quick, to give him, as it were,
almost a new marvellous sensation of life.
What had roused him? what was that
slight passing touch, which seemed to
have recalled the spirit to the dead body,
and quickened both?

A mere instinctive movement had
caused Maud to raise her hand to her
face, partly to conceal her tears. A mere
accident had caused that hand slightly—
scarcely perceptibly—to touch one of
those dark coils of hair; and yet that
minute, that chance decided their fate for
life, that little movement opened the
secret recesses which nought else had
revealed. John sprang up, their eyes
met, and all was told. No need for a
single word, each knew the other's whole
heart and soul, and that moment con-

tained a life. Scarce believing his happiness, afraid to think, lest it should prove a delusion and vanish away, John instinctively opened his arms, opened them to clasp Maud in a wild, fierce, dreamlike embrace. Was it flesh and blood he held, was it Maud? his Maud? Was that indeed true which he had never dared to hope or confess to himself? She loved him, it *was* true, and Maud was really his.

He kissed her fiercely again and again, as if to make sure she was indeed his very Maud, and she resisted not. Oh, moment all too short, and yet how intense! oh, if he could, if they could but die together so, that there might never be any waking from this trance of exquisite joy! He held her to himself, he felt her heart beat impetuously against his breast in wild bounds, he felt her warm breath on his cheek, he felt her perfumed hair, as it lay in rippling masses on his shoulder. It was such a moment as when we hold our breath during some exquisite passage of melody, and do not care to speak, or stir, or think, lest we should lose one note, one strain. He, at length, whispered softly, "Maud," and just caught the faint echo of his name. Did that word dissolve the spell? Did the sound of his own voice rouse her from her dream, recal her to herself? With a start she released herself from his enfolding arms, and, panting with alarm, sprang back away from him. Her great dark grey eyes gleamed with a wild light, as might the eyes of one before whom a chasm had suddenly yawned.

"Go! go!" she cried, with intense energy, retreating as in fear. "God forgive me, I am mad, I forgot! Oh, go, John! Mr. Fordyce, if you pity me, if you love me, go! I implore you to leave me now. Think I was mad, think we both were; forgive me, but go !"

She sank down in a chair, and hid her face in her hands. All terror and amaze, John approached, but she waved him back, the dream was at an end. Hand in hand, they had wandered through flower beds to the very edge of a deep abyss. The earth had shaken and sundered them. He began to speak, he addressed her as " Maud—dear Mrs. Harcourt !" but still she shrank back, and would not look up. Then at length he said,

" Mrs. Harcourt, Maud, my own dearest, I swear I think no thought which may not be harboured of you. I swear you are, and always shall be, my best, truest, only love ! Forgive me if I have offended you, forgive me the expressions of love I cannot help or recal !"

He stooped down low, and pressed to his lips the very edge of the light scarf she wore, not so gently, however, but that she felt it, and quivered with the thrill it sent through her. And then she found herself alone !

*   · *   *   *   *

CHAPTER XII.

NEXT morning the following letter was placed in John's hands by a little messenger from the school :

"After a night, sleepless from grief, doubt and anxiety, I rise to perform the most cruel duty of my life. Surely I may say no other woman has been tried as I am, when my very food turns to poison, and that which should cause me the most exquisite delight that woman's heart can know, plunges me deeper in misery—and, did I not trust in the merciful Father of all, I might add, despair. Mr. Fordyce, last night in a momentary madness, I listened to your declaration of love, and carried away by my own heart's passion, forgetful of all save those welcome words after the long period of desolation I have known—I was culpably weak, I was wickedly selfish. I ought at once to have aroused myself, I ought at once to have done what I do now, and told you that love, as between us, is impossible—is sinful.

"Pardon me this, and do not think harshly of me for my giving way to the temptation of the moment, or for my repentance and the reparation I make now. Think of a life passed in thirst intolerable, and imagine how hard it is for the sufferer to reject the proffered cup of water held to his lips. Let me tell you my misery in one word—I am a married woman, and my husband is alive! I force myself to write this be-

cause you must know it for your sake
and for mine; but remember, my tale
is one of sorrow and suffering, not of
sin. My marriage was a crime, not of
my commiting, and though tied by man's
laws and fettered by a chain which only
death can break, I am not guilty in
Heaven's sight. My real name is Armytage, Harcourt is my maiden name. Oh,
that it had never been changed! My
mother died in my infancy, and left me
to my father's care. Other relations,
save distant cousins, I had none. I was
brought up at home, indulged, caressed,
flattered, and yet at times treated with
capricious tyranny. As long as my
father's whims were obeyed, no one
could be more lavishly fond of me than
he was. He was accustomed to and demanded absolute obedience, this conceded, his affection knew no bounds. I
was treated more as a favourite and

petted slave than a child, and my relationship to him was a strange mingling of fear and love, not that perfect love which casts out fear.

"He was very wealthy, and all his riches were to come to me alone. He was very proud, and would rather have seen me perish at his feet than marry unworthily, or in a manner derogatory to the Harcourt name. His views of marriage were more those which prevail in France than in accordance with English notions. He believed that it was the place of the parents to make the match, and of the children to give an unhesitating consent. At the same time, I am bound to say that had he been able to foresee the miserable consequences of the match into which he practically forced me, I am sure he would have been the last to influence me. I was eighteen when Mr. Armytage

first came to our house at his invitation.
God knows I am only desirous to set
down exact truth here, and neither exaggerate the miseries I suffered, or bear
false testimony against the wretched
being who was the cause of them, and
who I pray may be forgiven.

"He was a young man, five years my
senior, rich, of good birth, and had received such an amount of polish as does
duty for education, and enables a man to
pass through the world unchallenged.
But his heart, his thoughts, his inner life!
I solemnly declare that I can conceive no
more revolting idea than he was the em-
bodiment of.   He may not have been
legally insane, and yet his mind and disposition were those of a madman. Cruel,
base, corrupt in thought and act, there
was no deed of wickedness he would not
do and find pleasure in. He seemed to
breathe only in an atmosphere of sin,

which choaked the life of good and purity.
His degradation was only equalled by his
cruelty, only surpassed by his cowardice.
And this man was—nay, is my husband—
that sacred word which is to command,
with a willing submission, a woman's
utmost reverence and love, only fills me
with shuddering and horror. I need not
say how ignorant I was of his real nature
when I obeyed my father's wishes, or
rather submitted to his will, and united
myself to him.

"Like most thoroughly bad men, he
had cunning enough to restrain and conceal his most offensive characteristics as
long as there was anything to be gained.
To my father he was the most attentive of
prospective sons-in-law, omitting no little
mark of respect and homage with which
he knew my father was pleased. To me
he was an assiduous suitor, and if his
manners had little of the warmth I might

s 2

have expected, at least they were respectful, and indicative of a desire to please.
When, therefore, I was informed by my
parent of his desire that I should marry
the man of his choice, I was at a loss for
an excuse. In position and birth he was
my equal, his wealth was little less than
mine would be. Any objection I might
make as to manner, I knew my father
would instantly put aside; the fact that I
did not love him, he laughed at and ridi-
culed as absurd girlish scruples and pru-
dery. I was in his hands and was too far
accustomed to obey to offer strong resistance, even in this the most important act
of my life.

"My ideas of filial duty gained the day,
and, in a fatal hour for myself, I consented
and was married according to his wish.
When once I had given him my word, all
preparations were hurried on with a speed
which allowed me no time for reflection or

drawing back. Delighted at obtaining
the wish of his heart, he would suffer no
obstacle to arise to prevent its immediate
fulfilment, and he told me that my wedding day would be the happiest of his life.
Alas! it was a fatal day to us both; to
him, ultimately, the cause of death;
to me it brought a life far worse than
death, compared to which, death would
have been happiness unattainable. A
very short time opened my eyes to the
character of the man who was to be my
partner for life.

"As soon as his end was gained, he
threw away the mask he had worn, and
cast aside the restraint he had put upon
himself. I saw him in his true colours
and found that, until death, I was tied to
a drunkard, a profligate, an abandoned
wretch, who combined cruelty, cunning
and dastardly cowardice. Before many
weeks, and while we were travelling

abroad, so that I was separated from my only friend, I was subjected to the very extremity of insult and even to personal violence.

" He, my husband, made it no secret that he hated me, and had only married me for my money—that he desired my death above all things, and that he loved the vilest of his creatures better than his wife. Daily was I exposed to fresh injuries, and, at last, it seemed as if his aim were to drive me to suicide or madness. I prayed earnestly to be kept from worse than either, for at length a deadly spirit of hate and resistance was aroused within me, and I trembled at the thoughts which sometimes entered my heart. On the very first opportunity after our return to England, I left the man who was my legal master, and fled to my father's protection. I cannot tell you the shock which my appearance gave him. The wreck of all his hopes and plans for me, was too much for his proud spirit to bear, and he was unable to forgive himself the injury he had done me. Within three months I was left an orphan and friendless; but before that time my poor father had made all arrangements necessary for my release from the wretch I had married.

"The Harcourt pride could not endure the thought of my name being dragged through the mire of the Court, where I could claim legal redress, or being bandied about as the subject of idlers' talk and gossip. We desired to conceal our disgrace as much as possible, and all legal proceedings were instituted and completed privately, to enable me to live separate from my husband, and to restore to me a large part of that fortune which had been the cause of my sorrow.

"From the day of my escape to the

present time, I have never seen him, although occasionally I have heard of his existence. My life has been one long effort to forget my grief, and to bury my troubles by labouring for the welfare of others. At first I had little taste for it, took little interest in the work. Gradually, my heart became warmed towards the miserable objects to whom I ministered, and in their sorrows I was sometimes allowed to let my own slumber.

"And then I saw you! Oh, Mr. Fordyce, had I known, had I guessed your feelings sooner, I would have hastened to spare you this trial—cost what it might to my own heart, I would have removed myself beyond your reach, and never innocently have permitted a passion to grow up which might be fatal to both. Pardon me this, forgive me the selfishness which only thought of my own love, and the necessary effort to keep it from finding outward expression. I trusted that I had commanded myself sufficiently, and that to you I was only a friend, not more. And now my eyes are opened. For one moment last night, I succumbed and was weak. But I will no longer delay the execution of a duty, necessary for both our sakes. We must not meet again. I shall leave this place, where I have dared dream of happiness and will encounter the stern realities of life elsewhere. Think of one who will ever think of you, pray for you; but think of me as for ever removed from you as if by death.

"God bless you, and keep you for ever, will always be the prayer of

"MAUD ARMYTAGE."

But Maud did not know the full depths of John's nature. Perhaps he did not of his own. But he knew her, and the letter which spoke an eternal farewell, and would have plunged most in despair, revealed a vein of hope to him, small indeed, but still of hope. Within an hour of its receipt, he stood before her—no longer trembling and downcast as at their last interview, but calm and firm.

"Oh, Mr. Fordyce; why have you come? this was wrong—was wrong and cruel to me!"

"No, Maud; neither wrong nor cruel; to stay away would have been both. I come to spare you an unnecessary trial, I come to prevent you from committing a wrong. Have you no trust in me? do you love me, and yet doubt me?"

"How can you ask? I trust you fully, entirely, with life itself. But I go to spare you and myself; it must be."

"No, Maud, it must not be. You who are so grand, so noble, shall not

fail here. Listen, you acknowledge that
you not only love but trust me. I
could not love you did I not trust you
as fully. And now, need such love and
such trust be parted by mere scruple?
Your sacrifice is unnecessary. I know
well how much our position allows, and
shall never claim more. Oh, Maud,
listen to me. I know and my heart
bleeds for your situation—aye, bleeds
perhaps selfishly, because in that I, too,
suffer. But is this to cut us off from
that bliss we may innocently enjoy?
Trust me, Maud, trust me, and do not
drive me away. By no thought, or
word, or deed will I ever disturb your
spotless, glorious purity. To me you
are and ever will be a sacred being. I
shall look upon you as I might do upon
an angel. What limits you appoint I
will keep, what laws you enjoin I will
observe, nay, anticipate. Only do not

drive me away from you; do not let
me have the torture of knowing that
your heart, your thoughts, wishes, sympathies and desires are all mine, and
yet I must never see you. I may not
call you by the most sacred of names,
but there is yet the title of friend to
which I aspire. Trust me, Maud, trust
me, and do not turn aside from a prospect where if only we will, we may
enjoy peace and happiness. Surely, after
our wanderings, here is land where we
may rest. Surely, after the dark night
through which we have passed in sorrow, here is the day dawn which brings
us light!"

And it was so. For his noble impetuosity would not be withstood, his
earnest pleadings might not be denied.
He asked for trust, and he asked as
one who had a right to demand. There
is a love founded on a loyal trust, and

a generous confidence which is content to wait. There is a love which to the world appears but as friendship, which *is* friendship—but a friendship of the highest, purest, noblest, the sweet communion of two perfectly concordant souls, the glorious unison of two voices which utter the same strain of melody. As after the Purgatorio, Beatrice was to Dante, so did these two pass onwards through life, approaching nearer and nearer to the perfect life which is all life and love. There was no expressed limit, no restraint in their intercourse, for none was needed. Each knew and trusted the other. Nor did either ever violate or betray the other's confidence; they knew it would have been the death of love. One in thoughts, and words, and wishes, and works, they went on hand in hand, through those labours to which their sorrows had brought them, now no longer as a refuge for concealed griefs, but as the outward expression of gratitude for an inward peace and joy which passed all understanding. A happy life it was, a brief moment in which they were content to bury the past and wait in confidence for the future. A life all too brief, too quickly passed, one of those supreme moments of bliss which crowns and ends a life, like a delicious strain of music, which as you listen dies away in a minor key. For "man goes forth unto his work and to his labour until the evening."

CHAPTER XIII.

IN the town of Marbury and parish of
St. Lazarus, there lived a man with
the elegant *soubriquet* of " Dusty Bob."
Like many other of the nick-names of
the lower orders, it was singularly inap-
propriate, inasmuch as his name was
Richard, and in his occupation as a
scavenger he had so much more intimate acquaintance with mud than dust,
that " Muddy Dick," or " Dirty Dick"
would have been far more fitting. However, Dusty Bob he was called by some
Marbury wit, and as Dusty Bob he was
known until the day of his death. He
was in the most literal sense of the

word one of the "unwashed." Public
baths might be established in Marbury
for all he cared; but he had nothing to
do with them. Sanitary lecturers might
lecture themselves hoarse, and demon-
strate convincingly the advantages to
mind and body of cleanliness; but he
didn't go to hear. them, and if he had,
would not have been convinced. Let
others wash and be clean, he would
none of it.

It is impossible to imagine a more
miserable, outcast, forlorn existence than
that of this wretched old man. His foul,
revolting, ragged, uncouth exterior was
only a true index to his inward man.
Outside, he was a thing of shreds and
patches and rags, held together by mere
cohesion of dirt. His garments were such
as to render it difficult to tell where one
commenced and another ended, and he
more resembled a filthy squamous mon-

ster that had just emerged from a roll in
the mud, than a human being, clad in
garments of man's devising and fashion-
ing.

To look at him, was to learn how thin
a barrier of circumstances separates a
man from a brute, and how the life of
some men seems but a series of attempts
to overpass that barrier, and divest
themselves of the burden of humanity
and civilisation. So, also, with such
spark of intelligence as made up his
mind. His history was a blank. He
saw that the generality of men and women
possessed, or had at some period possessed, father and mother, and so he
conjectured that some such might have
belonged to him. But he had never
seen them, or known them. Discovered
a foundling, " dragged up " by the parish,
apprenticed, starved, beaten, run away;
Stage the first. An idler, a beggar, a

doer of odd jobs, a porter, a fever patient in an hospital; Stage the second. A parish scavenger, a filthy bundle of rags with the accident of a soul, a drunkard; Stage the third. What was wanting but the short sharp agony to make him the unlovely corpse, and so end Stage the fourth? But the reader must fill in the intervals of these stages as he will, with starvation of body, and soul, and mind, utter black heathenism, stolid indifference, dogged hatred of the world and all it contained. He must imagine the ugly shadow of a life which had never known sunshine, or kindness, or the pleasures of social life and intercourse, or the joys and cares of wife or children.

His only idea of life was muddy heaps of refuse, in the midst of which stood a sordid figure, wielding a broom and spade. And yet we mistake, he had one other idea, though that was occasional and festive—drink. The pay of a scavenger is, as the reader may conjecture, not large, certainly not sufficient to allow of many luxuries,. but, by diligent and careful economy, Dusty Bob managed to save up enough wherewith to intoxicate himself once a week. He had passed one half of his life in experiments to discover with what spirituous mixture this might best be accomplished, and, in his insular ignorance, never having heard of absinthe, had finally decided on gin and rum in equal proportions, drunk neat. And so, for six days he was content to toil and labour on, interchanging no single word with his fellow-mortals, other than necessity compelled, in the expectation of that glorious Sabbath on which he had no mud to sweep together, and the whole day to get drunk in. He lay in bed until the public-houses opened after the morning service, and then took his bottle to be filled, and emptied with much despatch. A few scraps of food were afterwards produced from some hoard, and devoured beast-like, and then he would totter forth to some kilns outside Marbury, where the fires were always burning, and there, crouching down and huddled together, he would sit, waiting for night to come, and smoking his old black stump of a pipe. In the evening, he would gather himself together and slowly totter back to the squalid place he called home, fill his bottle once more, and then mechanically drink and smoke until he stole stupified to bed.

This was his life, and such as this he had lived for sixty years; he knew no other.

And now a few words about his chosen abode. In the lowest part of St. Lazarus parish was a public-house of evil repute, called the Green Dragon. It was celebrated for the number of tipsy rows and outrages which were continually occurring there, and the magistrates of the police-court had pretty frequently to hear statements from X, 21 commencing,

" From information I had received, your Worship, I went last night to the Green Dragon."

Close to the house-door of this delightful hostelry, gaped an archway, by which any one who was foolish enough to wish to do so, could enter into what was called Green Dragon Yard, a long narrow, foul yard, closed in by high buildings on either hand. On the right ran the storehouse and yard of a tallow-chandler, on the left, a grocer's premises abutted, towards the street, the archway and the public-house closed it in, while the head of the yard was formed by a tall, narrow, old-fashioned, beam and plaster house called the Palace, and reported to be two

hundred and fifty years old. From its
appearance, the spectator would have
been inclined to credit it with any
number of years posterior to the Deluge,
so unutterably crazy and tumble-down
and dilapidated was it.

It looked as if a strong man leaning
against it, must bring on himself the fate
of Samson again. A strong puff of wind
howling down the yard must inevitably
blow it down, one would have thought,
and yet it had stood many and many a
bluff December night, when stout old
trees had yielded to the blast. There it
yet remained sordid, weather-stained, foul,
hideous with blotches and fungus marks,
as though it had broken out with leprosy
and been forsaken by all respectable
houses in its misery and despair. And
yet this dreary mansion had once been
the abode of joy, and mirth, and laughter,
and prosperity. Out of its darkened

windows, now half closed with rags and dirt, merry smiling faces of children had gazed down upon the green fields around. Those crazy dormer windows, half sunken in the roof, had belonged to the nursery whose walls had echoed with the mirth of happy children. Up its broad staircases, each step of which now seemed to utter its separate shriek of pain and agony, had passed stately ladies in brocades and velvets and silks, led by gallant cavaliers with their plumed hats and falling collars of point lace. Often and often had the great Hall resounded with the shouts of laughter, the song, the joke, the hearty applause of the light-hearted revellers as they partook of the good cheer and generous wine with which the hospitable tables were loaded.

And now all had passed away together, and the only form to be seen in the great old Hall was that of a sordid old man slowly drinking himself into stupor. For in the Palace had "Dusty Bob" taken up his abode, undeterred by reports of ghosts, by its solitude, its desolation; influenced, indeed, mainly by these latter facts, and by the nominal rent he had to pay. In such a fit home did the miserable old man reside; house and master alike deserted, decrepit and dirty; house and master alike tottering to their fall, destitute of hope, or affection, or tender memories, mere useless plague spots to the eyes of men, and blots upon the face of nature.

It so happened that one cold wintry Sunday Dusty Bob had gone as usual to his favourite resort, the lime kilns, and stayed there until night came on. One of the lime-burners had been married that morning, and according to traditional usage, had "stood" beer all round to his mates, and of this beer the men, in rough good-nature, had made Dusty Bob par-

take no small share. Consequently the
old man, on leaving the kiln, had already
progressed a long distance towards the
intoxication which was his weekly bourne.
As he went along, he congratulated himself
on the unwonted treat he had enjoyed,
and staggered into the Green Dragon to fill
his bottle as usual, with which bottle in
hand, he entered the Palace, and having
fastened the door with the great iron bar,
a formula he never omitted, betook himself to the great Hall and went through
the same ceremony with the two windows.
Then having made all snug as he termed
it, he lit his miserable rushlight and
placed it on a small round table, which
with a broken chair formed the sole furniture of the room. By the side of the
rushlight he deposited his beloved bottle,
his short pipe, and a box of matches; and
then seating himself began his solitary
carouse.

A strange, Rembrantesque figure he looked in the gloom of that great deserted hall, a little island of dim light of which his pipe made the focus, in a vast ocean of shade and gloom. The wretched rushlight did little to dispel the dark, and only cast a sickly beam on the immediate vicinity, showing its sordid and ruined details fitfully and by starts. The occasional shrieks of the rats, the starting of the old panels, and the measured " puff, puff," of the old man's pipe were the only sounds which broke the dead calm of the place. All the rest of the house, all the rest of the room were in silence and shade save that little patch of light in which the scavenger sat, an ugly, black spot in a halo of dim light. All through the evening, and late into the night the old man continued to sit and drink. In spite of all he had had given him

it took very much to make him drunk,
and he sat for hours smoking and drinking, removing his pipe with one hand
to apply the bottle with the other.

The world of Marbury beyond was
engaged in its various ways, and the
bright stars were looking down alike
upon happy, peaceful slumbers, and
couches sleepless from sorrow or suffering, upon the weary watch of the
student, and the reckless dissipation of
the abandoned; when, at length, the
potent spirit began to exercise its influence, and Dusty Bob to sink and
sway about from the effects of the unusual amount of drink he had taken.
He stretched out his arm to have one
final draught, but his unsteady hand
knocked over the bottle, and the remaining spirit, perhaps half a tumbler-
full, was spilt in a little pool under
the table. With a sullen oath the old

man arose, and steadying himself by his chair, contrived to reach and grasp the rushlight, upsetting, however, at the same time, the box of lucifer matches. After an ineffectual attempt to re-light his pipe at the flame of the rushlight, he suddenly remembered some flaming fusees given him by the lime-burners. Having discovered one in his pocket he accomplished his desire, and then casting the still blazing fuzee aside, slowly and doubtfully groped his way upstairs to bed.

He had done all he could to secure a good conflagration and roast himself alive in his bed, and now it was left to certain laws of nature, and to the agency of inanimate objects to accomplish the rest, which they did accordingly. The reader must be good enough to see "in his mind's eye," first the dirty, rotten floor, whose boards were perforated with dry rot and anointed with grease from the refuse-food and scraps of months' accumulation. Upon this, and immediately under the table lay, (1) the broken bottle of spirit, from which ran a stream towards (2) the still flaming fusee, and (3) the little heap of lucifer matches fallen against the leg of the chair. The rest is easy and momentary. As soon as the mingled stream of spirit reached the lighted match, a silent, blue, flickering flame was the result, which ran quickly along, encircling the sulphurous matches, kindling them, and with a fiz and spurtle raising a greenish yellow blaze, which in its turn licked and lapped on the floor, and twisted up the rotten legs of the chair. The grease-stained floor was not unresponsive, and spluttered by way of reply; it gave its grease and fat, and strewed half-gnawed bones to feed the flames; yes, and it gave its very rotten self to feed the flames, for soon the worm-eaten boards were in a blaze, and soon a tongue of fire ran up the chair leg, and that took fire and blazed; the flame leaped up and caught the table, and that blazed. A sober man and a bucket of water would yet have saved the Palace. Instead, you have an old man lying in a drunken sleep, two stories up in a back room; you have rotten, old, greasy boards, dry oaken and deal panels, no water, and a cancer spot of flame spreading fast on all sides with no one to stop it. The eternal fitness of things would have it so.

The day of doom for the old house was come. Good-bye, old house! deserted and unloved, the spirit of joy and peace and innocent love had long ago fled from thy worm-eaten old carcase, and now the weary, time-worn body must follow! Come crashing down in clouds of flame,

and blaze of blue and red and yellow,
and showering sparks, and shouting
throng and dull uproar! Thy day of
doom has come, and thou must give
place to a better. And so the fire stole
on and on.

The two sides of Green Dragon Yard
consisted of mere sheds and stores, as we
before said. When, therefore, the flames,
grown bold, began to climb and lick the
pannelled window-seats, then crack the
small upper panes which the inside
shutter did not protect, and dart their
forked tongues through and beyond,
there was no eye to see and give the
alarm. And so many a delicate spiral
puff of smoke had given way to many
an angry shooting tongue of fire, before
their ravages were noted. One window
of the " Green Dragon " looked upon the
yard behind, and from this window was
it that the fire was seen at length. About

one o'clock in the morning, the landlady awoke, and remembered that she had left a certain key in the bar-parlour. Well aware of the importance of that key—it opened her money-box—well aware, also, that her staff could scarcely be deemed immaculate, and that, like Autolycus, they " were snappers up of unconsidered trifles," with many a grumbling word, she arose, and, casting a shawl around her buxom shoulders, began to descend the staircase.

As she passed the window before-mentioned, she first smelt. a burning smell, then heard a crackling sound, and putting her head out, she saw the old Palace alive with beautiful winding sparkling serpents of fire, darting this way and that, turning, and kissing, and hissing, and leaping up, and wrapping the whole ground floor in their embrace. Being a woman of quick wit and powerful lungs, she raised her voice with a great shout of " fire !" which awakened the barmaid, who screamed " murder !" which awakened the pot-boy, who shouted, first " pots !" and then amended that for " thieves !" Then every one arose, and gathered together, some half awake, some half sober, most half witted, and all half dressed. And then, when, at last, everyone seemed convinced of the fact that the old Palace was on fire, they all crushed into the street with one accord, and raised the alarm, until the place echoed with their shouts. Then came clamour, and confusion, and rushing, the maximum of noise and the minimum of utility. Then, in five minutes did Green Dragon Yard fill to the brim with as many eager men and women as could squeeze through the archway, while those who could not, stayed outside and fought.

At length, one original brain conceived the idea of going to the turncock, and went. And another offered to run one mile and a half to the suburban water-works, and ran.

We may remark, *en passant*, that there was telegraphic communication from Marbury to the waterworks ; but the directors of the company, with that foresight and sound sense which distinguishes such, forbad its use between twelve o'clock on Saturday night and seven o'clock on Monday morning. Doubtless, by this they hoped to prevent the course of Time, and keep the Sabbath, and yet, strange to say, people were proud, perverse and misguided enough to break the day of rest by falling ill and dying.

So, before the fire-engine came, there was a good long delay, and another before the water arrived, and another before hose

or buckets could be passed through the
narrow archway, and through the surging,
close-packed crowd beyond. And when
all this was accomplished, the old Palace
was a sheet of crimson, and violet, and
angry yellow, and emerald-green flames.
And Dusty Bob was asleep on his back,
snoring loud and long.

* * * * *

On the Sunday night, John Fordyce
had been to the old brick mansion,
Mostyn Hall, and stayed until about ten
or eleven with Maud. Never had they
felt more peaceful and happy, never had
they felt greater confidence in each other,
and in the future. Their talk had been
long and deep. They had discussed the
wondrous laws which influence and govern
human affinities and, direct the affections
of the heart into their proper channels.
They had pondered over the inscrutable
wisdom of the Father of all, which brought

at length into intimate connection two
hearts so balanced as to make up each
other's wants, whatever circumstances of
time and place had sundered them. And
they had agreed that their several troubles
and sorrows of the past only intensified
the pleasure of that sweet present, and
held forth promise of a happy future.

And then, at John's request, Maud had
sung while he sat by and listened in a rapt
silence which was almost pain. Her
fingers wandered over the notes, and her
voice, now rising, now falling, sometimes
swelling in triumph, and then hushed in
solemn awe, gave vent to those lovely
strains which immortalize the names
and memories of Haydn, and Mozart, and
Mendelssohn. At last she began playing
the 'Recordare' from the Requiem, now
and then singing a few strains of the
soprano part. And as John listened, the
tears rose to his eyes, and he whispered,

"Maud, I should like to die with that in my ears : I could die happy."

And she had smiled, and bade him chase away the melancholy thought, and to aid him, had sung in her rich glorious tones that triumphal hymn, "Let the bright Seraphim." And then came the long tender parting, when these two pure loyal souls separated with a mutual blessing, which was more than a caress. And then the last "good-night," and John turned on his way homeward. He was in high spirits, and laughed and joked with Maxwell, and teased him about his cocoa and his short pipe, till Maxwell told him he was "fly," and "a great fond booby" and had better go to bed. And then to bed he went; first looking out over the city, as was his wont, from his bedroom window.

And he dreamed he was toiling down a long dark avenue, thick strewn with dead

leaves, and fallen boughs, and slimy reptiles
which writhed across his path, and as he
plodded on, weary and sad, at length he
saw a beam of light which expanded more
and more as it approached, and then in
that luminous halo stood Maud enwreathed
with a lovely coronal of bay and roses,
and she held out one of cypress to him in
which were mixed *immortelles*. And as he
stretched out his hand towards it, the halo
increased into brightness unbearable; and
he awoke to see a brilliant, angry, red
over the sky, and to hear a dull uproar in
the street. In a moment he was up, and
after a hasty glance through the window
had thrown on the necessary garments
and run down to Maxwell to give him the
news that there was a fire in St. Lazarus.
And then the two men started together,
and ran down the High Street guided by
the quickly gathering throng and flying
crowds to Green Dragon Yard. It was

by exertion of no mean strength that they forced a passage under the arch and through the crowd, and when they stood in the court, they perceived that there was no hope for the old Palace. The heat was so intense in the narrow space, and the fear of the flames spreading to the grocery stores, where some gunpowder was said to be kept, was so great as to paralyse the workers and render them almost helpless. There was little order and system, and the fire had it all its own way, and swept round windows and shot through doors, and played round the lead pipes till they melted and poured their blistering stream down on the crowd below. As they arrived, there was dispute raging as to whether Dusty Bob was there or no. Some affirmed that he slept at the lime kilns, others declared he was in the Green Dragon, while one man swore that he had met him in Marbury an hour ago.

But as John looked up, he saw that which refuted these statements and made his blood chill with horror.

At one of the upper dormer windows appeared a greenish-white, agonised face, on which the reflection of the flames played fiercely, revealing with horrible distinctness the ugly, scared, satyrlike features, distorted and convulsed with the sufferings of eternity condensed into a sublime moment. And then with hoarse shrieks and cries like some wild animal in torment, he wailed and bemoaned his fate, and the cowardice of the crowd who would let a man roast before their eyes. The stairs were all on fire, he said, and the floors had fallen beneath, and there where he stood, a dark object against the flaming background, the smoke rolled round in volleys, and the sparks flew up, and the flames crawled up nearer and nearer. And still the old man shrieked and cried, and beat his sweat-stained face in impotent despair, until one strong, loud voice below shouted for a ladder to be brought. It was John who kept repeating to Maxwell's dissuasions,

"I will not let him die if I can help it. I cannot see him die before my face. It is no use, I must go!"

With difficulty a ladder was brought through the yard and fixed against the blazing front, while the hose were directed on it. But time was lost in doing so, and the old man's strength had failed, and with a doleful cry he sank back and was no more seen. But spite of this, and spite of the fact that the top of the ladder was five feet beneath the window-ledge, John rushed on. He grasped Maxwell's hand tight as he stood at the foot of the ladder, and then with a beating heart and

firm-set lips commenced climbing up.
The smoke nearly blinded him, and the
darting flames singed his hair and beard
as he ascended, and it needed all his
strength to hold firm against the shock
of the water from the hose-pipe. But
he persevered, and regardless of blistered
fingers grasped firm the window-ledge.
Once and again he hung by his hands
and heaved himself up; the third time
he succeeded, and raised himself first
on and then within the window. Happily he had no search to make, for the
old man lay crouched in a heap, there
where he had fallen. In a moment
more, as a bright flame and a cloud
of dense stupifying smoke shot through
the floor close at hand, he raised his
half-senseless burden and placed him
on the window-ledge.

By this time another man, a fireman,
had ventured up the ladder, and into

his arms, as he stood almost on the topmost step, was Dusty Bob consigned. Then John again twisted himself up, and taking firm hold of the heated window-ledge prepared to descend, and felt his feet firm upon the ladder once more, stooping forward and throwing his weight upon the wall.

The crowd, who stood in breath-less suspense, had raised their voice in a great shout, when from a lower window a sudden volume of smoke and flame rushed forward and shot out towards the court. Blinded, scorched, and already blistered by the heat, John relaxed his hold for a second. Then there was a crash, a downward rush, a vain attempt to catch to any-thing, and the next moment he lay a shattered mangled form on the pave-ment below. At the same moment, with a roar like thunder, the roof and front of the old Palace sank into the rejoicing flames, and the sparks shot up to the skies in triumph.

CHAPTER XIV.

THAT worthless life—to the eyes of men —saved, that noble existence cut short! Strange anomaly to those who look on, strange twist in the Gordian knot of life, ravelled and twisted in vain by men, till Death comes and solves it by one stroke. So thought Maxwell, as he bent over the crushed, blackened body of his friend, not dead, but so near death as to have his shadow resting upon him.

* In that clever novel "Creeds" will be found a scene much resembling that here described. The author of "Beyond the Church," thinks it only fair to state that this chapter was written almost in its present shape, four years ago, and that he never read "Creeds" until a few months back.

They raised him carefully, tenderly, as a mother raises her sleeping child, and then they bore him to the Rectory. Many a tear gathered in the eyes of those rough, hard men in the crowd, as they followed, which their stoic northern nature bid them conceal. Many had known him and loved him, and were grateful to him in their honest, independent way.

Two swift messengers departed with hastily pencilled notes from Maxwell, one to his friend the doctor, the other to Maud. And they came, in the darkness of the chill, wintry light, and ascended to the large upper room of the Rectory, where John had been carried. The room downstairs was in confusion, and blocked up with lumber, and so they bore him where there was space and air.

Little did it matter then, for he knew

not where he was, and when he awoke,
as from a painful dream, his wandering
thoughts had gone back to his early days
at Oxford, and Brydges' death, and he
beckoned to Maxwell to stoop down, and
whispered,

"I did all I could."

But in a moment or two, his eye fell
on more familiar objects, and the tide of
thought flowed back to the present, and
he remembered the fire, and knew that
he was dying. One glance from the
doctor was enough, although, to satisfy
Maxwell, he made such slight examination
as could be undergone without pain. One
leg, one arm, and several ribs fractured,
one perforating the lungs. Verdict whispered to Maxwell :—

"No human being can survive it, perhaps
he will last until morning. Best let him
be quiet."

No need to whisper, though, for John

knew it all, and smiled back upon the doctor.

" I know, I know, doctor, never shake your head, man." And then he turned his face to his friend, and whispered, " Have you sent ?"

And Maxwell nodded assent, for then Maud entered, as the doctor left. She came tearless, white, deadly white, but calm as a statue. She knew the worst, and knew that now all her strength was needed. Afterwards, time enough for tears—God help her !—but now she must think for him alone. As she flung her bonnet aside, and sat down by his side, her short, clustering curls fell forward, and, in some degree, hid her face.

" Oh, my love! my life !" was all she could utter, and then stopped, but her eyes said the rest.

And he replied :

" I cannot say much, my own Maud,

but why should I ? You know all I would
say, you know all I think. My heart and
all its thoughts have been yours, and the
only joy my life has known has been your
gift. I go where there is no doubt or
sorrow, and, if one may remember the
past, my thoughts and memories will be of
you alone. Thank God we have been true
and loyal !"

And, as his poor, broken, gasping voice
ceased, she could only murmur, again and
again,

"Oh, my love, my life !" and gaze
as though she could look him back to
life.

But the end was coming, and coming
speedily. The last struggle was at hand.

* * *

The night dragged on slowly and
wearily with the watchers, as they sat
beside their friend. The doctor had declared he would last until the morning,

but at times it seemed doubtful. All the fearful agony and pain had long ceased, and John lay utterly worn out. The only noticeable expression was one of extreme weariness. All the features, save his eyes, were at rest and unmoved by any motion; but they looked out and forward as of old, only now with a more awe-struck gaze, as though on the threshold of the mystery for which so long they had searched. He lay in utter silence, one hand clasped in Maud's, who sat by, struggling against her tears, and endeavouring almost in vain to continue calm.

Maxwell had read a few prayers at intervals, to which John's lips had framed an Amen—they could not utter. At length, as Maxwell rose from his knees, cramped and weary, seated himself on the bed and took the disengaged hand, once so strong, but now powerless as an infant's, with a soft smile John turned his eyes on Maud, and half whispered "Music."

She, too, well knew what he meant, and her heart gave a great throb and then stood still. But was this the time for breaking down, for distressing him, for indulging her own feelings? No, she would struggle bravely till the last. She moved to the harmonium near the bed, and began to play and occasionally join in the exquisitely mournful strains of the Recordare of Mozart's Requiem Mass. But it was too painful to continue long, her voice choked her utterance. The music died away, and with one great sob she resumed her place, raising his hand reverently to her lips. The candle flickered and went out.

They were not long in darkness, however, for as Maxwell went to the window and withdrew the heavy curtain, he saw by the dim grey light that they were close on daybreak. He gazed out a moment on the long chain of the M—— hills, coldly blue at that hour. The eastern horizon only waited for the finger of God to smite upon its portals, and let out the pent up flood of light as the waters of Horeb. A cock crew in the distance, and the air felt chill and keen. A low cry from Maud recalled him to the dying man. No longer the sufferer—the dying man. Already the last change was taking place. Pale before, he was ghastly now, and yet the weary wishful look was gone, and the eager eyes seemed about to realize their longing.

When raised up, he motioned to Maud to bend down, and pressed one long loving kiss upon her lips, then, his hand feebly clasping Maxwell's, he whispered, "Credo," as he steadily directed his eyes towards the gray line of the horizon. And Maxwell understood him, and began, in the language of universal Christendom:

" Credo in Deum patrem omnipotentem, creatorum cœli et terræ et—"

He paused, and looked back. A strange bright light came into John's eyes, a strange smile grew on his lips, as with firm loud voice he repeated the word, " Credo ;" then his head sank back, and the rosy gleam which at that moment issued from the East smote upon the face of a corpse.

The day had dawned, and the day star risen.

Light dawned upon his body as he died, what inner light had dawned upon his soul, it is not for us to say. It had passed already into that place where there is no day dawn, because there is no night, and the day star shines without ceasing

and light and knowledge issue from the
same bright source.   Bathed in the all-
golden light of the day dawn, he lay silent.
But with a grief which already had its
consolation Maxwell and Maud, sat silent
in the presence of

> " The shadow cloaked from head to foot,
> Who keeps the keys of all the Creeds."

And then at length, with an irrepres-
sible soul cry, Maxwell uttered words in
which all we may join,

" O Orient! Brightness of the Eternal
Light and Sun of Righteousness, come
and lighten them that sit in darkness and
in the shadow of death."

*   *   *

In Marbury town there still lives and
works among the sick and suffering a grey
haired woman, whose head, sorrow and
not age has silvered.   She is a widow
now, but the mourning garb she wears is
not for her husband but for one to whom

her release came too late. She has learned a quiet resignation, which is content to labour on and wait the appointed time, but her heart has gone before her and lies buried in the grave of John Fordyce, expecting that day-dawn which shall come to those who dwell "where the wicked cease from troubling and the weary are at rest."

THE END.

LONDON : PRINTED BY A. SCHULZE, POLAND STREET.